Though Flayzeranyx valued many things, he treasured nothing so much as the skull he had claimed from Skull-cap following his battle with the brass dragon.

The dragon didn't know what it was about the bony artifact that made it so compelling to him; he merely understood that it gave him a sense of power and well-being to look upon the object. Now he rose, spreading his wings to add a bit of lift to his gliding leap across the searing rock of the moat. He came to rest before the skull and squatted, staring into those black eyes.

He felt it again, a sensation that had become increasingly common when he regarded the thing. It was a feeling that the skull was trying to talk to him, to communicate something that was terribly important.

"What is it, my skull? Show me . . . speak to me!" he urged. . . .

Saga

DragonLance® Saga

Lost Legends
Volume II

Fistandantilus
Reborn

Douglas Niles

DRAGONLANCE® Saga
Lost Legends
Volume II

FISTANDANTILUS REBORN

Distributed to the book trade in the United States by Random House, Inc., and in Canada by Random House of Canada Ltd.

Distributed to the hobby, toy, and comic trade in the United States and Canada by regional distributors.

Distributed worldwide by Wizards of the Coast, Inc. and regional distributors.

Cover art by Todd Lockwood. Interior art by Jeff Easley.

First Printing: October 1997
Printed in the United States of America.
Library of Congress Catalog Card Number: 96-60810

9 8 7 6 5 4 3 2 1

8384XXX1501

ISBN: 0-7869-0708-8

U.S., CANADA, ASIA,   EUROPEAN HEADQUARTERS
PACIFIC, & LATIN AMERICA   Wizards of the Coast, Belgium
Wizards of the Coast, Inc.   P.B. 34
P.O. Box 707   2300 Turnhout
Renton, WA 98057-0707   Belgium
+1-206-624-0933   +32-14-44-30-44
                   Visit our website at http://www.tsrinc.com

Prologue

The River of Time is eternal, flowing inexorably toward a mysterious destination along a channel gouged by the continuing history of Krynn. A tide broad and stately over the course of decades, centuries, and ages becomes torrential and violent through other stretches of lives, generations, and years. Languishing within murky depths or churning around the obstacles that periodically constrict the flow into an angry cataract, the current progresses—and millions of individual beings entangle, each bringing a tale with its own beginning, middle, and conclusion. Yet each, as well, is a part of the great river, an often indistinguishable mote in the onward rush of time.

It is the historian's task to place these widely disparate truths into context, to illustrate how the mote of a single life must inevitably blend into the great flow. Be it a tale of light or darkness, of great men or small, the historian's pen must record honestly and impartially the perception of the truth that is viewed through said historian's eyes.

Most often the droplet of an individual's story is swept along by the greater flow, contributing its almost imperceptible weight in ways that even the astute chronicler must struggle to perceive. These are the teeming millions of the world, and despite the relative insignificance of each individual, it is their collective mass that gives majesty to the current and power to its flow.

Occasionally, however, a speck of a specific life will develop a momentum of its own, setting a course that will have impetus far beyond its own weight. Such an individual will twist the motes around it, perhaps swirling into a deep eddy, even pulling much of the river into an isolated and powerful orbit. Sometimes it will dip below the surface, vanishing by all appearances, yet in fact creating a powerful vortex, with currents rippling far downstream.

But even such mighty waters, these mortal cataracts and whirlpools, cannot escape the confines of the river. Ultimately they, too, are swept by the relentless, unstoppable current that is time, until even the ripples have faded away, vanished as if they had never been.

In a sense, the historian's task is to demonstrate otherwise. He must draw these rivulets up from the past and reproduce them to one who would study the river's channel, who would try to understand even a small segment of the overall course. The diligent chronicler pushes through the murky depths, identifies the key strains, and finds at the bed of the river the firmament that provides the proof.

Of historians who are perceptive and capable of recording the truth there are many, though one in particular comes to mind at present. Of tales worthy of the telling, the same may be said. Though the river is wide, this is a channel of the current that has always held great fascination to all who would hear the history of Krynn, perhaps because this tale concerns a mortal who strove constantly to hold the frailties of mortality at bay.

And he very nearly succeeded.

Now I find it fitting that this historian, and this tale, should come together. It is a story of life and death, though not necessarily in that order, and of a man who stirred the River of Time like no one else. His passing, when it became known, was celebrated by all who knew of his villainy and his might. His return to life, conversely, was conceived and executed in secret, and bore with it the seeds of overwhelming terror for the future of the world.

Yet I precede myself—or, rather, I precede the telling. Let it be noted that the river must at first be observed in portions upstream from the main channel of our story, segments of time that will place our story in context. Those glimpses, naturally, have been selected by the chronicling historian. He knows, as do I, that the story in fact begins much closer to the great stream's headwaters, and that its currents will ripple farther, into cataracts that remain to be revealed.

But herein lies the heart of the tale.

From the Chronicles of Astinus,
Lorekeeper of Krynn

Chapter 1

A Seed of Survival

*In the Name of His Excellency Astinus, Lorekeeper of Krynn
Notes Pertaining to events 2 PC-1 PC
Scribed this Fourth Misham, Deepkolt, 369 AC*

One of the greatest challenges in recording the story of
Fistandantilus arises from the fact that he—and the archmage Raistlin Majere—caused the River of Time to
divide for a period into two parallel channels. There are
two versions of history, and though in many respects
they are identical, in some significant aspects the
flowage takes a decidedly different appearance between
the two tales.

The divergence occurred a short time before the Cataclysm. In one history, Fistandantilus made preparations
for his journey to Istar, where he would forge an alliance

with a white-robed priest and cast his mighty spell of time travel. In the other course of the channel, Fistandantilus was mastered by Raistlin Majere, who had traveled from the future for the confrontation. It became the younger man's destiny to escape the Cataclysm, to befriend a priest, and to follow in the steps that (he learned too late) were ordained by destiny.

In either case, one hundred years after the Cataclysm there occurred an epic battle of magical power and violence, and the Dwarfgate War culminated in the massive destruction of Dergoth. In one current of history, Fistandantilus was killed here. In the other, Raistlin was banished to the Abyss—but there, too, it seems likely that the remnant portion of Fistandantilus met a matching end.

I shall focus this consideration of my research upon the time leading up to the confrontation. Raistlin and Fistandantilus were two entities before the melding of their lives by the magic that would so stir the River of Time. While the gods of Krynn and the Kingpriest of Istar moved ever closer to their inevitable clash, the Tower of Wayreth became the center of magical mastery on Ansalon, and the archmage Fistandantilus rose to the highest pinnacle of his power.

The elder wizard was the black-robed archmage, Master of the Tower of Sorcery, and—subsequent to his creation of the time-travel spell—Master of Past and Present as well. He had existed for centuries and scribed spellbooks that unlocked arcane secrets no mage before—or since, with one exception—would ever be able to grasp. Already Fistandantilus was widely known to be an ancient being. Even a study of elven lore must progress to the earliest volumes to predate him. Certainly for a long time prior to the Cataclysm he was the undisputed lord of magic upon Ansalon.

Central to his longevity, we now know, was the parasitical consumption of young lives—specifically, the blood and souls of the most skilled among his apprentices, those who were strong and who bore the seeds of magic deep within them. He harvested them as coldly as any butcher might a hog. The frequency of these cruel and murderous episodes is hard to judge, but it seems likely that he claimed a new apprentice's life at least every couple of decades.

Yet still the young men came to him, perhaps not quite believing in the horror stories they surely must have heard. They were drawn by ambition, knowing that he was the only teacher who could show them the secrets of true magical power. Desperate for the keys to this knowledge and to its attendant might, they traveled from far and wide to seek the great wizard. And indeed, many a black-robed sorcerer emerged from that tutelage with his life, if not his soul, intact, progressing to a reign of greatness and high influence in the world.

But there were many who never came out, who gave their lives to the archmage's insatiable hunger for young, vital hearts. And ever did the ancient one remain vibrant with eternal health, vigorous youth, and the greatest magic that the world had ever known.

And this brings us to Raistlin, whose mission has been well documented. In the aftermath of the War of the Lance, he journeyed into the past so that he could learn from, and inevitably challenge, the archmage. He mastered the spellbooks of Fistandantilus and had the advantage of knowing the history that he would attempt to revise. Indeed, one of the ironies of Raistlin's story is that the man who was so determined to change the course of the river found instead that he was trapped into reliving one of the most violent and disastrous segments of the flow.

The contest between Fistandantilus and Raistlin would be a battle with enigmatic results, a cataract of the river that tumbles well beyond the bounds of my current research. However, on one thing, the archmage's notes provide impeccable confirmation. (Incidentally, this act occurs *only* on the historical path involving the confrontation with Raistlin; in the original occurrence, I assume that the life of some unfortunate apprentice was successfully consumed by the archmage.)

In any event, of the preparations made by Fistandantilus immediately before he attempted to devour Raistlin's soul, one sequence must be noted.

Perhaps it was because he sensed the great power of his adversary that he performed this enchantment. Certainly Raistlin was a potential victim who stirred a great hunger in Fistandantilus. At the same time, the villainous sorcerer needed to approach his newest conquest with a measure of respect. To this end, he took a precaution prior to his spell that was unique among the countless castings he had done before.

As usual, the archmage had several apprentices besides the young man of mysterious origins whom he had selected as his victim. The historically astute reader may well be aware that, prior to his soul-devouring ritual, Fistandantilus invariably discharged his other apprentices. The unchosen were sent from the tower immediately, with no awareness of how fortunate they had been. It has been documented—by both parties, in fact—that he did this prior to his attack against the disguised Raistlin.

The archmage's own notes detail his precaution, which required the use of a complex enchantment, a spell that he cast upon himself. It is a complicated procedure to understand, similar to the magic jar spell that allows a powerful sorcerer to place his soul, his spiritual essence, into some sort of object for a period of time, protecting the wizard, as it were, from the vicissitudes of the world.

In the case of Fistandantilus, this casting split his essence into an animate and inanimate portion, allowing his mortal self to remain intact, but preserving a precautionary reserve of his entire being. The potion embodied a portion of all his essences—mental, physical, spiritual, and arcane. This enchanted liquid he collected in a silver vial and bestowed upon one of his departing apprentices as a gift. Even at the time, according to the archmage's notes, he was not certain whether or not the magic worked.

Our current tale is not concerned with the history-shaping conflict between Raistlin and the archmage, although later we shall be peripherally concerned with the subsequent events regarding the Dwarfgate War and the convulsion of magic that would shape the mountain called Skullcap. For the time being, instead, we will follow the steps of this discharged apprentice, one Whastryk Kite of Kharolis.

Foryth Teel,
In unworthy service to Gilean

Chapter 2

Whastryk Kite

1 PC
First Palast, Reapember

The young magic-user tried to walk softly, to bring his smooth-soled boots soundlessly against the forest trail. But with each footfall came a whisper of bending grass or the tiny slurp of suction from moist, bare dirt. Once, when he raised his head to look through the brush before him, he carelessly cracked a twig, and the noise was like a lightning bolt stabbing through the silent woods and into his pounding heart.

He told himself that it should not be so, that his fear, his extreme caution, were illogical reactions to a danger that he had by now left safely behind. In fact, it was a threat that was probably imaginary. There would be no pursuit—indeed, he had been sent away from Wayreth by the master of the tower himself, and Fistandantilus was no doubt glad that young Whastryk Kite was gone.

But still he was afraid.

Nervously he cast a glance over his shoulder, along the tangled track of Wayreth Forest. The tower was invisible now, screened by the intervening foliage. That same greenery had parted invitingly before Whastryk, leading him away from the sorcerous spire and its two remaining occupants. The tower, with its arcane legacy and wonderful trove of magic, had been Whastryk Kite's home, as well as his school and the residence of his companions, for several years. Yet abruptly the course of all the apprentices' studies had come to an end. Now, as he suspected that he had left that place behind him forever, he felt a strange mixture of emotions.

Despite the midsummer warmth in the woods, when he thought of the pair of magic-users who still occupied that arcane spire, the young mage shivered forcefully enough to send ripples shimmering through the smooth silk of his black robe. What powers, he wondered, would be wielded by them before the issue was resolved?

And that resolution, Whastryk had come to suspect, would be the death of the young apprentice, the lone representative from among the archmage's pupils who had been selected to remain.

He shuddered at the thought of ancient Fistandantilus, the lean and wolfish man with the vitality and temperament of a caged feline. Whastryk had seen the hunger so clearly etched in his master's ageless eyes. The archmage craved something precious and vital from the young men who came to study at his table, to learn from his words. He lusted for their youth and vigor, and from one he would claim his very soul.

Whastryk had felt his master's hunger himself, had chilled to the knowledge that the elder's gaze seemed to penetrate to every fiber of his being. The touch of those eyes had been a terrifying sensation, yet strangely exciting and alluring as well.

Even now, as the discharged apprentice hastened away on the forest trail—even now, when he suspected that the chosen one was doomed, would quite possibly be dead before the sun rose on the morrow—Whastryk felt a surge of jealousy, of pure, raw hatred directed at the one who had been selected to remain.

Why had that apprentice, and not Whastryk Kite, been found worthy?

Bitter thoughts raged in the young mage's mind, and he felt again the familiar resentment, the knowledge that in every aspect of life, his lot was unfairly restricted. Orphaned and abandoned as a boy, he had survived on the rough streets of Xak Tsaroth by his wits and eventually by the knack for magic that had persuaded bigger, stronger thugs to leave him alone. Then Fistandantilus had summoned him to the tower, and Whastryk had seen things he could never have imagined. For his own benefit, he had learned to wield his power, an arcane might that would allow him to master many other men and further the causes of the Order of the Black Robe.

And yet he would have given it up for a chance to stay behind, to share the powerful—and undoubtedly lethal—enchantment of his master's greatest spell.

Still, the young mage carried a valuable legacy from the Tower of Wayreth. It was not a treasure in his pouch, a value in steel or even in arcane trinkets. It was the knowledge of magic, the memories of his master's teaching, that he now held in his mind. He was free, and that knowledge would be the key to great power among the world of humankind. Whastryk merely had to choose where he would go and how he would wield that power.

And he also had one memento of his tutelage in the library of Fistandantilus.

The magic-user's hand settled around the silver vial in his belt pouch, the treasure that his master had given him as a parting gift. The liquid within was clear, and his fingers could sense the unnatural coldness through the smooth metal of the tiny jar. He remembered the solemn sense of ceremony with which Fistandantilus had bestowed the treasure upon him.

And once more he wondered, Why me? The archmage had been secretive on that point, telling his young apprentice to save the potion, retaining it for all the years of his life, unless, at some point, Whastryk Kite was threatened with imminent and seemingly inevitable death. If he drank the potion at such a time, Fistandantilus had declared, then the magical liquid would insure his survival.

A rumble of thunder trembled through the woods, and the black-clad mage paused. The tiny patches of sky visible between the dense canopy of leaves were invariably blue, and the sky had been cloudless when Whastryk had departed the tower barely two hours earlier. When the deep, resonant noise came again, the man knew: This thunder was born of magic, not nature. The source was the tall tower, the spire of sorcery that lay at the heart of Wayreth Forest.

Light flashed, a sparking glow brighter than the sun, penetrating deep among the trees with a cold, white glare. More thunder smashed, and shivers of force rolled through the ground. Whastryk stepped faster now, trotting, then running along the trail. His earlier regrets vanished, washed away by a wave of pure fear that—like the noise and the light—certainly emanated from that distant tower.

Winds lashed through the trees, hot blasts of air that bore none of the moist freshness of a rainstorm. Instead, this was a stinking, sulfurous gale, a wash of putrid breath that pushed him even faster along the trail. Lightning crackled with growing violence, and he shuddered under a clear impression that the sky itself screamed in raw horror. He heard a clatter, then felt a sharp stab of pain against his shoulder as black hailstones rattled through the trees, bouncing and cracking against the ground.

And then he was sprinting like the wind, driven by the force of his own terror. Branches lashed his face, and unnatural gusts tore at his hair, whipped his robe. It seemed that the two magic-users behind him, the tower, the woods, and the very world itself were being torn to pieces. If he slowed even a half pace from his full run, Whastryk sensed that the destruction would extend even to himself.

Finally the woods were gone. Wayreth Forest vanished into the mists over his shoulder, a place of his past. He was surprised to learn, at the first village he came to, that he was in the foothills of the Kharolis Mountains. After all, the magical forest had grown outside the great trading city of Xak Tsaroth when Whastryk had first encountered it. But he had heard that was the way of the enchanted wood. The worthy traveler did not find Wayreth Forest, so much as Wayreth Forest found the worthy traveler.

Now he saw no sign of the woods behind him, and the young mage thought it was good to be removed from the place. He set his sights upon the future, sensing that he would never see that forest again—and the knowledge was more a relief than a fear.

Chapter 3

Ends and Conclusions

In the Name of His Excellency Astinus, Lorekeeper of Krynn
Notes Pertaining to events 2 PC–1 PC
Scribed this Fourth Misham, Deepkolt, 369 AC

I have regrettably concluded that, for the most part, the tale of Whastryk Kite is the story of a relatively unremarkable life. He left the Tower of Wayreth and made his way to Haven. (It should be noted that in this he was fortunate; several of the other apprentices who departed at the same time as Whastryk journeyed to Xak Tsaroth and Istar; naturally they perished at either site during the Cataclysm. Apparently Whastryk Kite had better instincts—or information.)

In any event, upon entering the city of Haven, Whastryk took up residence there and prepared to put his magic to use. He established himself with the name of the Black Kite and immediately started building a reputation as a sorcerer to be feared—and one who was willing to perform services, for the right buyer at an adequate price.

Within a short time, of course, Krynn was rocked by the Cataclysm. Haven was spared much of the damage that befell other regions of Ansalon; in fact, the good fortune caused the city to swell with immigrants fleeing from regions that had been sorely wracked.

Never a godly place, Haven eventually became rife with the Seeker priests, purveyors of false religions who pronounced their doctrines on every street corner in the teeming city. However, immediately after the Cataclysm, conditions were terribly unsettled. He who had such power and wielded it to his advantage would be able to gain great influence.

Over the years, the Black Kite became well known in Haven as one who not only had such power, but was also willing to employ that power to serve his own ends. His services were used by brigands and warlords, by jilted lovers and jealous wives. Some of the city's most powerful nobles paid him handsomely, for no service other than that he left them alone—and that the rich folk could let it be known that the dark wizard was an acquaintance of theirs, if not a true friend.

Whastryk Kite modeled himself after his master, and the calling of the Dark Mage suited him. Of course, he was never to be as powerful as Fistandantilus, but he was able to wield great influence in the relatively isolated orbit of post-Cataclysmic Haven.

Fortunately the wizard left some rather extensive notes and records regarding those years. I have studied them and reached firm conclusions:

Firstly, Whastryk Kite heard only rumors of the fate befalling the wizard Fistandantilus, his former master. It was said that the archmage had been in Istar when the wrath of the gods smote the world. Since there were no reports of his presence anywhere in Ansalon, Whastryk—

and the rest of the world—made the not illogical assumption that he had been killed.

For Whastryk, it was enough to be his own master. Even more, he became one of the foremost black-robed magic-users of post-Cataclysmic Krynn. Of Fistandantilus he thought only rarely, most often when he held the small silver vial that had been the wizard's parting gift. It is clear from his notes that he did not know what the potion was for; nevertheless, he kept it ready. Occasionally he would examine the clear liquid, sensing its deep enchantment, its abiding might. He always carried it on his person, holding it for the time when he feared that his death might be at hand.

In the later years of his life, Whastryk became the target of many an ambitious hero. These were people who had come to hate the wizard for wrongs he had inflicted, directly or indirectly. Some were bold knights acting alone, while others were bands of simple folk anxious to avenge an evil deed. At least one was a woman, daughter of a merchant Whastryk had destroyed for his failure to offer the mage proper respect.

All of these attackers were killed, usually with great quickness and violence as soon as they passed through the arched entry into the wizard's courtyard. He developed a tactic effective not only for its deadliness, but also for the sense of terror it instilled in potential enemies. Whastryk would cast a spell from his eyes, twin blasts of energy that would strike the victim in the same place, tearing the orbs of vision from his flesh and leaving gory, gaping wounds. Such blinded enemies, if they still presented a threat, were very easy to kill.

The notes reveal in graphic detail that some of the wizard's foes—including the bold, doomed heroine— were only slain following a long period of imprisonment and tortures of mental, physical, and spiritual assault. (Indeed, the details of this suffering may cause even the dispassionate chronicler to weep with sorrow for the victims.)

By this time, the wizard exerted his control over a very

significant part of the city—a region that included many
prosperous shops and approximately one quarter of
Haven's entire area. It was an area ruled by evil, selfish-
ness, and greed, but it was also a place of one undisputed master. Whastryk collected a great deal of money
from those within his orbit, and he commanded the obedience of a great many sword arms.

By thirty years after the Cataclysm, the theocrats were
beginning to lay their claims to official rulership of
Haven, and Whastryk did nothing to usurp their authority in a visible or ostentatious fashion. Indeed, it is
known that he performed many favors, including assas-
sinations, magical disguises, and surreptitious recon-
naissance, for the powerful Seeker priests. No doubt the
underhanded use of magic served to awe the populace
and enhanced the authority of the corrupt theocrats and
their false gods.

And always the wizard's power grew, and his influence spread wide across the world—until, in 37 AC, his
writings abruptly ceased.

Though this might be regarded as occurring at the
height of Whastryk's influence and power, a careful
study of the records arrives at a different conclusion.
Indeed, I have discerned that, during the five or six
years preceding (say, from 31 AC on), the notations of
Whastryk increasingly indicate the effects of advancing
age. I see a hint of palsy creeping into what had once
been a steady hand, and the last volume of records is
shoddily kept, at least in comparison to Whastryk's
early notes. Eventually, with no reason given, the notes
cease altogether.

Perhaps boredom simply caused the mage to lose
interest in his record keeping (a historian's worst nightmare!), or perhaps he met some kind of sudden end that
has been lost to the history books. Furthermore, though I
have pored over the records from Haven during that and
subsequent periods, I have found no mention of the silver vial given to Whastryk by Fistandantilus. Whatever
the archmage's purposes with that uncharacteristic gift,

it seems conclusive that those purposes were thwarted. The vial and its contents, like the life of Whastryk itself, were brought to a terminus in that chaotic city.

Perhaps I shall get to Haven some day to pursue the matter; until then, it seems that there is nothing more to learn.

Foryth Teel,
In Research for the Scale of Gilean

Chapter 4

An Unlikely Hero

37 AC
Third Miranor

On the way home from the smithy, Paulus Thwait turned as he always did into the street where he lived. It was more of an alley, he was inclined to admit in moments of honesty, but—more important to him than any outward appearance of status or grandeur—it led the way to the place that he called *home*.

A smile played across his face, brightening the young man's normally intense features as he thought of the wife and baby awaiting him a hundred steps away. He ignored the close quarters of the taverns and tenements pressing from each side, the squalor of Haven that was so rank around him, and allowed his step to be buoyed by the thought of the cramped rooms that would be warm and aromatic from the cookstove, and by the knowledge that his family would be there, waiting.

It was strange to feel so happy, he thought, remembering that a few years earlier he would have guessed such a life to be as removed from his future as a visit to the farthest of Krynn's three moons. Indeed, how easily he could have fallen into a life of thuggery, playing the role of one of the Black Kite's bullies as so many young men of Haven did. After all, Paulus had proved that he was strong and brave, and keen and steady with his blade. And he had a temper that insured his fighting skills stayed in good practice.

Yet he had talent with his hands and eyes as well, talent that had been recognized by one of the city's premier silversmiths. That artisan, Revrius Frank, had taken the young man as an apprentice, allowed Paulus Thwait's talent to grow through the working of an honest trade.

The brawny apprentice had progressed to journeyman in a surprisingly short time, and lately Revrius had slyly hinted that he would soon have competition in this city quarter from another master silversmith. Now, making his way home at the end of a long, hard day of work, Paulus felt a flush of pride at the notion, and his pride swelled into a determination that tomorrow he would do an even better job with his metal and his tools.

But even beyond the gratification of his developing craft, the young silversmith had the best reason of all to be happy. It had been nearly two years ago that a caravan of settlers had come through the city, on their way to the good farming country reputed to exist to the south, in Kharolis. Belinda Mayliss, the daughter of one such farmer, had immediately caught the tradesman's eye, an attraction that swiftly proved mutual. The two had been married before Belinda's family had moved on, and now his bride—and, recently, their young, husky baby boy— had given Paulus all the reason he could hope for to work hard, do well, and be happy.

In the quarter of Haven where Revrius Frank maintained his smithy, Paulus was already developing a reputation as a man who could be trusted to perform skilled work. Indeed, for the last week he had been working on his most elaborate project to date: a silver mirror of perfect reflectivity, a sheet of metal hammered thin so as to be easily transportable, in a frame that would be highly pleasing to the eye. Tomorrow he would put the final polish on the piece, which had been commissioned by the most successful garment maker in Haven.

It is safe to presume that, as he walked home this pleasant spring evening, Paulus Thwait had no inkling of the role he would play as a small but influential mote in the current that makes up the River of Time.

He moved easily up the lane, stepping over the refuse that was scattered in the gutters, skirting the elder hermit who snored noisily, as he did every afternoon, on a small patch of greening grass. Close now, Paulus caught the scents of garlic and pepper, and knew his young wife had found the ingredients for a marvelous stew. The silversmith's stomach growled loudly as he clumped up the steps that led to the narrow balcony outside of their humble lodgings.

"That fat horse merchant tipped me two steel pieces for my work on his bridle," he announced as he burst through the door. Belinda, the babe in her arms, rushed across the room to him, startling Paulus with a gasp of relief as she threw herself against his chest.

Only then did he notice the mysterious figure across the room, in the corner farthest from the fire. It resembled a man cloaked completely in rags of dark cloth, but as he looked closer, Paulus felt a shiver of disquiet. Though the stranger seemed to stand upright, its lower reaches vanished into tendrils of mist! It had no legs, nor did it seem to be supported in any way on the floor.

"It came here a moment ago!" Belinda declared in a rush of fright. "Just appeared—in the corner, where it is now."

"Did it harm you? Threaten you?" His voice choked as

Paulus looked at the thing, fear and fury mingling in his emotions.

"No, nor young Dany. It just stayed there, as if it's waiting for something."

Paulus was a brave man, but he knew that it was only sensible to fear magic and the supernatural, both of which seemed well represented by the disembodied figure that now swirled threateningly toward the middle of the tiny room. But this was *his* home, and that knowledge brought courage and determination to the fore.

"What do you want?" the silversmith demanded in a voice thick with anger. All his brawler's past came flooding back, and he crouched, fists clenching at his side.

"Two steel pieces will be an adequate start," hissed the stranger in a voice that reminded the silversmith of water rolling at a steady boil.

"Why should I pay you?"

"Because you wish to live, to see your family survive, and to ply your trade in my city."

"I am doing all that now." With great effort, the smith restrained himself from striking the apparition.

"Ah, but for how long? That is the question every mortal dreads to answer, is it not?"

"Go away. Leave my home!"

"I will take the steel for now," insisted the ghostly interloper.

"You will take nothing!"

"Hah! You will pay, as do they all. You will be in my master's thrall from this day forward! And if you do not give steel, then I claim by fee in dearer coin!"

Infuriated, the young man attacked the figure, only to find that his fist punched through a cowl of black, cold air. He felt a chill of fear, but in his anger, he flailed wildly, both hands swinging through the intangible form. The vaporous messenger slipped past him in a hissing spoor of gas, a sound punctuated by a manic, cackling laugh.

Belinda screamed as the insidious vapor swirled around her and the squalling baby. With a whoosh of wind, the gaseous cloud swept the child out of her arms. "You *will* obey. And to be certain, I will keep the child— one year, to begin with."

The ghostly vision danced laughingly away as Paulus lunged after his son. "After that time, you *might* get him back. And if you come after him, know that you shall be struck blind, and he will be killed."

With a gust of wind, the ghost whirled away, carrying the baby through an opened window and out of sight in the darkened skies.

The pair charged out the door, but already the apparition—and the child—had vanished into the night air.

"Where did they go?" The young mother's question was an anguished wail. "Where did that thing take my baby?"

Paulus, frantic with grief and fear, knew the answer.

"The Black Kite!" He whispered the exclamation, as all citizens of Haven whispered when they mentioned the name of the feared and hated wizard. "This was *his* work!"

"But why did he come here—why *us?*" Belinda turned to him, seizing him by the shoulders. "And why would he take Dany?"

"He wants me—he wants power over me," Paulus declared, stunned by the realization. "I should have expected this. He holds all this corner of Haven in his thrall."

"You can't matter—not to him!"

"I can." Paulus was beginning to understand. "I know that Revrius Frank is forced to pay him, though he never speaks of it. Indeed, he's ashamed of the fact. But the Black Kite takes his steel and leaves him otherwise alone."

"Then why did he take Dany?"

"Because I was a fool," Paulus admitted, slumping in dejection. "I should have paid him."

"No!" Belinda was suddenly adamant. "It's more than that. He *fears* you. He knows you might stand up to him."

His wife continued, speaking with firm conviction—and affection. "He knows what a stubborn, bullheaded fool you are, and he knows the reputation of your fists."

Paulus flushed with shame, not wanting to recollect the part of his life spent brawling and fighting, but he knew that she was right.

"I won't pay him," he vowed. "But I'll get Dany back for us, and I'll see that Whastryk Kite is the one who pays."

"But how can you? You heard him. You'd be struck blind as soon as you try to go in!"

"I know, but I have a plan." Or at least, he amended privately, I *will* have a plan. Indeed, Paulus was no longer an impetuous man. Yet his son was gone, and he was certain that if he was going to save him, he would have to act fast.

Leaving his wife with a promise that he would be careful, Paulus went quickly to the smithy of Revrius Frank. There he spent several hours polishing to a high sheen the mirror of pure silver that he had been crafting for the garment maker. The reflective metal had been hammered so thin that it was of very light weight, easily transportable, and perfectly suited to the silversmith's plan. Finally he attached a leather handle to the mirror's back, ignoring the deep gouges he scored in the once immaculate frame.

Next the silversmith girded on a sword, suspending the weapon from his own belt, which was secured by a sturdy silver buckle of his own design. The metal clasp represented most of the saved wealth of his young family, and it seemed appropriate that he wore it now, when he went to fight for that family's very survival.

It was a grimly determined Paulus Thwait who started through the streets toward the wizard's home, which was a great mansion and compound that occupied a full block of the city. Black towers jutted from beyond a stone wall. The barrier was breached only in one place, by an arched gateway, an opening wide enough to allow passage of a large carriage.

The reputation of the place was well known to everyone in Haven. There was no gate that ever closed across
the entryway, but anyone who had entered there with
hostile intentions had been met by the wizard, then
struck blind by those searing darts that emanated from
his eyes. Once sightless, the victim was usually captured
or killed. Those who had been taken prisoner invariably
vanished forever from the ken of the rest of humankind.

"Whastryk Kite! I demand the return of my son!"

Paulus loudly announced his presence, and then made
as though to enter the low archway in the gatehouse
wall. Here he waited in the shadow underneath the arch,
watching the great door of the house.

In moments the door swung wide, and something
black swirled forward with impossible haste. The figure
was cloaked heavily, its appearance blurred like the
ghostly apparition, but Paulus knew this was the wizard, the Black Kite's speed clearly enhanced by some
arcane spell. The silversmith took care to keep his eyes
low, away from his enemy's face.

"Fool!" cried Whastryk Kite, in a sharper, more immediate version of the voice that had bubbled from the leg-
less visitor. "You dare to challenge me, silversmith?
Know that your child, and your bride, shall pay!"

The laugh turned to a sneer. "But take comfort that
you will not have to witness their suffering!"

Paulus still did not look at his enemy. Instead, he held
the mirror before his face and stepped forward as he
heard the mage bark sharp, guttural words of magic.

Crimson light flashed in the courtyard, and the silversmith heard a wail of anguish. Now he drew his weapon,
dropped the mirror, and charged.

The wizard known as the Black Kite was reeling backward, both hands clutching the bleeding wounds that
were his eye sockets. Paulus's boots thudded on the
pavement as he rushed closer, and he raised the sword
for a single, killing strike.

Then the man saw the mage, with his left hand, pull a
small silver vial from a pouch at his side. Ignoring the

danger and the blood pouring down his face, Whastryk tossed back his head and instantly swallowed the vial's contents in the face of Paulus's attack.

A moment later the silversmith's sword cut through the wizard's cowled hood, slicing deep into his brain. The Black Kite stiffened and toppled heavily to the ground, where he lay motionless in a spreading pool of blood.

The bold young silversmith stepped back only far enough to keep the sticky liquid from his boots. After a minute, he probed with his sword, making certain that the wizard was truly dead.

Then he went into the house to look for his child.

Chapter 5

Further Evidence

Scribed In Haven
371 AC
To my mentor and inspiration, Falstar Kane

As I had hoped, Esteemed Master, a chance to study the local records has allowed me to penetrate closer to the truth. To wit: I have learned of the fate of the wizard Whastryk Kite.

The tale was yielded up from the depths of Haven's oldest records. He did, in fact, die in 37 AC, killed by one of the citizens of this wretched city, a silversmith whose son the Black Kite had kidnapped. (The man's infant son was found, unharmed, within the magic-user's stronghold.)

As to the potion given to Whastryk Kite by Fistandantilus some thirty-eight years earlier, nothing is revealed by these records. It seems clear that, whether or not the magic was imbibed by Whastryk in his last moments, the enchantment had no effect on the outcome of the fight. The wizard was unequivocally slain; indeed, his passing was cause for more than a few celebrations.

Of the silversmith and his family a little more is known. The man became a hero for a short time: His quest had regained the baby, and an entire quarter of Haven was able to emerge from the shadow of the evil wizard's reign. Reputedly, there was enough gratitude among the merchants and tradesfolk to cause them to pay the young couple a handsome stipend.

Enriched by the rewards, the pair and their son removed to a small village in the country. There it is said that the baby grew to manhood, well versed in the tale of his father's heroism. Beyond that reference, however, the line disappears from view, offering no more disturbance to the waters of the great river.

Regarding the wizard Fistandantilus during this period of history, the records reveal no more. We know now that he used his time-travel spell to move forward to an age a hundred years following the Cataclysm.

But of his scheme to transport his essence via the potion of the magic jar, it must be concluded that he failed.

Your most loyal servant,
Foryth Teel

Chapter 6

Gantor Blacksword

251 AC
Third Mithrik, Dry-Anvil

The dwarf had been wandering for weeks, a span of time that seemed like years in the tortured ramblings of his mind. The Plain of Dergoth was a shattered, wounded landscape around him, everywhere waterless, parched into a barren desert by a midsummer sun. He had no destination, but he simply kept plodding along, leaving the tracks of his cleated boots like the trail of an aimless snake coursing through the dust and silt layering the hard, baked ground.

As he had done so many times since the beginning of his exile, he spun about, staring wildly into the distance, seeing the lofty bulk of the High Kharolis rising into the skies. Raising a knotted fist, he shook it at the massif, crying shrill challenges and insults, spitting loudly, stomping his feet, venting his fury against rock and sky.

And as always, the mountainous ridge remained silent and impassive, ignoring the dwarf's railing hysteria.

"I'll come back there, I will!" Gantor Blacksword shrieked. His hand came to rest on the hilt of the once splendid weapon that had girded his waist. Several times he had drawn the thing with a flourish, waving it at the mountain dwarf stronghold, but even through the feverish agitation of his despair, Gantor had come to see the gesture for the foolish act that it was.

Not foolish because the target of his rage was distant and unassailable, but because the hilt, steel-hard and wrapped with the hide of an ancient ogre, was only that: a handle, with no blade attached. Thane Realgar himself, lord and master of all the Theiwar clan, had snapped the weapon asunder as he had pronounced the sentence upon Gantor Blacksword.

The bearded, perpetually scowling Theiwar had been prepared to face death for his crime, even public execution or a painful demise following a long period of torture. Indeed, both were common fates handed to Theiwar murderers under clan law, and there was no dispute over Gantor's status as a killer of a fellow Theiwar. The best he had hoped for—and it was a slim hope—had been a forfeiture of his rather extensive personal wealth and a sentence to a lifetime of labor in the food warrens.

He could have faced torture and death bravely, and he would have gone willingly into the warrens, even knowing that he might never see the lightless waters of the Urkhan Sea again.

But he had never been prepared, could not have imagined, the utter horror of the sentence that Thane Realgar had pronounced.

Exile, under the naked sky.

The very concept had been so foreign that, upon first hearing the words, Gantor Blacksword had not fully grasped their meaning. Only as the thane had continued his dire pronouncement did the full sense of disbelieving fear seep slowly into Gantor's wicked and hateful brain.

"Your crimes have extended well beyond the boundaries that will be tolerated by our clan," declared Realgar, tacitly acknowledging that assassination, robbery, assault, and mayhem were common tactics for the settlement of disputes among the Theiwar.

"It is well known," Realgar continued, "that your conflict with Dwayal Thack was deep and true; both of you claimed ownership of the stone found between your delvings, and had you limited your activities merely to the killing of Dwayal in a fair fight, your presence before this board of judgment would never have been required."

Gantor had glowered and spat at the time, refusing to accept the words, though now he admitted to wishing that he had handled the problem exactly as the thane had suggested. Dwayal Thack had been a larger dwarf than Gantor, more skilled in the use of sword and axe, but even so the aggrieved miner had not been without recourse. After all, a fair fight among the Theiwar did not disallow the use of ambush or a stab in the back, and even the hiring of a trained assassin would have been acceptable, though in the latter case, Gantor might have been required to a pay a small stipend to the victim's family.

Instead, however, he had decided to take care of the problem himself. His plan had been simple but well thought out, and undeniably lethal.

It had been a simple matter to use carefully chiseled plugs of granite to block the two ventilation shafts connecting the Thack apartments to the rest of vast Thorbardin. Then Gantor Blacksword had visited one of the Theiwar alchemists, who were always willing—for a price—to aid the nefarious activities of their clients.

Armed with a smudge pot full of highly toxic vileroot, Gantor had approached his neighbor's front door during the quiet stillness that descended over the Theiwar city in the midst of the sleeping hours. Gantor had ignited the highly toxic mixture of herbs, hurled open the barrier, tossed the smudge pot inside, then slammed shut the door and fixed it in place with several carefully tooled steel wedges.

The rest of the killing had only taken a few minutes. There had been screams and gasps and a few feeble bashes against the door, and then silence.

Gantor still remembered his elation as he had awaited outside the door. Dwayal, his wife, his collection of brats—three or four offspring, so far as the murderous Theiwar had remembered—and whatever slaves and servants Dwayal Thack had employed had been inside the crowded apartments. They were inevitably dead by poisonous suffocation within minutes, though they suffered horribly during their last moments. The telltale stink of the vile-root extended into the corridor, so those who came in response to the commotion had no choice but to wait. Fortunately one of the things that made vile-root such an effective tool for this kind of work was the fact that the toxins in the smoke settled into a layer of soot within a few hours of vaporization.

When it was safe to enter, Gantor and several Theiwar wardens had entered the apartments—and then the true horror had been revealed.

One of Dwayal Thack's sons—may his name be cursed by the gods through eternity!—had been friends with one Staylstaff Realgarson, a favored nephew of none other than the Theiwar thane. Worse, Staylstaff had been visiting his friend, engaged in a bout of gambling, at the time of the murder. Naturally he, too, had perished as a result of the toxic fumes.

And Thane Realgar had proved utterly unwilling to treat the mishap as the unfortunate accident that it had surely been! Instead, the ruler of the Theiwar clan had reacted to the killing as if it constituted some sort of heinous, even unprecedented, crime. Gantor had been called before a clan tribunal, forced to listen to all sorts of accusatory remarks, and eventually came to realize that he would be punished for his natural and understandable—by Theiwar standards—attempt to defend his right to contested property.

Faced with the deliberations of the august body of wild-eyed, bristling dark dwarves, the accused had been prepared to accept his sentence bravely. He had vowed to himself that, no matter how heinous the tortures, he would not give the thane the satisfaction of seeing him, Gantor, lose his dignity or his pride. Indeed, he had been prepared to spit contemptuously when he was confronted by the terms of his punishment.

Yet all that resolve had vanished in the face of the actual sentence. Exile! Never in his worst nightmares— and Gantor Blacksword suffered some very horrible nightmares indeed—had the dwarf pictured a punishment so terrifying, so unutterably bleak, as that which cruel fate had delivered unto him. Thane Realgar's pale and luminous eyes had gleamed with a wicked light when he pronounced sentence, and the cheering of Dwayal Thack's many relatives had echoed from the rafters of the vaulted Judgment Hall when he had made his announcement:

"Gantor Blacksword, you are banished forever from the Theiwar Realms, and as well from all attended and allied steadings of the Kingdom of Thorbardin. You are sentenced to the world above, where you will live out your miserable days under the cruel light of the sun and without the comfort of your fellow dwarves."

His own scream of shrill terror had been drowned out by the delighted cheering of the gathered throng. With bitterness, Gantor remembered his own wife and elder son joining in the celebration. No doubt the faithless female had already taken a new mate, and the worthless offspring was certainly in the midst of squandering his father's hard-earned fortune. Such practical and unsentimental avarice was neither more nor less than the Theiwar way.

Of course, there was always the hope of revenge. . . . Someday Gantor Blacksword would find a way to make all his enemies suffer!

For a time, here under the horrifying, endless sky, the exiled Theiwar had failed to let reality dissuade him. He had spent the first days of his banishment in picturing the many vengeances he would inflict: his treacherous wife, slow-roasted on a spit over the family hearth. His son, skinned alive, but only over the course of many months. Indeed, perhaps the wronged patriarch could exact a whole year's worth of diversion before the wretched wastrel was at last put out of his suffering.

And Thane Realgar, too, would suffer the wrath of Gantor Blacksword, though not so mercifully as wife and son. No, the thane could only be sufficiently punished in the same fashion as he had sentenced Gantor Blacksword: He would be condemned to wander under the sun, banished from the comforts of stony Thorbardin for the rest of his days.

But over the initial weeks of his wandering exile, Gantor had at last realized that thoughts of revenge took him down a useless road. Without any real hope of returning to Thorbardin, he had no practical prospects of harming any of his enemies. And though the hatred, the desire for death and mayhem, never faded far from the forefront of the Theiwar's awareness, he had gradually realized that those urges would remain mere fantasies, unrealized by acts of truly gratifying bloodshed.

Instead, Gantor was reduced to this, to shaking his fist at the distant mountain, crying out his frustration and rage, then turning away in defeat to continue shambling over the trackless, dusty plain.

The dwarves of Thorbardin had equipped him with a meager pack full of provisions before they had summarily pushed him out of the South Gate of the great undermountain fortress. Gantor was given a small hand axe and a bone-handled knife with a blade of black steel that served as a mocking reminder of his once-honorable namesake. In addition, he had several skins full of drinking water, a blanket, a net, and many cakes of the hard, nourishing bread that was the major foodstuff of the mountain dwarves. As a final insult, Thane Realgar had taken Gantor's sword of black steel and snapped off the blade at the hilt, a further symbol of the disgraceful state to which he had fallen.

For a long time Gantor Blacksword had been sustained by little more than his rage. He had plodded through the Kharolis foothills during the nights and sought whatever shelter he could find during the day. When the sun was high, the Theiwar's eyes burned from the painful light, and when no cave or shady grove offered itself, he had been forced to pull his cloak over his head and lie, a huddled ball of misery, on the open ground until sunset.

The early days of his exile had carried him through lands of plentiful water, and during the nights he had been able to find fungus in the deep, wooded groves. Sometimes he had caught fish, using the fine webbing of the net to pull trout and sunfish from shallow streams. He ate the scaly creatures whole and raw, as was Theiwar custom, and the meager feasts had provided the few bright memories of his recent existence. Gantor's dwarfcake bread had lasted him for several weeks, thus augmented by the food that he could gather for himself. And he had been sustained.

But then his rambling course had progressed, coming all the way around the mountain dwarf kingdom until he had found himself on this trackless plain. There were no streams here, no groves wherein he could find the tender mushrooms. Worst of all, there were not even any caves, nor any tall features that would offer even minimal shade from the lethal sun. Day by day he had weakened, until his water was gone, and he shambled blindly onward, delirious and full of despair.

Since beginning his trek across the plain he had survived by eating . . . what? Gantor knew he hadn't killed anything, and there was nothing even remotely edible growing on the parched and arid desert. He had vague memories of carrion, rank and putrid meat surrounded by a maggot-infested pelt, but the gorging upon that foul meal had been a reflexive act, driven by mindless hunger.

And afterward he had been sick, his gut wracked by spasms and cramps that had dropped him in his tracks. Now he lay where he had fallen on the cracked plain, in this place, for more days than he knew. Several times since, just when he thought that the merciless sun must at last kill him, must finally bring to an end the awful suffering, he had been spared by sunset.

In fact, it had just happened again. Gantor's tongue was thick and dry in his mouth, and his parched lips cracked and bled with every effort of movement. He pushed himself over to lie on his back, staring upward at the vault of sky, seeing the pale wash of illumination, so cool and distant, that characterized the heavens on clear nights such as this. He had no knowledge of stars—Theiwar vision was far too imprecise to pick out the distant spots of illumination—but he knew there was something bright up there, something aloof and mocking.

He wanted only to die, but it seemed that Krynn itself conspired to keep him alive.

"Hey, fellow? I don't want to be rude, but that's an odd place to make a camp."

At first Gantor thought the words to be the products of another feverish dream, an attempt to drive him still further into madness. Yet he forced his aching tongue to move and parted his blistered lips enough to articulate a reply.

"I sleep where I will! I am dwarf, master of all beyond Thorbardin!" he boldly proclaimed. At least, he tried to boldly proclaim; the dryness of his throat reduced the proud boast to little more than a prolonged croak.

"Wait. I can't understand you. Do you want something to drink?"

Gantor couldn't reply, and in fact wondered why anyone who possessed such a magical voice would have trouble understanding his own profound response. Yet before he could voice his question, he felt a warm trickle over his lips. Reflexively he swallowed, and the water sent a jolt of pure pleasure through his parched body.

"How's that? More?"

Now the dwarf could see a dim shape, a shadow out-lined against the glow of the sky. Close before him, won-derful wetness dripped from the end of a waterskin. With a reflexive grab, fearful that the precious nectar would be snatched away, Gantor reached up with both hands, tearing the skin out of small fingers, thrusting the nozzle to his lips.

Water gushed into his mouth, soaking his bristling beard, causing him to choke and sputter—but still he guzzled desperately.

"Hey, don't drink it all!"

Gantor felt those small fingers touch his hands, and he growled a wet, splattering exhalation fierce enough to drive the figure of his rescuer hastily back a couple of steps.

"Well, I guess you can drink it all if you want," said that same voice, with a sigh of resignation. "Still, we might be better off saving a little for later—that is, if you want to. Well, I guess you don't."

Gantor, in any event, needed no permission. Indeed, he would have been halted by no command. When the skin was empty, he sucked on the small spout, chewing frantically, as if he would devour the very vessel itself.

"Wait! Don't wreck it!" Insistent now, the small hands came out of the darkness, seizing the drained waterskin and pulling it away.

The dwarf made an effort to resist, but his gut was taken by an abrupt spasm that wrenched him into a ball, then threatened to send all that precious water spuming back out of him. Clenching his jaws, tightening his gorge, Gantor resisted the nausea with the full strength of his will, forced the life-giving sustenance to remain in his belly. Gradually, over the course of minutes, he felt the water seep into his limbs, his brain, invigorating his thoughts, restoring some measure of acuity to his eyes, his ears, and his skin.

Finally Gantor Blacksword took note of his compan-ion. The stranger was traveling light and alone, so far as the dwarf could see. The fellow was not as tall as—and far more slender than—a dwarf. His face had high cheekbones and was narrow and weathered, lined now by furrows of concern as the twin eyes regarded the dwarf cautiously. He had a great knot of hair tied atop his head, a sweep that extended in a long tail across his shoulder. That mane flipped gracefully as the visitor looked to the left, then the right, then back down to the dwarf.

"What are you?" Gantor Blacksword demanded, fingers instinctively inching toward the bone-handled knife concealed at his belt. His voice was still a rattling croak, but at least his tongue and lips seemed to move.

"Emilo Haversack, at your service," said the fellow, with a bow that sent the topknot of hair cascading toward the dwarf.

With a whimper, Gantor recoiled from the sudden attack, until he realized that it wasn't an attack at all. His blunt fingers firmly clasped around the knife, the Theiwar tried again. "Not who—*what* are you?"

"Why, I'm a traveler," said Emilo. "Like yourself, I guess—a traveler across the Plains of Dergoth. Though I must say that I've traveled to a lot of different places, and every one of them was more interesting than this. Most of them a *lot* more interesting."

The dwarf growled, shaking his head, sending cascades of water flinging from his bristling beard. His eyes, huge and pale by normal standards, glared balefully at his diminutive rescuer.

"Oh, you mean *what*, like in dwarf or human!" declared Emilo with an easy smile. "I'm a kender. And pleased to make your acquaintance."

Once again the stranger made a threatening gesture, thrusting a hand forward, palm perpendicular to the ground, fingers pointing toward the Theiwar's chest. This time Gantor was ready, and the knife came up, the black steel carving a swooshing arc through the air.

"Hey! You almost cut me!" cried the kender, whipping his fingers out of the path of the assault. "Haven't you ever shaken hands before?"

"Keep your hands away from me." Gantor's voice was a low growl, barely articulate, but apparently impressive enough to deter the menacing kender, who took a half step backward and cleverly regarded the dwarf behind a mask of hurt feelings and morose self-pity.

"Maybe I should keep *all* of me away from you," sniffed the long-haired traveler. "I'm beginning to think it was even a mistake to give you my water. Though I guess you would have died here if I hadn't. And anyway, I can always get more." Here the kender shivered slightly, looking nervously over his shoulder. "But I guess I'll have to go back to those caves to find it again."

"Caves?" One word from the kender's ramblings penetrated the Theiwar dwarf's lunatic mind. "There's a cave? Where?" Gantor tried to scramble to his feet, but his legs collapsed and he fell to his knees. He reached forward to seize the kender, but the little fellow skipped back, causing the dwarf's hands to clasp together in an imploring posture.

"Why, over there. In the big mountain that looks like a skull. The one they call Skullcap."

"Take me there!" Gantor screamed, lunging forward. The promise of darkness, of shade from the merciless sun, was a more enticing prospect even than the thought of more water.

"I'm not sure I want to go anywhere with you," declared the kender, his narrow chin set in a firm line. "Didn't you just try to kill me? And after I saved your life, to boot. No, I don't think—"

"Please!" the Theiwar croaked the unfamiliar word, a reflex action that achieved its purpose: For the time being, the kender stopped talking about leaving the wretched dwarf here in the middle of the plain.

For his own part, Gantor Blacksword tried to force his newly revitalized mind through some mental exercise. This was a foreign creature, more dangerous by far than the hated Hylar and Daewar of the other mountain dwarf clans. Every enraged fiber of his being, every treacherous and double-dealing experience from his past, told the Theiwar that this kender was a threat, an enemy to be defeated, one whose valuables rightfully belonged to the one who killed him.

Yet right now the greatest of those valuables was knowledge, an awareness of a place where a cave, and water, could be found. And despite the dark dwarf clan's propensity for torture, for theft and illicit acquisition, no Theiwar had ever figured out a way to pry knowledge from a corpse.

And so, for now, the kender would need to stay alive. That settled, the dwarf tried to focus on the current of prattle that seemed to issue from the kender's mouth at such an impossibly high speed.

"It was awfully nice meeting you and all, I'm sure," Emilo Haversack was saying. "But now I really must be going. Important wandering to do, you understand . . . have to see the coast, as a matter of fact. Do you know which way the ocean—oh, never mind! Actually, I'm sure I can find it myself."

Gantor croaked a response that he hoped was friendly.

"Anyway, I can see that you have matters of your own to keep you busy. As I said, it really has been pleasant, at least by the standards of a chance meeting during the dark of night in the middle of a desert. . . ."

"Wait!" The Theiwar articulated the word with a great effort of will. "I—I'd like to talk to you some more. Won't you join me here in my camp?"

He gestured to the featureless, cracked ground around him. It was the place in this gods-forsaken wasteland where he had collapsed, nothing more, and yet the kender beamed as if he had been invited into a grand palace.

"Well, I don't mind if I do, really. It has been a long walk. . . ." Emilo shivered suddenly, looking over his shoulder again, and the dwarf wondered what could make this clearly seasoned wanderer so nervous. "And I could use some company myself."

The kender crossed his legs in a fashion no dwarf could hope to mimic as he squatted easily on the ground.

"I hope you're feeling a little better after the water. You know, you really should carry some with you. After all, a person can die of thirst out here."

"I *wanted* to—" Gantor started to speak in his habitual snarl, to tell this kender that he had desired nothing but death.

Yet now, with the wetness of water soothing his throat and the knowledge that there was a cave somewhere, perhaps not terribly far away, the Theiwar admitted to himself that he did not want to perish here. He wanted to survive, to go on living, even if not for any particular reason that he could name at the time.

"That is, I wanted to bring enough water to drink, but the desert was bigger than I thought it was," he concluded lamely, looking sidelong at the kender to see if he would swallow the lie.

"I see," Emilo Haversack said, nodding seriously. "Well, would you like a little hardtack?" He offered a strip of leathery meat, and the dwarf gratefully took the provision, chewing on the tough membrane, relishing the feel of saliva once again wetting his mouth.

"I meant to ask you," the kender continued, speaking around a tough mouthful of the jerky, "why doesn't your sword have a blade?"

Gantor gaped in astonishment, which quickly exploded to rage as he saw the kender examining the broken weapon. "How did you get that?" the dwarf demanded, making a clumsy lunge that Emilo easily evaded.

"I was just looking at it," he declared nonchalantly, allowing Gantor to snatch the weapon back.

Suspiciously the dwarf patted his pouch, finding flint and tinder where it was supposed to be. As he did, he remembered some of things he had heard about kender, and he resolved to be careful of his possessions.

"If you feel well enough, perhaps we should get going," Emilo suggested. "I've found that it's best to do my walking at night, at least here in the desert. If you want to come with me, I think we can get back to Skullcap—er, the caves—before sunrise."

Once again the dwarf heard that tremor in the kender's voice, but he took no note. The promise of a cave over his head before cruel dawn! The very notion sent a shiver of bliss through the dark-loving Theiwar, and he pushed himself to his feet with a minimum of pain and stiffness. Again he felt alive, ready to move, to fight, to do whatever he had to do to claim the part of the world that was rightfully his.

"Let's go," he said, making the unfamiliar effort to make his voice sound friendly. "Why don't you show me where those caves are?"

Chapter 7

Skullcap

251 AC
Third Adamachtis, Dry-Anvil

"There—didn't I tell you that it looked like a skull?" asked Emilo Haversack. "And doesn't it make you wonder how it got to be this way?"

Gantor leaned back, allowing his pale, luminous eyes to trace upward across the pocked face of the mountain, past the eye sockets and mouth that gaped as vast, dark caves. The visage did indeed look ghastly, and so realistic that it might have been the work of some giant demented sculptor.

"It might," the Theiwar said agreeably, "except I've heard a lot about this place, and I know how it was made. It serves as a monument to ten thousand dwarves who died here and an emblem of blame for the mad wizard who brought them to their doom!"

"Really? That sounds like a great story! Won't you tell me? Please?"

The kender all but hopped up and down beside the Theiwar, but Gantor brushed him away with a burly hand. "Time for stories later. I think we should head inside before the sun comes up."

They had plodded steadily through the remaining hours of darkness, with the kender claiming that he could see the pale massif of the garish mountain rising against the dark sky. This had been the first clue to Gantor that creatures on the outside world had much farther-ranging vision than did the Theiwar dwarves. Of course, even under the moonless skies, the under-mountain dweller had been able to make out every detail of his companion's features, and he had realized that his own eyes seemed to have a greater affinity for the darkness.

In fact, to Gantor, the ground underfoot had been clearly revealed. The dwarf had once pointed out a shadowy gully that the kender had almost rambled right into. Without missing a beat in his conversation, which consisted for several uninterrupted hours of preposterous stories of wandering and adventure, Emilo had hopped down into the ravine and scrambled up the other side. Still overcoming his stiffness and fatigue, Gantor had followed, pondering the difference between Theiwar and kender, not only in perceptions but in balance and movement as well.

Now, however, they stood at the base of the white stone massif, and Gantor did not need the slowly growing light of dawn to reveal the skeletal features, nor the gaping black hole—the "mouth" of the skull—that offered protection from the imminent daylight.

"Well, this is it," Emilo announced, drawing a slightly ragged breath. "Though I'm not sure that we have to go in. In fact, I'm pretty certain we can find water around here somewhere else, if we look hard enough. Now that I mention it, it might even be *better* water. I don't know if you noticed, being so thirsty and all, but the stuff I got in there was kind of bitter."

"I'm going in," Gantor announced, with a shrug of his shoulders. Faced with the nearby prospect of shade and water, he didn't care whether the kender came with him or not.

But then his thoughts progressed a little further. No doubt the kender knew his way around in there. And the place was certainly big, there was no denying that. Who knew how long it might take him to find the water once he started looking?

Furthermore, though the dwarf wouldn't consciously acknowledge the fact, there was another reason he desired Emilo Haversack's company. Perhaps it was just the grotesque appearance of the mountain, but there was something undeniably spooky and unpleasant about the place. Gantor didn't want to go in there alone because, in all utter, naked truth, he was afraid.

"Why don't you come along?" he asked. "You can show me where the water is and finish telling me that story about your cousin Whippersink and that big ruby he found in . . . what was that place again?"

"Sanction was the place." Emilo sighed in exasperation. "But you're not getting *any* of it right. First of all, he was my *uncle!* Uncle Sipperwink! I told you—his mother was my grandmother's older sister! Or younger sister, I'm not sure which. But it was an emerald, not a ruby, that he found in Sanction. And it was in a temple of the Dark Queen. You know, like in the days when there were still gods, before the Cataclysm."

"I'm afraid you lost me again," Gantor declared. "But why don't we find that water and make ourselves comfortable? Then you can tell me all about it."

"I'm not even sure you want to hear it!" snapped Emilo, a trifle peevishly.

"Well, what about my story, then? I can tell you about Skullcap."

The kender brightened immediately. "Well, *that's* something to look forward to. All right. It's this way."

Emilo stepped up the sloping approach to the vast cavern, the gap that, even at this close perspective, looked so very much like a sinister maw waiting to devour an unwitting meal. A smooth pathway, like a great, curving ramp, allowed them to easily approach the dark, sinister cave.

The dwarf clumped heavily along beneath the lofty overhang, instantly relishing the coolness of the eternally shadowed corridor within. The air was drier here than in Thorbardin, but for the first time since his banishment, Gantor Blacksword had the sense of a place that was fully, irrevocably underground. Each breath tasted pure and good, and the Theiwar's wide, pale eyes had no difficulty seeing into the darkest corners of the vast rubble-strewn cave.

Overhead, tall stalactites jutted sharply downward, like great fangs extending from the upper jaw of a preternatural mouth. Gantor saw piles of great rocks heaped across the floor, many of them showing jagged cracks and sharp edges, establishing that this was a cavern of violent creation. And that, of course, matched well with the stories he had always heard.

"Let's try this way. I think the path was around here somewhere," the kender suggested.

"You—you don't remember?" growled the dwarf, spluttering in suspicious indignation. "How can you forget something like that?"

"I remember." Emilo's tone showed that his feelings were hurt. "It was this way, I'm sure. Pretty sure, anyway."

He led the way before the Theiwar could make a further protest. It took perhaps an hour of wandering, of guessing between this passage and that, before Emilo had rediscovered the small circular chamber enclosing a pool of still water. The two explorers had descended a steep passage of stone, where a few steps remained visible through the wreckage of boulders and gravel that had tumbled onto the floor. Gantor Blacksword wondered idly how the kender had managed to make his

way through the impenetrable gloom, for he noticed that
Emilo was likely to stumble over rocks and other
obstacles that stood clearly revealed—to Theiwar eyes,
at least—in their path.

Perhaps it was by sound. There was, in fact, a faint
trickling that penetrated the deep chamber, suggesting
that the water in this pool was subject to some sort of
flowage. Still, the surface was utterly still, free of ripples
or waves, as if it had been waiting here for a century and
a half for no other purpose than to quench the thirst of
these weary travelers.

"Why did you say a century and a half?" asked Emilo
when Gantor, his thirst quenched, had belched, leaned
back, and voiced his supposition.

"'Cause that's how long this place has been here—as
Skullcap, I mean." The dwarf, feeling sated and expan-
sive, decided to grant the kender the privilege of the
story that was the birthright of every dwarf born beneath
Thorbardin's doming cap of mountain. The Theiwar
exile gestured vaguely to the massif rising far over their
heads. He was in a fine mood, and he decided he would
let the kender live for now.

"What was it before?" Emilo had settled nearby. Chin
on his hand, he listened intently.

"This wasn't a mountain. It was a huge tower, a complete fortress, Zhaman by name. A place of mages, it
was. We dwarves left it pretty much alone. Even the
elves"—Gantor said the word as if it were a curse—
"were content to halt at Pax Tharkas. They, like us
dwarves and the humans, gave the fortress of Zhaman to
the wizards and their ilk."

"Why would anyone *want* to come here, into the
middle of a desert. I mean, anyone except a kender who
really had to see what it was like?" asked Emilo seriously.

"Well, this much I know: It wasn't a desert back then.
That parched wasteland out there was one of the most
fertile parts of the kingdom of Thorbardin. Farmed by
the hill dwarves, it was. They brought the food in barter

to the mountain dwarves for the goods—steel, mostly—that they was too lazy or ignorant to make for themselves."

Emilo nodded seriously. He pulled the end of his topknot over his shoulder and chewed on the tip, his eyes far away, and Gantor knew that he was visualizing the scene as the Theiwar described it.

"And just like that it would have stayed, too, 'cept for there came one of the greatest banes of Ansalon since Paladine and the Dark Queen themselves." The Theiwar spat to emphasize the truth of his words.

And as he cursed and growled over the gods, Gantor spoke with utter sincerity. Indeed, the dark dwarves differed from many of their clan mates in scorning both of the mighty deities. To the subjects of Thane Realgar, any god except Reorx himself was viewed to be a meddling scoundrel, and no self-respecting member of the clan would allow himself to be persuaded otherwise.

"Fistandantilus, it was, who goaded the hill dwarves into thinking that we of the mountain had cheated them. Now, I've got no love lost for the Hylar—self-righteous, prissy little martinets, for the most part—but they had the right idea when they closed and barred the gates. We had no choice but to leave the hill dwarves to fend for themselves. Not room under the mountain for 'em all. Never was and never will be," Gantor stated with finality.

"And then the Cataclysm came?" asked Emilo, trying to follow along.

"No! That was a hundred years before! It was *after* the Cataclysm, when flood and famine scarred all the land, that the hill dwarves came begging for help. They forgot that they had turned their backs on the mountain years before, when they wanted to mix with the folk of the world." Gantor shuddered at the very idea; his time in exile had convinced him that the ancestral rift was a true and fundamental parting of the ways.

"But then they wanted to come back inside the mountain?" the kender prodded.

"Aye. And when the Hylar and the rest of us turned 'em away, we kicked them as far as Pax Tharkas and told them not to come back. But that's when they went and got that wizard and a whole lot of hill dwarf and human warriors."

"And the wizard . . . that was Fistandantilus?"

"And who'd 'a' thought he'd put together an army like that? Coming onto the plains around Zhaman, ready to move against the North Gate. That was when the North Gate was still there, of course. So we came out, and dwarven blood was shed across the whole valley. The Theiwar stood on the left flank, and their attack was sending the hill dwarves reeling back toward the elven-home."

"And the wizard? Did he do magic? Did he fly?" Emilo pressed excitedly.

"Well, that was one of the strange things at the time. It seems he wasn't there . . . didn't take part in the battle. Instead, he came here—or rather to Zhaman, the tower that used to stand here."

"So did you mountain dwarves win the battle?"

"We would have!" declared Gantor with a snort. "'Cept for the damn wizard. Like I was trying to tell you, he came here, worked some kind of spell, and the whole place was blown to pieces. Including my father, with the other Theiwar on the front lines."

"That's too bad." Emilo sounded sincerely regretful.

"Bah! The blackguard was a scoundrel and a thief! Besides, I got his sleeping chamber, and first pick of the family treasures." Gantor chuckled grimly at the kender's shocked expression, then leaned over to noisily slurp some water from the pool.

"Was Fistandantilus killed, too?" Emilo asked, studying the walls of this round grotto.

"Yup. Everybody knows that."

"It looks like some parts of this place weren't damaged too bad," observed the kender.

"Whaddaya mean?" argued the dark dwarf. He pointed across the chamber to a series of stone columns, now broken and splintered, cast casually along the far end of the large chamber. A deep crack, as jagged as a lightning bolt, scarred the wall all the way to the ceiling. "Surely you can see that. Right?"

"Well, of course," Emilo agreed breezily. "But down below here, I found a whole bunch of tunnels. Even a place where there's a jewel. . . ." The kender's voice trailed away with a shiver.

"Jewel?" Gantor froze, his luminous eyes staring at the pensive kender.

"What? Oh, yes. It was kind of pretty. I might even have taken it, except—"

"*Where?*" The dwarf had no ears for the rest of Emilo's story. His mind was alive again, sending a cascade of pictures through his imagination. Vividly he expanded the vista of his desires, imagining mounds of glittering stones, gems of red and green and turquoise and every other color under the rainbow. His fatigue and despair were forgotten, swept away by a tide of avarice.

His next instinct was as natural as it was swift: This kender was a danger, a threat to the treasure that was rightfully Gantor's! He must be killed!

Only after the dwarf had already begun to calculate the most expeditious means of accomplishing his companion's demise did further reality again intrude. Faced once again with the inexorable truth that you couldn't wring information from a lifeless witness, Gantor was forced to acknowledge that Emilo Haversack continued to be more useful to him alive than dead.

He forced his trembling voice to grow calm. "Where was this jewel? Far from here?" He cleared his throat and spat to the side in an elaborate display of casual interest.

"Well, quite a bit below here, actually." Once again Emilo displayed that strange sense of disquiet. "It wasn't really much to look at, kind of scuffed up and all that. Besides, there was something else . . . something I didn't like very much."

Gantor didn't want to hear about it. "Take me there!"

"Well, if you really want to. But don't you really think

we should rest for a—"

"Now!" snarled the Theiwar, instantly suspicious of the delay. "You'll just wait for me to fall asleep so you can get the treasure for yourself!"

"What? No, I won't! I don't even want it—not anymore, at least. But all right, then, if you're so worried about it, I'll show you. But don't say I didn't warn you."

Muttering about bad manners and pushy people, the kender rose to his feet and plodded out of the chamber where he had discovered the pool of water. They passed through a maze of broken walls and tumbled ceilings, but the dwarf could clearly discern that this had once been a structure of large hallways and broad, sweeping stairways.

Now the shadows were thick through the corners, and a stairway was as likely to be lying on its side as standing upright. They picked their way through the ruins with care, Emilo apparently guessing which path to take at several junctures. Eventually the kender came to a large circular pit, a black hole with a depth extending beyond the limits of the dwarf's darkness-piercing vision.

"This must have been a central shaft," Emilo said. If he still begrudged the dwarf's peremptory commands, his voice revealed no trace of the resentment. Instead, he was as chatty and conversational as ever. "You can see that it goes up through the ceiling as well as down."

Indeed, Gantor observed a matching circle of blackness in the arched surface over his head. A spindly network of strands dangled through space, connecting the upper reach of the shaft to the pit on the floor level. When he clumped over for a closer look, the Theiwar saw that these were the rusted remnants of a steel stairway that had once spiraled through the central atrium of the great tower of Zhaman.

And now those same stairs offered a route into the deep heart of Skullcap.

"That's how I went down before," Emilo said, joining the dwarf. "You have to hold on a little bit carefully, and in some places the metal sways back and forth. But it's strong enough to get you down."

Gantor blinked, glowering at the kender. "How do I know you're not trying to get me killed?"

Emilo shrugged. "Do you want me to go first?" He reached for the rusty remnant of a railing, only to be slapped away by the suspicious dwarf.

"Don't you try it!" Gantor seized the railing and stepped onto the top step, which was a small web of iron bars anchored solidly into the bedrock of the fortress.

Immediately the bars creaked, and there was a distant clatter of some scrap tumbling downward, clanging off the jutting wreckage of the stairway. The Theiwar yelped and clung to the railing with both hands as the frail support leaned outward, the vast gulf yawning like an unquenchable, eternally hungry mouth. As Gantor clung to his precariously dangling perch, more bits of metal broke away, the sharp sounds fading into the depths, banging, jangling, continuing to fall for a very long time.

"Here," said Emilo, extending a hand. He, too, stepped onto the bending bars of the platform, casually swinging into space with a grasp of the railing, then hopping to rest on the next intact stretch of stairs several feet below. "Just do it like that."

"I'll do it my own way!" snorted Gantor, gingerly inching along the railing, grunting as his feet swung free. He clumped to a rest beside the kender, and this time he didn't slap away the supporting hands that wrapped around his waist and helped pull him to safety.

"Come on," Emilo said cheerfully, scampering farther along the rapidly descending framework.

"Wait!" The Theiwar followed as quickly as he could, his temper growing more foul with each swinging traverse, each heart-stopping leap through the darkness. Quickly the hole in the floor disappeared overhead as they continued to descend steadily down the inside of the cylinder of stone. And always the kender proceeded jauntily, spanning long gaps with the same lack of concern with which he stepped over easy, solid footholds.

Abruptly the dwarf halted, seized by a new suspicion. Gantor clasped a shaft of metal and glowered at the kender, who was quite a few feet below him. "How come you're not scared going down here? Don't you know you could break your neck with one little slip?"

"Oh, we kender don't worry about much of anything." Emilo made a breezy gesture with one hand, ignoring the darkness yawning below. "The way I look at it, if it's going to get me, it will. Doesn't make much difference if I waste my time being afraid."

"That's crazy!" With renewed muttering, the dwarf started after the kender, trying to conjure up those images of treasures that had once flitted so seductively through his mind. But another, deeper thought intruded.

"What was that you were talking about, that thing that had you worried?" He remembered Emilo's nervousness, even fear, when they had first talked of the gem. "I thought you said you kender didn't get afraid of stuff?"

"What do—oh." Emilo's voice fell. "You mean down by the jewel?"

Gantor nodded silently.

"Well, there—there was a skull on the floor right beside the jewel. It kind of gave me the creeps. Just when I was thinking of taking that pretty stone along, I got the feeling that the skull was watching me with those shadowy eyes. I decided I would leave the gem and get out of there."

The Theiwar snorted in quiet contempt. Here was a person who didn't have the sense to worry about a bone-crushing fall into a yawning abyss, yet he let himself get alarmed by a mere piece of skeleton!

With a renewed sense of smugness, the dwarf struggled to follow along. He still cursed at frequent intervals, and his fury at the kender's seeming ease of movement grew into a cold determination, fueled by his instinctive antipathy for one who was not Theiwar, was not even mountain dwarf. His resolve was clear: As soon as Emilo showed him where the jewel was, the kender would die.

Finally a lower platform emerged from the darkness,

and Gantor sighed, relieved that the interminable descent was almost over. Yet he soon saw that there remained one more challenging section to traverse, for the tangled wreckage of the spiraling steel stairs dangled from the ceiling of a high passageway. Suspended in space, it formed a tenuous connection to the stone floor far below.

Emilo scampered like a monkey down the network of girders, railings, and steps. Even the slight weight of the kender was enough to set the whole mass to spinning slowly, and the dwarf grimaced at the sight of a single bolt, a stud of steel anchored into the bedrock of the cylindrical passage that seemed to support the entire remaining mass of metal. A shrill creak wailed through the air, and Gantor imagined the bolt giving way, carrying the kender into a tangled mass of killing metal.

Of course, the death of his companion would be inconvenient to the exiled Theiwar, since the kender knew where the jewel was. Still, if he were to be left here alone, the Theiwar felt little doubt that he could eventually locate the stone. More significantly, such a collapse would remove Gantor's route down to the treasure that he coveted now with even more fervor than before.

"It's easy!" cried Emilo, and the high-pitched echo— *easy, easy, easy*—seemed to mock the dwarf's hesitation. "Just jump over there and slide down the pole."

"Wait!" growled Gantor. He removed his small axe and reversed the weapon in his hand. With a few sharp blows, he drove the bolt back into its socket, secure in the knowledge that the deep pit in the stone was solid and the metal of the support uncorroded and strong.

Only then did he swing onto the framework, feeling his stomach lurch sickeningly as the beams and girders shifted. Again the creak of metal assaulted his ears, but the movement of the mass was less extreme than it had been when Emilo descended. Gritting his teeth, the dwarf scrambled down the rest of the way. When his feet were firmly planted on solid rock, he shifted his weight back and forth, glowering fiercely. His pale eyes were wide, absorbing the darkness, then settling upon the agitated figure of the kender.

"Well, that took a while," said Emilo, a trifle sourly. "It's over this way."

Once again Gantor suppressed his murderous urges, seeing that the wreckage of chambers and corridors around them still created a fairly extensive maze. Yet here the kender seemed to know where he was going with some degree of certainty, for Emilo started along one of the passages, winding easily between great pieces of stone that had fallen from the ceiling. Judging by the coat of dust over the scattered rubble, the Theiwar assumed that the place had been pretty much undisturbed since the convulsive explosion that had rendered Zhaman into Skullcap.

Again he found himself descending, following the kender down a series of stairways, but these were honest, stone-carved steps, cutting through squared passages that had been gouged into the living bedrock of the fortress's foundation. Gantor recognized dwarven work and admitted to a measure of racial pride when he saw that most of these stairways remained relatively undamaged.

Finally they emerged into a maze of small rooms. Despite the dust and rubble, Gantor discerned that these chambers were furnished with far more attention to detail than were any of the bare stone passages that had marked the rest of the catacombs. Woven carpets had once lined the floor, though most of these had rotted into a layer of moldy paste. The smell of decay was pungent here, and doorframes and beams of punky dried wood were visible in each of the four directions where the Theiwar could see corridors.

"It's this way," said the kender. "If you're sure you want to—"

"Don't try to back out now!" Gantor's heart pounded at the notion of the treasure that he sensed must be very near. He sniffed, and the spoor of riches was an almost tangible scent in the air. Unconsciously his fingers closed around the hilt of his knife.

They passed through several more chambers, and the Theiwar was vaguely aware of tables, of the wreckage of bottles and vials, of leathery tomes that, though layered in dust, had somehow escaped the rot and mold that had claimed the wooden and fabric objects within the deep cell.

"It's right there," Emilo said, halting abruptly and pointing to a shadowy archway. "Y-You go in if you want. I think I'll just wait here for—"

"Oh, no, you don't!" Gantor's suspicions, always bubbling near the surface, burst into full boil. He gave the kender a hard shove, ignoring the sharp yell of protest, and then clumped after Emilo into a small room.

Only it wasn't a room at all. Instead, the corridor seemed to continue until it ended in a blank stone wall. At first the dwarf was convinced he had been tricked, but when he glared downward at the kender, he saw that Emilo was paying him no attention. Instead, the little fellow's eyes were fixed upon an object at the base of the featureless wall.

Gantor shifted his gaze and then gasped as he beheld the eyeless skull, lying on the stone floor, gaping up at him from those empty sockets. It was just a piece of white bone, identical in appearance to any of a hundred other skulls that the dwarf had seen. Yet there was something disquieting, undeniably menacing, about the morbid object. The skull did not move, nor was there any visible trace of illumination around it; neither did it emit any kind of noise that the dwarf could hear.

But he could still not banish the sense that it was glaring, waiting, *watching* him. Shivering, he took a step back, his pale Theiwar eyes still fixed upon the piece of bone.

In fact, the fleshless visage was so distracting that it was several moments before the dwarf even thought to look at the other object lying on the otherwise featureless floor.

"The jewel!" he declared, suddenly wrenching his

gaze to the side. Trembling, he approached and knelt, though as yet he did not reach out to touch the gem.

A golden chain, still bright amid the dust of the floor, indicated that the thing had once been worn around a person's neck. A filigree of fine gold wire enwrapped a single large stone, a gem of pale green that was unlike anything else Gantor had ever seen.

He didn't need to identify the piece to know that it was tremendously valuable. This was an object unique in his experience, and that experience included very many encounters with precious gems of numerous varieties. And then he knew, his memory triggered by thoughts of a few odd stones of a type he had not seen for many decades.

"It's a bloodstone," he said gruffly, greed thickening his voice. He reached out, touched the chain, then looped it over his wrist to lift the gem up to his eye level. "You can see traces of red fire—the same color as fresh blood—there, right below the surface."

Avarice welled within the Theiwar's cruel heart, and he knew that he was holding the most precious object he had ever seen.

"Maybe you want to look at it outside," said Emilo, edging toward the door. "Right this way."

But Gantor wasn't listening. He stared at the stone, convinced that he was seeing flickers of light—hot, crimson bursts of illumination—deep within the gem. The pulses were faint, but visible to his keen eyes.

"Uh, Gantor?" asked Emilo. "Can we get going now?"

The dwarf snapped his head around to see that the kender had his back turned as he looked longingly up the corridor. With a snort of contempt, the dwarf realized that the little fellow was still nervous, unaccountably distressed by their presence here.

And finally the dark dwarf remembered his other intent, the determination that he would leave no witnesses, none who knew where he had found this treasure, or even who knew of its existence, its possession by the rogue Theiwar.

Gantor's face was distorted into a leer as, grinning, he lifted his knife. But then his eyes lighted upon the skull, the object that the kender found so discomforting. Enjoying the irony, the Theiwar sheathed his knife and reached down to pick up the bony artifact.

"What are you doing?" demanded Emilo, whirling back to stare, wide-eyed, as the dwarf raised the skull over his head.

"It's called murder," replied Gantor Blacksword, bringing the piece of bone down hard, feeling the satisfying crunch of the blow as the skull struck Emilo square between the eyes. Soundlessly the kender fell, rolled over, and lay still. The dwarf dropped the skull on the kender's motionless back. Then, clutching his treasure to his breast, Gantor scuttled from the room and started to make his way back to the world above.

Chapter 8
A Host, of Sorts

251 AC

His world had focused around one burning, constant feature:

Pain.

Everything was a throbbing ache, beginning in the back of his head, spreading through his jaw, his neck, his shoulders. It swelled out of the darkness, reaching with clutching, fleshless fingers, growing stronger with each stab of anguish, like hot blades piercing his skin and his mind. The agony reared high, like a kicking horse, and then the black void swallowed him again.

Later, the pain was there once more, but he took some comfort this time, realizing vaguely that the sensations could be taken as a sign of hope. At least it meant that he was still alive. Even so, the swelling momentum of his suffering sickened him, set his stomach to churning. Before his eyes, all was blackness, save for occasional sparks of red and white that appeared in the far distance, whipped forward like shooting stars, then blinked away.

Even in his confusion and his pain, he knew that these were not external lights, that they existed only in the bruised and battered passages of his mind.

My mind. He told himself over and over that this was his body, that the thoughts meant that he was alive. And all along a deeper question arose, as menacing as a fang-tipped serpent, to leer at him out of the darkness. He tried to ignore the question, tried to tell himself that it didn't matter. But it hissed insidiously, this mystery that would not be ignored, whispering itself over and over into his ringing ears.

Who am I?

This was a new question, he knew—at least a new mystery to him. Once he could have rattled off the answer without difficulty, with no hesitation. He had a past, a mortal life with parents, with a childhood, and . . . and travel. He had seen much of the world in the guise of that mortal life.

Why, then, could he not remember the person who had lived that life, the person he was?

The question was as frightening, in its own way, as the sickening anguish that threatened to pin him into his place. The first attempt to move brought a fresh wave of agony, a sickening assault that sent bile surging violently into his throat. Ignoring the shrieking protests resounding within his head, he rolled onto his side and vomited, spilling his guts onto a flat stone floor.

The floor, for some reason, triggered a suggestion of familiarity. He knew that he was inside, of course—the stale, musty air was confirmation of that. But now he perceived that he was far, far underground. There was no clue in his lightless surroundings to suggest that truth; it was simply a fact that he felt inclined to accept.

That was a victory of sorts, and he collapsed onto the

floor again, drawing ragged breaths, trying to remember *where* under the ground. While he thought, the aching in his head receded somewhat, and before he had considered the challenge of movement, he found that he had risen to a sitting position. Resting his back against a wall—also smooth, solid stone—he tried to stare through the darkness.

There was nothing to see.

His hands, familiar hands with short but dexterous and nimble fingers, probed into one of the pouches that he knew would hang from his belt. He found a flint and a short-bladed dagger right where they were supposed to be. And here was a bit of tinder, dry and brittle, protected by a soft leather folder. Beside that was a scrap of oily cloth.

His movements were smooth and practiced, clearly well rehearsed, though he could not remember a specific instance of ever having done this before. He scraped sparks from the flint, blinking at the sudden brightness, watching as they sizzled and faded. Again he struck, and this time one hot speck caught in the web of tinder. A small breath, carefully puffed, brought the tinder into flame. Twisting the oilcloth into a knot, he touched the frayed edges to the fire, and now orange light flickered all through the confines of the subterranean chamber.

And he felt a sharp stab of terror.

A skull was staring at him, the dark voids of its eye sockets cast even further into shadow by the flaring of the makeshift torch. With a gasp, he scrambled backward, holding the flaming cloth high, unwilling to take his eyes from the glaring death mask. Only when he had scuttled, crablike, around a corner did he allow himself to draw a deep breath.

He stood and, mindful of the rapidly burning cloth, began to search through the dark corridor. Soon he found what he sought: a creosote-soaked timber that had once been the leg of a table or laboratory bench. When the rag was wrapped around the blunt head of the tapered stick, the flames took slow root on the tarry timber, and soon a growing light flared brightly through the darkness.

This was a flame, he knew, that would last him for many hours. And it would take him a long time to get out of here—though it still irritated him to realize that he didn't know where *here* was. He hoisted the torch and looked through the surrounding wreckage for clues. He saw overturned tables, a litter of vials and flasks, even some tomes and scrolls, but nothing that looked even vaguely familiar. With a shudder, he turned his back and left the place behind.

For a time he wandered through a maze of stone passages, seeking only to avoid that menacing skull that had so startled him when he awakened. Yet despite his care, he found himself once again coming around a corner to confront the eyeless face that stared dispassionately upward from the floor. The bone-white visage had startled him when he had awakened, and he had the feeling that it was a dangerous object, lethal and powerful in ways that he could not understand.

Yet now, as he looked at it in the yellow light of his torch, he saw it for what it was: a lifeless piece of bone, sitting motionless on the floor where it had been dropped. He stepped closer, banishing the nervousness that once again churned his stomach. A trailing end of his long hair had somehow found its way into his mouth, and he chewed absently on the end of the thick mop.

"You're dead."

He spoke the words aloud, taking comfort from the sound of his own voice. He knelt beside the bone, noticing a fleck of rusty red on the back side. The blood was dried, but far fresher than the skull, and instinctively his hand went to his own forehead.

There was a lump there, a bruised patch of skin and a scab where he had been struck, where his own blood had flowed after the blow of a hard object.

He knew then that it was his own blood on the skull, that the piece of bone had smashed against his head and felled him here, in the depths of this shattered place. But why couldn't he remember?

"Who *am* I?"

He made the demand loudly, challenging the skull, the darkness, the stone walls—anything that might have been witness to the attack, that might offer him some hope of an answer. But of course, no answer was forthcoming.

Again the black eye sockets drew him, and he knew that the skull should have been a terrifying thing—indeed, some time before it *had* frightened him, and he knew that he was a person who was not easily scared. Yet now he perceived little of that earlier menace. It was as if the skull was a vessel that had been full of something dangerous, but now, perhaps shattered by the force of the blow, the danger had flowed out and left the fleshless head as a silently grinning remembrance.

Resolutely he turned his back on the skull and started to walk. Soon he found the iron framework of an old stairway, and he didn't even pause before starting what he knew would be a long climb. Ascending steadily, he held the torch in one hand, except during the most difficult parts of the climb. Then he clenched the narrow, unlighted end of the brand between his teeth so that he could use both hands to scale steadily upward.

He stopped once, startled by a distant sound. Listening, he discerned a thumping pulse, like the beating of a heart. As he strained to locate the sound, he saw a sudden image: a greenish stone, red lights flaring within the gem in cadence to the mysterious heartbeat.

Once again he suppressed a shiver a fear, knowing without understanding that fear was a strange emotion to him.

After the iron stairs there were more corridors, and a room where there was water. He stopped here, grateful for the drink, and took the time to fill both of his waterskins. He remembered that, beyond this ruined labyrinth, he would find very little water.

But how could he know this and not know where *here* was?

Finally he emerged beneath the muted blue of a clear sky fading softly after the sunset. He was not surprised that the great edifice behind him rose so high, nor that it was cast so perfectly into the shape of a great skull. Now he knew that this place was called Skullcap.

And then he had another vivid impression as the skull that he had left underground seemed to rise into his mind. He stared into those black, empty sockets and shivered under the feeling that it was still watching him.

"But who *am* I?"

He found the answer when he collapsed for rest in a shallow ditch. Under the fading light of day, he pulled out the contents of his pack. There was the hardtack—he remembered exactly what it tasted like, but he didn't know where it had come from. He found a soft fur cloak and knew that it would be useful on a colder night than this.

And he found an ivory scroll tube that was certainly one of his prized possessions. Within the cylindrical container, he found several maps and pieces of parchment with strange symbols and indecipherable notes scrawled across them.

At the top of several of the sheets, he discerned two words: *Emilo Haversack*. Taking a stick, he scribed the symbols into the sand, and he recognized that the words on the parchment had been written by his own hand.

"My name is Emilo Haversack," he declared, as if the repeating of the words would make the truth that much more evident.

But still, how had he come to be here?

And where were the rest of his memories?

Chapter 9

From Black to Life

259 AC

For a long time he had done nothing, been no one.
This was his protection as it had been in ages past, a tactic for use when those who sought his life for crimes real
and imagined became too powerful. And so he had
escaped the vengeful, had given pitiful humankind the
false notion that he was finally and irrevocably slain.

He recalled the fateful casting, the mighty spell that
should have yielded passage to the Abyss, allowed him
to challenge the Dark Queen herself. Instead, the
enchantment had erupted in violent convulsion, tearing
him to pieces, destroying him.

Indeed, by now the whole world must believe that he
had been killed.

But he had only been hiding.

How long had he lurked here, so far beyond the ken of humankind? He didn't know, really didn't care. As ever, he trusted to certain truths, knowing that the nature of human, dwarf, or ogre would eventually accomplish his task. The folk of Krynn tended to be violent peoples, and he needed their violence to give him flesh and blood and life.

Finally violence had been done, and the gift had been given. Again his essence was cloaked in flesh, the blood pulsing through a brain that, while it was not his, had been given to him to use. He could not discern immediately whether it was a human or perhaps a dwarf or even an ogre that had bestowed this gift upon him. Nor did he particularly care. He could make any of these peoples his tool, use whichever body was offered him until he could exert full control, reclaim his rightful place in the world.

So he had been content for a measureless time merely to rest within this mortal shell, to absorb the life and vitality of the body that gave him home. He did not need to take control, at least not yet, for he was still weak, still unready to reveal himself to the enemies who, experience had shown him, always lurked in the eddies of time's great river, waiting for his reappearance, for a chance to hurt or kill him.

Such enemies waited with vengeance and treachery in mind, and they sought him out whenever his presence became known.

And always he had killed them. He won because he waited until the time was right, and the same wisdom that had guided him then told him now that the time was too soon. He was content to let his host wander this far-flung corner of Ansalon, and the timeless one paid little heed to that body's travels or to its intentions and pleasures. For all this time he, the spirit of the ancient archmage, would grow stronger, would wait for the right moment to strike.

Gradually his vitality returned. He began to feel warmth, to sense desires such as, initially, thirst and hunger. And then later he knew stronger, more deeply ingrained lusts, cravings for power, for lives, and for blood, and these desires confirmed for him that he was ready once more to plunge his life back into the great river's flow.

Finally the time had come for him to emerge from hiding, to once more claim the prizes—in treasure, realms, and lives—that were rightfully his. He would take a new body, find the flesh of a strong young man, as he always had before. And he would once again claim the world of which he had once been master, in fact if not in public knowledge.

He shifted then, steeling his essence toward the mind of the man—or dwarf, or ogre—who was his host. He was ready to seize control, to destroy the host's intellect, to make the mind, the body, the life of this person his own.

But something was wrong.

The will of Fistandantilus surged more strongly, and he sensed the host body's agitation, its ignorance and its fear. This was the time it should begin to respond, when the will of the archmage would vanquish the hapless individual who was doomed to become fodder for his future life. Again he surged, twisting, driving the force of his mighty presence, the vast power of his magic, the full awareness of the hundred or more souls he had devoured during the long course of his rise to power.

And once more he failed.

His host was not responding to his will. He could sense the coil of mortality, the flesh and being of a person. But there was a capricious, free-spirited mentality in this host that would not yield to his great strength—indeed, it seemed to delight in thwarting his attempts to assert control.

His immortal essence had come to rest, as always before, in someone who could bear it, unawares, through the world. But now he desired to claim the host for his own, to consume him in the process of restoring himself to might.

Yet the host would not respond.

There were times when the power of the ancient archmage would reach out, seeking with ghostly skeletal fingers to lodge in the brain, or the heart or guts, of this unsuspecting person. But at best those grasps were fleeting, with the stuff of control always slipping away.

The essence of Fistandantilus settled back in frustration, and inevitably the knowledge that he was being thwarted brought a rising sense of rage, a murderous intent that should have erupted in a burst of magic, sizzling the flesh and searing the brain of the unwitting host.

But now he lacked the power, the means to work that arcane might. And as he struggled and railed against the fate that had imprisoned him in such a place, he began to consider the reasons. Any human, dwarf, or ogre, or even an elf should have yielded to the overwhelming force of great magic. The archmage would have preferred to have mastered a human, for that was the state of his normal, his original form, but he knew that he could make any of the others feel his power if need be.

The answer seemed to be that his host was none of those victims, those earlier targets of his will. It was a being of capricious habits, carefree and fearless sensibilities, and a life of confusion and chaos that at last allowed Fistandantilus to perceive the truth.

And it was a truth that filled him with horror and fear, for his spirit, his essence, and his desires for the future had been imprisoned in the body of a *kender.*

For a time, he could only shiver with uncontrolled fury, but gradually he came to the realization that he would have to change his tactics. And he was not without tools, without alternate plans.

He reached out first toward a distant skull, but all that he could see through the lifeless eyes was a barren and abandoned underground.

But when he sought for another talisman, a stone of blood and fire, he felt a more powerful, vital presence. There was a dwarf there, and dwarves had been known to yield to the archmage's power. The archmage strained to see while he felt the pulse and ultimately the perceptions of the one who carried the stone. A cursory study showed that this dwarf would be of only limited use: He was a cackling maniac, wicked but weak.

Still, Fistandantilus had a place for his power to take hold. The dwarf was a fool, but he was a malleable fool. The archmage felt the power of the stone, used it to penetrate the simple mind.

The dwarf would carry the bloodstone for a while longer, but ultimately he would bring it to someone who could be put to better use.

And the wizard's path would open, leading him once again toward the enslavement of the world in past, present, and future.

Chapter 10

A Stone of
Power and Command

263 AC
Paleswelt-Darkember

Kelryn Darewind rode out of Tarsis about two minutes before the captain of the city guards smashed through the door of the luxurious suite he had been renting in one of the landlocked city's finest inns. The fact that Kelryn had failed to pay for those lodgings, as he had failed to reimburse numerous merchants and vendors for goods and services during the half-year he had spent in the crowded city, was a significant reason behind the captain's—as well as the chief magistrate's—diligent attentions.

Yet the sense of timing that had allowed Kelryn to live well in cities as far separated as Caergoth, Sanction, and Haven had once again served him well. He had even been able to gather his few belongings, saddle the fine horse he had won gambling with a trader, and ride through the city streets and out the north gate without a sense of immediate urgency.

The man knew that he cut a lordly figure astride the saddle of his palomino charger. A cape of black silk trimmed by white fur of sable draped his straight shoulders. Fine leather boots garbed his feet, newly made by a leathersmith of Tarsis on a promise of payment by the handsome nobleman who had cut such a dashing swath through the city's social scene over the long, temperate summer.

It was the change of seasons, more than any concerns about the enemies he had left behind, that contributed to Kelryn's bleak mood as he rode generally north and west from the city. He was used to moving on, but he hated to be uprooted at the end of summer. Nevertheless, he put the spurs to his horse, urging the strong gelding to increased speed, just in case anyone from Tarsis should take his thievery as a personal affront. Of course, Kelryn was ready to fight to protect his freedom, but he would just as soon avoid any such potentially messy conflict by getting out of the area as quickly as possible.

The lone traveler made camp at a narrow notch in one of the long ridges north of the city. Here the road crossed the elevation, providing Kelryn with a good view to the south. He stayed alert through the long night, and when dawn's light washed over the plains, he could detect no sign of pursuit. Quite possibly the folk of Tarsis were just as glad to see him on his way—certainly, he thought with a chuckle, there were many fathers of young women who would shed no tears over his departure.

Yet the laugh was a dry sound and little consolation. In truth, Kelryn desired the company of other people, wanted to have their admiration and even affection. He knew he was a charismatic fellow. How else could he have lived luxuriously in the strange city on nothing more than the promise that funds would eventually be forthcoming from his faraway, highly esteemed, and utterly fictional home and family?

In the case of his stay in Tarsis, Kelryn Darewind had claimed that home to be Sanction. His identity as the proud scion of a wealthy mercantile family—aided, of course, by his natural charisma and striking good looks— had granted him admission to fine parties, had brought wise and powerful men to his dinner table, and had lured more than one of their daughters to his bed. It had, he reflected with a sigh, been a very pleasant half a year.

But where to go now?

For several days he followed the northward road. Approaching the town of Hopeful, he detoured across the plains to the east. Since he was still so close to Tarsis, he didn't care to take chance that word of his exploits had preceded him to the bustling highway town. Still camping out, he crossed the corner of the Plains of Dust as quickly as possible before turning his course back to the north. He saw few people and was impeccably courteous and helpful to those he encountered, so that any who looked for the trail of a thief and scoundrel would gain no information from interviews with the travelers Kelryn met.

The great massif of the High Kharolis formed a purple horizon to his west, lofty mountains that, he knew, sheltered the ancient dwarvenhome of Thorbardin. The highway led into those mountains, to its ancient terminus at the Southgate, but before he reached the foothills, Kelryn Darewind again altered course, avoiding the rising ground surrounding the vast range. He chose to skirt the realm of the dwarves. They were ever a suspicious people, hard to fool, and thus poor choices for the traveler's next stop.

Instead, he guided his horse through the lightly populated coastal realm, a place of a few poor farm villages, with tiny fishing communities huddled close beside the many sheltered coves along the coast of the Newsea. Several times he considered stopping at one of these, perhaps even to spend the winter, but a cursory examination of each of the prospective way stations revealed not a single dwelling that was suitable to serve as his shelter. And these communities were places of hardworking, honest folk; he knew they would make him welcome, but also that, if he were to stay for any period of time, he would be expected to pitch in and help with the many tasks necessary to survival in those isolated outposts.

And that alternative was quite simply unacceptable to him.

Instead, he continued on, wrapping his sable-fringed cloak around his shoulders against the increasingly chill winds sweeping from the vast wasteland of Icewall Glacier. His course took him past the desert of Dergoth, and he made the decision to try to reach Pax Tharkas before the Yule. There, he concluded, he would probably be forced to spend the winter; snow would make the lofty roads impassable, and there were no cities significant enough to offer him entertainment on this side of the forbidding mountains.

Beyond, of course, there were places such as Haven and New Ports, but Kelryn realized that he would have to wait until spring before reaching one of those bustling locales. Thus he was in a sour mood as he passed into the barren gorge that sheltered the road leading to Pax Tharkas from the south.

He knew that the ancient fortress lay astride a pass that was several dozen miles ahead, and that it was a fair-sized town in its own right. Unfortunately, the massive compound would also inevitably be under the military administration of some sort of local governor or warlord. Like the dwarves, such men were hard to fool with tales of forthcoming riches and intangible family worth. Grimly Kelryn was coming to terms with the fact that he may, in fact, be reduced to actual work in order to see his way through the winter.

He traveled light, though he had purchased several hard loaves of bread in the last village he had passed through. Too, he carried in his saddlebags several skins full of the strong ale favored by the mountain folk. These would make for meager rations when he camped, but at least he had the provisions to see him all the way to Pax Tharkas.

Stern and practical when necessary, Kelryn Darewind was in fact a very hardy man. He could survive in the cold, and he was good enough with his sword to protect himself from brigands or even an ogre or two. But he was frustrated now, because he preferred it when the living was easy.

If only he could reach Pax Tharkas before it started to snow. Now, as the wind penetrated his cloak, whipping his mane of lush black hair forward, he began to doubt that this would be possible. There was a strong hint, a taste and a smell in the air, that suggested he would be caught in a blizzard if he tarried outside for too much longer.

The waft of campfire smoke, carried from a side gully by the bitter wind, reached his nostrils at sunset of his first day in the gorge. Knowing he had at least another day or two to ride before reaching the great fortress, he decided to seek out the fire builder and, with any luck, receive an offer of warmth and hospitality—perhaps even including food—that would see him through the long night.

The gully leading toward the source of the smoke ascended steeply from the road, and the palomino skittered nervously as it tried to negotiate the grade. With a muffled curse, Kelryn slid from the saddle, took the reins in his hand, and started upward on foot. He discerned a narrow trail, but he was more concerned with the damage to his once fine boots. Weeks on the trail had taken their toll in scuffs, scrapes, and even one long gouge along the side of the leather footwear.

As he pushed higher up the gully, the curve of the ravine wall took the road out of sight below him, and he began to wonder if he had imagined the scent of smoke. And even if he hadn't, would someone who camped in such a remote location be welcoming, or even tolerant, of an intruder?

He had no answer to these questions, but he knew he would find out soon as another bend of the steeply climbing trail brought him in sight of a shadowy cave mouth. He could see a faint glow of crimson from within; this was clearly the source of the fire and the smoke. Scrambling up another few steps, he reached a flat swath of gravel before the mouth of the cave. His hand tightened around the hilt of his sword, but he didn't draw the weapon as he stared warily into the depths, wondering about the nature of the fire builder within.

"Hullo!" he called, trying to keep his voice cheerful. "Anyone here?"

A stocky, hunched figure moved from the wall of the cave to stand and face him. Silhouetted by the fire as it was, Kelryn quickly determined by the bowed legs and the barrel-sized torso that the cave's occupant was a dwarf.

"Who's there?" demanded the fellow suspiciously. Kelryn was startled to realize that, despite the backlighting, he could see the dwarf's eyes: two spots of milky white illumination, gleaming at him with uncanny brightness.

"A traveler—a poor horseman," he replied in the smoothest, friendliest tones he could muster. "I only hope to share the warmth of your fire."

With a snort, the dwarf turned his back and sat in the shadows of the cave's interior.

Kelryn waited a beat, wondering if the fellow would make more of a reply. When no sound, no sign of invitation or refusal was forthcoming, he cleared his throat. The horse's breath steamed at his ear, and the fire within the cave crackled atop a heap of embers that looked very warm indeed.

Finally the man determined that he would take charge of the situation. He moved forward slowly, tethering the horse in the entrance of the rocky shelter where it would be protected from the worst of the icy wind. Then he stepped inside, bowing to pass underneath a low mantel of flinty granite. Within, he found that the rocky ceiling rose high, giving him plenty of room to stand. The cave was a fine shelter, he observed, seeing that it even offered a natural flue near the back, where the smoke from the fire crept along the wall and then wafted upward, to be lost in the frigid night—and occasionally carried down to the road by a lucky gust of wind.

Kelryn noted idly that the stone around the flue was soot-stained and shiny black. He suspected that it had served as a fireplace for a long time and wondered if perhaps this dwarf had made the cave a more or less permanent home.

Advancing into the shelter, the man allowed his eyes to adjust to the darkness. He held his hands to his sides so that the dwarf, who glowered silently from his seat near the fire, would know he meant no harm.

"I'm Kelryn Darewind," he said, offering his most beguiling smile. He gestured to another flat rock beside the fire, opposite the position of the still-silent dwarf. "Would you mind terribly if I made myself comfortable?"

"Hah!" the dwarf snapped, and again those pale eyes flashed, luminous and staring. "Let me see."

Abruptly the fellow clasped both hands to the front of his jerkin, pressing the garment tightly to his chest. Kelryn was surprised to see that the piece of stiff clothing was filthy and torn, lacking the usually fine workmanship of other dwarven garb. The cave dweller's scalp was covered with a bristling mane of stiff, spiky hair, and his beard was a greasy, tangled mat covering most of his chest.

Kelryn was wondering what the dwarf's last remark meant when he heard the wretched fellow begin to speak. He listened, prepared to formulate whatever reply his host might find agreeable, until he realized that the creature was not speaking to his visitor.

"He wants to stay, he says," mumbled the dwarf. His pale eyes were vacant, staring past Kelryn, apparently focused on nothing at all. The fingers still clenched into tight fists pressed against his chest. "Wants to warm himself by the fire, he says."

"And it's the truth," Kelryn noted genially. "I wouldn't be surprised if we get some snow tonight."

"Snow, he says," cackled the dwarf, casting a wide-eyed glance at the human before turning his attention back to the vague distance.

Kelryn was mystified, yet intrigued. He suspected that the dwarf was mad, but the filthy cave dweller did not seem terribly dangerous, and Kelryn Darewind had a highly developed sense of danger, at least as it pertained to the protection of his own skin.

"You can stay," the dwarf said suddenly, releasing his shirt and sighing in what seemed to be exhaustion, or perhaps resignation.

"Thank you. I'm very grateful," replied the man. He considered a further question and decided to chance it. "Um . . . who is it that you were talking to? Or, I should say, to whom do I owe my gratitude?"

"Why, himself, of course," said the dwarf with a sly grin.

"Well, please convey my thanks."

"He knows . . . he knows."

The dwarf suddenly burst into activity, throwing several pieces of dry wood onto the fire, pulling out a crude bowl that he set in the coals beside the blaze. Kelryn realized that the dish was in fact a steel helm, probably of dwarven make, that had been ignominiously converted to duty as a soup caldron.

"And you are Kelryn," the dwarf noted, as if confirming his own memory.

"Quite right. And you . . . ?"

"My name is Gantor Blacksword, but you can call me . . . call me Fistandantilus!" crowed the filthy fellow, as if he had just been struck by inspiration.

"Fistandantilus . . . the wizard?"

"The same. 'Twas he who gave his blessing to yer staying, he I was talking to." The dwarf patted his chest smugly, as if the great wizard himself was compactly stored in a pouch beside his skin.

"But you just said that I should call *you* by that name, yet you seem to indicate that it belongs to someone else."

"It belongs to *me!*" shrieked the dwarf, hopping to his feet, standing with legs bowed as if ready to do battle. "You can't have it!"

"Nor do I want it!" Kelryn hastily assured the dwarf, utterly convinced that the wretch was indeed hopelessly mad. He watched warily as the dwarf, apparently mollified, sat back down. Gantor swept aside his beard and pulled out the loose neckline of his shirt, peering downward, apparently at his own belly, then slyly raising his wide, unblinking eyes to stare at his visitor.

"And are you of the Thorbardin clans or the hill dwarves?" the human asked, hoping to change the topic quickly.

"Bah! None of them are worthy of me, though once I numbered myself among the clan of Theiwar. I am of myself, and of Fistandantilus."

"But you told me that you *are* Fistandantilus." Kelryn, keeping his hand ready near the hilt of his sword, was rather enjoying the verbal sparring. And he was mightily curious about the dwarf's cloak. What did he have under there?

"That's for protection—mine and his." The dwarf looked out the entrance of the cave, as if he suspected someone might be sneaking toward them. Apparently satisfied, he settled back to stir his soup.

"May I offer some bread? A taste of ale, perhaps?" suggested the human. He went to the palomino and unsaddled the horse, resting his own supplies in a sheltered niche within the cave. Searching through his saddlebags, he pulled forth some choice selections from his store of provisions.

The dwarf watched with glittering, hungry eyes as Kelryn ambled back to the fire and resumed his seat on the flat rock.

"In truth, it's been many a year since I've had the taste

of real ale," Gantor admitted, maintaining his vivid stare. He reached out to snatch the skin as soon as Kelryn started to swing it over, as if he expected that the human would take it back at any instant.

"Take it. Have the whole thing," the man urged with utmost sincerity—not from any charitable sense, but rather because he knew the power of ale to loosen the tongue of dwarf or man.

The dwarf drank deeply, lowering the flask with a satisfied smack of his lips. He was surprisingly fastidious for such a filthy and disreputable creature, for not a drop of the amber fluid trickled over his lips or spilled into the tangle of his beard.

"Good," Gantor Blacksword allowed before taking another large swig. The second draft apparently confirmed his initial impression, for he belched loudly, then eased backward to lean against the cave wall, his feet stretched casually toward the fire.

A dreamy smile appeared in the midst of the dwarf's mat of whiskers. "Yes, it's been a long time since we shared a good taste of the barley," he sighed.

Kelryn was about to reply that they'd never shared a drink before, when he realized that the dwarf had not been talking to him. "Does Fistandantilus care for something a little stronger?" asked the man. "I have a small nip of wine that I've been saving for a special occasion."

Abruptly the dwarf stiffened, sitting upright and scowling with a menacing tuck of his brows. His eyes, usually so wide, were narrowed to white slits in the wrinkled map of his face. "What did you say?" he asked, his voice a low growl.

Kelryn silently cursed himself for trying to move too fast. Still, his curiosity would not allow him to backtrack. "You mentioned—that is, I believe you said—that you were here with the wizard, Fistandantilus. I merely asked if he desired a taste of wine."

"He's not here," the Theiwar declared. Once again his voice became friendly, conspiratorial. "As a matter of fact, he's dead."

"I'm sorry," replied Kelryn disingenuously. "I had hoped to make his acquaintance."

"You can." Gantor's head bobbed enthusiastically. "I know him."

The man ignored the contradiction. "Splendid! What does he want?"

"He wanted me to kill the kender. I knew that as soon as I picked up the bloodstone." The dwarf nodded in affirmation of his statement. "He told me to use the skull to hit him, and I did."

"That was wise," Kelryn agreed sagely. "He's not one you'd want to argue with."

"No." Gantor's beard and hair bristled as he shook his head vehemently.

The human thought about his companion's remarks, which he had at first been inclined to dismiss as the ravings of a lunatic. But now he was not so sure.

"You said something about a bloodstone. Is that how you talk to Fistandantilus? Do you see him or hear him in the gem?"

"That's it!" the dwarf agreed enthusiastically. Once more he cast a look to the outside of the cave. "I've never shown it to anyone before, but it's all right. He says I can let you see it."

Apparently satisfied by his own explanation, the dwarf reached under his beard, into his tunic, and pulled out a golden chain.

Kelryn gasped as the bloodstone came into view. Never had he seen so large a gem, and the finespun gold surrounding the stone was worth a small fortune by itself.

But it was in fact the bloodstone that caught his eye, that held him rapt, almost hypnotized. He could see flickers of light, like tiny magical fires, bursting into brightness within the pale, greenish depths of the polished gem. Despite himself, he felt that cadence calling to him, drawing him to the stone with powerful allure.

And he knew that he would have the gem—he *had* to have it!

"Fistandantilus was a great man," Gantor declared seriously. "He had many enemies, and they have smeared dirt and garbage upon his name. But he was strong and true. He would have been a light in this dark age of the world but for the treachery of his enemies."

"You know all this? You have learned it from the stone?" Kelryn tore his eyes from the gem, staring intently at the addled dwarf. "Tell me!" he insisted, his voice taut with impatience as Gantor hesitated.

"Yes. It speaks to me, guides me." The Theiwar spoke eagerly now, clearly anxious that the human understand. "It brought me here a month ago and bade me wait. And so I do, though he has not told me why."

"You were waiting for me," Kelryn asserted, once again looking deep into the stone, hearing the summons, knowing the will of the one who spoke to him from there. Gantor *had* been brought here by the will of the bloodstone, put in this place so that Kelryn Darewind could find him. The man was utterly convinced of this fact.

"But why you?" asked the dwarf, puzzled.

Kelryn made no reply, except to grasp the hilt of his sword in a smooth, fluid gesture. In an eyeblink, the blade was out, silver steel gleaming red in the firelight, the weapon striking forward before Gantor could move. The man lunged, cursing the awkward posture of his attack but unable to postpone his response to the presence, the irresistible summons that he felt within the enchanted gemstone.

As it turned out, his clumsy attack was more than adequate. The Theiwar waited, as still as a statue, as if he himself had been commanded or compelled to do so. Only after the sword cut through the bristling tangle of the beard, sliced into the throat, and the dwarf slumped with a gagging burst of air and a gush of blood did the man understand.

Like Kelryn himself, Gantor Blacksword had only been doing what he had been told.

Chapter 11

A Cult of Darkness

314 AC
Fourth Misham, Reapember

"Bring in the new supplicants," Kelryn Darewind declared, leaning back in the thronelike chair he had had installed in the nave of his ornate temple.

"Aye, Master!" Warden Thilt snapped to attention, bringing the claw of his baton upright beside his face. Kelryn smiled, knowing that his lieutenant clearly understood his wishes and his intentions.

Thilt stalked down the aisle of the temple. Rows of golden columns rose from the floor to either side of the man, pillars that were lost in the heights where, so far above, arched the marble ceiling. Two acolytes—dressed, like the warden, in golden kilts and chain-mail jerkins—

pulled open the huge silver doors and barked commands. Standing to the side of the entry, Thilt called out numbers, and one by one the recruits to the Temple of Fistandantilus dropped to their knees and began to crawl toward Kelryn.

The high priest, for his part, leaned back in his seat and watched as the file crept forward. A nice lot, he thought, counting a dozen men and a few women. They would swell the ranks of his congregation nicely, adding still further to the influence of the sect of Fistandantilus in the Seeker-ruled city of Haven.

The first supplicant was a man, and even though the fellow knelt at his feet, Kelryn could see that he was a strapping specimen, broad-shouldered and sturdy. When the man raised his face, the high priest saw that a jagged scar, crimson and angry, slashed down the side of his face, giving him a perpetually menacing scowl.

Finally Kelryn rose, standing before the kneeling supplicant. The priest lifted the golden chain from around his neck, allowing the crimson-speckled bloodstone to dangle before the man's eyes. His eyes lit with hunger at the sight of the gem, fixing in an unblinking stare as the gold-framed jewel slowly swung back and forth a few inches from his face.

"Do you swear by the new god Fistandantilus to offer yourself to his temple, body and soul and mind? Swear you to follow the dictates of his faith and to unfailingly obey the commands of his appointed servants? And do you accept me, Kelryn Darewind, as high priest of his faith, and will you follow my orders as the very words of your god himself?"

Kelryn intoned the ritual oath in the singsong cadence that had become so familiar to him over the last few decades. He had created the rote phrases himself—it had been one of the first things he had done, once he decided to install himself in this city of theocrats—and he was quite proud of the questions and the wording.

"Master, I so swear!" pledged the scarred man.

"By the power of the dark robe, I commend you into

our ranks," declared Kelryn, placing a hand on the man's shoulder, smiling thinly as the supplicant's face was suffused by a glow of inner happiness.

"Now, rise. Take yourself through the door of red. You will serve our god in the ranks of the Faithguards."

"Thank you, Master. Thank you from the bottom of my heart!" cried the recruit. He stood, and Kelryn thought for a distasteful moment that the fellow actually intended to embrace him. Perhaps the expression on the high priest's face was enough of a deterrent, for the supplicant merely stammered something, bowed, and started for the indicated door, one of three exits on the side of the chapel.

"In the Sect of the Dark Robe, we show our gratitude through our actions, through faithful service to the church!" Kelryn snapped as the man made his way to the red door. The high priest hoped his stern words would forestall any other such displays from the remaining supplicants.

The ceremony continued, with the next few men also being sent into the ranks of the Faithguards. These recruits swelled the number of Kelryn's private army to more than one hundred strong, dedicated and ruthless fighters all. The Faithguards were charged with the protection of church property, property that was increasing in extent and value on an almost daily basis. The armed acolytes also served to discourage the efforts of nearby sects that seemed to present too much of a threat to the cult of the black robe. More than one temple in this district had been mysteriously burned, its faithful priests found strangled, flayed, or charred in the ruins.

Several of the supplicants were young men, too slight or benign to serve in the Faithguards. These were assigned to temple duties, cleaning and other servant tasks. One would become the high priest's house servant, replacing a lad that Kelryn had been forced to torture and kill only the previous week, when that youth had fancied himself a manly lover and had dared to visit the quarters of the temple maidens.

Even now Kelryn scowled at the memory of the lad's insolent disobedience. Everyone in the church knew that those sanctified quarters were reserved for the maidens only, except for Kelryn Darewind himself. The priest made a mental note: He would have to warn the new recruits about the restrictions, since he wanted very much to avoid a similar infraction. Indeed, he had rather liked the previous boy, so much so that the high priest had actually required the aid of a burly Faithguard before Kelryn had been able to muster the resolve to gouge out the lad's second eye.

The last three of the supplicants were female. The first, a toothless hag who leered up at the priest with an expression of fawning adoration, was assigned to the sweepers; she would join a group who maintained the temple grounds and the high priest's mansion, insuring that the Sect of the Black Robe presented a gleaming and impeccable facade to this city of so many and varied temples. The second was a younger woman whose large, beaklike nose gave her a rather homely appearance; she was assigned to the Faithguards, and Kelryn knew that the men would make good use of her. No doubt within a few years, if she lasted that long, she would come to resemble the hag he had just assigned to the sweepers.

The final supplicant—positioned at the end of the line by Warden Thilt, who knew his master's tastes—was a young woman of unblemished skin, golden hair, and clear blue eyes. He had her maintain her kneeling posture for a little longer than was necessary and took great pleasure in her smooth voice as she stared into the depths of the bloodstone and reverently chanted the vows.

"You are assigned to the Temple Maidens," Kelryn declared, his voice already thickening with desire. "Pass through the white door. You will find a garden there, wine and fruit as well. Sample the food and drink as you wish. Then remove your robe and wait for me."

"Yes, Master," she intoned, and the high priest pulled away the bloodstone so those blue eyes would rise to regard him. He nearly fell into them, so pure was their color and so willing, so devoted, their expression.

This one really was a beauty, he thought, and he made a private vow that he would take his time with her. Too many times in recent years he had found a treasure like this, only to ruin her with his uncontrolled passion on their first encounter. Afterward, such tarnished beauties were useful only to the Faithguards. Sometimes, in fact, an unfortunate girl had been so frightened and disillusioned by her first encounter with the high priest that he had been forced to sacrifice her in the temple dungeons. Not that such executions were not without their own form of pleasure, but Kelryn Darewind was a pragmatic man and knew that his recruits were always more useful to him alive then dead.

Yes, he repeated silently, I will be patient with this one, that she may please me for a long time to come.

The woman walked to the white door, and Kelryn stared hungrily, watching the smooth curves of her body shifting gracefully beneath the gauzy cotton of her robe. He thought momentarily of dispensing with the rest of the day's business, but quickly he discarded that notion. He could be patient, and there were important matters of the church that needed his attention.

He flopped back into his chair, reflecting that it had not always been so. Had it actually been fifty years ago that he first arrived in this rich, lively, and utterly corrupt city? Kelryn knew it had, though none who saw him would have guessed his age to be much more than three decades. Indeed, he knew he looked very much the same as he did when he had ridden out of Tarsis so many years ago.

Now, however, when he thought back to those days, it seemed that he was recalling an experience from a different life. His hand closed around the stone that pulsed within his fingers, and he knew he owed a great transformation in his own life to his chance encounter with the dwarf, now a half century dead, on the Pax Tharkas road.

Except that he did not believe, had not even believed then, that it was really a chance encounter. It was the stone—or, more accurately, the spirit that throbbed within the stone—that had brought Gantor Blacksword into his path, that had summoned Kelryn up the steep gully to the Theiwar's smoldering fire.

The bloodstone had known that the raving dwarf had served his purpose. A pariah to his own kind, terrified and suspicious of everyone else, Gantor had been unable to carry the powerful artifact into the centers of life and vitality that it craved. Kelryn Darewind, on the other hand, with his easy social grace, his handsome smile, and his flowing, charismatic speech, had been a much better choice.

When the man first held the stone, he had felt its compelling power; even more, he sensed that the artifact was appealing to *him* personally. Then, when he had replied, had offered his acquiescence—for a price—he understood that the gem had respected Kelryn's strength. The stone needed the man, and the man needed the stone. Together they had helped each other for many years.

And Kelryn Darewind, for his part, had no complaints as he proclaimed himself a high priest. He knew he was a tool for the power within the stone, but he had been quick to grasp that his role called for him to maintain a position of great wealth and high status. He had strong men who would obey his every command and as many women of all ages, shapes, and sizes as he could possibly desire. And there had been another benefit as well, one that he had not perceived for many years after the founding of his sect. But now the truth could not be denied: Since he had been carrying the bloodstone, he had not been subject to the ravages of age that were the lot of every mortal man.

It had been that fact that accounted for so much of the sect's recent success in recruitment and donation. In an age when the gods had abandoned Krynn, when the pseudo-doctrines of charlatans hailing the virtues of false gods could be heard on any of a dozen street corners in Haven, even the barest suggestion of a miracle was enough to bring people flocking to his door. And word of a sect presided over by a young man who had been a young man for fifty years was clear enough evidence that he was a wielder of supernatural power.

At first, Kelryn had been dependent upon the hypnotic power of the bloodstone to gather his faithful. Since that fateful encounter in the chilly night he had worn the gem on its chain around his neck, taking comfort in the sensation of the stone against his chest. There were times he could even imagine it pulsing in time with his own heart, though he could never be certain if it was his own body that was setting the cadence of the measured beats or if he was reacting to some abiding force within the bloodstone.

From the comfort of the temple throne, he spent a few pensive moments reflecting on the long-ago encounter in the cave and its immediate aftermath. As he had planned, he had reached the gates of Pax Tharkas before the worst of the winter snows. He had spent the cold season in the isolated fortress, though he had not been forced to work for his keep as he had originally feared. Instead, he found that the stone seemed to enhance his insight into men he had gambled with, and by the time he had departed for the north in the spring, he had earned a respectable purse and recruited a band of tough and ruthless men, the first of his Faithguards.

At the same time, Kelryn had shaped the plan that, he hoped, would see to the comfort and security of his future. Accompanied by his thugs, he had journeyed to Haven, where it seemed that one or another new religion was arising almost every other week. Due in part to the burly nature of his assistants and in part to the hypnotic powers of the stone, Kelryn quickly gathered a fiercely loyal group of followers.

Supported by hard-earned donations, they had purchased a ramshackle shack in the New Temple quarter of Haven. Within a year, the sagging building had been replaced by a sturdy chapel. Twenty years later that church had been razed to make way for the current temple as new recruits steadily flocked to the banner of a sect that offered power, prestige, and the prospects of plenty to eat.

As the years had passed, his original Faithguards had grown old and died, though the high priest had remained as a young man. Rumors spread through the city about a cleric who was living proof that his god bestowed actual power, and more and more people came to see, and many of them to join, the thriving church. Simultaneously other temples that occupied neighboring plots in the district had been afflicted by poor luck. Some of these churches had burned, while others had mysteriously lost all their members. Many of the disenfranchised turned to the Sect of the Black Robe, while others merely disappeared.

As each neighboring temple was abandoned, Kelryn and his followers had been quick to move in. Now, fifty years later, the sect occupied an entire city block. The black robe compound was surrounded by a high wall, diligently protected by the fierce and well-armed Faithguards. Within were gardens and dungeons, garrison buildings and hallowed halls of worship.

And Kelryn Darewind was master of it all.

Again the high priest's mind turned to the new maiden, no doubt even now sipping strong red wine, waiting for his pleasure in the nearby garden, and with the thought, he resolved to dispense with the remaining business as quickly as possible.

"Where is the prisoner?" he asked of Warden Thilt, who stood by the door, patiently awaiting his master's command.

"Bring in the traitor!" called Thilt.

A pair of Faithguards, their leggings splattered with mud, stalked into the temple. They supported a sagging, broken man between them. Half-dragging the wretch, they advanced to the front of the chapel, then tossed the captive, facedown, onto the floor before their high priest.

"You found him on the road south of the city?"

"Aye, Master—halfway to Kharolis," growled one of the guards, giving the hapless prisoner a kick.

"You did well to catch him." Kelryn remembered the hook-nosed female he had assigned to the Faithguards. "As a reward, you two shall have first use of the new supplicant. You are dismissed, with my gratitude."

"Thank you, Master!" chorused the pair of guards, exchanging measured leers as they departed for the door. Kelryn knew they were sizing each other up, determining who would have the wench first.

"Ah, Fairman," the high priest said with an elaborate sigh, walking a circle around the man who still lay, face-down and trembling, on the floor. Thilt had retired to just outside the front doors, so the two were alone in the high-ceilinged temple. "Why did you decide to leave us? Have you had a weakness, a question in your faith?"

The man on the floor drew a ragged breath and found the strength to rise to his knees. He dared a sidelong look at the priest, shaking his head wearily.

"Rise from the floor, my good son," said Kelryn, indicating a nearby bench and using the comfortable honorific he reserved for those acolytes who had come to his church as young men. "Have a seat and clear your mind. I really *do* desire to hear your explanation."

Fairman, who had been a long-standing enforcer in the Faithguards, looked helplessly at the high priest. He knows his life is forfeit, Kelryn thought with an agreeable thrill of pleasure. But he also knows that the difference between a quick and merciful execution or a slow, lingering death by torture would depend upon the answers he gives.

"It was the skull, Master. I had a dream, and I saw the skull."

Kelryn froze, chilled more than he cared to admit by the words. "And where was it?" He tried, successfully, he thought, to keep the tension out of his voice.

"I don't know. It was dark, but I could see it clearly. And I heard it calling, telling me to go."

"And you chose to obey the voice of a dream rather

than the doctrines and the commands of your high priest."

Fairman looked at Kelryn with an unspoken plea in his eyes. He really wants me to understand, thought the priest, mystified by the sincerity of the doomed man.

"I—I had no choice," Fairman said miserably. "Even when I awakened, I saw those eyeless sockets, heard a summons . . . calling me, making me move."

"I see." Kelryn did not, in fact, understand the strange compulsion. Still, he was worried. He had lost more than a dozen of his once faithful followers in the last decades. Though that wasn't a terrible rate of attrition, those fugitives his Faithguards recaptured always reported a similar dream.

"You know, of course, that your treachery cannot be abided."

"I know, Master," declared Fairman miserably. He drew a breath, apparently trying to decide if he should say anything further.

"Speak, my good son," the priest urged gently.

"There was something else in the dream—and in my thoughts, when I was awakened."

"Something else . . . ?"

"It was a kender, Master. The skull became a kender, and then it was the kender I was chasing. He was important. He *was* the skull, it seemed, though the bone was not of his own body."

"A kender?" Kelryn mused, trying to keep his voice casual. But despite his bored facade, his alarm deepened. He himself had dreamed about a mysterious kender on more than one occasion, and fifty years ago Gantor Blacksword had ranted something about one of the diminutive wanderers as well. What could it mean?

"Yes . . . a kender who was afraid, lord. In my dream, he was afraid of me, afraid because I knew his name."

Kelryn Darewind had little concern for kender as a rule. Though these portents were mildly disturbing, the high priest's mind had turned inevitably toward other, more immediate, issues. Indeed, as Fairman babbled away his last minutes, the high priest's thoughts wandered.

He vividly remembered the maiden waiting for him beyond the nearby door. Suddenly he wanted her very badly. With a curt command, he summoned Warden Thilt.

"That is not important," he declared with an abrupt, breathless determination. He turned to Warden Thilt. "Take him to the dungeons. Kill him with a single strike."

"Thank you, Master!" cried Fairman pathetically, falling forward to wrap his arms around the high priest's feet.

But Kelryn was already up and walking, taking long strides toward the white door. His mind was aflame, full of the mental image of the young woman. He was sure the reality would not be a disappointment. Behind him, he heard low sobs as Fairman was lifted to his feet and escorted without a great deal of force toward the stone-covered trapdoor that led into the temple's nether reaches.

The woman was waiting, and she was even more beautiful and willing than Kelryn had dared to hope. He enjoyed her through the rest of the morning, and she seemed more than happy to devote her considerable skill to the advancement of her faith.

Only later, as he lay in languid half-consciousness, did Kelryn's thoughts turn back to the hapless Fairman. The man had been dead for several hours when the priest sat up, cursing softly at his own thoughtlessness. He should have been more patient, more thorough as he questioned the traitor about his dream.

Specifically, he should have asked what the kender's name was.

Chapter 12
New Dawn of the True Gods

351 AC
Second Bakukal, Gildember

"Stop them!" High Priest Kelryn Darewind cried, standing on the wall above the gates of his temple compound, commanding the Faithguards to steady the bar that held shut the wide portals.

But the force of the mob in the streets would not be denied. Though Kelryn quickly descended, joining his men to throw his own weight against the gates, the bar splintered like a toothpick, and slowly the massive barriers of the gates were forced inward.

As soon as there was a narrow opening, people began to stream into the courtyard of the Sect of the Black Robe. The force of the crowd swelled the gap, and Kelryn abandoned the lost effort, falling back as the gates swung wide and a great throng of terrified humans charged into the high-walled compound. Even worse, he saw several kender ambling along with the crowd, unaffected by the hysteria that gripped the humans.

The refugees scattered through all portions of the temple grounds, filling the chapel, spilling through the gardens and drill grounds, pouring into the barracks, even seeking refuge in the bloodstained dungeons beneath the temple floor.

"Try to fix the gates after the throng is through," growled the high priest. "And by all that you value, get rid of the kender! Kill them if they won't leave!"

Warden Horec, the most recent chief of the Faith-guards, saluted and promised to do his best, though they both tacitly acknowledged that the force of the mob was a thing that no mere human could be expected to control. Still, he knew his master's aversion to the small folk, and he would make certain that any kender within the compound was quickly discovered and tossed over the wall.

Furious, Kelryn pushed his way through the crowd into the temple, then climbed the spiral stairway to the blessed solitude offered by the high tower. Two strapping Faithguards stood at the foot of the steps, barring passage—at least, thus far—to any trespasser who tried to follow.

The view from above offered little consolation. Kelryn could see many places where Haven was burning, the fires ignited by the cruel red dragons under the command of the villainous highlord, Verminaard. As he watched, the priest saw one of the massive serpents glide between two towering pillars of smoke. Banking gracefully, the wyrm uttered a shriek in the air above a crowded avenue, sending people spilling in panic toward any shelter they could find.

It was just such a panic that had driven the throng into the Temple of Fistandantilus. For days the news had been clear and harsh: Armies were marching on

Haven, and the city would inevitably fall. As to his sect, the high priest was determined to do what he could to make sure it survived.

Kelryn touched the comforting weight of the bloodstone and wished that he could pray to Fistandantilus for help—wished that there really *was* a god that would protect him, that would see to the safety of his faithful follower.

As if to mock his hopes, the gliding red dragon dipped low, jaws gaping as it belched a great cloud of flame along a row of buildings not far from the temple. The structures, mostly taverns, ignited immediately, and moments later panicked folk came diving out of the doorways. Many of the victims were aflame, and they rolled in the street, screaming in agony, only to be ignored by their fellow citizens who fled past, desperate for any suggestion of safety.

Haven had fallen, as Kelryn, and everyone else who had a grasp of reality, had known it would. The dragonarmies that had swept southward from Abanasinia were clearly unstoppable, a horde of flying serpents, cruel riders, and teeming hordes of men and monsters on the ground. There were even rumors that the elves of Qualinesti were withdrawing from their ancestral home, taking ships across the Straits of Algoni toward the imagined safety of Southern Ergoth.

Kelryn wondered, as he had wondered before, if he had been a fool to stay. Perhaps he should have abandoned the temple, left the faithful to fend for themselves as he sought a new place to begin. Much as he had done nine decades earlier, he reflected bitterly.

He had not remained in Haven out of any sense of loyalty to his followers. Rather, he had been unwilling to abandon the riches, the comforts, the women that had been his lot for so many years. The highlords would come, would claim this place and establish their rule, but Haven would remain a city. Kelryn merely hoped to maintain something like his old status when the new regime took power.

The dragon veered again, winging past the tower, and Kelryn grimaced at the sight of the rider sitting astride the crimson-scaled back. The man bore a long lance with a bloodstained tip and a shaft of black wood. His face was concealed behind a grotesque mask, and the high priest longed to tear that mask away, to punish this warrior for his insolence and to see the fear in his eyes as Kelryn Darewind delivered a blistering incantation of lethal violence.

Alas, it was not to be.

Hate flaring in his heart, Kelryn watched the dragon and its rider bank again, veering smoothly back to the north. There, some of the city's garrison had been determined to make a stand against the advancing army, valiantly trying to hold the gate and low wall. That defense had lasted for a few minutes, until a trio of the red dragons had flown overhead. Those men with the courage to remain at their posts in the face of the inevitable wave of mind-numbing dragonawe had died there, seared by the killing flames or crushed by claw and rended by fang. The rest of the defenders, driven into flight by terror, had scattered into every corner of the city or fled into the wilds of the south.

By the time the enemy ground troops, the draconians and their human and goblin allies, had reached the city wall, the barrier had been scoured clean of defenders. Now those land-bound invaders were spreading through the city, burning, looting, and raping. It was these tactics that had driven the frenzied mob to the gates of the sect's compound, though Kelryn wasn't sure why the mindless folk felt they might be safe here. He was pragmatic enough to realize that the high stone walls and the sturdy gates would present no barrier at all to an army determined to sack the place.

However, as the day waned into evening and then blended into the following dawn, there came no attack against the compound. At sunrise, Kelryn resumed his place in the tower and saw that the fires in the northern districts of the city had, for the most part, burned themselves out. There was no sign that the destruction was continuing.

Throughout the day, a steady stream of injured people made their way into South Haven. Many of these were burned, while others had been wounded by weapons or the crush of the mob. They gathered in a miserable huddle outside the gates of the temple compound, pleading for entrance, but Kelryn was adamant that the gates remain shut.

Late that afternoon he sensed an ominous change as the crowd outside grew still, an expectant silence that swiftly extended to those within the temple compound as well. From the height of his temple wall, Kelryn saw a masked and armored officer marching at the head of an escort of scaled, hissing draconians. The company advanced down the street toward the Sect of the Black Robe, the throng of refugees parting almost magically before the horrific visage of the officer's leering mask. The awe-inspiring warrior confidently presented himself at the gates of the temple, sending his respects and a message that he wished to speak to the high priest.

Kelryn knew that the time had come to talk. He ordered the gates opened, and the dragonarmy officer, his stature and presence heightened by the grotesque mask, strode boldly into the courtyard. The draconians remained outside, but many more of the sick and wounded citizens of Haven took advantage of the opened gate to pour inside the compound, despite the presence of the sinister warrior.

Meeting the man in the middle of the courtyard, conscious of hundreds of eyes upon him, Kelryn bowed stiffly. "I am the high priest," he declared. He guessed that this was the man he had watched in flight on the previous day—at least, the garish mask and armor were identical to that dragonrider's. The priest felt a small shiver of gratitude that, for now, the great red dragon was nowhere to be seen.

Kelryn Darewind stared at the mask, hating the fanged maw portrayed there, reviling the tiny eyes that glittered at him from the narrow slits above the nose.

"And who is the god you serve?"

"My faith is that of Fistandantilus," Kelryn Darewind proclaimed. "Archmage of the black robes, he has joined the gods in the constellations of the heavens. I merely strive to see that his memory receives its proper due here upon Krynn."

"I see," murmured the officer, though there was something in his voice that belied the statement. Again Kelryn wished to rip that mask away, to confront the human face underneath.

Surprisingly, the officer suddenly obliged by lifting the heavy metal plate from his head and shoulders. He was astonishingly young, the priest thought, with a face masked by strains of sweat and grime, the sparse stubble of several days' beard blue-black on his chin, cheeks, and neck.

With a curt gesture, the man swept his arms outward to indicate the attentive gathered crowd. "If you are in fact a priest, then you should cure those who have been injured. It is not enough that you merely offer them the security of your compound."

Kelryn laughed, a sharp and bitter sound. "Surely you know that no priest, not since the Cataclysm, can heal the hurts of mortal flesh. I merely strive to instruct my flock—"

"*No* priest?" The officer was mocking, and Kelryn flushed, sensing the tension among his faithful like a lute string pulled taut through the air. He feared suddenly that he was being drawn into a trap.

The dragonrider spun on his heel, turning his back to Kelryn and addressing the gathered populace. "I come to you with a warning and with a promise of hope. For years has Haven been filled with charlatans and pretenders." He spat over his shoulder, and the high priest was forced to sidestep quickly to avoid the spittle.

"You should know that Fistandantilus is not a god, no more so than any of the Seeker deities. These are make-believe faiths, created by fakers such as this man to gather you into his power, to rob and abuse you."

"Liar!" shouted Kelryn, terrified of his own audacity, yet knowing that he could not allow the verbal onslaught to continue. He didn't want to fight, not here, not under these circumstances. Still, he wished that he were wearing his sword, and he resolved to defend himself with the small dagger he wore under his robe if the officer's affronts became even more direct.

Instead of attacking, however, the officer half turned, a sardonic smile upon his lips. He gestured to one of the refugees nearby, a child whose right arm dangled limply in a bloodstained sling. "Come here, lad. It's all right. I won't hurt you."

Wonderingly the boy came forward. Kelryn could not tear his eyes away as the warrior knelt, pulled off his gauntlets, and extended a gentle hand toward the gory cloth. "Know, my son, that there is a goddess who is real and who cares for you."

The man's voice rose as he swept his gaze over the whole throng. "Hear me, all! The Queen of Darkness, Takhisis herself, commands your obedience. But know that she offers rewards, riches, and power in return!"

The warrior touched the injured arm. The boy stood still, trembling, as the man ducked his head. "Listen to my prayers, Dark Lady who is my mistress and soon shall be queen of all the world. This child is innocent; he has done you no wrong. I beseech you, grant me the power to heal his flesh, to make him well that he may serve us, might bring further glory to your name."

"It—it doesn't hurt anymore," stammered the youth, looking with wonder at his arm.

"Take off the bandage." The officer's voice remained gentle, soothing.

Quickly the boy tore at the filthy cloth, casting it aside and raising his arm in the air. A joyful voice cried from the crowd and a woman rushed forward, sweeping the boy into her arms. "He is healed! Yesterday he was certain to lose his arm, and now the wound is gone!"

A gasp rose from the throng, and people, awestruck

and wondering, shuffled forward to see this proof of godhood.

"I tell you today of our queen's might and her mercy," proclaimed the officer, rising to his feet, speaking in a voice that resounded from the high temple walls. "There are more priests waiting to soothe your hurts, to teach you the rightness of our new faith. All who would open your ears to the truth, go to the great square of Haven, and there you will learn the ways of the true gods!"

Those people closest to the gate were already leaving at a run. With a restive murmur, a sound that grew into a low cheer, the rest of the crowd seemed to understand the command, embrace the hope it offered. Kelryn stood still, seething, watching the sardonic smile play across the dragonrider's face as the congregation, the refugees, even many of the Faithguards fled the temple in the face of this miracle. Only when the last of the once loyal followers had departed the gates did the man turn back, regarding Kelryn as if the high priest were a mere afterthought.

"You are an affront to true faith," barked the officer. "You deserve only death!"

Kelryn Darewind felt the hot pulse against his chest and pulled the bloodstone of Fistandantilus forth with a sudden, instinctive gesture. The officer stared at the stone a moment, blinking as his stern expression grew soft and vague.

"Lord Verminaard will use your temple compound as his headquarters." The man shook his head, visibly struggling to gain control of his thoughts and words. "You have one hour to gather your belongings and leave. If the highlord finds you here upon his arrival, you may expect to die—very slowly."

Kelryn made no reply. He saw the few of his Faithguards who still remained, those who had been the most loyal of his followers, watching him questioningly. Unconsciously he touched the bloodstone, once again secure under his robe.

"I carry all my needs with me," he said grimly. With a curt gesture, he summoned his remaining men—no more than a dozen—to his side. They fell into step behind him as he stalked through the gates, past the company of leering draconians, to march along Haven's suddenly foreign street.

Chapter 13

An Historical Analysis

To his Honor, Patriarch Grimbriar
High Priest of Gilean
Inscribed this year of Krynn, 372 AC

Your Eminence, I have been surprised to discover, during the course of my research, references of interest in the dragonarmy records pertaining to the fall of Haven and the subsequent occupation by the minions of the Highlord Verminaard. Specifically, there is some reason to believe that one of the great artifacts of Fistandantilus may have found its way to that chaotic city at some time following the creation of Skullcap and preceding the arrival of the dragonarmies.

Of course, the fall of Haven and the occupation of Abanasinia, Qualinesti, and the Plains of Dust have been well documented in the official histories, not to mention the detailed military accounts available in the rolls of Solamnia and the Highlord Ariakas. It would be presumptuous, and wasteful, of me to attempt to improve upon that body of work.

Rather, my patriarch, I shall strive to clarify several pertinent facts.

It is known, for example, that most of the Seeker priests were thrown down by the arrival of Verminaard's army. Some (the weakest and least influential, it seems) were allowed to maintain their holdings and congregations. Most were incorporated into the ranks of the dragonarmies, and a few—the most powerful, those who were perceived as a threat to Takhisis—were cruelly executed, their cults violently disbanded.

There is a strange tale regarding a red dragon rider, one Blaric Hoyle. The officer was sent to destroy a sect created for the worship of a false god, a faith dedicated to the archmage Fistandantilus. This temple was one of the more successful of the false faiths, reputedly because the high priest had demonstrated some small measure of immortality. At least, many witnesses claimed that he had lived in the city for perhaps a century, but during all this time had remained a very young man.

The hapless dragonrider apparently did not fully grasp the lethal intent of the order. He confronted the Seeker priest and closed the temple as he had been instructed. However, he then allowed the false cleric to leave the city of Haven before the executioner arrived.

Blaric Hoyle was tried by a military tribunal presided over by Highlord Verminaard himself. Apparently the officer was unable to offer a very good defense of his actions; the notes indicate that he seemed confused, even forgetful, about the circumstances of his confrontation with the false high priest. However, he made several references to a "sparking stone," and once claimed that he saw "sparks within the gemstone." These were vague perceptions, related without specificity, but they aroused my suspicions.

Hoyle did not know why he allowed the false priest to leave, but his responses to the question imply that the mysterious stone had at least something to do with his disobedient choice.

Alas, we hear no more from him. (As usual, he who failed to please his ruthless highlord master was granted only a very short appearance on history's stage.) However, it seems at least possible to me that the stone referred to could have been the bloodstone of Fistandantilus.

I know that all previous reports have indicated that the stone was destroyed during the convulsion that created Skullcap. However, Haven is not terribly distant from that place, and there was a strong belief that the "priest" of this faith came from the south (the direction of Skullcap) when he arrived in the city to establish his sect. And, too, there is the previously mentioned business about the man's strange propensity to resist the effects of aging.

The fugitive Seeker and his few remaining followers are believed to have made their way into the Kharolis borderlands. There it is reported that he established a camp as rude as any bandit's. They survived by preying upon weakness, plundering from the local citizenry, even stealing from the dragonarmies when they could find a detachment or supply center that was weakly defended.

The arrival of the dragonarmies in Haven and the closing of the Temple of Fistandantilus began to draw the threads of history closer together. Another occurrence, pertinent to future events, also happened during this interval:

The Heroes of the Lance, on their epic journey toward Thorbardin, visited the mountain of Skullcap, where it is rumored they discovered an artifact, the skull of Fistandantilus, which had lain untouched in the depths of that place for more than a century. It is possible that they brought it near to the surface, though certainly they did not take it with them.

In any event, while I have been unable to confirm everything that has happened in regard to this story, it can be deduced from subsequent events that the skull was no longer languishing in the deepest depths of that horrid fortress.

As Always,
Your faithful servant,
Foryth Teel

Chapter 14

Dragon Reign

356 AC
Mid-Yurthgreen

Time is a highly subjective reality. Hours, days, weeks, and years all mean different things, are held to different values by the many versions of mortality. For example, two days might encompass the entire lifetime of a certain bug, and for that creature, the ticking of a minute is an interval for great feasting, or for traveling a long distance. To a human, a minute is a more compact space—time, perhaps, for a sip of wine, a bite of bread, a phrase or two of conversation.

Yet to a truly long-lived being—an elf, for example, or a dragon—minutes can pass tenfold, a hundredfold, without arousing interest or concern. A single such interval is space for a slow inhalation, or an idle thought. It is certainly not time enough for serious cogitation, *never* enough for the making of an important decision.

And, by extension, the counting of months and years by such entities can also assume insignificant proportions. When compared to the more frantic pace of humanity's existence, very long times may pass in nothing more than a haze of quiet reflection.

Or in the case of a dragon, an extended nap.

It was thus for Flayzeranyx, who awakened in the cool depths of his cave with no awareness of the season, nor even of the number of years that might have passed since he had commenced his hibernation. Even the red dragon's return to consciousness was a gradual thing, an event spread over the span of several weeks.

Only after he had lifted the crimson, heavy lids that completely concealed his eyes did the great serpent notice the gradual increase and decrease of light from the direction leading toward the mouth of his cave. Through the gauzy inner lids that still cloaked the slitted yellow pupils, Flayze realized that these shifts in brightness represented the cycles of day passing into night, and then merging into the following dawn.

Idly he counted the cycling of five such periods of dark and brightness. By then he began to notice a nagging thirst, a dry rasp that cracked around the base of his tongue and made his mouth feel as though it were full of dust. And then, very vaguely, he noticed the first traces of hunger rumbling in the vast depths of his belly. There was still no real sense of urgency to his awareness, but he realized that it was time for him to move.

Slowly Flayze rose, pressing with his four powerful legs to lift his serpentine body, supple neck, and sinuous tail from the floor. A few old scales snapped free, chips of scarlet floating to the floor. The dragon wriggled, a violent shiver that rippled the length of his body, and many more scales broke loose. Those that remained, at last bared by the sloughing of the ancient plates, gleamed with a bright slickness suggestive of fresh blood.

Climbing toward the dimly recalled cavern entrance, Flayze ascended a rock-strewn floor, slinking with oily ease over steep obstacles, relishing the grace of movement, the power incumbent in his massive body. He sniffed the air, smelling water and greenery, and he was glad that he had not emerged during winter, when the hunting—and even the quenching of his thirst—could be rendered much more problematic by the presence of snow and ice. The odors from outside became more rich, and he smelled the mud, the scent of migrating geese, and he knew that it was spring.

And then the sun was there, shining into the mouth of the cave as it crested the eastern horizon. Flayze lowered his inner eyelids and hooded his vision with the thick outer membranes as he squinted into the brightness. He ignored the momentary discomfort, feeling the hunger surge anew, fired by the tangy spoor of a great flock of the waterfowl he had earlier scented.

A stream flowed, as he had remembered it would, just past the mouth of the deep cave. Lowering his massive muzzle into the deepest pool he could reach, Flayze drank, sucking the water out of the natural bowl in a long slurp. Downstream, the creek momentarily halted its flow, as if startled by the sudden absence of its source. The red dragon lifted his head, allowing rivulets to drain from his crocodilian jaws. In moments the pool was refilled and once more drained.

Now Flayze sniffed the breeze in earnest, anxious to eat. Again he was tantalized by the scent of the geese. He tried to recollect his surroundings, remembering a vast wetland, a flat expanse of marsh that lay at the downstream terminus of this very brook. The dragon extended his blood-red wings, stretching them up and down, working out the kinks of his long hibernation. The exercise felt good, but he was too impatient to limber himself fully; instead, he leapt into the air, pressed down with the vast sails of his wings, gliding just a short distance off the ground. He followed the grade of the descending streambed, hoping to surprise the flock by his sudden appearance over the marsh.

Flying felt good, as always. He didn't mind the cool air stinging, feeling strangely vital in his flaring nostrils. Then he was there, and the expanse of shallow water below him was choked with plump birds, thousands of them, cackling and murmuring in a great mass. With a roar of exultation, Flayze dipped his head, opened his mouth, and expelled a huge cloud of searing fire. The flame boiled into the waters of the marsh and killed a hundred geese in the first instant of its explosion. Banking steeply back, Flayze settled into the sticky mud, ignoring the thousands of other birds, the vast flock that took wing in a honking cacophony on all sides.

He used his dexterous foreclaws to lift the charred birds to his mouth, one or two at a time. He crunched and swallowed with sheer pleasure, relishing the hot juices running over his tongue. He didn't particularly like the sensation of mud against his beautiful scales, and by the time he had gulped down the last of the geese, he had sunk to his belly in the sticky stuff. Still, his stomach was full and his mood benign as he wriggled to the shore and flopped into the cool stream, allowing the brisk current to wash his body.

Finally he was ready to investigate his surroundings. The bulk of the High Kharolis rose to the south, purple against the horizon as the sun settled toward evening. To the north, he knew, lay Pax Tharkas, and beyond that the forested elven realm of Qualinesti.

The last Flayzeranyx remembered of that sylvan reach, he had been flying above the seemingly eternal canopy of trees on a routine patrol. He had still been getting used to the fact that he bore no rider; his knight, a man called Blaric Hoyle, had recently been executed by the Highlord Verminaard for some failure that had occurred during the sack of Haven.

As Flayze had flown, riderless, over the treetops, a pair of dragons had swept from the clouds, plunging toward him. Since every dragon he had ever seen had been allied in the Dark Queen's cause, he had at first been unconcerned, until he was startled by the brilliant reflection of the sun off silver wings.

Thus had the dragons of Paladine entered Flayze's war, and in the next moments, they summarily ended the red dragon's participation in that campaign. The scales on Flayze's back were cruelly shattered by a blast of frost, and a vicious silver lance had pierced his wing. It had only been his good fortune to dive away from the silvers and to be abandoned by his foe in favor of some more pressing concern.

After that fight, Flayzeranyx had returned to Sanction to meet with Emperor Ariakas himself. The mighty serpent had been ordered to return to the Red Wing, which was occupying much of Southern Solamnia at the time. There he was to be assigned a new rider, and he would return to the war to avenge the losses brought about by the sudden and unwelcome involvement of the metallic dragons.

Instead, Flayze had decided he'd had enough of fighting, at least, enough of the kind of violence required for the execution of the emperor's grandiose plans. The rogue red dragon had veered south, crossing the Newsea, finally coming to rest in this rugged region of Kharolis. The cave where he had recently secluded himself had been a fortuitous discovery on his earlier campaign. Subsequently it had provided a refuge wherein he could wait out the war in safety and comfort.

Now clean of the sticky mud, Flayzeranyx took to the air, flying high through the night and wondering about the fate of the world during the interval of his long nap. For a long time he glided through the skies, skirting the massif of Thorbardin—he knew that even the most deadly attack of Ariakas's legions was not likely to have reduced that dwarven stronghold—and seeking familiar spoors on the night breeze. He smelled proof of humans and elves in the forests and plains below and caught the acrid stink of a hill dwarf village well to the north.

Finally he detected the reptilian scent that he had been seeking. He soared low, silently gliding through the skies, drawing closer to the source of the odor that brought so many familiar and tangible memories. Acrid smoke tickled his nostrils, and he suspected the creatures he sought were gathered around a dying fire. A glance at the stars showed him that it was nearly dawn, and then he crested a low ridge and saw a dozen or more human-sized figures wrapped in cloaks and lying motionless around the embers of a large blaze.

Settling to the ground in a rush of wings, the dragon lowered his head and glowered balefully at a lone sentry, one who dozed, half standing against a nearby tree.

"Y-Your lordship!" stammered the draconian, dropping its sword as it scrambled to come to attention. "Get up, useless scuts!" it barked at the sleeping company. "Greet his crimson lordship!"

Alerted by the shout and the wind of the dragon's landing, more of the reptilian dragonmen rose from their sleep, muttering and cowering, regarding the monstrous serpent with slitted, fearful eyes.

Flayze was pleased to see that the draconians reacted to his august presence with instinctive obedience and fear. The red dragon huffed a deep breath, a thudding sound like a distant boom of thunder, and the creatures cast themselves facedown onto the ground.

"Tell me, little snakes," he hissed, slowly articulating each word. "What news of the war?"

The draconian guard, apparently used to the slower time sense of great wyrms, raised his head to ask a question. "You refer to the Draconian War, Mighty Lord? The campaigns of the Highlord Ariakas?"

"I do."

"Sad to say, Excellent Fire Breather, the dragons of Paladine and their cruel lances inflicted tragic defeat. The highlord is dead, his armies disbanded."

"I see." Flayze was not terribly displeased by the news. "And what of these lands? Who rules?"

"Much of this land is wild, O Mighty Wyrm. That is why we are able to survive here. The Plains of Dergoth, to the north, are a barren desert. But we have seen a brass dragon there, near the mountain of the great skull."

"Aye, Skullcap." Flayzeranyx remembered flying over the place. He had been curious during that earlier exploration, had even thought to land and investigate, but his rider had ordered him on, no doubt driven toward some other pointless matter of the war.

"He is a bold one, that brass," declared one of the other draconians in a sibilant accusation. "He killed Dwarfskinner, just last month."

"Aye, a killer," murmured several others. They looked at Flayze hopefully, and he understood why: They wanted him to kill the brass.

"Perhaps Dwarfskinner may be avenged," Flayze allowed. "But tell me more. How many winters have passed since the coming of the metal dragons?"

"Four, Excellent Flaming One," replied the sentry who had done most of the talking. "The latest just recently melted into water."

"Good," Flayze declared, with a nod of satisfaction. That meant that enough time had passed for certain concerns, such as his disobedience to the commands of Ariakas, to become irrelevant. At the same time, however, there were likely to remain aftereffects from the war, factors of chaos and violence that would make the red dragon's existence a little easier.

"Would his lordship care for a taste of jerky?" asked one of the draconians, with obvious reluctance.

Flayze snorted contemptuously, looking at the scrawny dragonmen as he remembered his sumptuous repast in the marsh. "No," he replied curtly. "I take wing again— and I shall look for scales of brass."

Chapter 15

Two Skulls

356 AC
Third Kirinor, Yurthgreen

Recalling the location of Skullcap, Flayze flew toward the great mountain with unerring accuracy. Fire pulsed in his belly, and his mind was inflamed with eager thoughts of battle. A brass dragon! None of the metallics was more hot-tempered, nor more irritating to the presence of a beautiful chromatic such as Flayzeranyx. The thought of a vicious battle, of the killing that would follow, drove him near to a frenzy as his broad wings soared northward through the dawn.

A brownish-gray fog lay low across the Plain of Dergoth, and the fire-breathing dragon had to forcibly resist the notion that he flew through a realm of ether, a place lacking substance and boundary. Occasionally the vapors would part to reveal a glimpse of the cracked and broken ground below, and this was enough to reassure Flayze about his bearings. So he swept onward, slicing the vaporous cloud with his sharp wings and smooth body.

He could have risen above the blanket of mist, but it suited him to remain within the concealment of the fog. He remembered that the plain below him was featureless and flat, offering no upthrusting obstacles that would suddenly burst from the fog to endanger him. And if there was in fact a brass dragon at Skullcap, Flayze felt no obligation to give the serpent a great deal of warning about his approach.

Other reds might have handled the situation differently, Flayzeranyx knew. Perhaps they would have concealed their flight beneath a spell of invisibility, or even altered their beautiful, perfect shapes with a polymorph spell, flying in the feathered guise of an eagle or condor. The red snorted, scorning such arcane deceits. Like all of his clan dragons, Flayze had an arsenal of magic at his command, but as he had throughout his life, he now disdained the casting of spells. He preferred instead the integrity of hot fire, the trustworthy strength of powerful sinew and sharp, rending claw and fang.

By the time the sun started to burn away the fog, the red dragon was only a few miles from the skull-shaped mountain that gradually materialized in the middle distance. He approached the mountain from the front, flying at an altitude that was even with the great pockmarks in the cliff that so resembled the eye sockets of an actual skull. The rounded dome formed a smooth summit of whitish-gray stone, and the whole edifice was still and ominous.

Drawing closer, he saw no sign of any inhabitant, not in the yawning maw of the entrance cavern at ground level—the skull's "mouth"—or in the large apertures that gaped above the craggy cliffs of the preternatural cheekbones. Any one of the three entrances was large enough to have concealed a good-sized dragon, so Flayze didn't allow his caution to recede. Instead, he banked, gliding through a leisurely circle around the edifice. On the back side, downwind from Skullcap, he caught a hint of sulfurous, steaming heat, the distinctive spoor of the brass confirming the draconians' reports.

Flayze dived past the face of the ghastly mountain, bellowing a challenge, turning to spit a gout of fire that raked all three of the entrances scarring the rocky face. Then he veered to the side, circling sharply, looping to come to rest on the smooth, rounded summit.

His blast had no sooner dissipated along the craggy rock than did the front of Skullcap explode in a hiss of blistering air, a gout of heat that seared outward, emerging from the skull's left eye to linger in the space before the mountain. Flayzeranyx prepared to leap, expecting the serpent to burst out of that same hole.

But the brass took him by surprise. It lunged from the right eye socket, curving sharply down and away. The red leaped after it, breathing fire, only to see the brass tail flicker out of sight around the side of the mountain.

Reacting by sudden instinct, Flayze flew upward, tilting to the side, flying in a wild, rolling cartwheel over the rounded crest of Skullcap. Immediately he saw brass jaws gaping before him, realized that the metallic had tried the same tactic—but the red was faster. Flayze's lethal fireball exploded around his enemy, searing the scales back from its face, boiling the glaring eyeballs in their sockets.

The two dragons met in a crash of talon and fang, but the brass was blinded and too sorely hurt to make an effective attack. Flayze seized his enemy's supple neck in his foreclaws, then struck with a single, crushing bite. The serpents, coiling together almost like lovers, collapsed to the dusty ground, shivering and lashing about for a moment, then settling into utter stillness.

Slowly a single head—a head cloaked in scales of bright crimson—rose from the corpse of his foe. Flayze twisted, uncoiling from the tangled body, shaking the sulfurous stench away. One final sniff confirmed that the brass was utterly dead.

Finally the red dragon turned toward the mountain. Already he entertained thoughts of making this his lair. Indeed, with the forbidding aspect of the skull visage, it seemed a perfect place for a red dragon. He padded through the entrance, ducking low to pass beneath the stalactites jutting down like great fangs.

A short distance into the cave he drew up short, puzzled by an object on the smooth floor. Squinting, Flayze discerned that it was a skull—a human skull. Surprised, the dragon picked it up, balancing it between two massive foreclaws. He felt a pulse of magic in the bony object, and at the same time knew a strong sensation that he should leave this place.

He scuttled out of the cavern with alacrity, looking over his shoulder at the mountain with a newly critical eye. In fact, he now perceived, this place had many faults as a lair. Most notably, it was stuck here in the middle of a desert. His comings and goings would be observed, on a clear day, by any creature within dozens of miles.

No, Flayze decided, taking wing again, he would find another lair. There was certain to be a better place around here; perhaps he would even return to the cave where he had hibernated.

At the same time, he pinched the piece of bone between his powerful claws. For some reason that he didn't clearly understand, he was utterly determined to keep the skull.

Chapter 16

A Window Through Time

374 AC
Fourth Bracha, Paleswelt

Flayze lounged easily in the steaming depths of his cavern. Water spilled from a narrow chute high in the cave wall, pouring in a cheery rivulet down the steep slope, then splashing into a pool of crystalline water. The overflow of that pool sloshed down a sloping slab, then gushed into the depths of the lower caverns. There it spattered onto rocks that were deceptively dark, but the sudden burst of hissing vapor provided quick proof that those stones were very hot indeed.

In fact, Flayze knew that, should he break one of those lower rocks in half, he would find that the center was a fiery red core of viscous lava. He knew because, more than once, he had done it. He relished the fiery depths of his lair, delighted in the fact that living, flowing rock slowly oozed into the lower reaches.

The perch where the mighty dragon coiled was, in fact, a sort of island surrounded by a gulf of black space. In the depths of that space, lava oozed and occasional spumes of fire burst from cracks in the rock, wafting upward to flicker soothingly through the lair.

He had discovered this cavern a decade or so ago, after abandoning the cave where he had gone to avoid the end of the Draconian War. That place, in truth, had proved to be too close to the dwarves of Thorbardin. This cave was larger and lay much farther to the south and west, overlooking the Plains of Dust from the terminus of the Kharolis Range. The climate outside tended to be a little frosty, by red dragon standards, but Flayze relished the natural heat of these deep caverns. He was content to remain here during the deepest months of winter, when the frigid expanse of Icewall Glacier seemed likely to extend all the way across Ice Mountain Bay and grind against the very base of this massif.

But now it was spring again, and Flayzeranyx was restless, ready to fly, to plunder and kill. As befitted an ancient and lordly wyrm, first he would do some planning.

His huge yellow eyes, the black slits of the pupils spread wide in the darkness, swept across the glorious extent of the fiery cave. Beyond the lava bubbling around his perch, he could see grotesque shapes, smooth and flowing formations frozen into the shapes that outlined the manner the molten rock had cooled into natural stone. Smoke wafted through the air, and several deep niches were illuminated with more or less permanent flares of glowing rock or wisping, flaring fires.

From one of those niches, black eye sockets stared back, and the dragon uttered a grim chuckle. There were many treasures scattered about the niches and corners of the cave: piles of steel and golden coins, weapons of dwarf-crafted steel, gems and jewels of spectacular value and sparkling beauty. Nearly every other item had an intrinsic value or purity of beauty that was far more tangible than the piece of dry bone. And though he valued many things, he treasured nothing so much as the skull he had claimed from Skullcap following his battle with the brass dragon.

The dragon didn't know what it was about the bony artifact that made it so compelling to him; he merely understood that it gave him a sense of power and well-being to look upon the object. Now he rose, spreading his wings to add a bit of lift to his gliding leap across the searing rock of the moat. He came to rest before the skull and squatted, staring into those black eyes.

He felt it again, a sensation that had become increasingly common when he regarded the thing. It was a feeling that the skull was trying to talk to him, to communicate something that was terribly important.

"What is it, my skull? Show me . . . speak to me!" he urged, his words a whisper hissed on a breath of soft flame.

As always, there was no reply. Gingerly, carefully, Flayze reached out and picked up the skull. He looked at it from every angle, flicking his forked tongue into the mouth, through the empty sockets of the eyes. He felt as though there was a mystery here, a locked treasure that he should know how to reach, to understand.

Yet though he had possessed the skull for nearly twenty years, he had never been able to learn how to release the secrets held within. Naturally he had tried many times. Perhaps sorcery would have helped to decipher the puzzle, but as always Flayze disdained magic, scorning the arcane arts as the tools of weaklings.

On an inexplicable impulse, he lifted the skull and placed it atop his own head, the eyeless face turned toward the front.

And for the first time he felt the power of the artifact take hold.

Abruptly he could not see the cave, couldn't smell the smoldering rock or the acrid taint of sulfur on the air.

Instead, he was looking at a different place.

This was a small fortified manor house on a rocky knoll. The terrain was suggestive of the Kharolis borderlands, though Flayze did not recognize the specific location. As he observed, mystified and intrigued, the dragon's perspective whirled inward, slicing through the manor's walls as if they didn't exist. He found himself in a room filled with a dozen or more rough-looking men. These were warriors, bandits most likely, to judge from the motley clothing, the ill-kept nature of hair and beards. Though they were inside, apparently at a place of safety, each of the men was armed.

And one of them stood out from the rest, a man who was well groomed, young, and handsome. He regarded the others with a tolerant gaze, and Flayze sensed that, despite his apparent youthfulness, this was the leader.

Something about the young man compelled the dragon's attention more firmly, and Flayze sensed the hot pulse of blood and magic, a cadence that was pounding beneath the stiff leather armor of the human's shirt. Finally the dragon's perspective fell further, through that material, and he beheld the bloodstone. The gem seemed huge, and he could sense its power—and its link to the skull that still rested upon the dragon's head.

These ruffians were an interesting lot, Flayze decided. Someday before too long he would seek them out, perhaps to kill them or take the bloodstone. Yet he felt a reluctance as he considered those options, a sense that the skull did not want him to attack—at least, not in a way that could endanger the precious stone. On the other hand, the wyrm might try to find a way the men could be useful to him.

Abruptly his attention shifted, pulled back from the bloodstone, out of the manor house and across the valleys of Kharolis. Soon he had the sensation of diving downward, sweeping along the banks of a shallow river until he hovered over a small village, a place of humans.

His attention was riveted upon a large house in the center of that village. There was danger to him there, in that house, a menace that the red dragon could not identify. Yet he knew that it was the skull that was showing him this danger, and the skull that was compelling him to act. Vaguely he perceived that the danger there was to the skull, not to the dragon, but even that threat was an affront to his draconic pride.

With a growl, Flayze lifted his head, dislodging the skull and breaking the spell that had bound him. He caught the treasure in his claws, setting it back upon the natural dais he had found for it. He was restless, uneasy, mystified by what he had seen. The men in the manor, he suspected, had a role to play in his future. Someday he would find them and bend them to his will.

But before then, there was the matter of the village. All sorts of alarming notions had stampeded through the dragon's mind when he beheld the place. Flayzeranyx didn't understand the nature of the danger, but he recognized a threat when he saw one. And with that recognition came the drive for action.

The village would have to be destroyed.

Chapter 17

A Day of Fire

374 AC
Fourth Misham, Paleswelt

Danyal scooted down the ladder from the straw-bedded loft that served as the bedroom for himself and his brother Wain. Wain, and Danyal's mother and father as well, were already outside tending to chores—milking the cow, getting the sheep into pasture, perhaps gathering turtles from the traps by the stream bank.

The lad felt an almost guilty thrill of pleasure as he thought of his own personal duties. His "chore" today was to go fishing, to bring home enough plump trout for the evening meal—and more, if possible. It was useful business, to be sure, valuable to his family and the rest of the little village of Waterton. But more importantly, fishing was about Danyal's favorite thing to do in all Krynn.

Of course, the lad did his share of the other chores as well. Though Bartrane Thwait was the most important man in the whole village, he made sure that his sons, Wain and Danyal, worked as hard as anyone else. They took turns helping with the traps, gathering potatoes from the field, tending the sheep, and milking the lone cow that was the most obvious sign of the Thwait family's exalted status in the community.

And the boys took turns doing the fishing, Danyal reminded himself. He shouldn't feel remorse just because it was his day to drown a worm or two. In all honesty, he admitted to himself with a private smile, he really didn't feel guilty at all.

He found his willow fishing pole just outside the house and checked the fine catgut line, insuring that it was free of snags. The supple pole, its length nearly three times the boy's height, whipped back and forth satisfactorily. Danyal had several hooks in his pocket, each painstakingly sharpened by his father last night, and a pouchful of plump worms that he had gathered several evenings ago under the silver light of a full Solinari. Finally he took up the creel, the wicker basket that hung on the hook beside the house's only door.

It was when he reached to his waist, looking to attach the creel to his belt, that he remembered that the strap of tanned leather he usually wore had broken just the day before. A piece of rope would suffice to hold up his trousers, but the creel—especially if he managed to fill it with fish—called for a sturdier support. Putting down the pole, he went back into the house.

Sunlight flashed off a surface of silver on the other side of the room, and Danyal saw his father's belt in its place of honor above the mantle. Of course, he knew it wasn't the belt that was being honored—it was the silver buckle that was a family heirloom, a treasured memento that had been worn by Danyal's ancestor.

The lad hesitated for a moment, knowing that the importance of that treasured buckle suggested he find some other way to attach the creel. But the late-summer breeze was already freshening. Soon the trout would drop deep to wait out the brightest part of the day.

With a quick decision, Danyal snatched down the belt, passed it through the loops on the creel, and wrapped it around his waist. As a last touch, he took a wool blanket and wrapped it over the belt; if questioned, he could always claim that he had taken the blanket in order to have something to sit on.

Even with the concealing blanket, he hoped that no one would notice as he stepped outside and carefully closed the door behind him. Grabbing his pole, he jogged along the track that led behind the village, heading for the undercut bank that dropped toward the stream. As he hurried along, he heard laughter from the village commons, where he knew that many of the townsfolk were stomping on grapes in the large wine tuns.

Glad that everyone seemed to be occupied, the young fisherman followed the railed fence around the back of the blacksmith's stable, knowing he was unlikely to meet anyone here. He was startled by an angry whinny and reflexively ducked out of the way as a large black horse that had been lurking on the other side of the fence reared on its hind legs. The animal snorted and lashed out with a steel-shod hoof, a blow that Danyal barely avoided by skipping out of the way.

"Better luck next time, Nightmare," he muttered, not very loudly. He shook his head nervously, admitting that the blacksmith's ill-tempered nag really frightened him—as she did anyone who came too close to the small corral.

Still, the woods and the stream beckoned, and within a minute the village was out of sight, lost behind the willow and cottonwood trees that lined the banks on both sides. Danyal headed for the first of a series of deep pools, where he and his brother had met with frequent success. If the nearest of the holes didn't offer an ample supply of hungry fish, he would cross the stream on the makeshift bridge formed by an old willow, a tree that had fallen across the waterway before he was born. There were deep pools within easy reach of the other bank as well, and though they were a little more inaccessible, they were also a little more likely to yield positive results.

For several minutes he meandered through the sun-speckled woods, watched the sparkling reflections from the stream, smelling the cool wetness of clean water. Everything seemed perfect as he reached the streambank beside a deep, still pool. The blue-green depths of the water concealed many fish, he knew, and he took care to approach the bank in a crouch, so as not to disturb his prey.

The shadow that flickered across him was moving too fast to be a cloud and was too large to be a bird. Danyal gaped upward, then fell to his rump, stunned beyond words by the sight of a massive red dragon. Rocked by a numbing wave of dragonawe, he could only stare, trembling in all his limbs, feeling his guts turn to water in his belly.

The serpent was gliding low, so low that the tip of the creature's sinuous tail trailed through the tops of the tallest cottonwoods. As the monster drifted out of sight beyond the trees, Danyal's first conscious thought was that he was safe. The serpent obviously had flown past without taking notice of him.

His next thought was of the village.

"Mom! Pap! Wain!" he cried, leaping to his feet, his voice shrill and urgent as it pierced the woods. And then he was running, his fishing pole forgotten, desperately sprinting toward the village where all the people that he knew in the world resided.

Before he had taken twoscore steps, he heard the first of the screams, cries of horror that rang even louder than his own urgent shouts. By the time he was halfway home, the smell of soot and ash was heavy on the summer breeze.

And when he scrambled up the bank and burst

through the last of the trees, toward the rear of the blacksmith shop, he thought he had stumbled into the aftermath of a terrible war.

Smoke was thick in the air, stinging his eyes and nostrils. Even worse was the heat, a physical blow against his face that slammed him to a halt, brought his arms up in an effort to shield his skin from the searing blazes that threatened to blister his forehead and cheeks. He squinted, trying to see through the smoke and tears.

It seemed that every building in the village was ablaze, and most of them had been smashed into kindling. Bodies—the corpses of his neighbors, his family!—were scattered everywhere, many gored by horrific wounds, others burned beyond recognition by lethal flames. He staggered sideways and caught a glimpse of the common square. The tuns full of grapes had been shattered, and the spilled red wine provided a grotesque carpet for the torn and shattered bodies that lay motionless among the wreckage.

A great scarlet wing sliced through the roiling smoke overhead, and Danyal fell to the earth, crawling frantically under the shelter of a broken door. He watched the lashing tail of the dragon as the beast flew away, toward the north, returning along the direction from which Danyal had first seen it.

Slowly Dan stood up. The fires had settled somewhat, though his face still burned from the surrounding heat. He edged around a nearby building, skirting the destruction as he stayed beneath the shelter of the trees alongside the riverbank.

Something moved and the lad lunged backward, tumbling into the underbrush as a great, black shape emerged from the burning wreckage of the blacksmith's shop. He saw the shining pelt, the wild eyes, and then noticed the cruel gouge of a fresh, bleeding wound on the panicked animal's shoulder.

"Nightmare!" he shouted as the horse plunged past him, skidding around the first bend of the stream trail at a full gallop. The lad was not surprised when the frightened creature ignored his cry.

And then he was possessed by a panic as deep as the fear that had driven the horse. Danyal, too, turned his back on the village. Without conscious thought, he felt his feet carry him onto the streamside trail, away from the ruin, away from everything he had known in his life.

Chapter 18

Ashes

374 AC
Fourth Misham, Paleswelt

Danyal's feet pounded the smooth dirt of the trail as
he relied on subconscious memory to avoid the rocks
and roots that jutted forth from so many places. Certainly he did not see these obstacles; his eyes were
blinded by tears, and his mind refused to let go of a
specific picture: the remembered shape of a child's
body, someone his own age charred black and stretched
on the ground, reaching with outstretched arms toward
the edge of the village, the stream, toward Danyal
himself.

It was that last recollection that all but shouted aloud,
dominating his awareness. Somebody had been reaching

out for him, had desperately needed his help, and he had not been there.

He had identified none of the bodies in that first horrified glimpse, but a new wave of tears spilled freely as he thought that any one of them could have been his father or his mother, or Wain. And if they hadn't been there, in the small commons square, then they had certainly been killed in the crushed barns or the incinerated char of the torched outbuildings.

In truth, Danyal didn't want to know any more. His only comfort was running in this mindless dash through the streamside woods.

Eventually, however, the straining rawness of his lungs, the stinging ache in his side, slowed the pace of his flight. Shambling with fatigue, he stumbled over a thick willow root, staggering a step farther before he collapsed. On the ground, he sobbed until he had no tears left, until his panting breath faded to raw, painful gasps. His eyes, clear once more, stared at the twisted trunk of the aged willow tree, saw sunlight flicker from the rills of the stream.

Numbly he tried to absorb the fact that this was the same stream he had seen that morning, but it didn't seem possible. His grief had gone, a fact that he thought very strange. Trying to think about that, he realized that he had no feelings of any kind. He lay there for what seemed like a very long time, considering the reality of this, amazed that he wasn't crying or frightened.

Or angry.

When he was able to summon the strength, he rose to his hands and knees and pushed himself around to sit with his back to the smooth bark of the huge-boled tree, watching the water. He recognized this place, and it amazed him to see that he had run so far upstream. In fact, he had already passed the last of the trout pools that had seemed so remote that morning.

A fish jumped, a beautiful flash of silver scales in the sunlight, spattering a rainbow cascade of shimmering drops before splashing back to the rippling water.

Strangely, Danyal wasn't hungry.

Only then did he notice that his throat was quite dry. He rose, stumbling awkwardly to the bank, and when he knelt on the bank, he had to catch himself as he almost pitched forward. The surface of the stream danced and dipped in ways he had never noticed. It was as if he had never seen flowing water before. Lowering his cupped hands carefully, he lifted the clear liquid to his lips and slurped draft after draft of the drink.

Thirst quenched, Danyal blew his nose, then looked around the sun-speckled valley. It occurred to him that he would have to decide what to do. He thought of the village again, and his next breath was ragged, but when he shook his head sternly, the numbness returned. The secret, he saw, was not to let himself feel anything.

Again he faced a decision. He knew he couldn't stay here, though a small part of him quibbled with the notion, suggesting that he might as well flop down right here and sleep till he died.

But where was he to go, then? And what to eat, how to live?

With a flash of hope, he thought of his fishing pole, knowing he must have dropped it around the time he first saw the dragon. His feet took to the trail and he backtracked, again amazed that he had run so far.

It took a long time to reach the pole, and by then he could smell the acrid stink of the burned village. Crows jeered each other from the trees overhead, and he saw buzzards wheeling high in the sky.

He picked up the supple shaft of willow. Again he thought of the village as he had last seen it, and he told himself that he could go no farther. His eyes filled with tears and he shook his head in frustration as a nagging, unwelcome question intruded into his thoughts.

What if somebody had lived, had miraculously survived the onslaught of fire and destruction—a person who was injured, maybe badly, someone who needed help?

Uttering a sharp, bitter laugh, he knew the notion was

ridiculous. The devastation was too complete. Still, he also realized he couldn't leave, couldn't go away from this place, until he knew for sure.

Slowly, hesitantly, he stepped along the trail, following the bend away from the stream, stopping for a moment, taking the time to carefully lean the pole against a gnarled willow, then climbing the low bank that marked the end of the trees. He was grateful now for the smoke that seeped through the air, trailing upward from countless burned beams and charred foundations. At least he could only see a small portion of the place at once.

He went first to his own house, the largest building in the village. It was hard to recognize the building he remembered amid the twisted wreckage of broken stone and charred, splintered timbers. He saw the paving stones of the front walk and a pit full of black timbers that he tried to tell himself was the cellar.

But it wasn't, couldn't be. Surely this was some strange location, a spot in some infernal realm that bore only a surface resemblance to the place where Danyal had spent the first fourteen years of his life.

The blacksmith's shop was recognizable by the anvil and forge that still stood in the midst of charred wood and the splintered stone of the building's back wall. Danyal staggered away, gagging reflexively at the sight of a brawny hand, burned fingers stiff around the hilt of a heavy hammer, the limb and tool extending out from the base of the rubble.

And everywhere else it was the same. He stepped around the pool of wine and the blackened bodies that had been gathered around the wine tuns in the commons, vaguely deducing that most of the villagers had died here—probably in the first lethal blast of the dragon's attack. Many of the corpses were so burned as to be unrecognizable, and he kept telling himself that these were just carvings of wood or charcoal, inanimate things that had been formed into grotesque caricatures of actual people.

In the small pasture on the far side of the village, he turned away from the sight of the shepherd boys—including Wain, he knew—who had met death from the dragon's rending claws. These bodies were even more horrifying because the former humanity was apparent, undeniable, in the small, cruelly torn shapes.

Danyal wanted desperately to turn and run, to leave this place behind forever, but he forced himself to complete his grim circuit. In the center of the village, before the remnants of his house, he turned through a circle, peering through the smoke for any sign of life.

"Hello!" he shouted, startling a hundred crows into loud, cackling flight. "Is there anybody there? Anybody at all? Can you hear me?"

He waited while the birds grew still and the soft echoes faded. The stillness, then, was absolute, and he accepted the truth: He was the only living person here.

Before he knew it, he was back in the woods, at the streamside, where he had set the fishing pole before entering the village. And again he wondered, Where should I go?

For the first time in his life, Danyal considered the fact that he really knew very little about the world beyond this valley. He knew that somewhere downstream, far along a distant forest road, there was a city called Haven. His ancestors had come from the city. Occasionally some adventurous person from the village would go there and return with stories of exotic people living strange, crowded lives.

Upstream, to the north, there was wilderness, and there was the dragon. The creature had come from that direction, then returned along the same path. Danyal knew the waterway rose in some of the mountain heights that a person could glimpse, on a clear day, if he found a vantage where he could get a view through the trees. It seemed likely that the dragon lived there, too.

As soon as he reflected on the two options, he knew he would be going toward the mountains. An emotion was beginning to creep through his curtain of numbness, a feeling of anger, of bitterness and of hate. The dragon had taken everything about his life from him. He would do the same thing to the great crimson serpent!

The notion gave him a surge of energy. Excited about the prospects of a real objective, he was immediately ready to start out. He could worry about the details of his mission later.

Picking up the fishing pole, the youth started on the upstream trail. His step was firm, his intentions clear. He had a fine creel and a sharp knife, as well as flint, tinder, and the warm wool blanket wrapped at his waist.

Anger propelled him as he strode quickly along the trail. He decided he would walk until sunset and then hope to catch a fish or two before dark. As to where he would sleep, he had a good chance of finding a river-bank cave or a hollow tree. Often he had camped with his brother, using nothing more than the arching foliage of a weeping willow as their shelter. If he had to, he could do that tonight as well.

But Wain wouldn't be there, would never be there again. Thoughts like this kept intruding on his anger, threatening once again to drag him down with grief. He resisted courageously, though more than once he was startled to realize that he was crying.

A crashing in the brush nearby nearly sent him sprawling. He drew the thin-bladed fishing knife reflexively, brandishing blade and pole as he heard a large form pushing through the trees. Then a black shape burst into view, ears flattened against its skull as it uttered a shrill neigh of fear. With a thunder of hoofbeats, the animal turned to gallop along the trail, swiftly disappearing from view.

"Nightmare!" he cried again, his hopes bizarrely inflamed by the sight of the once familiar creature, however ill-tempered, that had shared the village with him.

But then he was weeping again, this time in frustration, as the horse vanished from his view. He plodded along, his earlier energy rapidly dissipating into bleak despair.

Nearly an hour later he came upon the animal once

more, now standing passively at the side of the trail. Walking softly, approaching from the rear, Danyal was startled to hear a gentle, feminine voice—someone who sounded very much like one of the girls from the village.

"Have a taste of this, you poor old mare. I know you've had a bad scare. Believe me, I know what that's like. There, take another bite. There's plenty more apples on the ground in the orchard."

Danyal's next step brought him in view of the speaker, and he was surprised to see a kendermaid. He recognized her race immediately. Several times a year, one or more of the diminutive wanderers would travel through Waterton, to the dismay of honest and gods-fearing folk. But they had always been friendly and entertaining to the village's children.

This one was the size of a human girl, but wisps of gray streaked her thick, dark hair, a mane that she had bound in the typical kender topknot, except that it split into two tails, one draped over each of her shoulders. Her face was round and becoming; only the spiderweb of wrinkles at the corners of her mouth and eyes suggested that this was other than a pretty girl. That, and the pointed tips of her ears, Danyal realized, as he recognized the elfin shapes framing her face. She wore practical and well-worn leggings, moccasins, and jacket, and had an assortment of pouches and purses dangling from her neck, shoulders, and belt.

Her eyes widened as she saw him, but then she smoothly raised a finger to her lips, silencing him before he could speak. She pulled an apple from a voluminous bag at her side and allowed Nightmare to nibble on the ripe fruit. At the same time, she slipped a halter line over the horse's muzzle and carefully drew the rope over the now upstanding ears.

Danyal, having previously seen this maneuver attempted upon Nightmare, inevitably with disastrous results, was surprised when the horse nickered softly, then probed toward the pouch in search of another apple.

"There, there." Now that he watched her speak, he could see that the stranger spoke with a maternal, soothing tone that belied her diminutive size. She gently patted the horse on the neck, and Nightmare's head bobbed in response—or perhaps the motion was simply an effort to chew the next apple.

"Hello," she said at last, looking at Danyal with an expression of sympathy and concern. "I saw the dragon. Are you from the village?"

He nodded dumbly.

"I'm sorry," she said. "I guessed that this horse came from there. Is there anyone else . . . ?"

She let the question hang in the air, and this time his mute response was a shake of the head.

"Well, here," she said, offering him the end of the halter. "I think you should have him."

Reflexively Danyal took the rope, though he was vaguely surprised that Nightmare didn't immediately take off running. "Th-thanks," he said, also by reflex.

"I wouldn't try to ride him just yet," she said. "He got kind of burned on the shoulder there. I was thinking that maybe a mud poultice would help it heal."

"You're right!" The youth was suddenly infused with enthusiasm, with the thought that there was something he could do to help. "I'll be right back."

He skidded down the slope, into a silty patch of the streambed, and quickly scooped a double handful of the smooth, gooey stuff. Scrambling back up the bank, he struggled to keep his balance without using his hands. At the horse's flank, he reached up to gently place the poultice over the hairless, seared patch of flesh. Nightmare shivered, his pelt rippling along his flank, but he didn't shy away from the ministrations.

"That was a good idea," he said, speaking softly to the kendermaid, who had been standing on the other side of the animal. Questions suddenly occurred to him, and he blurted them out: "Who are you? What's your name? Do you live somewhere around here, in the valley?"

When he got no response, he dipped his head, looking

under Nightmare's neck. He felt a chilling sense of surprise, wondering if, for a moment, he had imagined the kendermaid's presence.

She was nowhere to be seen.

Chapter 19

Autobiography

To His Excellency Astinus, Lorekeeper of Krynn
Inscribed this year of Krynn, 353 AC

As Your Excellency can well imagine, I am moved and flattered by your request that I provide a summation of my own life story. Of course, it has always been my belief that the proper historian should be a reporter, a chronicler of great deeds, and not a participant. Whether the fortune be good or ill, however, it has been my luck to have been thrust into the role of participant in some of these occurrences. Overcoming my reluctance, suppressing my discipline and training, I have forced myself, as it were, to stir the river's waters with a paddle of my own.

Naturally my humble role is dwarfed, virtually to insignificance, by the deeds of the great actors on the historical stage. Indeed, it seems presumptuous of me even to take up quill and ink for the discussion of such abjectly inconsequential deeds of my own, though admittedly those trivial occurrences did involve a certain level of risk to me. My blood still chills at the knowledge of the perilous circumstances that I repeatedly encountered. With nothing more then the steadiness of my spirit, the keenness of my observer's eye, and the sly wit of my tongue, I went into contest with villains of monstrous capability, fiends who would have flayed me alive as soon as looked at me.

And with all humility, I have overcome my modesty enough to describe how my encounters in these adventures were indeed met with some measure of success, however small and unportentous it may have been.

But, of course, I digress, forgetting that you have requested a history of the time *preceding* those sublime accomplishments. As ever, I shall strive my best to be the equal of Your Excellency's requirements.

To wit: My studies commenced during the autumn of 366 AC, when I was accepted into the Temple of Gilean in Palanthas as a novice. I was commended upon my literacy, though (as Your Excellency is no doubt aware) several of the elders held certain misgivings as to my suitability for the priesthood.

My studies progressed in two directions. In areas of research, of scribing, recording, and of accurate description, I was universally praised. However, in matters representative of faith in our god of neutrality, I confess that I displayed a rather extreme impairment. A typical novice, of course, has learned the basics of casting a spell after the conclusion of a year or two of study. And naturally it is not uncommon for the learning to increase in rapidity as the apprentice spends more time in the monastery.

In my own case, sadly, I passed the better part of a decade pursuing my studies devoutly, yet failed to so much as stir the dust in the library by means of magic. It was as if a light, a discernible spark, was glowing in the spirit of each of the other monks. In my case, however, the ember had been long ago doused, and so thoroughly soaked that it could never be relit.

In the course of my academic accomplishments, however, I did manage to make such a name for myself (or so I was told by the masters and Patriarch Grimbriar himself) that it drew even the attention of Your Excellency. It was the matter of my writing, of course, and not my faith that resulted in this notice. Specifically it was the study of Fistandantilus, the topic that became such a focal point of my early research.

The archmage of the black robe, so utterly corrupt and yet so immortally powerful, was a figure unlike any other in the long history of Krynn. His was a story full of contradictions and indeed is one of the powerful side currents wherein the River of Time goes through such tumultuous cascades in order to draw the various streams together. The tale began in the mists of ancient times and carries through the present, and it even, during the future that is my past, bears a relevance to the ongoing course of the great river.

Too, it is a tale that is known to be entwined with another of history's great figures, the archmage Raistlin Majere. In places, in fact, the currents of the two archmages in the stream of history seem to run together, mingling in such a fashion that they are truly indistinguishable.

It was my choice to make the study of Fistandantilus my first area of specialization. I derived great pleasure during those years in the monastery in tracing the accounts of the archmage's presence in this or that portion of Ansalon, during times when he was active, times when he was dormant, and even during epochs when it seemed that he was in two places at once! I did a bit of traveling in the course of these studies, most notably a journey to Haven in 370–371, where I unearthed key details. There you will remember that I did (or should I say "I will"?) unearth the first mention of Kelryn Darewind, though at my first encounter, I did not learn the name of the false high priest.

And there was a great deal that had been written about my subject, enough to keep me occupied for those years of research. (Forgive me, Excellency, if I now dare to think that my own body of work has significantly expanded that material, that it might provide months or years of inspiration to the diligent student historian who might someday follow in my tracks!)

Yet inevitably I reached a time when I had exhausted the available sources. And still I had displayed no aptitude for the casting of even the most basic spells of clerical magic. In truth, it seemed that my aspirations toward the priesthood were destined to end in failure.

It was in the spirit of a last chance that Patriarch Grimbriar and my own tutors at last called me into their presence. I remember still the flickering tapers casting yellow beams of light through the dark, lofty library. My heart was hammering, for I feared that I was to be dismissed as a failure, sent from the place to make my way in the world as one who could not find his true calling.

Instead, my mentor, Falstar Kane, opened the meeting by giving me a gift. *The Book of Learning*, it was, and I well recognized the treasure that I held and the level of trust that the temple hierarchy had placed in me.

I opened the enchanted tome and was confronted with a blank page. I knew enough of the meaning to wait expectantly for the further words of the masters. (Of the book, more later.)

"We have decided, Foryth, that your learning must continue along a different path than it has to date," Falstar Kane declared, his tone gentle.

"I await your commands, your inspiration!" I pledged with utmost sincerity.

"We are sending you once again into the world beyond the walls of our temple," continued my mentor gravely.

"Where, my lords?" I inquired in tones as bold as I could muster.

"Your diligence in the matter of the archmage is well

known," declared Thantal, one of the other masters. "It has been suggested that you journey to a place where you might continue that study, where you might seek to add to your work . . . and at the same time seek something else as well."

I was admittedly intrigued. Even at that moment, I had determined upon an initial target for my studies.

"Field research—and a quest for magic," declared Patriarch Grimbriar, putting all the cards on the table (if Your Excellency is not repelled by a gambling metaphor).

"What kind of magic?" I dared to ask.

It was Falstar who replied. "*Any* kind, my son. You are to travel for a year, and it is hoped that you will take advantage of the time to further your studies on the matter of Fistandantilus."

"However, it is expected, nay, *required*"—the patriarch's tone was very stern indeed—"that you return to these premises in possession of a spell of clerical magic. You must do this within the allotted time of a year, or your course of study under the Scale of Gilean shall be terminated."

His words chilled into a ball of ice within my gut. I had struggled mightily to learn a spell, but if I had failed within the reverent, controlled environment of the monastery, it did not seem likely that I could succeed in the chaos of the outside world.

"Do you have an idea," Falstar asked, "of where you might commence your journey?"

To that, I replied with confidence. "You may recall from my research the discovery of a man, a false priest of the Seekers, who once lived in Haven," I replied. Encouraged by my listeners' apparent interest, I continued.

"During the time of the Seekers, he established a false religion, gaining considerable prestige until the coming of the dragonarmies. He left the city then, but I have encountered hints in my studies that suggest he may still live somewhere in the remote and mountainous country south of Qualinesti."

"Why does this particular cleric—a false cleric, it

should be noted—interest you?" There was honest curiosity in Brother Thantal's voice.

"Because his sect was based on a worship of Fistandantilus," I replied.

"Appropriate enough," agreed Grimbriar. "But the man must be very old by now. Perhaps he has died."

"He may have died," I agreed, "but I doubt that he is old." In the face of their questioning glares, I explained. "His sect lasted for some fifty years in Haven, yet at the time of its dissolution, he was still a young man. He had found a means to avoid the effects of aging." (I did not mention my supposition, but I believed even then that the bloodstone of Fistandantilus might have been the key to this longevity.)

"That *is* interesting," Falstar Kane declared with a pleased smile. "May the god of neutrality watch over you on your travels."

"And grant you good fortune as well," added the patriarch. (For all his sternness, I believe that he really did want me to succeed.)

So it was that I left the monastery in Palanthas behind, taking ship to New Ports, then following a rough overland road into the depths of the Kharolis wilderness.

And it is there, Excellency, that my story truly begins, in that future era when I was a much younger man.

In Devotion to the Truth,
Your Loyal Servant, Foryth Teel

Chapter 20

A Disturbance in the Night

374 AC
Fourth Bakukal, Paleswelt—First Linaras, Reapember

The apple orchard was right where the kendermaid
had said it would be. Tethering Nightmare to a sturdy
branch, Danyal gathered as much of the fruit as he could.
He placed the apples in his creel, for lack of a better
place, and then ate several while he sat on the grass and
watched the black horse graze.

Nightmare, for her part, glared balefully at the lad, the
relentless stare of the large brown eyes making Danyal
very uneasy. He imagined the horse thinking about a
way to break loose, perhaps to trample him or, at the
very least, to gallop away, never to be seen again.

"Maybe I should just let you go," he reflected aloud.

"You're probably going to be a lot more trouble than you're worth."

The horse's ears came forward at the words, and as Nightmare started to crunch another apple, Danyal felt a strange kinship to the animal. He knew he would be even more lonely if the steed was to run away, so he shook his head and laughed ruefully.

"I guess we're stuck together, the two survivors of Waterton."

It still didn't seem real when he thought about it, and so he tried not to do so. He wondered about the trail he would walk tomorrow, though these thoughts were troubling, too, because they led, inevitably, to the dragon that had flown away into the north.

When darkness descended, the lad pulled his blanket over himself and fell asleep, only to toss and turn anxiously. His dreams were troubled by images of fire, of giant crimson wings and a killing maw. Interspersed were episodes in which he saw his mother or the rest of his family, only to have them snatched cruelly away by some force over which he had no control.

He awakened before dawn, shivering despite his blanket, and feeling a powerful gnawing in his gut. It was a hunger that could not be addressed by apples, and he made his way to the stream as the first tendrils of light reached upward from the eastern horizon. Before half the sky had paled he had three nice trout. He built a fire at the edge of the grove and felt the warmth of the flames. Cleaning and splitting the fish, he speared the fillets onto sharp sticks and grilled them over the fire.

By the time the sun had risen into the treetops, he was well fed, warm, and dry. He changed the muddy poultice over Nightmare's wound, relieved to see that it had begun to heal nicely. Finally he took the tether in one hand, his fishing pole in the other, and started along the streamside trail.

Before the sun reached its zenith, he knew he was farther from home than he had ever been before. The valley here looked much the same as it did around Waterton, though he noticed that the stream had more frequent stretches of frothing rapids. The weather remained warm and sunny, for which he was grateful, and at times he would walk for a mile or more without remembering the horror that had driven him onto this trail. He would lose himself in a sense of adventure, the confidence of the fisherman that, just around the next bend, he would find the ideal pool, the perfect fish.

But then the memories would return, and he plodded forward under a melancholy that was more oppressive than the heaviest overcast, borne down by a weighty depression as dispiriting as any drenching shower.

The sun itself seemed to darken in the sky, and Danyal found himself slowing, stumbling, biting back the lump building in his throat. At these times, it was Nightmare that kept them going, the big horse leaning forward, hooves clopping at a steady pace, the tether in the boy's hand tugging him along, keeping him from a state of utter collapse.

That night he camped in a grove of cedars, again eating fresh trout with a couple of his apples. He built a small fire before falling asleep and, aided by the windbreak of the evergreens, spent a more comfortable and restful night than he had previously.

On the third day of his trek, the ground began to rise noticeably. He had seen no settlements, no sign of humankind or any other race of builders, in the time since the wrack of his village had been left behind. Now the distant mountains rose as a purple mass to the north and east, and in places he saw long, white snowfields and glistening white cornices draped across the lofty alpine ridges.

In the late afternoon of this day's trek, he came around a curve in the upstream trail and was startled to find that the waterway was spanned by an arched bridge of gray stone. Releasing Nightmare's reins, he scrambled up a slope of broken rock to stand upon a narrow, rutted cart track. The horse kicked and sprang, following him and coming to a standing stop in the roadway.

"Where do you suppose this goes? Or comes from?" he asked, looking up and down the little-used path.

Nightmare's muzzle dipped toward the ground. The horse tore away a clump of clover that grew beside the track, while Danyal tried to think. He saw no sign of tracks—hoof, boot, or cartwheel—in the road, and guessed that it hadn't been used in some time. Yet it suggested that there was something worthwhile in each direction, else why build the road in the first place?

He decided to camp nearby and consider the questions during the night. Just upstream from the bridge, he found a sheltered grotto with a soft, mossy bank and a deep eddy in the creek that seemed to promise good fishing. Though he wasn't sure why, Danyal also made sure that his makeshift camp was out of sight of the unused roadway.

After another meal of grilled fish, he made himself and the horse as comfortable as possible. Again he fell asleep easily, completely drained by the strenuous activity of the day.

This time, however, his sleep was interrupted by a sound that had him sitting upright, clutching his fishing knife, before he even knew what had awakened him. Then it came again, a shout of alarm followed by a cold, harsh bark of laughter.

There were men nearby! And judging by the sounds of confrontation, Danyal guessed that some unfortunate traveler had encountered another group, perhaps bandits or other roadside bullies.

Heart pounding, Danyal threw off his blankets and crawled to the edge of his grotto. The slope on this side of the road was steep, climbing into a cliff of broken, craggy rock. At the base of that precipice, barely a few paces off the road, he saw the glowing embers of a campfire. And in the dim light, as he stared, he saw one man backed against the rock wall while several others, large, hulking fellows, closed in on him menacingly.

Nightmare stood still nearby, nostrils quivering, ears cocked toward the disturbance. Abruptly Danyal realized that the horse might make a sound at any minute, a sound that would betray his own position. There was no way he could move the animal soundlessly, so to protect himself, he began to sidle sideways, staying above the strangers, moving along the slope of the hill so that he closed the distance between them.

Light flared as one of the bandits threw dry wood onto the fire. Danyal got a view of the lone traveler, who stood with his back to the rocks, weaponless, as he faced the others. Moving still closer, the lad was surprised to see that, while he was unarmed, the man was holding a book in his left hand. The tome was opened, and in his right hand, he actually held a quill and ink bottle, trying unsuccessfully to dip the pen while he addressed his attackers.

"Where did you say we are? And what was that name again? I'm sorry, but in this light it's terribly hard to see the page. Ah, thank you . . . that's much better," he declared as more tinder was thrown onto the fire.

"Never mind that," growled one bandit, a strikingly handsome fellow whose gleaming dark hair and firm facial features seemed incongruous above the filthy mat of his leather shirt. "Hand over your purse, if you have any thoughts of seeing the morning!"

Danyal gasped quietly. Despite his guess, he was shocked to hear the men's intentions confirmed. He shrunk down behind a felled tree, trying to remain invisible and silent, yet he pressed his eye to the gap under the log so he could still see the scene around the traveler's campfire.

"I daresay my purse hasn't much to offer," the fellow was saying. He seemed remarkably unconcerned, thought Danyal, for someone who might be facing the last minute or two of his life.

"This could go badly for you. Don't you have the sense to be scared?" demanded the handsome bandit, obviously wondering about the same thing. He swaggered around as if he were the leader of the group. "Here, Baltyar—give me a brand. Perhaps we'll make this fellow think twice about his answers."

"Aye, Kelryn," replied another, sticking a branch bristling with dry needles into the fire. Flames crackled into the night, exploding with a hissing, popping noise, flaring so brightly that Danyal was certain his own hiding place would be revealed.

Then he heard another sound, a clatter of movement to the side that drew curses from the bandits and pulled their attention toward the lad's camp. Instantly Danyal understood what had happened: Startled by the flaring branch, Nightmare had pulled away from her tether. The lad could hear the black horse stumbling over the rocks, charging past Danyal's hiding place.

"Look there! A horseman!" cried one of the bandits, pointing at the shadowy outline of the frightened steed.

Nightmare whinnied, the sound shrill and piercing in the darkness. With a leap and a kick, the frightened black horse lunged along the steep slope above the roadway, slipping and sliding on the loose rocks. Many of the boulders tumbled free, rolling downward with rapidly building momentum.

In seconds, the sounds of the rockslide roared louder than the shouts of the men or the shrill neighing of the mare. Danyal saw a large stone bounce into the air, then crash into the blazing campfire, sending sparks and embers cascading through the area.

Men were screaming now, scrambling to get away. In the surges of light, Danyal saw the bandits, with swords drawn, looking wildly back and forth, seeking signs of their attackers. Another big rock thundered through the camp, knocking down one of the bandits, leaving the man thrashing and moaning in the middle of the road.

The leader knelt over the injured man, who cried out in pain. A short sword flashed in the firelight, and the wounded fellow's cries swelled to a quick, feverish shriek before they died in a sickening gurgle of blood.

And then the bandits were gone, footsteps pounding down the road as the rockslide exhausted itself, loose stones and gravel still shifting, settling down the steep slope. Danyal smelled the powdered rock in the air, tasted the dust in his mouth, and tried to imagine what had happened to the lone traveler. His campsite was buried beneath a thick layer of rubble, and nothing seemed to be moving down there.

The lad gingerly picked his way down the slope, seeing that Nightmare had somehow reached the roadway. The black horse regarded him impassively as he probed through the boulders until he was startled by a voice from the shadows.

"Hello there," said the traveler. He came forward, and Danyal saw that he had been sheltered by an overhang of the bluff—the same place he had been driven by the extended swords of the bandits.

"H-Hello," the youth replied. "Are you all right?"

"I think so," said the man. "I'll admit that was bad luck with the landslide."

"Bad luck?" Danyal was amazed. "I think it just saved your life!"

"Oh posh," said the fellow. "It only chased away those men. And I could tell that one of them was just about to tell me his name!"

The youth wanted to reply that, to his eyes, it had looked as though the bandits intended something other than an informative conversation. Still, the stranger seemed so sincere, even genuinely disappointed, that Danyal changed his tack.

"My name is Danyal Thwait," he said tentatively. "Who are you?"

"Foryth Teel," replied the fellow, tsking in concern as he picked up the book that the bandit had thrown against the rocks. "It's not damaged," he said to Danyal, as if he never doubted that the lad was terribly concerned about the condition of the tome.

"Good," replied the youth. "But now, Foryth Teel, why don't you come with me? I think we should find a new place to camp."

Chapter 21
A Mind and Soul of Chaos

374 AC

On those instances when the essence of Fistandantilus became maddeningly, frustratingly aware, the archmage knew that he had languished within the kender host for scores of years. The spirit hungered for escape, craved the exercise of power that would bring him victims, souls that he could absorb, lives he would use to restore his unprecedented might. But always these desires went unsated, remained mere memories from a long-ago epoch of might and magic.

As more time passed, the archmage's hunger became starvation, and his need for vengeance swelled. He resolved that, when at last he celebrated his ultimate success, his killing would consume whole cities and countless thousands of lives.

In these times of lucidity, he remembered his talisman, the bloodstone. Upon occasion, he could almost feel the gem pulse in his hands, so vivid were his memories of its warmth and vitality. The artifact had ever been an eater of souls, and now it throbbed with the stored power of many consumed lives.

And the stone was still his best hope, for his efforts had brought that artifact into the hands of one who could use it—a man who had once been a false priest and had now become a lord of bandits.

Sometimes the soul of Fistandantilus tried to reach the bandit lord, using the stone as a conduit. The man had been pliable in some ways, and more than willing to use the powers of the stone. But he was also stubborn and independent, and instead of yielding, had learned to use the bloodstone for his own purposes. And because of the directionless kender, the archmage was unable to use his host to retrieve the stone.

Still, the archmage could be patient. Eventually there would come a chance for the kender to touch the stone, and then Fistandantilus could assert power and control: The false priest would become his tool, the wandering kender would be doomed, and ultimately the route for the archmage's return to flesh would lay open before him. Until then, however, Fistandantilus continued patiently to allow the power of the bloodstone to sustain the man, to prevent his aging.

And the ancient being was aware of another avenue of potential survival as well. He saw through a pair of eyes that occasionally gave Fistandantilus a specific view, and even in his ethereal state, he knew he was not beholding the environment surrounding his kender host. No, these were different eyes, eyes of power and magic, but lacking any substance of flesh, tissue, or tears.

When the image was clear, the archmage saw fire and smoke, a dark cavern where molten rock seethed and bubbled.

Sometimes he saw a villainous visage, a great head of

scales and fangs that rose to regard him, that met his fleshless eyes with slitted orbs of fiery yellow. This was a great dragon, attempting to commune with the skull. Fistandantilus was forced to be careful; he knew he could never control such a beast, even in the limited way he did the Seeker priest.

For brief instants, the might of the archmage would surge, rising to meet the power of the skull or the bloodstone. These spells inevitably overwhelmed the kender's intellect and will.

But inevitably the power of the ancient wizard could not be sustained, and then the chaos of the kender's mind would twist and pull at him, tearing his rising presence into shreds. His awareness would fade and he would shriek his soundless horror and frustration until the dissolution cast him once more into the eternal wasteland of his own ambitions. The kender, with his awareness and will restored, was once more free to continue the capricious wandering that had occupied him for such an interminable time.

Fistandantilus was barely able to sustain the power needed merely to insure that the kender did not age. Drawing upon the store of lives he had consumed, the archmage maintained the fool's youthfulness for decades, making sure that the host did not suffer the debilitating effects of advancing years. As with the holder of the bloodstone, the ancient sorcerer dared not allow his all-too-mortal tool to suffer the ravages of age, else the mortal might perish before fulfilling the archmage's purpose.

But would he ever be free?

In fact, Fistandantilus never accepted the possibility of failure. He was endlessly patient, and he knew that eventually the potent gem and the wandering kender would come together. In anticipation of that moment, he could almost taste the blood, hear the screams of his victims as the wizard worked his deadly, consuming magic. His vengeance would require many, many victims, and he exulted to images of mass conflagrations, of helpless mortals crushed, one after another, by his own hands.

And though such gratifications remained but a dim memory for now, he began to sense an impending confluence. His hope, his talisman, was coming closer. The sensation grew in strength and substance until he could hear the pulse of that constant heart, the bloodstone of Fistandantilus.

It was out there somewhere, and it was not far distant.

Chapter 22

An Historian at Large

First Palast, Reapember
374 AC

Instead of following the road in either direction, Danyal took up his fishing pole and creel, and he led Nightmare and Foryth up the streamside trail until they were half a mile or more from the gray stone bridge. The shadows were thick and the trail was rough, but the lad took heart, reasoning that the difficult going would also impede anyone who tried to follow them.

"We should be safe around here," Danyal finally suggested when the two humans and the horse stumbled upon a rock-walled niche near the bank.

"By all means," Foryth agreed, still displaying his air of bemused cheerfulness. "Gilean knows I'll be ready for a night of sleep after I take a few notes."

"Um, I think one of us should stay awake, just in case those men come back. We could take turns." The lad looked nervously into the woods, starting at each shifting shadow, each rustle of leaf or snap of a twig. He thought with a shudder of the young, handsome bandit with the curiously dead eyes, and he knew the man would as soon kill them as talk to them if he found them again.

Danyal had to admit, though, that this new camp was ideally situated for concealment. It was sheltered in another grotto, almost completely screened overhead by a canopy of trees, and as long as they remained quiet they should be safe from anyone who didn't stumble right into the midst of their hiding place.

Apparently lacking any of Danyal's practical concerns, Foryth had already knelt down to flick a spark into a pile of tinder he had gathered. With some difficulty, he brought the glowing specks into embers, waving his hand over the dry pine needles in an unsuccessful attempt to fan the flames.

"Don't you think we'd be better off without a fire?" asked the youth. "I mean, in case they come back? It could lead them right to us."

"Oh, I think those ruffians are long gone by now," the traveler said dismissively. "Now, where was I?"

"Here, let me help," Danyal said with a sigh. Admitting to himself that he was unusually chilly tonight, he knelt and puffed gently on the embers. In the sheltered grotto, it was hard to tell which way the wind was blowing, and Dan devoutly hoped the smoke would be carried away from the road.

Within moments, a finger of yellow flame danced upward, growing boisterously as he fed chips of bark and thin, brittle branches to the hungry fire.

Foryth used the flickering light to illuminate the page of the book he had retrieved from his pack by the rock wall. Once again he had his quill and inkwell out, the latter perched on a flat rock beside him.

"You're really going to write? *Now?*" Danyal couldn't believe his eyes.

"Why, of course. The best history is recorded while it's still fresh in the historian's memory. Say, you didn't catch the name of that fellow, did you? The young, handsome one who seemed to be in charge?"

"I don't *care* what his name was!" Danyal squawked, then bit his tongue as the sound of his voice echoed through the forest. He lowered his tone to a rasping whisper. "He's a bandit, and he could be coming back!"

But Foryth was already engrossed, his only response the scratching of the sharp quill across the page. "Let's see . . . the day is First Palast, month of Reapember, during this year of our chronicler 374 AC."

Foryth cleared his throat in ritual preparation. " `Bandits encountered on the Loreloch Road, fifth day out from Haven. My camp was interrupted following nightfall' . . . let's see . . . how many of them did you count?"

The sudden question took Danyal by surprise. "I—I guess there were six or eight of them, that I saw at least. There might have been—"

"Drat the luck that didn't let me get that fellow's name!" snapped the historian peevishly, though he didn't let the complaint still the pen-scratching of his scribing.

"Um—didn't one of them call him Kelry, or something like that?" Danyal recalled.

"Hmm . . . yes, I believe you're right. It *was* something similar to that." Squinting at his page, silently mouthing his thoughts, the man wrote with quick, smooth strokes. Once he looked up toward Dan, but it seemed to the lad as though Foryth didn't even see him.

"Why were you out here, anyway?" asked Danyal when Foryth, having busily written for several minutes, stretched out his hand and blinked a few times.

"What? Oh, thank you, yes. Some tea would be wonderful," the lone traveler replied as he returned his industrious attention to his page. The feathery plume of the quill continued to bob past his nose, casting a larger-than-life shadow across the man's narrow face. Features tight with concentration, Foryth Teel took a moment to dip his pen while he chewed thoughtfully on the tip of his tongue.

"Uh . . . I don't have any tea," Danyal interjected in the momentary pause of the pen's progress.

"Why, yes, that would be very nice." Foryth's head bobbed in agreement, though his face remained someplace very far away. "Help to take the chill out of the bones and all that. Now, where was I?"

Danyal sighed, figuring he could probably inform the historian that the sky was falling down on them and Foryth would merely suggest, politely of course, that he would really like a little sugar with that.

The lad stared into the flames, moping. For some reason, though he had a companion in his camp for the first time since leaving his village, he felt lonelier than ever. Foryth Teel couldn't even carry on a decent conversation. At the same time, the distracted traveler seemed as if he would be terribly vulnerable if the bandits decided to return. Again Dan wondered about the flames. He knew the fire was a beacon that would extend well beyond the confines of their narrow grotto.

It occurred to him that he could just take Nightmare and leave, moving farther up the streamside trail, but he wasn't ready to turn his back on the strange traveler. Foryth Teel, for all of his distractibility, at least did not seem likely to be any threat. And he *was* company.

Finally the historian drew a breath and raised his eyes. The book remained open on his lap, but he set the quill carefully on the flat log where he had placed his ink bottle. "Didn't you say something about tea?" he asked.

"No!" Danyal's exasperation crept into his voice. "I asked what you were doing on this road, and when you said you wanted some tea, I told you I didn't have any!"

"What? Oh, forgive me. *I* have tea. It'll just take a minute."

Danyal waited impatiently as the traveler pulled a tin pot from his pack, scooped some water from the stream—

almost falling in as he did so—and then looked vainly into the surging flames, seeking a place to rest his kettle.

"Here." With a sigh, the lad used a stick to pull a small pile of hot coals to the side of the flames. "Set the teapot on these."

"Splendid! Now, what was it you were trying to say?"

Danyal was about to shake his head in disgust, muttering that it didn't matter, when Foryth brightened with sudden recollection. "Oh, yes—why am I here? I daresay they'd have to let me into the priesthood if I could give a complete answer to that one!"

He laughed self-consciously, though the youth saw no humor in the statement. Foryth continued. "I'm on my way to a place called Loreloch. It's up in these hills." He gestured vaguely to the darkness on all sides.

"I've never heard of it," Danyal admitted. "But I've never been very far from Waterton."

"Well, it's kind of a secret place. In truth, most people don't even know it's there. It's a little village, so I hear, gathered around a fortified manor house, a stronghold of armed men. The lord there doesn't have much to do with the outside world."

"Why do you want to go there?" Danyal also wondered, but didn't ask, how the befuddled researcher expected to find the place.

"Fistandantilus!" Foryth held up a single finger, as if that one word held the key to all of his plans and ambitions. Apparently observing that Danyal wasn't terribly impressed, he continued. "I'm a historian, seeking to chronicle the story of Krynn's greatest archmage. Specifically, there's a man who lives in Loreloch who went there after the Seeker priests were thrown out of Haven."

"I've heard of Haven," the lad declared proudly. "That's where my ancestors came from, not too long after the Cataclysm."

Foryth might not have heard; at least, he made no adjustment to his own tutorial "This man, the disgraced Seeker, declared that the archmage Fistandantilus was a god, and that he himself was the high priest of the religion. For a time, he had quite a few followers—until, of course, the Seekers were shown to be false priests."

In spite of himself, Danyal found himself fascinated by the story. "That was when the dragons came, right? And people learned that Paladine and the Dark Queen were still here, could still answer prayers?"

"Aye, the two great lords live, and so do many other gods as well. Gilean, the patriarch of my own faith, and gentle Mishakal. And others who are less benign as well.

"But back to my story: This false priest was driven from Haven and, with a small band of followers, he seized the stronghold of Loreloch for himself."

"Didn't the highlords object?" asked Danyal. "I mean, I know I wasn't born yet back then, but I heard that during the war they even came to Waterton and made folks pay them with food from every harvest. Or else they threatened to send their dragons in and destroy the town." The lad shuddered as his mind conjured up a vivid memory of just that. He looked at the man out of the corner of his eye, relieved to see that Foryth had apparently not noticed his distress. For some reason, he wanted to keep that incident a secret for now.

"They may have done the same to Loreloch. Gilean knows, they could have sent a dragon to raze the place if they were displeased," the man admitted. "I don't know why they didn't, to tell you the truth. Perhaps they simply paid no attention, or maybe he was too small a pest to warrant the trouble."

Foryth cleared his throat, and Danyal realized the man was organizing his thoughts, restoring his direction after the question.

"There was another unique feature about this priest of Fistandantilus. Unlike most of the Seekers, this priest had at least one unnatural power: Though he had been the head of his sect for something close to a hundred years, he had never been known to age. It is said that he survived the war, which ended more than twenty years ago, of course. I'm wondering if he still possesses the same youthful appearance as he did back then, though his church was cast down and he was lucky to escape into banishment."

"Lucky?" queried Danyal.

"Compared to dead, I should say so. After all, no less a personage than the dragonarmy highlord had issued an order for his death. And now, from Loreloch, he makes occasional raids into neighboring villages, preying upon the highway traffic into and out of Haven and the coastal ports."

"Don't the Knights of Solamnia object to his robbing people and stuff?" On several occasions during his life, Danyal had seen one or two of the armored warriors pass through Waterton. He vividly remembered his impressions of dignity, might, and awe-inspiring competence and capability. "I'd guess that no one could get away with crossing them," he suggested earnestly.

"Well, you're right about that last. Still, the knights have been awfully busy since the war. They've tried to restore some order to their realms, and they had another invasion of Palanthas to face just a few years after the Dark Queen was defeated. Too, down here the Newsea cuts you off from the centers of knightly power, although there is one knightly marshal, named Sir Harold the White. Still, he has a great territory as his responsibility, so, no, I would say that Loreloch is a little too much of a backwater to call for the attention of our Solamnic protectors."

"But why do *you* want to go there?" Danyal pressed.

"I told you!" Foryth seemed exasperated, though the lad could not remember hearing an answer to that question. "Fistandantilus!"

"He's there? But you said he was dead."

"He's *not* there! But the leader of Loreloch is a man who claimed to worship the archmage, and this man doesn't get any older! Naturally I want to find out why."

"If it's a secret place, how will you find it?" Danyal finally asked.

"Why, my book, of course. *The Book of Learning*,"

Foryth explained, as if the lad should understand every-thing he was saying.

Danyal waited, hoping that the historian would say more. But then Foryth shook his head, discarding some private thought, and the lad wondered if there was still another reason the man had embarked on his journey.

The historian resumed his scribbling, muttering qui-etly to himself, as Danyal felt his eyelids growing heavy. He lay back, finding a smooth, rounded curl of root to serve as a pillow, and in moments he was asleep. His dreams were filled with images of dragons and knights, of a tall fort on a mountaintop, and dark forests that were full of dangers. For a long time, he ran, cutting between the trees, gasping for breath, but he couldn't escape.

The snapping of a twig was the sound that pulled Danyal up from the depths of his slumber—so abruptly that he wondered if he had just closed his eyes a second before. But, no, the fire had faded to a mound of coals, and Foryth, too, was asleep, leaning against the rock where he had been doing his writing.

"Wake up!" hissed Danyal, looking around worriedly. Through the memories of his sleep, he heard the echoes of the breaking stick and felt grimly certain that some-thing—something large—was out there.

He blinked as the shadows moved, then found himself looking up into a handsome face that he vaguely recog-nized. Gray metal reflected the pale firelight, a crimson glow running up and down a blade of sharpened steel.

"And what prize is this?" declared the young, dapper bandit, his dark eyes flashing back and forth between Danyal and Foryth. "It seems that our poor net has caught us two birds!"

Chapter 23

The Master of Loreloch

First Majetog, Reapember
374 AC

Another bandit pressed forward, and Danyal caught his breath in sudden fear. The newcomer looked every bit the villainous wretch. One eye was missing, covered by a crusty black patch. A scruffy beard, tangled with mats, coated the man's chin, and he opened his mouth to reveal numerous missing teeth. Dan recoiled from breath stinking of ale, garlic, and other, less readily identified odors.

"Let's have yer purse, laddie," growled the nearly toothless bandit, leering down at Danyal with an expression that churned the young man's stomach into a roiling mess.

"I—I don't have any money!" he stammered. He

thought fleetingly of the silver belt buckle, nervously pulling down the front of his shirt to make sure the heirloom was covered.

"No money? Then I'll have to take me booty from yer blood, I will!" The leering bully pulled out a long, wickedly curved knife, the blade gleaming sharp on both sides as he extended one edge to press against Danyal's neck.

"Hold a minute, Zack," said the first bandit, the one with the handsome, beardless face of a young man. Despite his ragged garb, there was a sense of nobility, or at least an element of graciousness, in the way he stood regarding the two captives with an expression of vague distaste.

"Aw, Kelryn!" Zack complained. "We'll get naught from these blighters. Let's just stick 'em and be on our merry way."

"No," declared the leader, studying Foryth Teel's slender figure. "I'm curious. Why weren't you frightened enough to go farther away? Instead, you build a fire that we can smell for a mile down the road! And what was all that about wanting to take notes?"

"I'm merely a humble researcher, attempting to conduct studies in the field."

"Studies?" Kelryn stared curiously at Foryth Teel. "You've picked a rather strange place for your library, stranger."

"The true historian must be willing to journey to strange places."

The one called Kelryn acted as if he hadn't heard. "You had a partner?" he mused, still studying Foryth Teel. "And all the time I thought you were alone."

He turned to regard the youth. Despite the man's smooth forehead, his strong chin and mouthful of clean white teeth, Danyal recalled—and confirmed—his earlier impression: This was a very dangerous fellow indeed. His eyes were dark and hooded, utterly devoid of compassion or any other human emotion. When he smiled, the expression seemed to Danyal like the toothy grin of a hungry cat.

The youth sensed that the situation had spun far beyond his control. "I wasn't traveling with—"

"This is my squire," Foryth interjected smoothly. "As a precaution, I had directed him to camp some distance away from my own sleeping place. I find it easier to complete my studies in solitude."

"Bah!" Zack was still impatient. The frightening man with the knife felt the edge of his blade, and his one eye shone with eagerness as he regarded Danyal. "Like I says, boss, let's be done about it."

Again the leader chose to ignore his henchman's suggestion. "What is the nature of your research?" he inquired instead.

Foryth Teel seemed quite willing to explain. "I journey to find a man, once a false priest of the Seeker cults, who is rumored to dwell in these mountains, in a place called Loreloch. I wish to converse with him on a matter of mutual interest."

"I see. It may be that I can help you. What is the nature of your business with the Master of Loreloch?"

"I seek information on matters regarding the ancient wizard Fistandantilus, who has been long dead from our world," Foryth was saying. "It is said that this Seeker is quite an authority on the topic."

"And you have come to sit at his feet?"

"Er, in a manner of speaking, yes. I have devoted many years of study to stories of the archmage. I had hoped his knowledge might help me to fill some of the gaps in my research."

Kelryn laughed easily, and Danyal saw those hooded eyes brighten with the first light of enthusiasm, of genuine feeling, that the youth had seen there. "I believe he might be willing to meet you. If, that is, I let you live."

"What about the kid?" whined Zack, plaintively. "Can I stick him?"

Danyal edged away from the one-eyed bandit and his sharp knife, but the rock wall of the grotto brought his movement to a sharp halt.

"I should say not!" Surprisingly, it was Foryth who

answered. "My work requires the presence of my squire, else there is no way that I should be able to compile my notes and maintain a precise record. I need the lad."

"It seems to me that we can make other arrangements for your assistance," Kelryn said, shaking his head dismissively. "And truthfully, if Zack doesn't get his regular entertainment, he can become rather . . . disagreeable. I think I should give him the boy."

Danyal's stomach churned in fear, even as he realized that he found the bored manner of Kelryn's words even more frightening than Zack's leering cruelty.

"Tsk, tsk." Foryth shook his head, though Danyal thought the historian didn't seem terribly agitated. "Remember, there is the matter of the reward. . . ."

"And what reward would that be?" Kelryn asked, staring intently at the priest-historian.

"Why, the ransom that my temple would be willing to pay for myself and my squire."

"What temple?" Zack spun, crouching as he faced Foryth. Danyal took advantage of the bandit's turn to draw several deep breaths, grateful for the clean night air. He watched, heart pounding, as the men continued to talk.

"Why, the Golden Palace of Gilean in Palanthas, of course. The patriarch of my order would be more than willing to ransom two of its lost sheep, should they be assured that neither of us has suffered harm in your hands."

"He's lying!" snarled Zack, his glaring eye swiveling back and forth between the historian and the youth.

"I'm not so sure," mused Kelryn Darewind, speaking to his henchman. "In truth, it seems that the temple masters might well be inclined to protect these lives with coin of good steel."

He regarded Foryth questioningly. "For the sake of argument, what manner of reward are we discussing?"

The historian shrugged. "I cannot say with any accuracy. This is a situation unique in my experience. However, you can always send a message of inquiry. While we're waiting for the reply, perhaps I can effectuate an interview with the Master of Loreloch."

Danyal watched the exchange with a mixture of disbelief, amazement, and fear. He was astounded that these men could discuss matters of life and death with such aplomb. At the same time, he felt as though he was a very unimportant piece in the game that was being enacted before him.

"Hey! They've got a horse over here!" A voice called from the darkness, and other shadowy forms moved through the woods, drawn toward the source of the sound.

Abruptly the night was split by a loud whinny, followed by a bone-crunching smack and a very human wail of pain and fear. Brush cracked and a body tumbled into view, a bandit who clutched the limp, twisted shape of his left arm as he collapsed on the ground and moaned.

More whinnies rang from the darkness, followed by curses, smashes, and finally the sound of rapidly receding hoofbeats clattering up the streamside trail. Three more bandits came into view, dragging a fourth, the latter bleeding heavily from a gash on the forehead. In another moment, another man crawled out of the woods, pulled himself onto a stump, and proceeded to wrap a filthy cloth around his knee as he cursed beneath his breath.

"Eh, Gnar," chortled Zack. "Break yer leg, did ya?"

"Bah! It'll set just fine!" growled the other, though the grimace tightening his face served to belie his bold words. He looked at Zack, then Kelryn, and Dan was surprised to catch a glimpse of the naked fear on the man's face.

"That was no normal horse. It was a beast possessed by a demon!" snapped the bandit with the broken arm, painfully rising to a sitting position. "I swear I saw fire come out of its mouth!"

"And it crushed my knee with a hammer," moaned Gnar, drawing his bandage tight. Meanwhile, the man whose head had been gashed by the hoof moaned and pressed his hands to the swelling lump of his face.

"A spirited animal, that's all," spat another, a stocky,

mustachioed man with a short bow and quiver of arrows. He looked at his fellows in scorn. "You're just not fit to hold the halter of a horse like that!"

"Why didn't you take the rope, then, Garald?" asked Kelryn smoothly.

"I tried, lord—I tried. But these fools had made such a mess of things that by the time I got there the animal had broken free. There'll be no catching it, at least on foot."

"Your horse?" Kelryn inquired, regarding Foryth with a raised eyebrow. "Undoubtedly the creature responsible for the attack against us at your first camp?"

"Er—" Foryth, who had winced and cringed at the sound of Nightmare's escape, looked around awkwardly.

"Our horse," Danyal blurted quickly. "I'm the squire, so I take care of her. Her name is Nightmare," he added, suppressing the urge to grin at the damage the mean-spirited animal had inflicted on these ruffians.

"Apt," replied Kelryn, his tone droll.

"Enough o' this!" snarled the one-eyed bandit, Zack. "Are we goin' to stick 'em and be on our way?" His filthy thumb, still caressing the edge of the big knife, left no doubt as to what Zack's desire was.

"No, I think not." Kelryn was firm, his expression pragmatic.

"Not even the boy?" Danyal gagged on Zack's fetid breath as the bandit leaned close, cackling in cruel mirth.

"I must say, the reward from my temple will be limited—perhaps refused entirely—if such a promising young apprentice is stolen from the church by untimely violence." Foryth's tone suggested that he thought his superiors were a trifle unreasonable on a matter like this, but that he, personally, was powerless to effect a more practical solution.

"No, Zack, not even the lad. At least not yet," Kelryn ordered with a tolerant shake of his head. "We'll find some other way for you to have some entertainment," he promised the sulking knifeman before turning to the rest of his band.

"Gnar, your leg is badly hurt. We'll have to see how you fare. And, Kal"—he addressed the man who had been kicked in the head—"you'll be able to walk, I have no doubt.

"Nic, let me see that arm." Kelryn gestured to the man whose elbow had been crushed by the rearing horse. The fellow came forward and knelt, while the bandit leader took the limb in both of his hands, ignoring the man's gasp of pain when the arm was lifted.

"Fistandantilus!" cried Kelryn Darewind, turning his face to the sky. "Hear my prayer and grant me the power to heal your unworthy servant's arm!"

A green light flared through the night, and Danyal gasped at a sudden, foul scent, like the odor released when someone turned over a rotten log. Kelryn Darewind stiffened, calling out strange words as he clutched the injured elbow.

"Stop! No!" The wounded bandit cried out in pain and twisted away, falling to the ground and writhing. He groaned, kicked weakly, and drew ragged breaths as he lay motionless, panting like a dog. After a few moments, however, he pushed himself off the ground with both hands, forcing himself to sit up.

"The—the pain is gone," he declared, extending the arm. To Danyal, the limb seemed stiff, still cocked at an unnatural angle, but the bandit seemed content that his agony had been dispelled.

"You called out the name of Fistandantilus, and then you healed him?" Foryth Teel, like Danyal, was clearly amazed. "What happened here?"

"A priest called upon the power of his god . . . and he cast a spell." The bandit leader spoke of himself in third person. He seemed dazed.

"That was astonishing!" Foryth Teel declared. He picked up his book, flipping through several pages. "Healing magic is the clear province of faithful priests and gods. But you called upon Fistandantilus. Does that mean that you . . . ?" The question trailed off. Then the historian blinked. "*You* are the Master of Loreloch?"

"Indeed. As I was the Seeker in Haven, the 'false' priest of Fistandantilus."

"But—but that was real magic! You actually *healed* him!"

"You are surprised?"

"Astounded, more truthfully." Foryth blinked again, scratching his chin. "And you claim the faith of a god named after the ancient archmage Fistandantilus? That is truly amazing."

"In fact, I worship the true faith of Fistandantilus, the sect of a god as genuine as Takhisis or Paladine!"

"But he was mortal. He was a man, not a god!" Foryth Teel was adamant. "There must be some other explanation. An inconsistency in translation, perhaps!"

"No, nothing like that, I assure you."

"But—but how could it happen? It's impossible. It must have been a trick—"

"In case you doubt the evidence of your own eyes, I dispute your preposterous suggestion about my actions. Are you as much a fool as the others?" The bandit sighed, with an exaggerated shrug of his shoulders. "It seems that I will have to prove it to you. Fistandantilus is a god, and I am his high priest! And you, of course, are my prisoners!" Once again Kelryn seemed to be in sudden good cheer, throwing back his head and laughing heartily. "Now, my unwilling guests, if you will be so kind as to gather your blankets, I wish to start out before the dawn."

"Where are you taking us?" Danyal dared to ask, keeping a wary eye on the menacing figure of the one-eyed bandit, Zack.

"Why, to your destination, of course." Kelryn spoke as if he was surprised by the question. "You will have a chance to become acquainted with the dungeon of Loreloch, but it is still some miles away."

"Splendid!" Foryth Teel declared. "Then we'll have plenty of time to talk!"

The amazing thing was, thought Danyal as his fellow captive excitedly gathered his quills, ink, and teapot, that the historian actually meant it.

Chapter 24

Another Detour on the Road to Faith

First Majetog, Reapember
374 AC

It is with a mingled sense of purest excitement and deepest regret that I at last address my notes. On the one hand, I have made a startling discovery that twists an understanding of history on its ear: Fistandantilus, a god! With a priest who is *not* a charlatan. Of course, the story must be examined, the evidence studied by my critical eye, but here is great meat for the researcher's diet.

On the other hand, there is a matter that lays such a heavy cloak of guilt upon my shoulders that I doubt I shall show these writings to anyone. (Of course, that cannot exclude the all-seeing perceptions of my ever neutral god, yet it is that very neutrality, I fear, that lies at the root of my failure. I shall expound momentarily.)

Who will believe me? Fistandantilus neither dead, nor undead; instead he has become immortal! It seems that the archmage has somehow vaulted himself into the pantheon of Krynn! Of course, it also seems unthinkable, but I saw the proof with my own eyes.

A priest of a self-proclaimed religion has demonstrated the power to heal! It was a limited healing; Kelryn all but admitted that the crushed knee of the bandit called Gnar was too badly damaged for the magic of his god to prevail. Yet the spell he demonstrated was enough to humble my own priestly ambitions—I who have yet to heal so much as a hangnail through the use of the magic of my faith.

Indeed, the proof was enough to whet my appetite, but I must learn more. Does Kelryn Darewind possess the bloodstone of Fistandantilus? And what does he know about the fates that cast the archmage into Krynn's pantheon? Though he was recalcitrant in conversation, the priest of Fistandantilus did promise me that I would have some access to his notes. (He claimed that his library was located in a lofty tower top, perfectly suited for reflection and research.)

But there weighs upon me that other matter, a fact that dulls the elation of my discovery, for I know that I have erred terribly.

Gilean, I confess to my utmost failure, though you doubtless know of my trespass already. How quickly I have abandoned the dispassionate viewpoint of the historian, allowing myself to become involved in the affairs of insignificant persons, while in full awareness that such involvement cannot help but steer my studies away from the truly impartial voice of the aloof chronicler.

Specifically, it is in the matter of the mistruth—oh, I must strip away obfuscation and call it by the proper name: the *lie*—I spoke on behalf of the young traveler who had made my acquaintance on that very night.

Of course, he is no more a squire than I am a high priest, or even any priest at all. My own actions served to obscure the truth, to twist my captors' perceptions of reality, all because of a realization that I would find the lad's execution unsettling. Indeed, Lord of Neutrality, it was this own selfish frailty that led to my weakness.

My actions kept the boy alive, but at what terrible cost to my objectivity? I have searched *The Book of Learning*, seeking some sign indicating the severity of the affront, but the tome has been ominously silent on the matter.

Even in self-recrimination I forget myself. It is my duty to put aside my distress and to continue with the task that brought me to this corner of Kharolis. The deception of which I speak has occurred some two days prior to my recording of these notes; I shall hasten to put down the events of the current day and to describe as best I can my situation and prospects.

Following the escape of that rather frightening horse and Kelryn's healing spell, the bandits tied my hands before me, prodding me through the darkness on the narrow trail (upon which I tripped several times, scuffing my hands and, once, bloodying my nose) until we again reached the Loreloch Road and the bridge of gray stone. It was not until then that I saw that the youth, Danyal Thwait, had been similarly bound and forced to follow behind me.

Footsore and weary, we ascended the winding, rough road through the remainder of the night. We were slowed by the need of Gnar to be helped by two men, and in this I was fortunate. Indeed, should the band have proceeded at its normal pace, I have no doubts but that it would have been me who restricted the pace of the rest of the party, with all the awkward attentions—particularly from the one-eyed bandit, Zack—that would have entailed.

By the time dawn began to color the sky, we had reached a small grove of pines in the protection of a low saddle. This was not a pass through the range—I could see higher and more rugged elevations rising on the north side of the ridge—but it provided a place for our captors to seek concealment and rest through the day.

I gather that, though they are bold and lawless men, the bandits of Kelryn Darewind's band do in fact fear the Knights of Solamnia. Else how can I explain the hidden clearing, deep in the woods, where we sheltered during the day? Also, consider the fact that one of the men trailed behind us after we departed the road; I looked back to see that he was sweeping a pine bough, heavy with needles, across our trail. Thus all sight of our passage was concealed.

Hearing the desultory talk of the men during the long trek and through the daylight hours of inactivity, I gather that they were returning from a successful raid on a specific enemy. Kelryn had taken them to kill the Solamnic Knight, Sir Harold the White, and his family, eliminating that enforcer of the law from the territory the bandits wanted for themselves. (Although I learned that their success was not complete; Zack complained loudly about a girl, a daughter of the knight, who somehow escaped their murderous net.)

The men's spirits were still inflamed by their cruel sport, and the gruesome stories of the murder could only enhance their villainy. At times I found it nearly impossible to consider their acts with dispassion, yet I was able to muster my faith, to forcefully remind myself that theirs was a current in history's river as worthy of telling as any other.

Danyal and I were bound together at one side of the encampment. My request that we be released and that I be provided with my book and writing implements was rudely laughed away.

Lacking the means to record events, I tried to talk to the lad, to explain my distress about the failure of my objectivity that had led me to lie about him. He was surprisingly appreciative, as I suppose is only natural. After all, as the old saying goes, even the meanest of lives is treasured by the one who lives it.

The boy showed traces of brightness and perception in our conversations, yet he seemed remarkably unsympathetic to my own dilemma. Indeed, so clearly did he treasure his own survival that he seemed rather put off when I mentioned my regrets at the loss of my historical dispassion.

Eventually I was released from my tether and taken to join Kelryn. I was able to gather much information from him, though he still denied me the chance to take notes as we talked. I can only hope that my memory has served me as accurately as does my pen.

He told me that when the True Gods returned to Krynn, with them came Fistandantilus, risen to the exalted status of a deity. Kelryn Darewind had demanded power of that god. He told me he used it to keep the memory and the knowledge of the archmage alive. His followers had woven great tapestries depicting the wizard's life, and he boasted of how those artistic fabrics still draped the halls of Loreloch.

It must have been the destruction of Skullcap, I mused, that somehow converted the archmage into godhood. After all, he had opened the portal to chaos, a path to the Dark Queen herself. But when I voiced my speculations, I discerned that Kelryn Darewind had not the slightest interest in my suppositions.

Instead, he made mention of something that he called "the skull of Fistandantilus." I gathered that this was an object that he sought with a great deal of interest, though he would share little information about it when I pressed him for further explanation. I speculated upon an unconfirmed rumor I had heard in Palanthas, a report that Fistandantilus had existed as an undead lich after the destruction of Skullcap, at which Kelryn Darewind scornfully laughed in my face.

When I sought response to my other questions, the bandit became suddenly reluctant to talk. I was again secured to my tree, and we two prisoners spent the rest of the day in boredom and slumber.

With the coming of darkness, again we took to the

road. The bandits prodded us with obvious urgency, and we followed the descending route down the north side of the ridge. At the base of the incline, we came to a rapid stream, here crossed by a sturdy bridge. After making the crossing, we proceeded upward again, and I sensed that we were drawing close to the lofty massif of the High Kharolis.

The long night of climbing exhausted me and many of the others, though Kelryn Darewind displayed no sign of fatigue. Finally we made camp again, this time in the depths of a mountainside cave. My captors have at last consented to provide me with the tools of my trade, and thus I hasten to write my observations, to record the history of the last few days with as much dispassion and objectivity as possible.

But as I look at the young lad who sleeps restively nearby and know that my interference was the act that kept him alive, I fear that I have already failed.

Chapter 25

Wyrmtales

First Majetog, Reapember
374 AC

Danyal pulled on the pole, saw the trout break the surface in a ripple of droplets and gleaming silver scales. He tugged gently, but then it was a violent force, and he ripped the hook from the fish's mouth. The pole felt stiff and heavy in his hands.

Then he heard the fish scream, a sound so full of suffering that his heart nearly broke.

And then he *was* the fish, and the water closed over his head, but he couldn't swim! He was badly injured, torn and bleeding, and held by the unbreakable strands of a long, tethering line.

He awakened, thrashing in panic, finally sitting

upright and blinking through the smoky shadows of the cave. His garments were soaked with sweat, his hair plastered to his forehead by the clammy perspiration. Danyal had to draw several deep, gasping breaths, reassuring himself that it had been a nightmare. Even so, only slowly did the sensation of drowning recede.

And he was still bound by the long tether—that part had not been a dream. The rope bit into his wrists, and the loss of circulation stung his hands, deadened his fingers. The other end of the twisted braid of tough leather was wrapped securely around a massive wooden stake that had been driven into the ground within the cave some time before their arrival.

He saw Foryth Teel, blinking slowly, stirring from slumber, and Dan guessed that his own thrashing had awakened the historian, who had been busily writing when the youth had drifted off to sleep.

But what was that scream? Danyal sensed that the sound had been a part of the real world. As he came to that conclusion, he heard an angry shout, then a man's voice that broke into sobs, broken by desperate pleading. "No—leave me here! Just go on without me. I'll stay out of sight till I can—"

"Get it over with, Zack!"

The last words, spoken in the voice of Kelryn Darewind, cut off the objections, though the sounds of soft sobbing still burbled through the cave.

Danyal crept forward, to the limits of the rope, and looked toward the entryway. He saw Gnar, the bandit with the broken knee, crawling slowly backward across the ground, while Zack advanced on him with his face split into a menacing leer. In the one-eyed bandit's hand was the gleaming knife.

"Yer too slow, old Gnar," cackled Zack. "Ya never were good for much, and now with that knee, yer just an anchor holding back the rest of us!"

"By all the gods, leave me here!" begged the injured man.

Abruptly Zack thrust. Gnar tried to roll away, but the blade snicked through his throat with a whiplike slice.

Danyal was horrified to hear the rush of air, the gurgling noise of death as the crippled bandit, his wrapped knee holding his leg unnaturally stiff, thrashed across the ground. Back arching, Gnar's hands scraped to either side for a long moment. Then, with a reflexive shudder, his struggles ceased and he lay still.

Kelryn Darewind turned away, and his eyes met Danyal's. The youth was frightened by the look he saw there—an expression of deep, unquenched hunger—but he found that he couldn't tear his gaze away. Instead, he imagined the bandit leader attacking, consuming him.

"His wound was infected," declared Kelryn. "He was doomed, and he was slowing the rest of us down. I merely gave the order to hasten the inevitable."

Zack was busy cleaning his blade on the dead man's cloak. His one eye gleamed as he cackled at Danyal. "And I *am* the inevitable!"

Shrinking back against the wall, Danyal tried to vanish into the shadows. He was startled to realize that he was shaking, and his mind echoed relentlessly with the horrid gulping slurp that had been Gnar's dying sound. Creeping as far back as he could, Dan tried to will himself to disappear. Memories of the bandits' stories, of the murder of Sir Harold, of spitting his baby on a sword, of the awful things they had done to his wife, chilled the lad. He found himself remembering the girl he had heard about and hoped that she was safe.

Foryth Teel, the lad was not surprised to see, busied himself copying down some notes. The historian had certainly seen the grim scene enacted before them, but his face gave no clue to any distress that he might have been feeling.

Trying to disappear into his corner, Danyal let his hands settle protectively over his belt buckle. He pulled on his shirt, insuring that the material drooped over the metal bracket. He had left behind his fishing pole and creel when he was captured, and the bandits had taken his knife, but he was determined to keep secret the existence of the silver heirloom.

Some time later Zack came toward them. Danyal was certain they were going to be killed, but Foryth merely held up his hands, allowing the man to cut the leather thong that had bound the historian to the stake. Hesitantly Danyal did the same, recoiling as the butcher wheezed a waft of putrid breath in his face.

The lad's tether was cut, and soon he and Foryth were standing, flexing their muscles, allowing circulation to reach into the previously deadened parts of their bodies. Their hands remained tightly bound together at the wrists, but at least they could move around, stretching their legs and working the kinks out of their backs.

"Hurry up there," snapped Kelryn Darewind, striding farther into the cave to address his two captives. "We've got to get started. It'll take us all night to get to our next shelter, and I want to be inside by the dawn."

Danyal thought the bandit leader seemed jumpy and anxious; he looked over his shoulder for a moment, then stared intently into the shadows at the edges of the cave.

"Tsk—it'll take a minute just to be able to move again," Foryth said, limping forward, leaning against the cave wall to help him balance. Kelryn glared at the man, and Danyal had a glimmer of terrible fear.

"I'll give you a hand," the lad offered, stepping to the historian's other side and taking his arm. Together, still hobbling, they made their way to the entrance of the cave.

Two of the bandits had already dragged Gnar's corpse away, but the place where he had died was marked by a great smear of blood, and Danyal found his eyes drawn to the place with magnetic inevitability.

"Lot of blood in a man—or boy, for that matter!" hissed Zack, his breath hot in Danyal's ear as the murderer cackled gleefully.

"Let's go!" snapped Kelryn, and Zack flipped an angry look at his leader before leading the party out of the cave.

Fortunately Foryth had restored the feeling to his legs by the time they reached the rutted road. Under the pale light of a half-full Solinari, they started northward again, climbing along the edge of one of the steep-sided valleys that cut into the heights of the Kharolis Mountains.

For several hours, they marched in grim silence. The bandits seemed surly and suspicious, cursing at the unexpected sound of a clattering stone or softly griping at each other about inconsequential matters. Danyal kept quiet, wishing he could just be forgotten, left to himself in this rugged wilderness.

Kelryn, who had been leading the band, eventually ambled to the side of the road and waited for the two captives to reach him. He fell into step beside Foryth Teel, regarding the historian with a pensive expression that seemed darkly sinister in the moonlight.

"I can't help noticing that it seems you have started out on your quest with a rather ill-suited selection of companions and weaponry. What, in fact, do you know of the dangers that might be encountered in these mountains?"

"Tsk," Foryth replied dismissively. "It is the historian's job to record the details of those dangers where they are discovered. It is not my place to do battle, to change the face of Krynn through actions of my own."

"Yet you very nearly didn't survive to record that history," replied the bandit. "And you should know that I am not the only thing you need to fear in these heights."

"And what other manner of danger might we encounter?" Foryth reached for his book, then, apparently deciding that the complications of writing and walking outweighed the need for immediate accuracy, dropped the tome back into his pack.

"There's a dragon." Danyal spoke boldly, forgetting himself enough that he wanted to contribute to the conversation.

"Ah, the squire speaks. And he is correct." Kelryn addressed Foryth Teel. "I assume that you caught sight of the wyrm in the days before our meeting?"

"No!" Foryth objected. "I would certainly have remembered such an occurrence."

"Um, you were asleep," Danyal said, giving the historian a nudge with his elbow. "I saw the dragon fly over, but I didn't want to wake you."

"What?" Foryth scowled at the lad, and for a moment Danyal had a glimpse of what a real squire might feel like after he had displeased his master. "You should *always* wake me up for a dragon!"

"Yes, sir. I-I'll make sure I do that," Dan replied, uncertain as to whether the historian was really making a point or simply going along with the youth's story.

"And was there enough light that you could see the nature of this serpent?" asked Kelryn, turning his own attention to the youth.

"Yes. It was red—and *huge*," Danyal said, his voice thickening as he recalled the monster.

He wanted to say that it had destroyed his village, flown from the sky to bring ruin and death to innocent Waterton. But he dared say no more, or he would risk revealing the charade of his relationship to Foryth Teel, the utterly fictional relationship with its promise of ransom that seemed to be the only thing currently keeping Danyal alive.

"You felt the awe?"

The lad nodded mutely, remembering the way his guts had seemed to liquefy in his belly at the sight of the monster, hating the tears that welled in his eyes with the memory. Fortunately Kelryn seemed to take his emotions as nothing more than the normal reaction in one who had encountered such an awe-inspiring beast.

"I suspect you saw the red dragon known as Flayze," the bandit lord declared. "He is the bane of these mountains, a bully and predator against elf, dwarf, and man. Wicked to the core, he relishes nothing so much as the slow death of one of his enemies, unless it is gorging himself on a haunch of charred meat."

"You know him?" Danyal was amazed to hear the man speak of the serpent with such familiarity.

"Indeed. He has something that I cherish, that I want very much. Yet even more, I have had cause to hate him for many long years."

"What does he have?" asked the youth, only to recoil as Kelryn's eyes went blank and his face lost every hint of emotion.

Any thoughts of obtaining further information about that history were blocked by the forbidding expression on Kelryn's face.

"Always wake me up for a dragon!" Foryth insisted once more, as if distressed that the conversation had proceeded so far without him.

"Why?" snapped the lad peevishly. "Would you try to kill it?"

"Of course not!" Foryth was horrified. "Why, such an act would completely shatter any historian's pretense of neutrality! It's hard to think of anything that could be more disruptive of the proper observer's role."

"Not to mention that killing a dragon is far from an easy thing to do," Kelryn noted. Once again his tone was light, and in spite of himself, Danyal felt a flash of relief that the bandit lord's aloof mood had passed so quickly.

"How can a dragon be slain?" asked the youth. He had a vague memory of his intentions when he had started up the valley from Waterton. From the vantage of a few days' distance, his goal of killing the monstrous serpent seemed laughably unattainable, not to mention suicidal.

"The best way has always been to get a bigger, stronger dragon to do it for you," Kelryn said with a bitter laugh. "It's how the Dark Queen was defeated during the last war."

"But this dragon wasn't killed."

"No." The bandit lord shook his head seriously, considering his reply. "If you live long enough, you will find that many dragons, wyrms of all the clans of metal and color, still dwell in many of the hidden corners of Ansalon."

"Why don't they rule the world, then?" Danyal couldn't think of any way that a serpent such as Flayze could be stopped, if the monster took it into his head to claim any kind of realm for himself.

"That's a good question. What does our historian have to say on the matter?"

Foryth scowled, tsking a few times as he pondered the subject. "The best reason seems to be that they don't want to," he said finally. "Gilean knows that any one of them could wreak a great deal of havoc if it decided to do so. But they fight among themselves all the time—at least, all the time when they're not sleeping. And a big dragon sleeps a lot, sometimes for ten or twenty years at a stretch. Each dragon is more concerned with its own comfort than with other matters."

"Don't the Knights of Solamnia hold them in check, sort of?" Dan asked. Remembering the gleaming armor, the brawny size, and easy, capable grace of the few such armored horsemen that he had seen, the lad tried to picture a human fighter competing with the massive killing force of a red dragon. Even that picture was scary, as Danyal was forced to conclude that the would-be dragonslayer would truly be facing a hopeless task.

Both Kelryn and Foryth were shaking their heads.

"Bah!" the bandit lord said with a curse. "The knights are old women now, weaklings who are afraid of their own shadows. There are none of the bold lancers left from the days of the war."

"That is open to debate," the historian disputed. "But you should know, lad, that the tales of a knight on horseback killing a dragon, no matter how courageous he is, how pure his heart and steady his hand, are merely the stuff of legend and fiction. No, a mighty dragon has very little to fear from anything except another mighty dragon."

"But there *has* to be *some* way!" insisted Danyal, so intently that both men turned to regard him with interest. "I mean, it's hard to believe all those stories, all the legends of dragonslayers and heroes and stuff, were just made up," he concluded lamely.

"Remember the old saying: `Never underestimate the imagination, nor the thirst, of a bard,' " Foryth noted with a benign chuckle. "Most of those tales you're recalling were invented by a traveling minstrel who needed a good tale in order to sing himself a supper and a pitcher or two of fine ale. Such poets and artists should not be confused with the true student of history—that is, the dispassionate historian."

"Ssst!"

The warning came from the darkness ahead. Danyal stiffened, watching the hunched figure of Zack slip off the road. The other men of the band, too, shrank into the shadows.

Then he heard whistling, melodic notes rising through the night air.

And he knew that the bandits had found another victim.

Chapter 26

A Heart of Blood and Fire

circa 374 AC

Fistandantilus heard the pulse through the ears of his host, and it was closer than it had ever been before. Blood quickened in the incorporeal stuff of his mind, and renewed hunger tingled in his tongue, tantalized his memories.

The bloodstone!

Fistandantilus lusted for the touch of that potent artifact, knew that its arcane force would allow him to master—and then destroy—this wretched kender. The wizard's essence churned with vigor as he tried—as he had tried for so many decades—to make his power felt.

And for the first time in the foggy expanse of his entrapment, he was close to succeeding. At last the bloodstone and his kender host were nearing each other, approaching the connection that would open the way to his freedom and his revenge!

For a moment, the spirit basked in anticipation of tormented victims, of the blood and the souls and the lives that would be his for the feasting. He was determined that there would be killing enough to satiate the hunger nurtured in this unthinkably long imprisonment.

But then another power intruded into his arcane awareness. This was a force that disturbed the true linkage between the essence of the wizard and his ancient bloodstone! It was a mysterious presence, a film of gauze that shrouded his control, masked his power, yet at the same time it was a force magical, spiritual, and ghostly. And it fought for the bloodstone with the same vigor and the same sense of proprietary ownership that drove the wizard's own hungry essence.

He sensed vaguely that this intrusive power was centered near the person of a human, and it was competing with Fistandantilus, powerful enough to block the archmage's best hope of success.

Seething, hateful of this new complication, the wizard sensed that the bloodstone was getting closer still. He heard the pulse as a loud cadence, thumping through his very self.

It was really, truly near! Now the talisman reached out to him with tendrils of glorious heat, close enough to be almost within his reach. Tingles of power and awareness shivered through the archmage's ethereal being. The cadence of life that had once been a distant suggestion was now a thunderous drumbeat resonating constantly, driving him with insatiable hunger and need.

But it was a bitter fact that the bloodstone was actually within the reach only of the pathetically directionless kender, the person who had been an unwilling and unwitting host to the spiritual essence of Fistandantilus for more than a century.

The ghostly spirit writhed and twisted, groping for a tiny snippet of control. But there was still that interference, the force that blocked him, competed for the power of the gemstone. And instead, the essence of evil could only despair as the fiery enchantment of the stone came so close that it all but sang out its message of vitality, of hope, of life itself.

Then the impending conjunction was shattered beyond restoration, cast aside by the shield he could perceive but not identify. Infuriated, Fistandantilus turned the full power of his attentions toward one of these companions. Quickly he saw that this was a human lad, a person easily distinguished from the faceless mass of humanity.

This was his enemy, the source of the mask that was a power equal to the ancient one's. The presence, the competing essence fought with him, brushed him aside. Overwhelmed, Fistandantilus felt his awareness slipping away.

The kender was once again his own master.

And another person, the human boy, was added to the list of those who had to die.

Chapter 27

A Whistling Wanderer

First Kirinor, Reapember
374 AC

Danyal watched as the whole group of bandits took shelter in the ditch, while Kelryn seized Foryth and him by the arms and pulled them out of sight behind a boulder beside the mountain road. The slope above them was steep and rocky, while across the way, the ground dropped into infinite blackness. From the remembered view at sunset, the lad knew that the terrain on the other side of the road plunged down a steep incline toward a mountain stream far below.

He tried to see through the darkness, but Dan could make out nothing of what was approaching along the track. All he could hear was the tuneful whistling, the sound growing slowly louder as they waited.

"Who do you suppose it is?" Foryth asked, the sound of his voice carrying through the night air.

"Silence!" hissed Kelryn, pulling the historian farther back from the road.

Danyal, meanwhile, lowered himself to the ground and peered around the edge of the large rock, seeking some sign of the approaching whistler. He could see the vague shapes of the huddled bandits crouching in the ditch, fading moonlight reflecting dully off exposed steel. The lad remembered Zack's keen blade, the bandit's willingness to wet that razor edge in the blood of seemingly anyone within reach, and he prayed that the unwitting traveler would suddenly turn around, would flee down that dark mountain road.

The next sounds he heard dashed all those hopes, even as they sent the bandits into consternation.

"Hi there! What are you doing in that muddy ditch? It's a lot drier up here on the road."

The eight men of Kelryn's band lunged forward to form a ring around the diminutive traveler Danyal saw in their midst. The thugs growled like wild animals, though their presence didn't seem to startle or worry the lone wanderer.

"Oh, were you waiting for me? That's nice. Pleased to make your acquaintance—Emilo Haversack, at your service. And you are . . . ?"

"A kender!" declared Zack in disgust, advancing on the unconcerned fellow.

"Why, yes. Haversack is a kender name, after all—one of the finest, oldest, and most honorable of all the kender clans, if I say so myself. And of course I do, because nobody else will."

Somehow the kender had passed through the ring of bandits to make his final remarks before Kelryn, Foryth, and Danyal. Though they hadn't emerged from the shelter of the concealing boulder, Danyal realized with vague surprise, the diminutive stranger had somehow wandered right up to them.

"Emilo Haversack, at your service," he repeated, clasping Danyal's bound hands and pumping enthusiastically.

"Hey—he got my purse!" shouted one of the bandits, a burly and sullen archer known as Bolt, as the group whirled toward the kender.

"What? Oh, this?" Emilo was holding a small leather sack, a pouch that jingled as he lifted it. "You must have dropped it. Here!"

The kender tossed the pouch back to Bolt, but as it sailed through the air, a stream of silvery coins tumbled out, bouncing and rolling across the road.

"My steel!" roared the bandit, dropping to his knees and trying to sweep together all the coins. Laughing uproariously, the other members of the band joined in the fun, snatching any of their compatriot's coins that rolled out of his reach.

Danyal watched in amazement as Emilo took Foryth's hands in a vigorous handshake, then bowed deeply to Kelryn Darewind.

"Anyone could see that you're the esteemed leader of these bold fellows. I'm honored to make your acquaintance. Emilo Haversack, at—"

"I know," Kelryn interjected drily. "At my service. But how, pray, can a kender offer service? And why should I accept it, if offered?"

Emilo chuckled good-naturedly. "Both very good questions, of course. Actually, I wouldn't think that you'd get many kender around here. But if there *is* anything I can do for you, well, I'd be glad to talk about it."

"Stop that confounded midget!" shouted Bolt, who was still upset about his lost steel pieces. "I'll take each missing coin out of his hide."

"Well, really," said Emilo in exasperation. "I'm the one who *returned* your purse. I don't see why you should be taking such an attitude."

It was then that Danyal noticed his bonds had miraculously fallen from his wrists. Remembering the enthusiastic handshake from the kender, he regarded Emilo

Haversack with growing awe.

And concern. Unmollified, Bolt was advancing on the little fellow. The bandit's short sword was raised, and he was clearly in no mood for fancy explanations.

"Hey! My purse is missing, too!" Zack's roar of outrage checked Bolt's menacing approach.

"Is this it?" Emilo was holding up another pouch full of coins. "You should really be a little more careful." Again the purse flew through the air, and again, to cries of outrage and glee, valuable coinage tumbled to the road, bouncing into the ditches, rolling along the ruts.

Even Kelryn had paused, hand on his sword as he watched in amusement, Danyal noticed. The bandit lord advanced to stand close behind Emilo Haversack and finally put his hands on his hips to laugh aloud at the antics of his followers.

The lad cast a glance at Foryth and saw the historian looking with amazement at the loose ropes dangling from his own wrists. Dan felt a flickering dawn of hope, but it was quickly dashed. Even free from their bonds, it didn't seem likely that the two of them could evade their captors for long before they would be run down and caught. And he didn't even want to think about the precautions the bandits might take if the pair showed an intention to escape, nor about the vengeance Zack might take if he should recapture his fugitives.

"Here, let me help with that," Emilo offered genially. He sauntered toward the men, who backed away, each unconsciously revealing the location of his valuables as he placed a hand at belt, side pouch, or, in one case, the top of his boot.

Ignoring their distress, the kender skipped through the group of suspicious bandits. "Here!" he cried, flipping a steel piece to Bolt. "And another!" This time the glittering coin tumbled past Zack's outstretched hand, bouncing onto the road, then rolling between Bolt's legs.

"That's mine!"

"Keep yer paws off it!"

Immediately the two bandits lunged, colliding heavily, then falling to the ground where they exchanged sharp punches. Rolling back and forth, spitting and swearing, the pair thrashed from one side of the road to the other. Steel flashed in the darkness, and Danyal saw that Zack had drawn his wicked knife.

"No blades!" Kelryn Darewind's voice cracked through the night, and the one-eyed bandit, cursing loudly, tossed his dagger aside and delivered his fist into Bolt's blunt nose.

"Hi again!"

Danyal whirled at the sudden voice, almost falling down as he saw that somehow Emilo Haversack had sauntered around the large boulder and now stood behind the youth and the historian, regarding them curiously.

"You stirred them up pretty good," Danyal noted, grimacing as Bolt bit down on Zack's wrist, drawing a howl of outrage from his writhing opponent.

"Yes," the kender agreed, nodding with a certain sense of justified pride. "I'd like to stay and watch, but don't you think we should be going?"

"Tsk—we're prisoners," Foryth Teel chided. "We're not allowed to—"

"We're not prisoners right now!" hissed Danyal urgently, seeing a design behind the kender's antics and hoping there was more to the plan than simply running as fast as they could into the night. "He's right. Let's go!"

"But—"

"Come on!" Danyal insisted, grabbing Foryth's hand and pulling. The historian reluctantly stumbled along, though he cast a glance at the bandits, almost as if he hoped Kelryn might see them and put a stop to this nonsense about escape.

For his own part, the lad felt certain their argument and departure would draw the attention of the bandits, but a quick look showed that Kelryn had joined the ring at the edge of the fight, which was building to a climax as Zack tore his bleeding hand from Bolt's mouth and tried to get a stranglehold around the burly man's neck.

"This way," Emilo said, leading them up the road. "I picked this spot on purpose."

The sounds of the fight receded in the distance as they sprinted into the night. Danyal was tense and fearful, expecting a shout of alarm at any moment, but if anything the intranecine duel raged with increasing intensity.

"Here." Emilo Haversack halted quickly, pointing to a niche between two rocks on the downhill side of the road. "Sit down, and you'll be safe."

"What? How?" demanded Danyal, who thought that the place offered precious little concealment, and even then barely enough for one person.

Any further objections, however, were overcome by a sound of real alarm down the roadway. Kelryn's voice barked through the chaos. "Find them. Bring them to me!"

"You go first! I'll follow!" whispered the kender, prodding Foryth toward the place he had indicated.

With a sigh, the historian stepped off the road—and immediately vanished from sight. Danyal heard an "oof" of alarm, but even that sound swiftly faded into the night.

"Now you go!" urged the kender. Hearing the sounds of running feet, the lad didn't hesitate. He stepped after Foryth and felt his foot lose purchase on the edge of a slippery, smooth-walled chute. Instantly he was on his back, skidding and sliding over a muddy surface with incredible speed. Only with the greatest of effort did he bite back the shout of alarm that threatened to explode from his mouth.

Instead, he tried to pay attention, to pick out the features of the hillside before him. A thin trickle of water drained down this smooth ravine, providing lubrication for a plummeting, headlong slide. Danyal had a fearful thought of Foryth coming to a halt below only to be smashed by the lad's uncontrolled plunge. Or what if this gully debouched into a waterfall and dumped them unceremoniously onto a waiting pile of jagged, unforgiving rocks?

But the slide seemed to continue smoothly for a very long way. Through the bouncing and scraping and the rushing of the wind, Dan gradually became aware of another body plunging along the gully behind him, and he guessed—and fervently hoped—that Emilo had accompanied them. He had to pray the kender wouldn't have recommended the route if he didn't have some hope of its success. Still, the lad was far from enjoying the slide as he skidded through a patch of mud, then felt a rough surface of rock scrape him painfully on the back.

And suddenly he was airborne, floating, falling, certain that he was doomed, yet even then some deep-seated instinct kept him from crying out.

He smacked into water that was icy cold and deep. The force of the impact knocked the breath from his lungs, but he was immediately stroking for the surface, kicking desperately until his face broke free and he could draw a deep lungful of air.

Another figure splashed into the water beside him, and only when Emilo popped to the surface, treading water easily, did Danyal hear the churning, choking sounds a short distance away. The two swimmers each grabbed one of Foryth's flailing arms and thrashed through the chilly pool until they could pull the historian onto a sandy bank. All three lay for several minutes, gasping for breath, slowly absorbing the awareness of their changed circumstances.

Danyal noticed heavy evergreens drooping overhead, and the lad felt certain they were concealed from the road on the mountainside so far above. He waded into the shallow water to look upward and saw the ridgeline, where the road was, silhouetted high against the night sky.

"My guess is that they'll figure we kept running and chase along that road for a long distance," Emilo explained. "The chute we came down is pretty much invisible at night, though if they're still up there at dawn, they won't have much trouble spotting our trail."

"Perhaps by dawn, then, we should be somewhere else," Danyal suggested. "And thanks for rescuing us."

He shivered, and the chill came from more than his wet garments. Indeed, as he considered the prospects of a long captivity, with Zack and his knife waiting always in the shadows, the lad didn't have any doubts but that the kender had indeed saved their lives.

Chapter 28

A Mysterious Affliction

First Kirinor, Reapember
374 AC

Danyal was startled by a sudden movement in the shadows of the pines. He whirled, reaching for the fishing knife that he no longer wore at his belt. Then, as his eyes focused in the dim light, he gasped in shock.

"A girl!"

She was hiding in the deep shadow of a streamside boulder but, seeing she was discovered, came hesitantly forth, taking Emilo's arm in a protective gesture.

"This is Mirabeth," said the kender with grave formality. "She was waiting here for us."

There was something familiar about the slight figure, who stood a little taller than Emilo. Danyal saw the topknot that split into two long tails, one over each shoulder, and he was certain.

"You're not a girl. You're the kendermaid who tamed Nightmare, who showed me where the apples were!"

"Yes . . . that was me." Again he heard the musical voice, soft and hushed but still delightful to his ear.

"Remarkable! Simply remarkable. Now, wait—I must get this down," declared Foryth, fumbling in his pouch for the tools of his trade. "You were feeding apples to our lad, here?"

"Forget about the book!" hissed Danyal. "Remember, we've got to get away from here before daylight!"

"The boy is right," Emilo said. "I picked this place for your escape carefully, and we've got a bit of a head start, but we don't want to dally any longer than we have to."

The historian looked as though he were about to argue, but Danyal stepped in front of him and addressed Emilo Haversack. He felt like a chronicler himself, wanting to ask a thousand questions—starting with why the kender had taken such a risk. Instead, he forced his thoughts along practical lines.

"Where do we go from here? What's our best chance of getting to some kind of hiding place before daylight?"

"If we go downstream, we'll meet the river in a few miles. We won't be able to cross, but there's thick woods in the valley, and we could go either right or left along the bank. The walking's easy, with lots of cover."

"So they'll assume we went that way?" Danyal was trying to think, remembering how easily their camp had been discovered late on the night when he had met Foryth Teel.

Emilo nodded in response to the question. "Upstream, there's still woods, but we'll find groves of evergreens, like this one, or aspens, with lots of meadows in between. Also, there's a few cliffs where the stream turns to a waterfall."

"I remember." In fact, Danyal had spent the hour of sunset looking over this same valley, though from the road high on the ridge, the terrain along the streambed had looked much less daunting than it did from here. Still, he didn't think any of the cliffs would prove unclimbable.

"We should go upstream," Danyal urged. "I don't think they'll try to look for us that way, and the route down the valley is too easy, too obvious."

"I agree," Emilo said, quelling any objections Foryth Teel might have raised.

Surprisingly, the historian also nodded in agreement. "Loreloch is somewhere up in these mountains, so I certainly don't want to waste a lot of time marching back down to the lowlands."

Danyal looked at the historian in amazement. "You *still* want to go to Loreloch?"

"My dear boy, a slight setback should never be allowed to deter the diligent research of the hard-working historian."

"Setback? You were *captured!* For Gilean's sake, he held you for *ransom!*"

"Tsk—and that provided me with a perfect opportunity to conduct my interviews. An opportunity which, through no fault of my own, has been indefinitely postponed. Now, am I correct in assuming that we should be on our way?"

"Quite right," the kender declared with a curt nod.

Emilo led the way, with Mirabeth at his side and Foryth stumbling through the darkness behind. Shaking his head at the historian's single-minded obstinacy, Danyal brought up the rear.

They tried to climb in silence, but the terrain was rough, and overhanging pines, as well as sharp crags of rock, cast much of the footing into deep shadow. As a result, they frequently stumbled over unseen obstacles, tumbled loose stones into the river, and generally made enough noise, Danyal thought, to rouse the dead from their graves.

Fortunately they encountered no sign of the bandits. Emilo postulated, reasonably enough, that the men would have backtracked along the road for quite a distance, assuming that in the darkness the escaped captives would not have dared to venture on the steep slopes above and below the rutted track.

Danyal had no difficulty keeping up, even over the rough ground. In fact, he found himself anxious to continue when Foryth and Emilo paused to catch their breath. They had progressed no more than a mile, and the youth was vividly aware of the dawn that must eventually illuminate the skyline and reveal the muddy slide that had been their escape route.

"I'll have a look ahead," he said, passing the historian and the kender, who had taken seats on flat rocks near the bank of the stream.

"I'll come with you," Mirabeth said.

"We'll be along in a minute," Emilo promised, while Foryth nodded weakly in agreement.

The kendermaid seemed unaffected by fatigue as she climbed along with Danyal. They picked their way between large rocks, seizing roots and branches to pull themselves upward. In one place, the human youth had to leap to catch a handhold. Scrambling up the steep face of a boulder, he saw that the distance was too great for Mirabeth.

Danyal stretched himself flat on top of the rock and reached down the face.

"Here—take my hand," he whispered, projecting just enough to be heard over the musical splashing of the nearby stream.

She jumped and caught his grip, her weight surprising as she was suspended momentarily by his clutching fingers. Quickly her feet, in their soft moccasins, found solid purchase and she scrambled up to join him atop the rock.

"Do you think we should wait for them?" Danyal asked, fearing that Foryth and Emilo would have difficulty over this portion of the route.

"Yes," Mirabeth replied softly. Her eyes were wide, almost luminous in the darkness, and—as when he had first seen her beside the horse—Danyal was struck again by her resemblance to a human girl.

"Were you traveling with Emilo the other day when I saw you beside the stream near Waterton?" he asked.

"We were following the road," she said with a nod. "And I saw the orchard and wanted to get some apples. Emilo was tired—he gets that way a lot—so he took a nap while I came down to the trees. I wasn't expecting to see you or your horse."

"She wasn't *my* horse," Danyal objected. "At least, not until you haltered her for me."

He cleared his throat and shook his head against a wave of melancholy, suddenly feeling a strong pang of sadness, missing the mean-tempered mare with more feeling than he would ever have imagined.

"Where is she—the horse, I mean? Did those men get her?" Mirabeth's smooth brow furrowed in concern, and suddenly the lines of her age were heightened, revealed like clear shadows in the starlight.

Danyal's chuckle was rueful but fond. "Actually, it was Nightmare that got some of them." His laughter died quickly at the memory of poor Gnar, crippled by the kick of the horse and then executed by his companions, who found his presence an inconvenience. He wondered about Nightmare, hoping the horse was all right.

Movement stirred below as Foryth and Emilo came into sight. Danyal helped them both up over the steep boulder, then resumed his place at the rear of the little party as they continued upstream along the course of the plunging, splashing brook.

Soon the steepness mellowed into a grassy valley, where the ground proved soft and marshy underfoot. Moving to the side, they hastened along a low ridge where the terrain was still open, though large clumps of gray-black rock jutted from the carpet of grass and flowers. The stream was a shimmering ribbon of silver, visible as it meandered back and forth through the flat, low ground.

Finally the valley walls closed in again, and the course of the waterway returned to its steep and rocky dimensions. More trees grew here. Conscious of approaching dawn, Danyal was relieved to have some semblance of cover overhead. They found a trail that, while narrow and winding, was clear of the obstacles that had tripped them up all night.

Padding through the dark woods, Danyal strained to see Foryth Teel's tan robe, following the blur of color as they moved more quickly than they had been able to before.

A gasp of alarm accompanied Foryth's skidding to a halt, and Danyal bumped into the historian roughly.

"What is it?" asked the lad, pushing for a view around the historian's side.

Foryth pointed mutely to the ground before them, where one figure writhed on the ground and another, recognizable by her twin ponytails as Mirabeth, knelt nearby and cooed soothing sounds.

"Emilo!" cried Danyal, in his alarm forgetting to hold his voice to a whisper He, too, knelt beside the kender, seeing that their rescuer was rolling from side to side, back arched, eyes wide and staring.

"What's wrong?" Foryth whispered, clutching Danyal's shoulder.

"I don't know."

Even as he spoke his quiet answer, the youth was remembering a man from his village, Starn Whistler, who had been subjected to spells like this—"seizures," the villagers had called them. Danyal had been frightened when he witnessed one of the attacks as a young boy, but his neighbors had been nonchalant. Soon he had learned that, though Starn looked as though he was locked in the greatest agony, the man would awaken slowly from the seizure without lasting harm. Within an hour, he would have returned to normal.

The symptoms had seemed very much the same as this violent spell, which now caused the kender to make choking sounds, bringing his voice gurgling inarticulately from the depths of his throat. Danyal felt helpless as he watched Mirabeth stroke Emilo's forehead, then lean down to whisper soothingly into the afflicted kender's ear.

"Can I help?" Danyal knelt beside the kendermaid, who didn't raise her eyes from the struggling figure of Emilo.

"I don't think so," she whispered. "This happens to him a lot, and the only thing to do is let it pass and to try and keep him safe until then."

Finally the kender drew a deep, ragged gulp of air, then collapsed limply. His breathing slowed, settling into a normal cadence of sleep. When Danyal felt Emilo's forehead, however, his hand came away wet with sweat. The long brown topknot was matted across the kender's cheeks, and every so often his body would shiver under the assault of violent trembling.

"He'll need to rest for a short time," Mirabeth said. "He'll be confused when he wakes up, but I think we'll be able to start walking again."

"I wonder if we should just camp right around here," suggested the human lad, realizing that they were well concealed by the cloaking evergreens. Even as he asked the question, however, he wished they could have put more distance between themselves and the scene of their escape.

"We should go farther if we can," the kendermaid said.

A few minutes later Emilo groaned and his eyelids fluttered. Finally they opened and he looked around, his gaze flicking from Mirabeth to Danyal.

"Who—who are you?" the kender asked.

"I'm Mirabeth, and this is Danyal. The man over there is Foryth. We're all your friends."

Dan was amazed at the obvious answer, but as he watched, he saw that Emilo really seemed to be absorbing the information. These were things that he really couldn't recall!

"And me . . . who am *I*?"

"You're Emilo Haversack, a kender," Mirabeth said frankly. "From one of the oldest, most honorable of the kender clans."

"What—what happened? Where are we?" Emilo strained to lift himself from the ground, and the pair assisted him into a sitting position.

"We're in a stream valley in the Kharolis Mountains," Danyal said. "You had a spell. We're waiting for you to get better."

"I had a spell?" The kender regarded the youth with confusion.

With a serious nod, Danyal replied, "Yes, but you're going to be all right."

"Thanks . . . I . . ." Abruptly the kender's eyes rolled back in his head, and with a strangled gasp, he fell backward to collapse upon the ground.

Chapter 29

A Strange Malady

First Misham, Reapember
374 AC

"It got him again!" Danyal cried, patting Emilo's cheek, trying to draw some response from the stiff, motionless kender.

Once again Mirabeth knelt beside the afflicted fellow, talking to him soothingly. They heard him gasp some strangled, inarticulate sounds, though Dan thought he heard the word "skull" in the midst of the ravings, and finally he drew a deep breath and lapsed into a more relaxed, normal-seeming slumber.

Some time later the kender stirred, then sat up, looking around with a dazed expression.

"Can you walk?" Danyal asked, shivering at the dull

look he detected in Emilo's eyes.

"Walk . . . yes . . . yes, I can walk." The kender's voice seemed to gain strength from the positive response.

"Good." Dan turned to Mirabeth. "Do you want to lead the way? I'll help Emilo."

"I think I should stay beside him," she said quietly. "Why don't you see if you can find us a path?"

Foryth brought up the rear as the lad started through the woods, trying to keep his feet on the smooth, winding trail that he could barely see. He felt a glimmer of fear, a moment of melancholy and longing for the secure bed in the loft of his parents' house. But then he banished the memory, knowing he would never be able to go back there. Trying to stare through the darkness, he concentrated on looking for a good path up the rough valley floor.

Moving at a fast walk, he gradually realized that he could, in fact, discern the path better than before. Looking upward, he saw a patch of the eastern sky between two conical evergreens; the rosy tint of dawn was already reaching toward the zenith.

Still making good time, Danyal focused his attentions on locating a good place for them to hide during the day. The copse of woods they traversed ended soon, and the small party broke into a jog as they crossed a meadow of tall grass and drooping, dew-laden flowers. The stream was out of sight to the left, running through a channel that was slightly deeper than ground level. Soon the enclosing arms of the pines were around them again as they entered a much larger grove.

"It looks like this woods goes some way up the side valley," Danyal noted as the four travelers paused to catch their breath. "Maybe we should get off this trail and try to hide ourselves up there, at least until dark."

"Are we running from something?" Emilo asked. His eyes no longer lacked focus, but he asked the question with obvious sincerity.

"Some men—evil men. I'll tell you all about it when we find shelter," Mirabeth said. "Until then you'll just have to trust us."

"I do," the kender agreed, chewing on the trailing end of his topknot. "But why don't I remember anything? Even my name?"

"I told you, you're Emilo Haversack," the kendermaid declared sternly. "And you're our friend, and you'll just have to be satisfied with that for now."

Silently accepting, Emilo mouthed the clearly unfamiliar sounds of his name several times. Danyal, meanwhile, ducked under the low branches of an evergreen and found a small clearing giving passage through the woods.

"Go on ahead," he told Mirabeth as she followed with Emilo and Foryth. "I'll brush our tracks off the trail to cover our route if we're followed."

"Good idea!" the historian agreed, absently grinding his heel into the ground as he tried to adjust his bootlace. "Would you like me to help?"

"Um, no," the lad demurred. Foryth followed the two kender while Danyal followed their backtrail to the edge of the meadow. The grass was trampled flat and would undoubtedly mark their passing for some hours to come, so he decided to concentrate on masking their route through the woods.

In several places, he could see footprints, mostly from the historian, in the soft loam of the needle-covered ground. He brushed these with a branch, starting to back carefully along the route they had taken.

Abruptly he was taken with an idea. He stepped into the meadow at the end of the trail the companions had made. Moving at a right angle to their path, he took low, sweeping steps toward the bank of the stream. Trampling the grass, he stepped firmly, holding his feet in place to leave clear marks.

When he reached the edge of the water, he saw that the banks of the streambed were slightly taller than his own height. A short distance below, the water babbled cheerfully along a flat, graveled bed, the flowage no more than a foot or two deep. At the lip of the tall bank,

Danyal skidded downward, intentionally leaving a gouge in the dirt and a footprint at the very edge of the water. Next he rinsed his feet free of mud, then climbed across several boulders until he reached the fringe of the wood. Seizing a root of pine, he pulled himself into the shelter of the trees. Here he stepped lightly as he returned to the original backtrail and continued to sweep away their tracks until he reached the place where the trio had turned toward the deep woods.

Danyal took care to obliterate every sign of their passage, feeling a strange thrill at the thought that he was deceiving Kelryn Darewind, Zack, and the other bandits. Of course, a stern and practical part of him was afraid that they might be followed, but another part was able to take grim pleasure in the knowledge that his careful masking would be certain to thwart the bandit chief and his villainous group of thugs.

After he had concealed a hundred paces or more of the connecting trail, Danyal tossed his broom-branch aside and jogged after his companions, following footsteps that were barely visible in the smooth forest floor.

However, he would have gone right past the clump of brambly wild rose that clustered at the base of a low rock promontory, except for the fact that the bush seemed to call out to him as he went by.

"Sssst! Dan—this way."

He stopped and stared, finally perceiving the outlines of a dark opening at the base of the rocky knoll. Gingerly he stepped around the prickly bushes, avoiding the thorns while at the same time taking care not to leave any sign of his passage.

Foryth, Mirabeth, and Emilo were huddled within a small alcove in the rock. The place was too tiny to be called a cave, but it was spacious enough to hold them all as long as nobody wanted to lie down, and, more importantly, it was well concealed from the woods beyond.

"You're Danyal, they told me," Emilo said as soon as the youth made himself comfortable in the small enclosure. "Pleased to make your acquaintance . . . again."

"Um, me, too." It was strange, this loss of memory, but the lad was glad to see that Emilo seemed to have regained his vitality. Dan wanted to ask questions: Why, for example, had Emilo taken it into his head to rescue them? But he doubted that the kender would know the answers, at least not now, and he didn't want to upset him further by posing queries that would only highlight the unfortunate fellow's loss of memory.

In any event, it seemed to be the kender who was determined to ask questions.

"Foryth said you were traveling into the mountains by yourself, and then Mirabeth told me that your village was burned by a dragon. I'm sorry."

"Don't be. It wasn't your fault," Danyal declared curtly, even as he was surprised by his own snide reaction. Still, one thing he knew was that he didn't want sympathy. He laughed bitterly as he remembered his plans in that long ago time—was it just four days ago?—when his world had died.

"I was on my way to kill that dragon," he admitted, sheepish over his earlier brusque attitude. "I guess I never gave any thought about how I was going to do it. All I had was a fishing pole and a little knife, and I don't even have those anymore!" Again he laughed, trying to sound harsh, sensing that he had wandered dangerously close to the brink of tears.

"And what about you?" Emilo, to Danyal's relief, had turned to Foryth. "Do your studies often bring you this far away from the temple library?"

"Er, no." Foryth cleared his throat, then repeated the mannerism, and Danyal sensed that he was reluctant to talk, a reluctance that made the lad all that much more curious about the historian's tale.

"Actually, I have been given a chance—sort of a last chance, to tell the truth—to be ordained into the priesthood of Gilean."

"This is some kind of a test?" Danyal guessed. "Getting to Loreloch?"

"Not that, specifically. You see, I have studied the

priestly doctrines for many years, but I have never been able to master the casting of a spell. I pray to Gilean with utmost sincerity, asking for guidance, for a hint of power. But there is nothing there."

"And if you don't cast this spell . . . ?" probed the youth.

"Then I shall never become a priest. My life's objective, all the fruits of my labors, the volumes of my writing, shall have been for naught."

"I don't think so!" objected Danyal. "You told me that story about Fistandantilus. It was good. You don't have to cast a spell in order to make the words you write on paper, the histories you tell, mean something. To make them be important, I mean."

"But the most highly regarded historians of Krynn have been priests of Gilean," moaned Foryth. "And all I need is *one* spell, a single, simple enchantment that would prove my faith. Then I could join their numbers!"

"I wouldn't count on a priest of the Seekers giving you one," Danyal muttered sourly. "And I can't believe you still want to go to Loreloch!"

"It's more important now than ever. I simply must see the writings, the records of Kelryn Darewind. How did the archmage become a god? Where does he reside? And are there other facets to his faith, sects in different parts of Krynn? These questions *must* be answered."

The historian drew a deep breath, continuing firmly. "There are very few things about Fistandantilus that have escaped the light of the historian's torch. But the details of his passing, at the time of Skullcap's creation and beyond, have always called for further investigation. And now it seems there was real import there, occurrences that we never suspected!"

"And you're going to study those things but remain aloof, uninvolved?" Dan asked, remembering the historian's concern over his intervention that had kept the lad alive.

"Er . . . yes, of course. That is, I have to be. Tsk." Foryth shook his head, flustered. "My efforts would be doomed to failure if I should let myself become attached to individuals or, worse yet, attempt to play a role myself."

"But how does all this study and research help you learn a spell?" Mirabeth voiced the same question that Danyal had been wondering about. "My father said— that is, I heard somewhere that priests pray for their spells, get them from their god." She halted, flustered, though only Danyal seemed to notice the kendermaid's distress.

"Well, I guess it doesn't, to tell the absolute truth," Foryth admitted with slumping shoulders. But then he raised his head, and his narrow chin jutted forward in an approximation of determination. "But I don't know where to find a spell, so I thought it made sense to do something useful while I was looking."

"You can't argue with that," Emilo agreed with an amiable chuckle.

Despite his willingness to do just that, Danyal was forced to concede that the kender was right—Foryth's decision made as much sense as anything else. "Good luck, then," said the lad. "I hope you find that magic."

"You know, in a way I envy you kender," Foryth said, leaning his head against the cave wall and shifting his eyes from Mirabeth to Emilo. "Your folk are, in many ways, the favorites of Gilean. True neutrals, that's the kender. Nary a care in the world as you go wherever your mood and your interests take you."

"I don't know about that," Emilo said seriously. He chewed thoughtfully on the tail of his topknot. "Of course, right now I don't known much about anything. But it seems to me that we have cares just like humans. And that business about being truly neutral . . . I'd like to think we know the difference between good and evil.

"And that we practice a little more of the former," the kender added with a soft laugh. He lapsed into silence, and for a time, the four companions just rested. They shared cool water from Mirabeth's canteen, and finally Danyal decided he would bring up some of the things that had been bothering him.

"About these . . . seizures," he said to Emilo. "Have you had them all your life?"

"Well, yes, I think so. Actually," the kender admitted, chewing on his topknot, "I'm not sure. You see, I don't remember my childhood or my early life. So I've had these attacks ever since I can recall."

"What's the first thing you remember? Where were you, and how long ago was it?"

"Well, those are good questions. I remember that I was in Dergoth, on the plains around Skullcap. I met some elves there, and they fed me and gave me water. From what they told me, I was about ready to die there in the desert."

"When did that happen?" Foryth asked, warming to the questions with the interest of the true historian. "Did they tell you the year?"

"As a matter of fact, they did. It was two hundred and fifty something, as I recall."

"That's more than a hundred years ago," Danyal said with a whistle. "I didn't think kender lived to be that old—not that you look old, that is. But that's part of it, isn't it? You don't look that old."

"More than a hundred years?" Emilo looked puzzled. "I could have sworn that it was just last winter, or maybe a little before that. But not a hundred years!"

"What do you remember of where you were, what you were doing, last winter?" Foryth took over the interview. "Were you and Mirabeth traveling together then?"

"Well . . ." Suddenly Emilo looked frightened. He cast a worried glance at the kendermaid and asked, "I didn't know you then, did I?"

"No," she said.

"But—but why can't I remember? When did I meet you? How long ago?"

"It was just a few days ago, actually," Mirabeth said. She turned her head, including the two humans in her explanation. "I was wandering on my own—that is, I'd been by myself for a little while. I was having some

211

trouble, I guess you could say, and Emilo came along and helped me out."

"Did he rescue you from bandits, too?" Danyal asked, only half teasing.

"No," she replied with a soft laugh. The lad decided that he liked that sound a lot. "I was trying to camp, but my lean-to had fallen over and my bedroll was soaked with rain. I couldn't get a fire going, and I was sitting in the woods, teeth chattering, feeling sorry for myself. He almost scared me out of my skin when he walked up and said—"

"Emilo Haversack, at your service?" guessed Danyal.

Mirabeth grinned at him. "The same thing he said to you, I presume."

"And he *was*—at our service, I mean. Really, you saved our lives," declared the young human. "I guess I haven't told you that, but you did."

"Oh, now, tsk," interjected Foryth Teel. "I admit that business of being tied up was unpleasant, but I hardly think Kelryn was going to do us in."

"Then you weren't paying attention! Do you remember Zack—the way he liked to play with his knife?" Danyal shuddered at the memory. "He wasn't ever going to let us get away, despite what Kelryn said."

Still, he admitted privately, it was Kelryn Darewind himself who was the scariest of all the bandits.

"You mentioned that wizard, Fistandantilus," Emilo said, drawing the historian's attention away from Dan. "It seems to me I've heard a lot about him. I just can't remember any of it."

"There's a lot to know," declared Foryth enthusiastically. "He was the Master of Past and Present, you know. The first wizard—and one of only a very small number—who learned how to travel through time. An archmage who manipulated history by altering his own position in the River of Time. He had an influence on ages of elves and men, in an era before the Cataclysm—"

"And in Skullcap and Dergoth afterward," noted the kender, bobbing his head.

"He must have been awfully old. Was he human, or perhaps an elf?" asked Danyal.

"Oh, absolutely human—in a way, human many times over," Foryth said with a grim chuckle. "You see, he absorbed the spiritual essence of other humans, for the most part young men who were gifted with magic. These sacrificial lambs were destroyed, and the power of the archmage was maintained and increased with the passing of years. Eventually he had consumed the essence of many men, and his power had become greater than any other mage's in the history of Krynn."

"How?" The lad had a hard time imagining the magical power, the bizarre consumption, that the historian described.

"It's said that he used a gem—a bloodstone. That's one of the things I wondered about, but Kelryn Darewind wouldn't discuss it."

"I saw a bloodstone once," Emilo said.

Danyal looked at the kender and gasped in shock. Emilo's eyes had gone blank and lifeless, devoid of expression or awareness. His jaw hung slack and he sighed sorrowfully, shoulders slumping as if the air had all gone out of him.

"A bloodstone?" Foryth was apparently unaware of the kender's sudden alteration, for he pressed forward with obvious excitement. "They're very rare, you know! Where was it? Could it have been—"

"It pulsed . . . hot, hot blood. . . ." Emilo spoke sharply, visibly straining to push out the words. His lips stretched taut over his teeth, and he grimaced between each quick, bursting phrase. The voice was deep and rasping, very unlike the high-pitched chatter of the kender's normal speech.

"Yes, I remember the stone. And then the portal was there, colors . . . whirling. I sensed the magic. It pulled me, drew me in!" Eyes wild, Emilo backed against the rock wall, recoiling from the three companions who watched, aghast. "And then *she* was there, laughing, waiting for me!"

The kender's sudden scream of terror reverberated through the enclosed space of the cave, and Danyal instantly pictured the sound resonating through the woods and valley far beyond their hiding place.

Emilo drew another breath, but by then the youth was on him, pressing him down, a sturdy hand pressed over the kender's mouth. Only when he felt the thin, wiry body relax underneath him did Danyal release his hold, rocking back on his haunches as he tried to offer his frightened companion a reassuring smile.

Mirabeth was kneeling at Emilo's side, and she took his hand and cradled his head against her shoulder. The kender's eyes were blank again, but this time Danyal was almost relieved by the lack of expression; it was certainly preferable to the awful, haunting terror that swept over Emilo Haversack's features a few moments before.

The sun was high in the sky when at last they relaxed. After sipping another drink of water, Danyal was relieved to lean his head on a mossy log and allow himself to fall asleep.

Chapter 30

A Telling Ear

First Bakukal, Reapember
374 AC

Danyal awakened with a strong feeling that it was late afternoon. The air beyond the rocky niche was still, and he heard cicadas chirping, the steady droning of plump, lazy flies. It was Reapember, he recalled, though the temperature—and the hot, stuffy smell of the air—seemed more suggestive of midsummer than early fall.

He saw that Mirabeth, too, was awake. Her brown eyes were staring at him as he stretched and slowly brought himself back to full awareness of their surroundings. Foryth and Emilo still slept, leaning together against the opposite wall of their little niche in the rock wall.

215

"I've been thinking we should go out and have a look around . . . before dark, I mean," the kendermaid whispered.

Danyal nodded; her suggestion was the same thing that he himself had decided. As quietly as possible they slipped between the cliff and the thornbush, crouching as they looked into the woods to the right and left.

The scent of lush pine was pure and overwhelming, seeming to deny the existence of anything dangerous. But Danyal wasn't in any mood to take chances. Still moving with care, he crept forward, under the branches of a thick pine. Fortunately underbrush was scarce and the going was relatively easy. The forest floor was a mat of brown needles broken from numerous branches. Some of the trees, like the one he currently used for shelter, were massive, while others were mere saplings.

He had the feeling that any one of them could have concealed a dangerous enemy.

Mirabeth crept forward to join him, and for several minutes they lay on their bellies, silent and intent, watching the woods for anything out of the ordinary. Abruptly the kendermaid nudged Danyal, almost causing him to gasp in alarm until he saw that she was smiling.

Following her pointing finger, he saw a doe and a fawn grazing a mere stone's throw away.

The two watchers kept completely still, scarcely breathing, as the pair of deer pulled at the tufts of grass that, in places, poked through the carpet of dried pine needles. Shadows dappled the rich brown coat of the doe, while the speckles on the fawn's back and flanks seemed to sparkle like diamonds as the creature cavorted through patches of sunlight. Alternately tense and playful, the young deer moved around its mother with upraised ears and stiltlike, unsteady legs.

For long minutes the animals moved slowly across Dan's and Mirabeth's fields of vision, and the lad took heart from the knowledge that the shy creatures would certainly have taken flight if any threat was lurking nearby. Finally the deer wandered away, lost behind the screening trunks of the woods, and the two wanderers rose to their feet.

"I tried to mask our path through the meadow beyond these woods," Danyal explained. "Let's take a look and make sure we don't have anyone on our trail."

Mirabeth nodded and moved away with lithe grace. With a flash of guilt, Danyal watched her from behind, thinking she was very pretty. She moves like a girl, he realized—a *human* girl—though she could have been sixty or seventy years old, for all he knew.

When she turned to see if he was following, he blushed furiously, even more so when he saw her shy smile and suspected that she knew he had been watching her. Lowering his eyes, he concentrated on following through the woods without making a lot of noise.

Taking a circuitous route away from their shelter, Dan and Mirabeth dropped into a rock-bedded ravine. The gully scored a straight path through the woods, angling generally toward the large meadow where the lad had created the false trail. Following the natural trench for several minutes, they finally saw the brightness of full daylight through the trees. It was easy to scramble out of the ravine, using roots and vines for handholds. At the top, they wriggled forward until they were concealed beneath a pine tree at the very edge of the forest.

"There!" Mirabeth's warning was a barely audible breath of air.

Danyal saw them at the same time: six scruffy figures, moving through the meadow along the trail that the four companions had left the previous night.

"I wonder where the others are." Again Mirabeth spoke in a hushed voice.

Indeed, though the men were too far away to see their faces, Danyal knew that two of the bandits were missing from this group. From the matted hair and beards that he saw, he guessed that one of those absent was Kelryn Darewind.

"They're coming up to the place where I hid the trail," he whispered, his stomach churning into his throat as the men reached the edge of the woods. Only when they turned toward the stream did he allow himself to relax, realizing as he exhaled that he was trembling.

"It worked," he breathed, his sense of elation sublime, but tempered by knowledge of the nearness of danger. "They're following the false path I made!"

He heard shouts in tones of disgust as the bandits came to the edge of the water, though he couldn't hear exactly what they were saying.

"It sounds like they've been that way before," Mirabeth deduced. "Looks like they've been double-checking the trail—and that's where they lost it."

Dan realized she was right. "They must have back-tracked once they lost the trail in the stream." But how persistent would they be in looking for the concealed trail? Would they keep searching? And where were the other two men?

Several of the bandits were engaged in a heated argument, pointing both upstream and down, while another of the fellows seemed ready to start back to the woods.

"We've got to get back to the cave and wake Foryth and Emilo if they're still sleeping," Dan urged. "It's time to get out of here!"

Moving as quickly as they dared while still preserving some semblance of silence, the two backtracked to the ravine. They leapt down to land on a patch of smooth moss and then broke into a full sprint, following the gully toward its terminus near their makeshift shelter.

"This is where we climbed in," Danyal said, pointing to the shelf of rock that rose as the left wall of the ravine. "It didn't seem so high when we jumped down."

"We can climb it," Mirabeth assured him. "There's plenty of handholds."

Danyal agreed.

"Don't start coming up until I'm all the way to the top. You shouldn't be beneath me, in case I slip!" the kender-maid called over her shoulder.

She kicked her foot into a crack in the stone wall and reached upward to find a pair of handholds. Pulling herself off the ground, she ascended smoothly and soon neared the top of the rocky face.

Watching nervously, Danyal saw her foot slip momentarily from its perch. He tensed, ready to catch her, trying to anticipate how she would fall, but the nimble maid maintained her balance easily. In another moment she disappeared over the rim of the top.

A split second later Mirabeth's scream of shrill terror split the woods, sending birds cawing into the air and filling Danyal with unspeakable panic.

"What is it?" Frantically the lad threw himself at the rock wall, scrambling up a short distance and then, slipping in his haste, tumbling back to sprawl on the ravine floor. He looked up and felt the hope drain from his body.

Kelryn Darewind stood there, and in his arms, he held the squirming figure of Mirabeth. His hand was clasped over her mouth as she stared, wide-eyed with terror, at Danyal Thwait.

"Well, there you are, my young friend." The bandit lord was cool, even dispassionate, and that aloofness brought Dan's hatred burning through every other emotion. But he could only stare in impotent fury as Kelryn continued. "It seems you must have wandered off in the night. It's really quite a relief to find you again."

Trembling, Danyal stared bitterly upward, knowing that even if he clawed his way up the cliff, it would be a simple matter for the bandit lord to kick him loose when he neared the top.

"I think I'll take this little prize with me to Loreloch!" taunted Kelryn Darewind.

Only then did another figure saunter into view, as Zack joined his captain. The knifeman fixed Danyal with a cackling glare, his one eye flashing wickedly.

"Run!" screamed Mirabeth, suddenly twisting her mouth free from Kelryn's hand. "He's going to kill you!"

Danyal couldn't make his feet move. He cried aloud as the false priest clapped a rough hand over the kendermaid's mouth. Only when Kelryn nodded forcefully at

Zack did the youth perceive the imminent threat and break into flight.

He heard the clump of something heavy landing on the ground behind him and didn't need to look back to know that Zack had leapt into the ravine. The bandit's thudding footsteps were loud and clumsy as he pounded after Dan, and the boy couldn't suppress a sob of terror as he felt that menacing presence closing in. He sprinted as fast as he could, dashing around corners in the winding ravine, desperately seeking some place that might let him scramble upward to safety.

And knowing that he left Mirabeth in Kelryn Darewind's merciless hands somewhere far behind him.

Zack uttered a bark of cruel laughter, and Dan knew from the sound that the man was only a few steps behind. Eyes blurring, the lad thought of Mirabeth, horrified at the prospect of her captivity among the merciless bandits. Strangely, that fear seemed much more real and more terrifying than the prospect of his own imminent death. He fought back another sob, his grief rising from the fact that he was so utterly unable to come to Mirabeth's aid.

When he attempted to leap over a rock that blocked the ravine bottom, Danyal's strength and agility came up a fraction of an inch short. His foot caught at the top of the boulder, and he tumbled headlong, landing heavily on a patch of sand. He rolled hard into the steep wall of the gully and looked up to see Zack's villainous face leering down at him.

"Well, laddie—looks like I get to wet my blade again after all!"

Danyal clawed to either side, trying to find a rock or a stick, anything he could use as a weapon. But his hands couldn't do more than scratch at the smooth, hard-packed sand.

Zack threw back his head and laughed—the last sound he ever made. A heavy piece of granite, jagged with a multitude of sharp edges, plummeted from above, striking the knife-wielding bandit in the middle of the forehead. Zack's head snapped back like a cracking whip, and he toppled like a stone statue. Danyal vaguely heard the thump as the man's head smashed onto the rocky ground.

Only then did he look up, squinting against the sky to see Foryth Teel leaning over the lip of the ravine. The historian dusted off his hands and shook his head in agitation, clearly distressed.

"Did you throw that?" Danyal asked, looking once more at the piece of granite that had smashed Zack's skull.

"I'm afraid—tsk, that is, yes, I did," Foryth admitted sadly. He sighed, as if he had just committed a grave act of injustice. "I just don't seem to be able to keep from getting myself involved. Er, is he dead?"

Danyal stepped over to Zack's still form, hesitantly taking a moment to look closely at the expressionless face, the blank and sightless eyes. Finally he nudged the bandit's knee with his toe, drawing no response.

"Yes, he is." He was about to turn away when he saw the big knife, the keen edge shining like quicksilver in the sunlight. The weapon lay in the stones where Zack had dropped it, and Danyal impulsively reached down and picked it up. The hilt was smooth and comfortable in his hand, and the blade was well balanced and clearly lethal.

At the thought of killing, an urgent thought grabbed him. "What about Mirabeth?" he shouted. "We've got to help her!"

"I'll meet you up ahead!" Foryth called back.

Danyal was already racing back along the ravine floor. When he reached the spot where the kendermaid had ascended, he stuffed the knife into his belt and climbed as quickly as he could, drawing himself onto the rim of the precipice as Foryth came huffing up to him.

"They went that way," the historian said, pointing into the woods.

Danyal was about to start along the trail when he caught sight of something unnatural on the forest floor.

It was a wedge of tan wax, and when he picked it up he clearly saw the resemblance.

"It's the tip of a false ear—a pointed ear!" he exclaimed, his mind churning.

"Do you think—that is, could Mirabeth have lost it?" Foryth asked.

"Yes!" Picturing the kendermaid with the twin top-knots, the pointed ears, and the webbing of age lines around her mouth and eyes, Danyal's mind whirled with questions. "Why would she wear something like this—a fake tip for her ear?"

The answer was obvious in his own mind, but just in case any doubt remained, Emilo Haversack came into view, trotting from the direction of their cave. He saw the ear, looked into the questioning faces of Foryth and Danyal, and nodded in understanding.

"I remember now," the kender confirmed. "Mirabeth is really a human."

Chapter 31

Pursuing the Pursuers

First Bakukal, Reapember
374 AC

"She *is* a human girl!" Danyal gasped, remembering his impressions of Mirabeth's bouncing walk, the shyness of her smile, and the musical sweetness of her voice.

"Yes—or, rather, a young lady, actually." Emilo's brow was furrowed, and the lad wondered if his companion was trying to recollect other details. But then he realized that the kender's expression was related to his news.

"Her story's like yours, in a way," Emilo told Dan. "She's the only survivor of a catastrophe, a murderous attack that killed everyone in her family, including their servants and guests. Mirabeth was lucky to escape with her life, and she only did so by donning a disguise."

"As a kender? But why?"

"Ahem." Foryth Teel cleared his throat with dignity. "I'm never one to ignore the details of a story, but I wonder if perhaps our discussion should wait for another time. If our attentions now might not be better directed toward pursuit?"

"You're right." Danyal was nearly overwhelmed by a feeling of helplessness, but the tautness in his limbs and the palpitating of his heart were caused by another emotion as well: He felt a burning fury, a rage that he knew could drive him to savagery and violence. When he thought of the way Kelryn Darewind went about calmly, arrogantly, destroying the lives of so many people, he wanted only to kill.

His hatred for the bandit lord roared into an angry flame. The man seemed to represent everything frightening, terrible, and unfair in the world. He was a deadly foe, but unlike the dragon Flayze, he was not invulnerable.

And he had Mirabeth.

"Which way did he take her?" Foryth asked. "I saw him here at the edge of the ravine with Zack, but then I chased after you, Dan. I'm afraid I lost sight of him."

"We saw his men down by the stream. I'm sure he'll take her there." Danyal started along the most direct route to the clearing, plunging between the trees, holding his arms before his face to brush the branches aside. He heard Foryth and Emilo charging behind him and, in a surprisingly short time, saw the open sunlight of the meadow expanding before them.

Instinctively the lad halted and crouched. Joined by his two companions, he squirmed forward to get a look without revealing himself to view.

A shout sounded from the far side of the clearing, and they saw Kelryn Darewind holding the still-squirming figure of Mirabeth in one hand. With the other, he waved, and one by one his men came into view, scrambling up the bank of the low streambed to rejoin their captain at the edge of the woods.

"I count seven of them," Foryth Teel remarked softly. "Plus the young lady, of course."

And then they were gone, vanishing into the woods at a jogging trot that, Danyal knew, he and his companions would be hard pressed to match for any length of time.

But they had to try. He rose to his feet, ready to dash across the meadow and chase the kidnappers through the woods, when he felt a restraining hand on his arm—one on each arm, actually.

"Wait!" Emilo hissed.

"Indeed. Wouldn't you think they've set someone to watch their trail?" Foryth asked, with what seemed like maddeningly casual curiosity to Danyal.

"Why?" snapped the lad. "He's got what he wants. He'll just—"

"Precisely my question," the historian continued. "What *does* he want? If we knew that, we'd know what he plans to do about us, among other things."

"Such as whether or not he wants to lure us into an ambush," Emilo added.

Danyal was infuriated at the thought of some cowardly bandit lurking at the forest's edge, but a cool, quiet part of his mind suggested—in a very soft voice—that his companions were right. He looked across the clearing at the opposite grove, estimating that a hundred paces or more of open ground separated that clump of trees from the wedge of forest where the three of them currently held their council of war.

"We could charge across the clearing together," suggested Danyal impulsively, remembering the big knife he wore at his waist.

"Tsk . . . a nice idea, and appealing to my own sense of bold adventure. But what if there are two, or even three of them?" Foryth demurred.

"Or an archer. It seems to me at least two of the bandits had short bows," Emilo chimed in.

Danyal's frustration welled anew, but again he saw the need for caution. He cast his eyes left, seeing only the sloping and fully exposed incline of the grassy ridge that formed the side of this stream valley; then he looked right, toward the stream that was currently invisible, running within its deep banks.

"The streambed!" he whispered. "Let's stay in the woods until we meet the stream. Then we can follow the channel, hiding below the bank until we get to the other side of the clearing!"

"Splendid idea!" Foryth exclaimed in an enthusiastic whisper.

Emilo was already moving back from the clearing. In moments the three were on their feet, concealed a short distance within the woods as they once more plunged between the trees with all possible haste. Soon they heard the trilling of water before them, and then the stream was there, spilling across its gravel bed some five or six feet below the level of the forest floor. To the left, they could see the waterway cutting its deep channel into the ground in the meadow beyond.

Without hesitation, Danyal led the way down the smooth, muddy bank. Emilo and Foryth came behind him, though the historian stumbled at the base of the bank and splashed to his hands and knees into the stream. Still, he rose to his feet with aplomb and hastened to follow.

Kicking through the shallows at the edge of the flowage, Danyal had a strong feeling that he was in a tunnel. The lofty trees closed in above the narrow stream so that no more than a small strip of sky was visible. Compared to the dappled shadows of the waters here, the bright, sunlit expanse of the meadow glowed brighter and brighter before them.

And then they were out of the woods, still following the streambed in its course through the meadow. Though the bank was already higher than his head, Dan leaned forward and down with instinctive caution. The shorter Emilo didn't have to worry, while Foryth, the tallest of the trio, ducked with exaggerated care as he splashed along behind.

Heart pounding, Danyal wondered if the bandits

would have thought to watch the stream as well as the clearing—or even if he and his companions were correct in their suspicion that one or more of the men had stayed behind. The lad couldn't help worrying that they were wrong, that perhaps all the precautions were a waste of time, allowing Mirabeth to be spirited away while the trio of would-be rescuers tried to sneak up on an empty patch of woods.

The branches of the next grove arced before them, and soon they felt the cool shade of the trees around them again. Danyal still led the way, trembling with a tingling awareness of the need for stealth and of the existence of potentially deadly danger.

The human youth found a niche where the stream-bank had yielded to the pressure of a gnarled root and dropped into a deep notch. With two steps, he was up, slipping through the forest with the wicked knife in his hand. He stayed low, trying to be stealthy, using all the techniques of rabbit-stalking that he had learned over his life. Gliding from one tree to another, he kept the meadow to his left and advanced on the place where the bandits had disappeared into the woods.

He was startled by a sudden waft of odor, an acrid stink of sweat and campfire smoke, and he knew beyond any doubt that an enemy was near. With a gut-wrenching jolt of energy, all his doubts disappeared and he was ready, even eager, for danger. Emilo, also moving sound-lessly, joined him behind the trunk of a massive pine while Foryth held back a few paces.

The kender wrinkled his nose, also sensing their enemy ahead. With a finger to his lips, Emilo pointed to himself, and to the right; then he indicated Danyal, and pointed left. The lad nodded, watching his companion draw a dagger almost as long as the weapon Dan had claimed from Zack.

Foryth, meanwhile, had armed himself with a stout stick that was nearly as tall as he was, a club that bulged with a solid knot at one end. He indicated silently that he would come after the two, moving straight ahead.

As Emilo disappeared behind intervening trees, Danyal was startled to realize that his fingers, clenched around the hilt of the knife, were stiff with cramps. He changed hands on the weapon and painfully flexed his reluctant digits. At the same time, he moved forward with extreme care, keeping the blade outthrust and ready.

After a moment, he caught sight of a man—or a man's boots, to be entirely accurate—extending from beneath a tree. Judging by his feet, the bandit was lying on his belly, no doubt looking out over the clearing that extended just beyond his vantage. There was no visible reaction from the lookout, who remained apparently unaware of the stealthy trio.

Dan had no more started to congratulate himself on his luck when he considered, for the first time, the realistic prospect of sticking the sharpened piece of steel that he held in his hand into another person's flesh. Practically speaking, the task should be easy. He was still unobserved; he should be able to fling himself forward and fall on the man's back. One quick stab and the fellow would be killed, wouldn't he?

All at once Danyal felt himself weakening, his guts once again churning with a feeling of despair as he wondered if he could, in fact, just murder this man in cold blood. But if he didn't, how were they ever going to rescue Mirabeth?

"Ssst!"

A harsh, clearly audible whisper split the woods, and Danyal all but groaned, certain that one of his companions had given them away. Still, he shrank back into his own concealment, surprised to see that the man under the tree was wriggling backward with no indication of extreme alarm. Finally the bandit rose to his haunches, turning his face away from Danyal as he replied with similar furtiveness.

"Yeah? What is it?"

Only then did Dan see the second bandit, a mustachioed bowmen called Kal. The fellow crept up to his compatriot and gestured into the field. "Any sign of 'em?"

"Nah." The reply was curt and disgusted.

"Me neither. They haven't tried to come along the ridge, or I woulda seen 'em for sure."

"D'you think we should head back to Loreloch, or at least meet Red at the bridge?"

The archer barked a dry laugh. "Boss said to wait until tonight. I'm not thinkin' I'd like to cross him."

"Yeah. Well—"

The snap of a dry twig was like a crack of thunder in Danyal's ears, a sound that overwhelmed everything else. It had come from behind him, near where the lad had last seen Foryth.

"What was that?" The bowman instantly had an arrow nocked, his weapon drawn as he peered into the thick woods. "Go check it out!"

"Me?" The squatting man was at first indignant. Then he looked at the other's weapon as he drew his own short sword, apparently reaching the obvious conclusion: His companion could cover him with an arrow, while his blade would only be useful at close quarters.

Rising to his feet, the swordsman advanced past the other side of the large tree trunk behind which Danyal crouched. Scarcely daring to breathe, the lad peered between the branches, saw the bowman moving closer to gain a clear shot past his companion's shoulder.

"Who's there?" demanded the swordsman, slashing at a few branches in an attempt to open up his view. "Don't make me come in there after you!"

"Tsk."

Suddenly Foryth Teel came into sight, stepping between two trees with his stout stick clenched in his hands. Danyal couldn't see much, but he was aware that the historian was trembling, staring at the bandit with wide eyes.

"Why don't you just drop that little club," suggested the swordsman with a grim chuckle. "Else I'll have to cut yer hands off first."

The historian lunged away with an abrupt movement, drawing a shout of alarm from the sword-wielding bandit.

"Hey!" Steel flashed as the man charged after Foryth, only to fall with a thud, then utter a shriek of pain. Emilo Haversack rolled free, his blade bright crimson as he bounced to his feet.

"Why, you little—" The archer lunged forward, ready to shoot, but he never released his arrow or finished his threat. As he darted past the tree, Danyal charged from his shelter with a yell of rage. He was so close to the bowman that he could smell the stink of his filthy clothes, and without pausing to think, he aimed for the spot where the ragged vest was laced with a few torn strips of leather.

The heavy knife stuck hard in the bandit's chest as the man whirled away, shocked by the sudden attack. His elbow cracked Danyal in the chin, and the lad staggered, feeling his hand slip from the hilt of his only weapon. He tumbled onto his back and waited for the arrow that would pin him to the ground.

But instead, the bowmen dropped his weapon from nerveless fingers. Both hands flailed at his chest, trying unsuccessfully to gain a grip on the weapon that, Danyal now saw, had plunged in very deeply.

A thick paralysis held the lad in place as he watched the man slump, saw the beady eyes grow dim and unfocused. Only when the bandit flopped heavily to the ground did Danyal release his breath, realizing that he was trembling all over and far too weak to stand.

"We make a good team," Emilo said, helping Foryth Teel to his feet from where the historian had fallen in his clumsy attempt at flight.

And then, seeing the handshake between the kender and the man, Danyal realized that it hadn't been clumsiness; it had been a plan! Foryth had acted as a diversion, giving the kender a chance to attack the much larger swordsman by surprise. The lad himself had then taken advantage of a similar chance when the archer had come to the aid of his companion.

"We do," Dan agreed.

He approached the man he had killed, feeling curiously empty. It made him squeamish to pull the knife from the fatal wound, and he gagged, almost vomiting when he saw the amount of blood that came welling from the puncture after the weapon had been removed. But when he turned away, drew a ragged breath, and thought of Mirabeth, he felt calmness returning.

"There's one more, the one named Red, waiting at a bridge," he reported, then added to Foryth, "And they're taking Mirabeth to a place you'll be interested in: Loreloch."

Chapter 32

Loreloch

Second Palast, Reapember
374 AC

The trio found the bandit named Red snoring loudly on the soft bank beside the next bridge. The man didn't stir as Danyal, Emilo, and Foryth Teel approached to within a few feet. When the breeze shifted, the companions caught the scent of brandy and quickly guessed why the heavyset swordsman slumbered so soundly.

"We should just kill him, shouldn't we?" asked Danyal, cursing his own reluctance as he looked at the defenseless man. He told himself that if it had been Zack or Kelryn, he would have had no trouble making a lethal thrust. Whether that was true or not, he couldn't say, but he knew that he could never stick the cruel knife into this drunken man.

"Er . . ." Foryth was also clearly hesitant. "Perhaps we should just ignore him and go on by. He may never even know that we've been past here." The historian pointed along the road that extended beyond the far side of the bridge. "Loreloch is that way, according to my map. Why don't we just move on?"

"Seems risky to leave him here," Emilo suggested. "Though I really don't know about stuff like that. Still, we don't want him coming along behind us."

Danyal was about to argue further when they heard a clatter of stones behind them. Whirling, he saw the shape of a large black horse coming forward at a fast trot.

"Nightmare!" he cried, irrationally delighted by the appearance of the great horse. At the same time, Red stirred with a snort. Sitting up, the man blinked at the plunging animal as the mare swept toward the bridge. The three companions dropped behind the bank on the far side of the road as the bandit staggered to his knees, gaping in astonishment.

"By the gods, it's the demon horse!" Red shouted, lurching to his feet. The horse pounded closer, looming black and large as she thundered toward the bridge. The great hooves smashed on the roadway, and Dan felt each thud reverberate through the ground.

Red spun around, apparently without even noticing the three figures on the other side of the road. With a wide-eyed glance over his shoulder, the man took off running.

Nightmare thundered onto the small bridge, snorting contemptuously at the trio of companions. Danyal scrambled to his feet in a rush and made a lunge for the horse's halter, but before he had taken two steps, the animal sprang into a gallop and bolted away, the sound of the hoofbeats soon fading in the distance.

"Where did she come from?" Dan asked, staring after the horse in frustration. He felt a bleak sense of abandonment, made even more painful by the thought of Mirabeth's captivity. He had no doubt that the lass would have been able to bring the mare to an easy halt.

"Her timing was good." Emilo made the more practical observation.

Foryth Teel was looking at the map in his book again. "And it seems that Red is running away from Loreloch. I don't suppose he'll be in a hurry to go home after abandoning his post."

"And Nightmare's going toward Loreloch. Maybe we'll catch up to her," Dan said, without a lot of hope.

They settled upon the direction, following the vague map in the book that only the historian seemed able to comprehend. With grim determination, the trio of would-be rescuers set out across the mountainside, staying uphill from the rutted mountain road. Alert to danger, they tried to move swiftly without exposing themselves unnecessarily to observation.

Now the three of them actually presented a rough approximation of a fierce and dangerous band. Danyal still had the big knife, and he had taken the short bow and a quiver of arrows from the man he had stabbed. He had been no slouch at shooting rabbits in the woods around Waterton, and he felt quite certain that he could deliver an arrow with accuracy at a far more dangerous target.

Foryth Teel had claimed the short sword from the bandit who no longer had need of such practical tools. Slinging the weapon at his waist, he had at first tripped over the scabbard frequently. By the second day, however, he had at least learned to walk with the blade handy, and he could draw it in a maneuver that was terribly impressive to look at, even if it might have been of questionable use in an actual fight.

They kept to the rocky ridges above the roadway instead of taking the smooth but easily observed track. Twice they camped on windswept slopes, not daring to build a fire that would have left them vulnerable to discovery.

At the first of these camps, Emilo shared the rest of Mirabeth's story—at least, as much of it as she had told the kender and that he could remember.

She had been the daughter of the bold Knight of Solamnia, Sir Harold the White. This was a man who had made peace in this portion of Kharolis his personal business. Eventually he had become too great a thorn in the side of Kelryn Darewind, and the bandit lord had exacted revenge in a brutal and murderous attack against the knight's house.

"I should have guessed it!" Danyal said. "Kelryn Darewind's men were coming back from those murders when we first ran into them!"

After slaughtering her family, Kelryn had made it clear that he was determined to find and kill the lone surviving daughter of the family. She had been found, by Emilo, as she had said: miserable and alone in the wilderness. Knowing the bandits were about, they had seized on the idea of the disguise, and together they had made the wax ear tips. Emilo had helped her to fashion her long hair into the topknots favored by kender, and Mirabeth herself had known enough about makeup to trace the thin age lines around her eyes and mouth.

The knowledge that her life was forfeit if Kelryn should discover the girl's identity was further incentive to their rescue attempt. This awareness caused Danyal to toss and turn miserably through each interminable night, terrified that Mirabeth's disguise would be penetrated by the shrewd villain. He could only hope that she had been able to use her hair or some other means to disguise the real shape of her ear.

On the second night of their pursuit, Emilo suffered from another attack, a seizure like the one that had claimed him on the night of their rescue on the road. Dan and Foryth tried to keep the kender comfortable as he thrashed on the ground and finally went rigid. Again he had awakened with little memory of their surroundings, though during the course of this last day, Emilo's awareness had slowly returned.

Finally their cautious approach brought them into sight of their goal.

The manor house rose like a small peak from the crest of what was, in fact, a full-sized mountain. A single tower of stone thrust high above the walls, and several peaked roofs were visible over the ramparts. Still, most of the structure was lost behind the steep barriers that enclosed the major portion of the mountaintop, giving the place the look of a small but formidable castle.

Danyal and his two companions looked up at the place from a neighboring ridge, and they immediately started to look for the best way to approach the place.

Only as they were discarding options and proposing others did the lad realize that a week earlier he would have been filled with despair at the prospect of approaching—not to mention entering!—such a fortress. Yet now the challenge simply reinforced his sense of grim determination, fanning the embers of hate that now burned steadily just below the surface of his awareness.

"That bridge looks like the only way to get up to the place," Danyal said, pointing to an arched span that crossed a steep-sided gully separating Loreloch's summit from a neighboring elevation.

The manor itself was a surrounded by smooth walls, though many small, rude cottages were clustered on the outside of the compound. Some of these were perched at the very edge of the precipitous slope, while others lined the narrow lane that led from the bridge to the front gates, currently shut, of the imposing edifice.

"Once we're across, we'll have to find some way other than the front gate to get inside there," Emilo noted.

"Maybe they left the scullery door open," Foryth suggested. When Danyal looked skeptical, he added an explanation. "It happened in the monastery all the time, even though the place was supposed to be locked up tight. A cook who's throwing out a full pot of scraps and garbage doesn't like to fuss with a lot of locks and latches."

"I guess that makes sense," Danyal admitted. "It'll be dark in an hour. Why don't we rest here awhile, then move in after sunset?"

The others agreed, and they waited for the seemingly interminable interval as the sun vanished over the horizon and the sky slowly faded toward black. Danyal's suggestion of rest, he realized, was wishful thinking; instead, he studied the mountaintop stronghold, looking for some weakness in what had clearly been designed to act as a small fortress. There were many windows, but they were all high in the stone walls. The only hopeful sign was that there seemed to be no guard posted at the bridge.

By the time full night had descended, Dan hadn't found anything else even remotely hopeful, but neither did he want to delay any longer. The trio started out by descending to the road, then held to the uphill edge of the narrow track, close beside a shallow ditch that just might offer them shelter if they needed to suddenly dive for cover. Still, they all knew their best chance lay in remaining undiscovered, so they concentrated on moving with stealth as well as speed.

It took a surprisingly long time to reach the bridge, and when they did, Danyal saw that the edifice of Loreloch was even larger than it had appeared from across the valley. At least there was still no guard posted at the terminus of the span, nor had anyone bothered to plant any torches or lanterns outside the cluster of hovels and small, enclosed pens that huddled around the stone-walled manor.

Crouching beside one of the low walls flanking the bridge, the three companions moved cautiously onto the narrow, low-walled crossing. Danyal had never been so high above the ground as he was at the middle of the bridge, and he had to suppress a wave of dizziness when he looked over the rampart into the ravine below.

But then they were across, with the first of the rude shacks just a dash away and the bulk of the manor rising beyond. Most of the smaller buildings were dark and silent, though candles flickered in a few windows. Lights flared from many high windows on the manor wall, and sounds of shouting or raucous laughter occasionally wafted through the still air.

"It's almost midnight," Foryth said, after a look at the stars. "I wonder if things will quiet down in a little while."

Danyal didn't want to wait, but he had to admit that the place sounded terribly active right now. This was a stark contrast to his village, which had invariably settled into slumber within an hour of two after sunset. Still, he was about to suggest that they move closer when Emilo spoke in quiet agreement with the historian.

"Let's give it another hour or so. I'd suggest you two go around to the right. Maybe you can find that scullery door. I'll take the other side and see if there's something I can do along the lines of creating a diversion."

The intruders crept around the few ramshackle out-buildings near the end of the bridge, finding a small ledge below the line of sight from village and manor. Knowing they could wait here without fear of accidental discovery, they settled about making themselves comfortable while they stayed silent and low. Time ticked by interminably, but when they finally lifted their heads to regard the edifice, they saw that many of the torches had gone out. Listening carefully, they heard no further sounds of revelry.

"I'll wait for a while before I make a racket," Emilo said. "No sense in stirring things up too soon. But if it sounds like there's trouble, I'll try to lure them away from you."

"How?" Danyal asked, but his only reply was a noncommittal shrug from the kender.

Stealthily the youth led Foryth around the edge of the steep mountaintop. They heard sounds of loud snoring coming from one of the huts and made as wide a detour as possible around the place. It took them fifteen minutes to move beyond sight of the bridge, and Danyal felt terribly exposed, conscious of the vast gulf of space to his right and the looming bulk of the apparently impregnable manor rising to the left.

"Smells like we're getting close to the kitchen," Foryth noted. Danyal, too, had detected the odor of rotting garbage, though he hadn't made the same connection.

Sure enough, they saw the shadowy outline of a small doorway in the base of the manor's wall. Below the aperture was a steep section of the mountainside, where clearly the cooks simply threw out whatever leftover food and other waste made its way to the great house's kitchen. A noise of scurrying and chattering startled the intruders, and it didn't help them to relax when they realized that the sounds came from dozens of rats, who scraped and scrabbled over the rancid pile of refuse.

Danyal was starting to look around for some sign of a guard when Foryth walked boldly up to the door and reached for the latch. His heart pounding, Dan tensed, expecting an alarm or challenge.

Instead, the door opened with a soft creak, revealing a large room that was dimly lit by the glow of fading embers. Scuttling forward, the lad joined the historian in stepping hesitantly into the stronghold of Kelryn Darewind.

The kitchen smelled of soot and grease. In the dim light, they saw large counters, a great stack of pots, and a brick fireplace that held the still-glowing coals.

"Where would she be?" Foryth wondered. "It's a big house, after all."

"Kelryn told us he had a dungeon, remember? I think we should look on the lowest level we can find."

"Makes sense," the historian agreed. "Should we split up?"

Danyal shook his head firmly, and not just because he didn't want to be left alone in the place. "There's twice as much chance of us getting discovered if we're in two different places," he pointed out. Foryth nodded in apparent agreement.

The kitchen door was a massive barrier of iron-strapped oak, but the hinges were well oiled, and the door opened with barely a whisper of sound. They stepped onto a woolen carpet that lined a wide hallway, with several doors visible in the dark-paneled walls to either side. A pair of candles, each set in a wall sconce, provided wan illumination through the wide, high-ceilinged corridor.

To the left, the hallway expanded, then turned a corner. Dan caught a glimpse of long tapestries hanging down from the top of the lofty walls, and he remembered Kelryn mentioning works of art that he had commissioned to display the glories of Fistandantilus. The brightest lights he had seen came from that direction, so Danyal decided, logically enough, to go the other way. He reasoned that the dungeon would be remote from the main gathering halls and dwelling rooms of the manor.

He passed several doors that were smaller than the kitchen door, fitted with brass hinges that had been polished to golden brightness. Continuing his process of deduction, he concluded that these, too, would be unlikely to lead to the dingy underground chambers he was imagining. After a dozen steps, the corridor curled around a curving stone wall; here he found a sturdy iron-strapped door.

"This is the base of the tower," Foryth whispered, gesturing to the rounded wall. "The door probably leads to a stairway that goes up."

"How do you know that?" wondered Dan, incredulous.

"I merely marked the location when we were outside," the historian said modestly.

"Such a mass of stone has to have a foundation on the ground. And this is it."

Realizing that the historian was probably right, Danyal continued on, finding flagstones under his feet now instead of the carpet. Shortly he found still another door, this one also banded with iron, and when he put his face to the frame, he caught the scent of mold and dampness.

His heart quickening, he turned to tell Foryth of his observation, but he saw no sign of the historian! Near panic, Dan padded back along their tracks.

The door that was in the base of the manor tower was open a crack, though the lad knew it had been closed when they first passed it. He could only assume that Foryth Teel had entered here and was perhaps even now climbing toward the upper reaches of the stone spire.

For the first time tonight, Dan felt a twinge of despair. He didn't dare waste time going after his wandering companion, nor could he risk calling out to him. With a soft groan, he hurried back to the door he had suspected led to a downward stairway. There was a heavy iron latch securing the door against being opened from the other side, and this served to confirm the lad's suspicions.

As carefully as possible, he lifted the hasp, then pulled on the door. In the dim light, he saw a stairway descending into utter shadows. Anxiously he looked around, seeing several unlit candles in sconces similar to the mounts holding the burning tapers. He took one and touched it to the wick of a burning candle. Thus armed, he went back to the door.

Just before he started down the damp, stone stairs, he heard a clatter from outside the walls. Men shouted, and Dan deduced that Emilo had begun his diversion. Hoping it was effective, he turned his attentions to the darkness before and below him.

The air was chill with a penetrating miasma that seemed to seep right into his bones. Tiptoeing carefully, clutching the knife in one hand and the candle in the other, he crept down a long flight of stairs.

At the bottom, a dingy corridor forked to the right and left, and he felt a return of his momentary panic as he wondered which way to go. Finally he guessed at random, starting along one branch, holding the candle up as he passed several small cells. The metal doors of these enclosures stood open, and with a quick pass of the candle, Danyal saw that each was unoccupied.

When he reached a door that was closed, he lifted the candle toward the grate at the top of the barrier and tried to peer within.

"Who's there?" demanded a stern feminine, familiar voice, and Dan's heart did handstands in his chest.

"Mirabeth! It's me, Danyal!" he whispered, drawing a gasp of surprise and hope from within.

"Can you get me out of here?" she asked, rushing to the door, coming into the light of his flickering candle. He was relieved to see that she appeared unharmed. One of her ears retained its wax pointed tip, and she had combed one of her twin topknots down to cover the other, undisguised ear.

In another moment Danyal had pried open the catch, which was a very crude lock. Mirabeth gave him a big hug, and he wrapped his arms around her as best as he could while still retaining the grip on his knife and candle.

"Come on!" he urged. "We've got to get you out of here!"

"And just where do you think you'll go?" barked a sneering voice out of the darkness—a voice that Danyal clearly recognized.

It belonged to Kelryn Darewind.

Chapter 33

The Eyes of the Skull

Second Palast, Reapember
374 AC

Flayzeranyx stared at the skull, sensing the desire there. For long years, he had felt the glare of those dead eyes, heard the hushed voice whispering into his mind, insinuating ideas, suggestions, wishes. He knew that the skull tried to use him, that it wanted to employ the dragon to slake its hideous hunger.

But the red dragon's belly rumbled with a hunger of his own.

The eyes in the fleshless skull gaped, unblinking, as they had stared for so many decades. They looked upon the fiery inferno that was the lair of Flayzeranyx, and they watched, and they waited.

For a long time, there was only the smoke, the bubbling of lava and the hissing of steam. Clouds of soot billowed, churning in angry clouds, and tongues of flame licked into the air. Nothing seemed alive here, until finally crimson scales coiled in the darkness and leathery wings expanded to fan the air, sending gusts of wind swirling through the cavern.

Bursts of yellow fire exploded upward, as if exulting in their master's arousal when the mighty serpent raised his head and neck far above the smooth, hardened lava of his perch.

The dragon studied the skull and sensed the need. He saw a pale green image and detected the sparks of crimson fire that burned there. The hunger, the lust, in the skull was an almost palpable force.

"And where is the talisman?" asked the wyrm in a silken voice. He probed, staring with his great yellow eyes, penetrating the depths within the skull.

Abruptly the serpent saw the image change, and he sensed the truth as he beheld the human lair in the mountains. "Your heart of blood and stone is there!"

The skull remained as ever, but did Flayze now detect a mocking leer in the eternally grinning teeth?

"I know the place," he whispered. "The mountaintop stronghold . . . I have seen it, tolerated it, for these many years."

The skull was silent, still. But the shadowy stare of those dead eyes seemed to penetrate the dragon's very being.

Instinctively Flayze hated that place, hated the powerful allure that drew the attentions of his artifact. The skull wanted the stone with a desperate, powerful longing. The red dragon, on the other hand, had many treasures. He could afford to scorn the chance to add another bauble to his collection.

Wings spreading, the dragon turned toward the world, ready to fly.

Behind him, the skull watched, silent and motionless as ever, its white teeth locked in an eternal grimace.

Chapter 34

The Master of Loreloch

Second Majetog, Reapember
374 AC

"I was wondering how long it would take you to come for her. I'm impressed, of course, that you seem to have dispatched Zack so handily, but I was a trifle disappointed when you hadn't broken into Loreloch by last night. I thought you were taking an awfully cavalier approach to this pretty kendermaid's rescue."

For a moment, confronted by that familiar, dangerous voice, Danyal froze. He pictured Kelryn Darewind lurking in the darkness, like a cat who had found two mice out of their hole. The candle in Danyal's hand flared weakly, and he saw Mirabeth's eyes, so hopeful an instant before, cloud with a mixture of fear and despair.

Dan, too, felt a growing measure of hopelessness. At the same time, he wondered how the man had known to wait here for him. Remembering the noise that had crashed outside the manor walls, the lad wondered if the bandit lord had been alerted by Emilo's premature diversion. In any event, he was here in the darkness, watching and laughing at them.

But then Dan's instincts took over; he tugged Mirabeth out of the cell and started down the musty corridor, away from the direction of that soft, menacing voice.

"Halt!"

Kelryn barked the word, and just like that Danyal's feet ceased to move. He tried to urge Mirabeth along but found that she, too, might as well have been glued to the floor. The two of them squirmed and strained but couldn't pull their boots free. This was magic, Danyal realized with sinking spirits, knowing that some sort of spell had acted to cloak them in this cast of immobility.

"You had no chance of really making a successful rescue, you know—no chance at all," declared the bandit lord, sauntering from the darkened recesses of the dungeon. Suddenly the two young people could see him, but not because of the candle that still flared brightly in Danyal's trembling hand.

No, the lad realized. Rather, it seemed that there was some kind of eerie light emanating from Kelryn Darewind himself. The man was outlined in a pale green glow, an illumination not unlike the natural phosphorescence Danyal had observed on some of the lichens that grew in shady places near Waterton.

Except that this glow was clearly, uncannily powerful, in a way that no natural glow could ever be. In fact, it seemed as though the greenish luminescence actually *smelled* of some sort of arcane power, some inner might that allowed it to freeze them so helplessly in their tracks. When the bandit lord came closer, he smiled, white teeth gleaming in the strange light.

"I knew tonight would be the night that you came for her. I knew it even before your friend made such an untidy racket outside the walls."

Now Dan could see that the pale light glowed from between the man's fingers, sickly beams of eerie illumination expanding from Kelryn Darewind's hand to spread through the dungeon. He held an object there, something small enough to be held within his closed fingers, but it was a thing that pulsed with frightening arcane power. Too, it was something terribly, unnaturally bright but not fiery, for clearly it was cool enough to be held.

"The bloodstone of Fistandantilus." The bandit lord held up a golden chain, allowing the pale stone pendant to dangle and sway before them. "It's too bad your friend, the historian, isn't here. I know he'd get quite a thrill out of seeing this."

Danyal stared at the bloodstone, unable to move. He felt the power of the gem in that terrible light, sensed that his eyes—and his brain—were being damaged even as he was compelled to maintain his unblinking attention. There was no doubt in his mind that it was this stone that glued him in place, that compelled his obedience to a command he would have given anything to disobey.

"It was the bloodstone that allowed me to trick him, to make him think that I was a real priest!" The bandit lord chuckled over his own cleverness.

Danyal tried to speak, worked to choke out a word or two of challenge, but he was unable to make his mouth and lips obey his will.

"Oh, very well. You may relax, but don't try to flee." Kelryn masked the stone again as he spoke, and the sudden darkness was a huge relief, like a wash of fresh air blowing away the scent of an open crypt.

Suddenly their feet weren't fastened to the floor anymore, and Mirabeth and Dan staggered in shock as the spell faded. They clung to each other for balance and reassurance. The youth desperately wanted to run, but now that he knew the power of the stone, he dared not take the chance—at least, not yet.

"The gem is the key to my success. It not only insures the obedience of reluctant listeners such as yourself, but it also protects me from those who would do me harm. There was a time when its power brought people flocking to my temple. Now I have learned—and only in the last few decades—that this gem of Fistandantilus even gives me the power to heal. Oh, it's not perfect, of course, not like a spell cast by a true cleric. But you saw it work."

Kelryn Darewind drew a deep breath, shaking his head in apparent wonder. "This bloodstone has a soul of its own, and it helps me! Over the years it has consumed countless lives and amassed a mighty power. It has taught me many things, shared wonders of history that others would never believe!"

Dan wanted to ask if the stone had corrupted him, made him evil and cruel as well.

"Hah!" Kelryn's bark was loud and abrupt. "Even that fool of a historian doesn't know the scope of his own ignorance. *I* know, because there is a voice, a spirit of knowledge, that talks to me through the stone."

The man came closer, looking down at his two captives, and Dan sensed that once again Kelryn really wanted to talk, wanted to make them understand. And the lad hated that smooth face, that calm expression, more than ever. He wanted to punch the man, to draw his knife and plunge it into Kelryn Darewind's evil heart.

"And it was the bloodstone, after all, that provided me with the knowledge that you were coming here tonight. It was really quite a simple matter to understand your objective."

Kelryn frowned suddenly, allowing the green light to ooze once more from between his fingers as he scrutinized Mirabeth. "Though I would have thought that the kender himself would have come after his woman."

Abruptly he squinted, as if seeing Mirabeth for the first time. He reached out, pushing her hair back from the rounded human ear. Roughly he slapped at the pointed tip of her other ear, drawing an immediate shout

248

of protest from Danyal but at the same time knocking away the wax ear.

Then he threw back his head and laughed.

"You're *her*! Sir Harold's daughter, the one who escaped!" he exclaimed, full of mirth. "I've had you locked in my dungeon for the past days, and I didn't even know it. Oh, what a splendid joke! What wonderful irony!"

He snarled then, his face distorted by a momentary naked cruelty. "Your father was a menace to me, a danger who lasted for too many years. It is good to know that you will soon join him in death."

Danyal felt an onrushing wave of horrible fury, combined with an agonizing awareness of his own helplessness. They were both as good as dead, he knew, and he felt utterly powerless to change their impending fate. His fingers itched toward the weapon at his waist as he considered the chances. Could he draw the knife and sink the blade into his enemy before Kelryn could work the magic of the bloodstone?

He knew that he couldn't.

"Raise your hands, both of you," declared the man curtly, as if reading Danyal's thoughts. Though he struggled valiantly to resist, Dan's arms moved against his will, extending themselves over his head until he stood with hands helplessly upraised. His weapon might as well have been at the bottom of the sea for all the chance he had of reaching it.

"I think we'll do this in a fashion my men will enjoy," the bandit lord declared in a tone of amusement. "Let's see . . . perhaps I should have the two of you leap from the upper battlement onto the rocks. They're at least a hundred feet below. Yes, that would be effective. And dramatic as well, I'm sure you'll agree."

Kelryn frowned, apparently confronted by a deeply distressing problem. "But should I have you jump together or one at a time? I just don't know." Kelryn Darewind sounded genuinely distressed over his difficult choice.

Dan's heart was pounding, and he felt the sweat

trickling down his brow, but he still could make no gesture nor sound of protest.

"Well, to get us started, we can climb out of the dungeon. You, girl, go first. The lad will follow, with me in the rear. Now proceed, but slowly."

Like zombies, Mirabeth and Danyal shuffled through the dark corridor of the dungeon. Once the lad tried to stop, to resist the commands of the bandit lord, but the feet that had been so unwilling to move a few minutes ago now refused to stop their inexorable march toward whatever doom Kelryn Darewind chose to devise for them. The pale, glowing bloodstone was like a physical prod behind him as Dan strained to turn, tried to resist with all his will the commands that marched them toward imminent execution.

"It shall have to be one at a time," mused the bandit captain, startling them with his casual return to the topic of murder. "The look on the survivor's face is not a treasure that I would care to waste. But which of you first? I really would like you to make a suggestion."

Once again Kelryn's fingers tightened around the bloodstone, and as green light seeped through the dungeon, Dan saw that the gem was pulsing with renewed power.

Danyal's mouth opened and his tongue jerked reflexively, but he gagged on words that seemed drawn to the power of the bloodstone, that rose like bile in his throat. Spitting and coughing, he shook his head, drawing a sigh of disappointment from the false priest of Fistandantilus.

"Now, climb!" barked Kelryn Darewind as they reached the foot of the stairway. Mirabeth still led the way, and Danyal allowed her to advance several steps before he started after her. Once more he thought of trying to resist, though he still couldn't manipulate his arms. Could he throw himself backward, try to carry the bandit lord down the steep steps? Perhaps he could badly injure, even kill the man!

Buoyed by the sudden hope, Dan worked his head

around, getting a glimpse of his captor. He was dismayed to see that Kelryn Darewind had drawn his sword as he followed them onto the stairs. Any maneuver such as the lad had contemplated would only result in a gory wound for himself.

Slumping in despair, Danyal turned his attention to the climb. Each step seemed to emerge from a haze before his face, and he found his feet rising without conscious direction as he gradually ascended.

They came to the door at the top of the stairs, and Mirabeth pushed it open, shuffling into the great hallway beyond. Danyal followed, and Kelryn came last. He still held his blade, but he seemed to be most concerned with the green gem that still glowed between his fingers.

"Go that way," he declared, pointing toward the curve that Dan remembered led toward the entry hall with the tall, tapestry-lined walls. The corridor had been illuminated by only a pair of candles before, but now a dozen or more torches burned in sconces spaced along each of the walls. The youth didn't see any of the other bandits, but he heard shouts from outside; he could only hope that Emilo, at least, had gotten to a place of safety. With a grimace of heartache, he wondered again what had become of Foryth.

"These depict great moments in the history of my temple," the would-be priest declared, gesturing toward the long strands of fabric. The artistry might once have been splendid, but the bright colors had faded, and the fringes of the tapestry were tattered and moth-eaten.

His hands still stretched over his head, Danyal couldn't have been less interested in the soot-blackened banners. Yet as he flexed his numbing fingers, trying to think of something, anything, useful to do, he suddenly had the flash of an idea.

"That picture," said the lad, pointing toward the nearest tapestry. He stepped right up to it, vaguely discerning a crowd scene and a depiction of a large square edifice. "What is it?"

"The tapestry displays the laying of our temple in Haven's outer wall." Kelryn spoke with animation and interest. "You see? There I stand to oversee the work."

The man stepped up to the embroidered illustration, indicating a figure outlined in green light, standing like a rod atop a small pyramid of square stone blocks. The Seeker priest stared admiringly at the handiwork, and the lad sensed that the man's attention and desire had shifted momentarily, coming to rest in his reminiscences of those days of glory.

Dan saw his chance. Hands still upraised, he seized the edge of the tapestry and threw himself backward, instantly hurling all his weight and momentum onto the support of the ancient fabric.

Please give way! His prayer was desperate and, apparently, successful: The long swath of cloth tore near the top, and a great, dusty shroud tumbled downward, burying Kelryn Darewind, his sword, and his green bloodstone.

As soon as the bandit lord disappeared, Dan felt his arms drop, freed from the spell as the green light was smothered. Instantly he had the dagger out, ready to slash at the form that struggled beneath the billowing layers of the tapestry.

"Danyal—this way! *Hurry!*" Mirabeth took his arm and pulled before he could make his attack. He heard footsteps and saw the flaring of bright torchlight from the direction of the kitchen.

Groaning in frustration but recognizing the need to flee immediately, Danyal followed the lass as she darted through the entry hall. The manor gates, he was surprised to see, were standing open. Torches flared among the crude cottages of the village, and he guessed that some of the men, alarmed by Emilo's diversion, must have charged out of the fortified structure to investigate.

And then the two of them were through the gates, plunging down the sloping ground beyond the wall. With a sharp turn away from the road to the bridge,

Danyal pulled Mirabeth into the deep shade of a small barn.

Panting, trying to breathe as quietly as possible, he looked around, assessing their surroundings.

But he wasn't expecting to see anyone as close as the figure who rose to stand right beside him.

With a reflexive twist, Dan raised his knife, pushed Mirabeth aside, and stabbed.

Chapter 35

Escape or Doom

Second Kirinor, Reapember
374 AC

"Wait!" The familiar voice jolted Danyal, giving the lad barely enough time to check the deadly blow he had intended to land.

"Emilo?" Danyal sagged backward, allowing the dagger to fall away from the shadowy figure. "I—I almost didn't recognize you! You could have—*I* could have . . ."

"Don't worry. It's me, and I'm all right. I see you heard my diversion. Oh, and hi, Mirabeth!" declared the kender. "I'm really glad to see you!"

"Thanks—thanks to all of you—for coming after me," she replied. But then she looked around, seeking someone else in their hiding place, which was the shadowy alcove behind a small barn. "Where's Foryth?"

"Still in there, I guess." Danyal shook his head in despair. "I told him to stay with me, to be careful, but he wandered off before we'd been inside for ten minutes!"

"I don't know if we can afford to wait for him," Emilo said ruefully. "It kind of puts the whole plan in trouble."

"What choice do we have, besides waiting here?" argued the youth. "Did you see how many men were gathered at the base of the bridge?" He gestured into the torchlight at the end of the little lane, where a small knot of bandits milled about.

"Yes." Emilo didn't sound concerned. "Actually, I don't think they'll be there long."

"Why?" asked Danyal incredulously.

The kender made no answer. Instead, he cocked an ear to the side, clearly expectant of some noise.

Within seconds, a great boom resounded through the night, echoing back from the neighboring mountain as a cascade of orange flame leapt into the air from the far side of the manor's walls. A heavy thud rumbled through the ground under their feet, and debris clattered around them while the fire flared into a brightness like false daylight.

"You did that?" Danyal asked, amazed and impressed.

"That used to be a shed just outside the stronghold," Emilo said smugly. "See if they'll ever store all their kegs of lamp oil in one place again!"

The band of men who had been guarding the end of the bridge now raced in a mob toward the scene of the explosion. Flaming oil had been cast in a great arc around the blast, and several neighboring cottages and a haystack were all crackling into a lively conflagration. The guardsmen were joined by others from the manor as everyone within sight labored to fight the flames, shoveling dirt onto the fire or, more rarely, casting a bucket of precious water on some particularly vulnerable outpost of the blaze.

"D'you think that will hold their attention?" asked the kender nonchalantly, leaning against the wall of the barn and trying to observe the gates of the manor. Flames soared into the sky, glowing like a beacon in the night.

"Let's get to the bridge!" Mirabeth urged, pointing to the route that had opened before them.

Ducking low, staying to the shadows as much as possible, the trio scuttled past the outbuildings of the small village. Finally they reached the last hut, still twenty paces from the end of the bridge. The whole surface of the span was visible from the manor, though the illumination naturally was brightest at this end.

"No point in hanging around and waiting for someone to find us," Danyal said, after checking to see that Kelryn's bandits were still busy with the fire.

The three of them raced onto the bridge, not daring to look back as they willed their feet to fly, and sprinted with all possible speed onto the surface of flagstones. In moments the deep chasm, black with night shadow, yawned to either side of them and the chilly air breezily washed away any trace of warmth that might have lingered from the fire in the village.

The first shout of alarm didn't come until they were halfway across, but even that was disastrously early, Danyal knew. Knowing their flight had been observed, he urged his companions to redouble their efforts, intending to fall back and try to gain them time, holding off the pursuing bandits with his dagger. But Mirabeth apparently sensed his intention, for she seized his wrist and pulled him sharply along at her side.

Finally the far end of the bridge was there, and they raced off the span and onto the dirt roadway. But now they heard the sounds of an angry mob, shouts and cries and hoarse, communal cheers as the bandits left the dying fire at the stronghold to give pursuit. Danyal sensed the bloodlust of the band and knew the three of them wouldn't live for a minute if they were caught.

"It won't work. We can't all make it!" he gasped. *"Run!"*

Again he tried to hesitate, to turn and buy more time, but Mirabeth pulled him hard. "You're coming, too!"

And so he followed, the kender and the two young humans dashing into the shadows of the mountainside while dozens of murderous bandits charged onto the bridge.

The crushing wave of awe that swept over Danyal was no less sickening for its familiarity.

"Dragon!" he gasped in horror, all but lurching forward. His knees turned to rubber, and he stumbled, staggering, then falling onto his face as Mirabeth collapsed and buried her face in her hands beside him.

Emilo skidded to a halt beside them, his face turned skyward. "Would you look at that?" he declared, his tone full of wonder. "A dragon!"

Danyal didn't want to look, but he needed to know. He raised his eyes and saw the serpent soaring overhead, blotting out the stars across a great swath of sky. Crimson scales reflected like rubies in the flaring light of the fire across the chasm, and then two massive wings pulsed downward, a blast of wind raising dust from the road.

"Take cover!" shouted the youth, reaching up from the muddy ditch on the uphill side of the road to seize Emilo by the wrist. He pulled the kender in beside Mirabeth and himself, hoping that they had been far enough from the lights around Loreloch to escape the serpent's notice.

The three of them lay in chilly water and sticky mud, staring in horror at the winged shape that had soared over them and now plummeted, intent upon the edifice of Loreloch.

Many of the pursuing bandits had come as far as the middle of the bridge. Now, confronted by flying death, they turned en masse and tried to flee back to the manor.

But the dragon was far too fast. The serpent closed the distance with another deceptively leisurely stroke of those great wings. The massive head lowered, and then the night became bright with a hellish assault of flame. The dragon flew onward in a rush, leaving behind a cacophony of crackling fire, screaming men, and rushing wind as the inferno sucked in the cool night air.

Next Flayze glided past the manor, ripping away one of the great walls with his mighty forepaws. Another gout of flame spewed from those cruel jaws, this time turning everything within the manor walls into blazing destruction. A billowing cloud of fire arose, swelling into a mushroom of oily flames as the stables were incinerated next.

Coming around the great edifice, the red dragon crushed the cottages and barns of the village with blows of its claws or the whiplike lash of its monstrous tail. Again it breathed, and a dozen small houses crackled into fire.

Finally it came to rest on the ground beside the stronghold. With a few rending blows of its powerful foreclaws, it pulled down the rest of the walls. It smashed into the sturdy tower once or twice, but then apparently decided that solid structure wasn't worth the effort to destroy it. Instead, the wyrm concentrated on crushing any buildings still standing, burning everything flammable, and killing anything that moved within the ruin that had, minutes before, been Loreloch.

Only when the destruction was absolute did the serpent once again spread those vast wings. Catching a rising updraft, air heated by fires kindled by the dragon's own breath, Flayze launched himself into the sky and soon vanished into the dark of the night.

Chapter 36

A Trove of Treasure

Second Majetog, Reapember
374 AC

Later, when I was asked to explain my decision to climb the tower in Loreloch, I could not recall the exact thought processes that led me away from my young companion and into the lofty aerie of the fortified manor. I can only recollect a feeling, a sense as though a muse was singing to me from atop those stairs, a goddess of historians and chroniclers who urged me to visit the chambers above. No doubt my recollection of Kelryn's statements—he had told me that his library was in the highest part of his stronghold—helped me to make the decision.

In any event, I was halfway up the long, spiraling stair before it even occurred to me that I should perhaps have let the boy know of my intentions. By then, of course, it was too late; I would have risked discovery of us both had I gone back down to look for him.

So, instead, I continued on.

By the time I reached the top of the stairs, excitement and anticipation had gone far in overcoming my earlier misgivings. I saw that the spiraling steps terminated in a small landing, a landing that was isolated from the upper room of the tower before a large, secure door. I was as certain as I had ever been about anything that behind that door I would find the keys to unlocking many portions of previously unrecorded history.

Questions whirled through my mind as I stood there considering the barrier of wood and iron. This was the heart of Loreloch, I was utterly certain, and Loreloch and Kelryn Darewind were the keys to understanding the remaining mysteries of Fistandantilus. What had happened to the archmage after the convulsive explosion that had created Skullcap?

The answers, I had no doubt, could be found on the other side of that portal. At the same time, I had an uncanny feeling of danger, and knew I couldn't just walk through the door.

The clatter of a great banging noise abruptly shattered the still night that had surrounded the mountaintop edifice. Immediately I heard a curse from within the room and barely had time to flatten myself against the wall of the tower when the door flew open and none other than Kelryn Darewind should dart out! From the shadows, I caught a glimpse of his face, saw his jaw locked in a wolfish grin of cruel anticipation. With a shudder of apprehension, I thought of Danyal and Mirabeth somewhere in this great house and knew that they were in terrible danger.

I also saw that the priest of Fistandantilus—I did not learn until later that he really was a charlatan, as I had first believed—was clutching something bright and greenish in his hand as he charged down the spiral stairway. He did not see me as I shrank into the darkness.

Indeed, such was his haste that he forgot to bolt the door behind him!

I wasted no time in taking advantage of that oversight. As soon as the bandit lord was out of sight, I slipped through the doorway to find myself in what was clearly a study. There were numerous tomes and scrolls on the heavy shelves that lined much of the room's wall space. The three windows were small, almost like tunnels looking through the thick stone walls of the tower. Each of them was secured by a stout wooden shutter that fit tightly into the round window.

One practical thought did intrude: I thought to bolt the door behind me before I settled down to work. A single candle was still flickering weakly, and I used the wick to fire several bright lamps. With ample light, I settled down to read and within moments was utterly engrossed in the information before me.

I learned that Kelryn Darewind was not a priest, and Fistandantilus was not a god. He had lied to me—his imperfect, limited healing power had come from the bloodstone. At the same time, I ascertained that the essence of the archmage had somehow survived through the centuries, and that it yearned to return to Krynn. Whether he had become an undead lich, or existed in the form of a disembodied ghost, I could not, as yet, tell.

But I learned more, as well . . . that Fistandantilus might not have been destroyed in the convulsion of Skullcap, but that he had laid plans that were in danger of reaching fruition. And with his success, I knew, his vengeance would bring a reign of terror and darkness akin to some of history's most dolorous epochs.

Then my hands trembled as I came upon a real secret, concerning an artifact that opened the doors of understanding. For the first time, I learned about the potential—for great power, and for great evil—of the skull.

And then I saw the real danger of the archmage's plan.

Chapter 37

Clues from the Ashes

Second Kirinor, Reapember
374 AC

Dawn broke over the sky as Danyal, numb with awe, looked at the flaming wreckage of Loreloch. Occasionally a stone broke free from the rubble of the once high walls, rolling through the burning cottages, then tumbling from the summit of the village's mountaintop to bounce and crash down the long, sloping incline. Two structures of stone still stood more or less intact amid the ruin: the bridge leading to the manor, and the lofty tower that had risen from within the high walls.

"Foryth!" the youth said with a moan. "He was still in there. He couldn't have survived!"

Emilo shook his head sadly. "I never saw him after

you two went around back last night."

Danyal tried to suppress his tears, but when he slumped back to the ground in the ditch, he felt his throat tightening and knew that the unwanted moisture was stinging at his eyes.

"Why did he have to go wandering off?" he groaned. "He should have stayed with me; he'd be out here with the rest of us now!"

"Quite possibly true," Emilo admitted. The kender's eyes remained focused on the ruined structure, and Danyal turned around to follow the direction of his companion's gaze.

The dragon had worked the destruction of Loreloch using the same methodical thoroughness with which he had devastated Waterton. As well as the bridge and the tower, a few chimneys, stone walls, and an occasional silo stood after the onslaught of flames, though the fires still searched hungrily through the ruins, eagerly seeking more fuel. The wrack seemed utterly complete, and it was impossible to think that anyone could be still alive in there.

"Don't you think we should get going?" asked the kender casually. "Just in case any of Kelryn's men happen to be around."

Danyal shook his head firmly. "Not yet." He found it inconceivable that anyone could have lived through the attack, but more to the point, he was not ready to abandon the place where he had last seen Foryth Teel. "Maybe he's hurt in there, or trapped somewhere."

He was surprised to realize that, despite the man's fussy nature and impractical priorities, the youth had become very fond of the aspiring priest. Also Foryth's knowledge and his sense of insight into the minds of other people, particularly the bandit lord and former Seeker priest, had been comforting weapons in the companions' meager arsenal.

"Let's have a look, then," Emilo agreed.

The far end of the bridge was littered with charred, blackened corpses. Despite the fact that, moments before, these men had actively been seeking his own blood, Dan felt a grim regret at the loss of human life, at the implacable fire that had swept down from the sky with such telling, lethal effect.

"The dragon even pulled down the cottages," Mirabeth said softly. Her own eyes were dry, but her face was as pale as a ghostly fog. "There were people sleeping in them, and now they're dead."

Another rock clattered into the ruins, and the three companions looked toward the tower, expecting to see another stage of Loreloch's collapse. Instead, they saw a small shutter slowly swing outward, a sturdy wooden plug that had secured a tiny window in the thick stone walls of the tower.

"Someone's alive there!" Danyal whispered, fear and hope mingling in his heart as he saw a slender hand emerge from the window. Even before that hand waved, he recognized the tan sleeve drooping around the slender wrist.

"It's Foryth!" cried the lad, leaping from the ditch and scrambling into the road, ignoring Emilo's fingers as the kender tried to slow him down. "Foryth!" he called again, dancing at the end of the bridge, waving both his own hands. "Are you all right?"

They couldn't hear the reply, though Dan clearly imagined the "tsk" as the historian leaned out of the small, lofty aperture. Foryth waved again, and the trio finally understood the nature of his gesture.

"He wants us to come to him." Mirabeth voiced the obvious conclusion. "Up in the tower."

"But—" Danyal could think of a thousand reasons to object, though none of them quelled the joy of discovering that his friend was alive. "I suppose he thinks he's found something we just have to see," he concluded.

"Well, let's have a look, then." Emilo was already sauntering back over the bridge. Dan and Mirabeth came behind, though the two young humans slowed appreciably as they neared the mass of charred bodies on the far end of the span.

"I wonder which one is—or *was*, I should say—Kelyrn Darewind?" The kender spoke breezily as he stepped among the blackened bodies.

Danyal took Mirabeth's hand and squeezed, grateful for the returning pressure of her fingers. They avoided looking at the corpses as they walked along the fringe of the bridge to avoid the killing ground. Even so, the scent of burned flesh, singed hair, and death was like a physical barrier across the roadway. Finally, holding their breath against the stink, the two stumbled onto the broken, shattered ground of Loreloch.

Allowing Emilo to pick a path through the wreckage, they reached the base of the tower. Danyal helped the kender pull rocks away from the doorway, where they found that the sturdy portal had been smashed in by the destructive force of the dragon's attack.

Quickly they scrambled up the stairs that spiraled around the interior of the tower. "Foryth!" Danyal cried as they pounded toward the top.

When they reached the landing and burst through the open door, they found themselves in a small library. The historian was seated at a large table. A huge book lay open before him. Nearby were stacked numerous other tomes, and several scrolls had been tossed casually on the other end of the table. One of these had been unrolled and was being held open by a pair of heavy stone paperweights.

"Ah, there you are," Foryth said cheerfully. "I heard a bit of excitement out there. Glad to see that the three of you were able to get away."

"Why did you take off like that?" demanded Danyal, suddenly furious at the historian's nonchalance. "You could have been killed! We were supposed to stay together! Weren't you paying attention?"

"What? Er, yes . . . I suppose not. That is—tsk! Look here, my boy. I've found something absolutely fascinating."

In spite of his agitation, Danyal leaned over the page that Foryth indicated. He wasn't surprised that he couldn't recognize the symbols written there. "What's that supposed to mean?" the lad demanded.

"Why, right here!" The historian could barely contain his excitement. "It says that there *is* a skull! The skull of Fistandantilus exists!"

"And why is that important?" Mirabeth asked.

"Because if Kelryn Darewind was to get both of those talismans, the results would be . . . well, they would be too horrible to talk about, that's what."

"Why? Kelryn is dead!" Dan objected. "The dragon surely killed him!"

"Perhaps. But the threat remains. If anyone of evil ambition should gain possession of the skull and the bloodstone, he would gain an unthinkable power."

"What power?"

"He could travel through time—become the Master of Past and Present, as Fistandantilus was in another era. That is, I believe that the combination of the skull and bloodstone would allow the holder to travel through time, much as Fistandantilus himself did."

"And that would be bad for Krynn?" Mirabeth wondered out loud.

"If the time traveler is wicked and ambitious enough, there are no limits to the damage he could do. Kelryn Darewind could easily become a virtually immortal dictator, a master of a realm greater than Solamnia. And he would be utterly, absolutely invulnerable, for he could use the same power to foresee any attempt against him before it was enacted!"

"Where is the skull?" Dan asked.

"*That's* the mystery that stopped Kelryn Darewind, that prevented him from going after the skull. And a good thing for the world, I might add."

"You told us. But does that mean you don't know where it is, either?" The lad was becoming exasperated with the historian's indirect responses. "Then why don't we get out of here?"

"Tsk. I said that Kelryn Darewind didn't know, but he lacks the keen eye of the researcher, the ability to perceive obscure clues. I myself have made a deduction."

"I think I understand. . . ." Emilo Haversack chewed on the end of his topknot. "The skull—"

"Precisely!" The historian could hardly contain himself. "It has to be in the lair of the dragon!"

Chapter 38

A Captive Once More

Second Kirinor, Reapember
374 AC

"I'll be going to the lair of the dragon immediately," Foryth Teel said. "I have already looked in my book. There's a fair approximation of a map on page twelve thousand, six hundred and forty-seven."

"You're crazy!" challenged Dan. "You saw what that monster did to Loreloch! You'd never even get close to the skull, much less have a chance to do your stupid research!"

"My sense of duty compels me to try," the historian retorted stiffly.

"Why? So you can learn that spell to become a priest? What good will that do if you're dead?"

Foryth Teel sighed. "No. That isn't the reason. I have realized that I've been fooling myself. I have no future as a priest. In fact, all of you have helped me to reach that decision. That is, you've come to mean very much to me. So much so that I'm no longer the impartial chronicler—and perhaps I never was."

He paused, clearing his throat awkwardly. He had accompanied the other companions down from the lofty tower, and they had crossed the bridge to stand at the end of the span across the chasm from ruined Loreloch. Finally the historian continued.

"I, tsk, that is, I think it would be best if the rest of you retired to a place of somewhat greater safety."

"You should come with us!" Danyal insisted.

"You're a brave lad and a good friend. But I have my job, and you have yours. You have to see to Mirabeth and Emilo, you understand?"

"I—I'm going with you," Emilo declared abruptly.

"But the danger—" Foryth started to object, but the kender shook his head firmly.

"I don't know why, but I have a feeling that I can learn something important from that skull . . . like I've seen it before, and it was significant."

"Then I'm coming, too!" Mirabeth interjected. "You won't know what to do if Emilo—that is, if—" She broke off and covered her face as she sobbed.

"I'll be all right," the kender said. "You should get away from here!"

"Indeed, you and the lad, at least. Go to Haven, or even Palanthas. But get out of these mountains to somewhere safe," Foryth Teel said gently. "You both have many years before you, and who knows? It might be useful to future historians to have you bear witness to these events. You can carry the word of Kelryn Darewind's death and the end of Loreloch."

"Do you think the bloodstone was destroyed?" Danyal asked, shivering as he looked toward the ruined stronghold.

The next sound came from behind them, however, and

the four companions whirled in unison as the rasping, dry laughter sounded from the darkness.

"The bloodstone was *not* destroyed. I still have it, safe and sound!"

The voice of Kelryn Darewind drew a gasp from Danyal and a low scream from Mirabeth. With one arm, the bandit lord held the lass in a grip of crushing force. His other hand held a knife, and its keen tip was already pressing into the young woman's throat.

Kelryn moved forward, lifting Mirabeth so that her toes barely touched the ground. Dan, Emilo, and Foryth could see that the once dapper bandit lord looked terrible. Much of his hair had been burned away, and a scar of red tissue covered his forehead and one cheek. His clothes were grimy and smelled of char.

Seeing their looks of incredulity, Kelryn chuckled bitterly. "I knew the dragon was coming, so I had a few seconds of warning. While my men were charging onto the bridge, I jumped into a ditch. I was half buried in mud when the fire came!

"And you are right, historian. The skull *has* to be in the lair of the dragon!" gloated Kelryn. "Apparently you are not the fool I took you for. Now you will take me there!"

Danyal's hand was already clenched around the hilt of his long knife and his knees were bent, ready to lunge toward the hated bandit who had somehow survived to follow them here. Before he could attack, however, he saw one more fact in the eerie red light.

A tiny trickle of blood dribbled from the wound on the young woman's neck, the place where the sharp knife point was pressed. Mirabeth held utterly still. Dan knew the cut must have hurt, but she revealed no trace of discomfort or fear. Instead, she looked at him with an expression that pleaded for him to stay calm, to listen, to *think*.

Overcoming his fury and terror, the lad tried to do just that. Still, he growled a warning. "If you hurt her, I'll kill you. I swear by all the gods, I don't care if it costs my own life. You will die!"

Kelryn nodded in acceptance, as if the lad's passion was the most natural thing in the world. "Just don't *you* do anything that gets her killed," he declared in an easy, conversational tone.

"And now," he added to Foryth, "I heard you say something about a map. Well, get it out, historian. You're going to lead us all to the skull of Fistandantilus!"

Danyal stared in disbelief, but it was Foryth who asked the question. "How could you have known about the dragon?"

"What do you mean?" The menacing swordsman was nonplussed by the question. Then Kelryn pulled the bloodstone, still attached to its golden chain, from beneath his tunic. "*He* told me—the soul of the blood-stone, who waits for my coming, my prayers!"

"Fistandantilus?" Foryth said with detached, schol-arly interest.

"The same. At last he has brought me to you, where my destiny and his shall come together!"

"What do you want?" demanded Danyal. "Power? Knowledge?"

Kelryn laughed. "I knew the historian had discovered my notes, and I suspected he would have solved the puzzle, learned where the dragon's lair is."

"And the skull." It was Foryth Teel who answered. Kelryn nodded, encouraging the historian to continue. "From the notes I saw in the library, you believe that the combination of the skull and the bloodstone will give you one of the great powers of Fistandantilus."

"The power to travel through time!" Kelryn Darewind could no longer contain his exultation. "The skull to show the way, and the bloodstone to give catalyst to my flight!"

"But why?" Danyal was mystified. He could under-stand a lust for riches or lands, could even see a vague purpose behind a man's desire to master other people, to make himself a lord or a king. But this was a craving that made no sense to him.

"There is no greater tool for one who would seek to

further his own ends," Foryth Teel intoned. "A man who knows what will happen on the morrow can position himself to take full advantage of his enemies' misfortunes. I'm afraid what I told you before is true: He could become unstoppable."

"And so he will!" gloated Kelryn. "My power in Haven, before the coming of the dragons, was a small and pathetic thing in comparison to the might I will wield when I am Master of Past and Present!

"Now lead us through the mountains, historian. We go to claim the skull!"

Chapter 39

Threads

Reapember, 374 AC

It was so close now—the bloodstone was right *here*. He could almost feel it, could almost touch and taste the powerful talisman that was at the very heart of his immortal existence.

But there was still interference, a fog of mysterious power that masked itself even as it competed for the artifact. It was a shield that refused to let him pass, denied him his ultimate triumph.

It wasn't the boy who was the cause of his frustration; he knew that with certainty now. Instead, it was an arcane force, a mysterious and extremely powerful essence that was for some reason centered around, but not within, the human lad.

He possessed a talisman of arcane might that acted to thwart the will and intentions of the archmage. Even worse, there was something strangely familiar about that competing power, and it was every bit the equal of the archmage's own might.

And that meant that it was most assuredly something to be feared.

Chapter 40

Firemont

Third Misham, Reapember
374 AC

"There—the twin peaks, with the smoking crater between them. That has to be the place," declared Foryth Teel. His excitement over the discovery apparently overcame the fatigue, fear, and anger that had been with the companions constantly on their long, difficult trek through the High Kharolis.

For a moment Dan felt his frustration and anger expanding to encompass the historian, who could be so detached about their own circumstances, but the lad quickly quelled the emotion, saving his antipathy for their real enemy.

"The lake is steaming," Kelryn Darewind added.

"That's got to be the boiling lake that shows on your map."

The bandit's knife remained pressed against Mirabeth's throat, though the man conversed about the view as if she weren't even there. "The lair—and the skull of Fistandantilus—has got to be somewhere up that mountainside."

"Let's see. . . ." Foryth Teel was not entirely convinced. He flipped open his book, tracing his fingers across the symbols on the page. "I see the boiling lake, and there we have the twin conical summits. But the glacier—there's supposed to be a glacier."

For the thousandth time, Danyal's hand closed around the hilt of his knife, and he cast a sidelong glance toward Kelryn Darewind. As always, it seemed the man had anticipated his interest. He winked, flashing the lad a smile as cold as the stare of a dead fish.

"I have to admit this looks like the place," declared Emilo Haversack.

"Sure," Kelryn chatted easily about the connection. "The two mountains are both pointed. And that one has a glacier on the south face, just like the map shows. Now, let's move."

"Then that means the lair should be a cave mouth about halfway up the right-hand peak," Foryth concluded triumphantly and with as much confidence, Danyal thought sourly, as if he were describing where in the marketplace one might find a vendor of melons. Still, the historian refused to be hastened as he scrutinized the view.

Dan fought valiantly against the misery and hopelessness that threatened once again to drop him in his tracks. His only desire was to rescue Mirabeth, to get her away from Kelryn's hands long enough to exact revenge upon the bandit lord.

And then . . . and then what?

He didn't know. Of course, in the eight days since they had departed ruined Loreloch, Danyal had come to share some of the historian's sense of their task's importance. He recalled grimly the warning Foryth Teel had issued about the menace presented by the prospect of Kelryn Darewind's success.

Indeed, Dan had spent some of the last long nights thinking about those prospects. If the cruel bandit gained the power to travel through time, he could use that might to create an awful regime, a place devoted to violence and the worship of the vile, corrupt sorcerer.

The journey had been difficult as the five of them had made their way through rugged mountainous country. Yet the days outdoors had hardened them all, and they had learned to take advantage of what shelter they could find. Usually they had camped without a fire, unwilling to draw attention to themselves, for they all feared the great serpent whose lair was the object of their quest.

Huddling together under their two blankets, they had weathered the first blustery chill of autumn, determined to bring their quest to a successful conclusion.

Three times they had been brought to a halt as the kender was violently afflicted by one of his spells. Each had seemed, at least to Danyal, a little more severe than those that had come before. The first time Kelryn Darewind had been ready to kill the unfortunate kender. It had been Mirabeth who had quashed that idea, making it clear that she would sacrifice herself before she would allow it. Kelryn had been unwilling to relinquish his hostage, and for the first time, Dan had seen that the bandit lord was, in fact, as frightened as the rest of them of being left alone.

For hours following that attack, Emilo had been unfocused, his eyes haunted by memories that he could not—or would not—recall. On the next occasions, Kelryn had reluctantly, and impatiently, waited for the kender to regain his senses and mobility.

Fortunately they had seen no sign of the dragon. If Flayze had returned to his lair after destroying Loreloch, then he had either remained there or flown into a different portion of his territory. Now they regarded the mountain, sure that the monster lived here and anxious to find the safest route of ascent.

Danyal wondered for a moment if, now that they had discovered the location, Kelryn might try to kill them. The lad resolved that wouldn't happen without a fight. But apparently the bandit lord was still frightened of the prospects of going on alone.

"You will go first, along with the kender and the historian," Kelryn informed Dan. "The lass and I will follow along behind, just to make perfectly sure the rest of you stay honest."

"If you harm her . . ." Danyal didn't complete the threat, but the fury burned hot in his eyes. Kelryn Darewind merely shrugged.

"Let's see . . . we can ascend the peak just about anywhere," Foryth Teel suggested, anxiously changing the subject. "It doesn't look like a real tricky mountain to climb."

"I think we should follow that gully," Dan suggested, pointing to a ravine that scored deep through the rough ground on the mountain's lower slope. "At least we'll stay out of sight from the lair."

The others agreed, and they used the waning hours of daylight to reach the foot of the conical summit. The lake of steaming water was nearby, off to their left, and even from a quarter mile away they could see that the surface of the water actually boiled in places, bubbles gurgling explosively upward, a roiled swath of waves churning into steam. A thick plume of water vapor rose from the lake, shrouding the valley in a nearly eternal fog, and they were grateful for the added concealment, even as the clammy air kept the perspiration on their skin from dissipating and matted their hair and clothing into a perpetually damp mess.

Despite the boiling lake, the air chilled rapidly with the coming of night. A cool wind blew down from the heights, and their breath frosted in the air as the four companions and their brutal enemy started the ascent.

At least the gully proved to be a good choice of a route. Though they occasionally had to maneuver around large rocks or short, precipitous drops in the sloping floor of the ravine, the party was able to climb in a trench with walls rising twenty or thirty feet high to either side. For hour after hour, they made their way upward, pausing rarely for a few minutes of rest, but then immediately turning back to the challenges of the steep ravine floor.

By mutual, unspoken assent, Danyal led the way. He and Emilo were the most nimble of the companions, but in the last days, the kender had seemed to lose some of his bold, carefree nature. Dan wasn't certain whether this was because of the frequency and violence of the recurring spells, or because of concern for Mirabeth. In any event, the change had been dramatic and saddening.

The lad carried a loop of short rope, the line one of a few things they had salvaged from the ruins of Loreloch, and over the steep stretches of the climb, he braced himself at the top and dangled the rope as an added handhold for his companions.

In these sections, Kelryn Darewind climbed one-handed, keeping a tight grip on the knife and Mirabeth with the other. Any thoughts Danyal had about dropping the rope were quickly dashed when he saw that he would inevitably injure the lass as well as the bandit lord.

It was after midnight when, having just completed a fifteen-foot stretch of vertical ascent, they paused for another gasping rest. It looked to Danyal as though they were only halfway up the steep, high mountain, and he suppressed a twinge of fear, not wanting to imagine what would happen if daylight revealed them to be far from cover, fully exposed on this craggy summit of bare rock.

"Tsk—there's a hole here," Foryth said wearily. "I almost fell in."

A waft of steam in Dan's face was the first indication that there was a deep break in the ravine floor. Following the warmth, Danyal came around a large rock to see a black hole in the ground, a gap large enough for a person—

but certainly not a dragon—to squeeze through.

"It's a cave!" Danyal exclaimed.

"It could be a vent for the dragon's lair," Foryth suggested thoughtfully, coming to stand beside the lad.

"Let's go in here, then," the lad suggested. The warmth of the air felt so good that for a moment he was able to quell the emotions of fear and hate that were raging in his mind.

The others agreed, so once again the human lad led the way. Danyal crawled on his belly, feeling the passage open up within a few feet of the first entrance. Trying to move silently, he reversed himself so that his feet were preceding him. Sliding on his rump, he came to a lip of stone. Despite the nearly complete darkness, he discerned a surface a short distance below his feet and was able to slide down until he was standing on a smooth, flat rock.

In short order, the others had joined him. Though they moved without speaking, each whisper of cloth scraping over stone, each scuff of a bootheel finding purchase on the floor, seemed like a loud, resonant noise in the still darkness. Kelryn tightened his grip on Mirabeth, and as Dan's face flushed, the lass looked at him with a mute plea. She wanted him to remain calm, and for her sake, he did.

Gradually Danyal realized that it was neither utterly still nor completely dark within the subterranean chamber.

"Go!" hissed Kelryn. "Lead the way!"

A dull rumble of sound seemed to rise from the very rock itself. Indeed, it was not so much a noise as a vibration, a trembling that was apparent in the air and the firmament in equal portions. The ground seemed unsettled, and Dan wondered momentarily if the cave was on the brink of collapse. Still, the walls seemed solid, and on a practical level, the noise seemed likely to mask at least the small, incidental noises made by the four intruders. Furthermore, though the narrow entry passage screened all the ambient light of the night, there was a pale illumination that marked the curving outlines of a narrow, stone-walled cavern.

There was a crimson tint to the glow, which suggested an origin in a hot furnace of fire or embers. Whatever its source, however, Danyal was glad for the light, relieved that they wouldn't have to grope through darkness or, even worse, carry some sort of light that would clearly announce their presence to any denizen with eyes.

By silent, mutual consent, they began to advance carefully along the cavern. The footing was surprisingly smooth. There was none of the loose rock or gravel underfoot that Danyal would have expected, indeed had encountered in every other cave he had ever explored. Instead, it was almost as though this stone had flowed here like thick mud, then hardened into the curves and whorls that made the footing in this smooth-walled passage such easy going.

Warm, dry air wafted into their faces, the temperature increasing gradually to a baking heat that suggested a source of deep and infernal fire. The illumination, too, increased, until they were advancing through a cavern limned in crimson, with a fiery center beckoning and threatening from ahead.

Finally they came to an end of their narrow tunnel, finding an aperture that was perhaps twenty feet above the floor in a much larger cave. The floor below them was crisscrossed with lines of bright red, like liquid flame, and a great black knob of stone rose from the midst of the vast circular chamber.

There was no sign of the dragon. However, Danyal stiffened when he felt Foryth touch his arm, then point toward a shadowy alcove on the far side of the cavern.

A skull, a *human* skull, sat there, regarding them with black, eyeless sockets. Despite its fleshless inanimation, Dan felt a shiver of apprehension as he beheld the piece of bone. He could not ignore a sensation that those sightless eyes were staring right at him.

"There it is!" Kelryn Darewind whispered, his face distorted by a leer of anticipation. Again he tightened his grip on Mirabeth, and his eyes found Dan. "You, boy. Go down there and bring it to me!"

Danyal's combination of emotions—his hatred for the bandit lord and his fear for Mirabeth's life—must have created an amusing torment on his face. In any event, Kelryn Darewind looked at him and laughed as he pressed the dagger a little harder against her skin.

"Why do you hesitate? Are you frightened finally?"

Kelryn pressed forward, still holding Mirabeth as he herded the trio of companions to the lip of the drop. Danyal saw a narrow ledge and started along the descending ramp, clinging to the wall as he inched his way along. Foryth, then Emilo, followed. Still clutching Mirabeth in the crook of his arm, the bandit lord came along behind, keeping the knife poised for a killing strike.

At last they worked their way down to the cavern floor, feeling the bedrock of the mountain quickly warm the soles of their boots and moccasins. In a small group, they crossed a stone arch that spanned one of the rivers. The crimson stuff was, in fact, molten rock, Foryth explained to Danyal.

Finally they gathered before the alcove where rested the skull of Fistandantilus. Its sightless eyes still glared, and Danyal squirmed under the uncanny sensation that they were watching him.

It was Emilo who took a step forward, scrambling up a shelf of rock below the alcove. He stared at the skull from only a foot or two away, and Danyal realized that the normally fearless kender was trembling.

"I remember," Emilo said, his voice a harsh whisper. "I saw this skull before. . . . There was a dwarf there, a wicked dwarf. . . ."

"Take the skull! Bring it to me!" snapped Kelryn, prodding the knife hard enough to draw a gasp from Mirabeth.

Slowly the kender reached out his small, wiry hands. Hesitating only for a moment, he took the skull between his palms and slowly lifted it from the smooth rock of the alcove. Danyal, realizing that he wasn't breathing, half expected the mountain to collapse or some sort of explosion to rock them.

Instead, there seemed to be almost a lessening of the vibrations in the deep, fiery mountain. With a sigh of relief, Emilo slumped to the ground, holding his grotesque trophy at arm's length.

It was then that the deep chuckle rumbled through the lair, a sound that could only mean one disastrous thing. And as he looked up and saw the slitted yellow orbs leering out of the darkness, Danyal knew.

Flayzeranyx was here.

Chapter 41

Shards Assembled

Third Bakukal, Reapember
374 AC

Fistandantilus felt the flush of power as the kender's hands touched either side of the skull. The circle was complete and needed only the explosion of blood and magic to bring the archmage's scheme to fruition. His will, his memories, and his presence coalesced into a single powerful entity, an entity with a growing semblance of control.

At the same time, he felt the pulse, the heated throbbing of the bloodstone. It was coming from nearby, and with the skull, it would make him complete.

Yet still there was that cursed, impenetrable interference that was somehow tied into the presence of the boy.

But that, too, would soon end!

Indeed, the kender was his slave now, the skull giving Fistandantilus the power at last to overwhelm his host's limited powers of resistance. The wretch would suffer before he died, but first there was another task to perform. Still maintaining his focus, Fistandantilus felt the nearness of the bloodstone. He gathered his might, plunging through the recesses of the kender's mind, taking full control.

Emilo Haversack sidled to the side, until he crouched next to the prone form of Kelryn Darewind. The bloodstone was there, and through the skull, the archmage could at last bring the kender under his control.

And Fistandantilus hungered for the nearness, the imminence, of killing.

Chapter 42

Dragons, Priests, and Magic

Third Bakukal, Reapember
374 AC

In the split second of recognition, Danyal knew that the wave of dragon awe was imminent and inevitable. Even so, the reality of the red monster's presence jellied his knees and felled him like a corpse—except that he was still alive, gasping and horrified as he lay helpless on the floor. Mirabeth, Foryth, and even Kelryn Darewind had been similarly staggered by the serpent's arrival, though the bandit lord had fallen on top of the girl, pinning her in place with his weight. The four humans stared, in various stages of immobility and fear, from where they had collapsed.

Only Emilo still stood. Danyal remembered the

kender's nonchalance when the dragon had flown over Loreloch, but even when he saw the proof repeated before his eyes, he wondered how it could be that his companion could remain upright, apparently unconcerned, in the face of that lethal and overwhelming presence.

In fact, Emilo, still holding the skull, now sauntered past Kelryn Darewind, without taking advantage of the fact that he was behind the bandit. He could have pulled Mirabeth to safety! Instead, he walked away from the others, head upturned to regard the massive dragon.

The serpentine monster's neck twisted, bringing the reptilian visage downward with a rasp of dry scales until the twin nostrils gaped before the companions. A small puff of black smoke emerged from the flaring snout, and Danyal coughed reflexively. Kelryn Darewind was still awestruck, staring at the wyrm.

Strangely, the explosive convulsion of his lungs seemed to bring some semblance of control to his limbs, and Dan was able to push himself to his hands and knees.

Crawling to Mirabeth's side, he took her hand, grateful for the returning pressure of her fingers.

"Now," he mouthed.

Mirabeth nodded, and Dan pulled on her hand as she tried to roll away. But the false priest overcame enough of his own terror to twist, to threaten with the knife pressed now against the young woman's back.

She groaned in pain and, with a grimace of bitter dismay, Dan froze.

"Look!" Mirabeth gasped.

Still clenching her hand, Dan turned to see Emilo standing, apparently dazed, before the dragon's broad nose. The scarlet jaws gaped slightly, revealing a multitude of teeth, the largest of which were easily as big as the blade of Danyal's knife.

"The skull of Fistandantilus belongs to me," hissed the dragon wickedly.

"No. The skull belongs to no one—no one except

itself," replied the kender.

At least, the words came from Emilo Haversack, but the voice was deeper and more forceful than the kender's familiar chatter.

Emilo studied the bony artifact that he held in his hands. Then he raised his head once again, calmly meeting the dragon's glare.

With a deliberate movement, the kender tucked the skull under his arm, the bony face looking backward. With the opposite hand, he reached into a pouch at his side and pulled forth a gold chain, from which dangled the pendant of a familiar gem.

"My bloodstone!" Kelryn Darewind's shriek was a thin, piercing blade of sound. Eyes wide, the man grasped at his shirt with his left hand. His right still held the knife with white-knuckled intensity, the tip of the blade digging cruelly into Mirabeth's back.

The skull stared from its black eye sockets, grinning with locked, rigid teeth.

"If you are wise, red serpent, you will withdraw immediately and you will have a chance to live."

The words came from the kender, but again this was not Emilo Haversack speaking. The diminutive figure cradled the skull as he allowed the glowing gemstone to sway dizzyingly back and forth.

The dragon snorted, and Danyal was momentarily certain that they would all be engulfed and killed by a lethal explosion of flame. But something—perhaps it was merely a desire to protect the treasures from harm— held Flayze's deadly attack in check.

Instead, the great serpent flicked a claw, striking Emilo in the chest, propelling him backward with violent force. The kender's body smashed onto the ground, bounced, and collided with Foryth Teel. The historian caught Emilo's limp form and gently lowered him to the floor.

Somehow the skull and the pendant had remained with the frail body through that violent assault, and now, as blood seeped from a deep wound in the kender's chest, the grinning death's-head lay between Emilo's feet while the pendant rested nearby on the floor. The pale green light pulsed from the stone, bright even in the fiery illumination of the dragon's lair.

Kelryn Darewind, his features locked in an expression of horror, lunged toward the stone, then whirled as Mirabeth took the chance to dive away from him. She scrambled across the floor, and the bandit lord darted after her, then backed off with a snarl as Danyal faced him with the large, curving knife. Foryth Teel, in the meantime, gently probed at the mess that was the kender's chest.

"Is he . . . ?" Danyal glanced at the bloody figure and was horrified to see the white flash of Emilo's ribs through the tear in his chest.

"He's alive." Grimly the historian pointed at a pulsing muscle, and the lad was vaguely aware that he was seeing a part of the kender's heart.

Abruptly Foryth raised his head. His eyes bored into the dragon, and his thin body went rigid and taut in a way Danyal had never seen.

"For years I have strived to remain aloof, to let history weave its tales without my interference or my judgment."

His tone hardened, and he shook a narrow fist in the air. Foryth's eyes were wild, and his forehead was slick with sweat. "But this is *too much!* Fate is too cruel, and I blame all you who would be the great shapers of history!"

The historian drew a firm breath and stood. "This one is *innocent*, and he has been wrongly used!"

Foryth Teel was shouting aloud now, in a voice that seemed powerful enough to overwhelm the volcanic tremors of the angry mountain.

"How *dare* you!" The historian's voice was choked with passion, a whiplike force of anger lashing at the monstrous serpent.

Flayze merely uttered an amused snort in response.

At the same time, Danyal noticed a newcomer in the cave: an incongruous image of a slight, elderly man dressed in a robe of drab gray. The stranger was standing nearby, clearly within the line of sight of the dragon, yet the serpent seemed not to be aware of his presence. And then, when Foryth Teel swept his gaze across the room, he, too, looked past the man without any sign that he was aware of the mysterious observer.

He *is* an observer! Danyal made the realization as the stranger raised his hands, revealing that he held a long scroll of parchment. With the scratching of a quill, he started to write, his eyes shifting smoothly from dragon to historian to bandit lord. Dan felt wonder at his own acceptance of the strange appearance; still, he couldn't shake the feeling that the man seemed to belong here.

Foryth Teel whirled, pointing an accusing finger at Kelryn Darewind. "And *you!*"

It seemed to Danyal that all of Foryth's self-control, his vaunted dispassion, had vanished under the onslaught of his rage. He raised his fists, then leaned back and shouted toward the ceiling arching so far overhead. "And all of you priests, and even the gods themselves! Paladine and Takhisis! I spit on your arrogance, your cruel manipulations. And Gilean, do you hear me? You are the worst of all!"

At that statement, the strange scribe turned with a start toward the priest. His eyes narrowed momentarily, and then he went back to observing the dragon.

"You strive for aloofness, dispassion, but how can you ignore the hurts?" the historian went on.

Fumbling in his pouch, Foryth Teel pulled out his *Book of Learning*, scornfully waving the tome in the air.

"All of you are corrupt. I condemn your immortal pretensions!"

Now the historian's voice took on a slower, but still accusing, tone. "I see that it's no use to simply watch. I have to do my part, to be a part of the story. And it matters who lives and who dies. People like this kender are more than just pawns. He deserves better than to have his life cast away in the middle of your contest!"

Foryth choked the sound of a strangled sob, then

straightened to stand tall. "I can't make a difference; it's a pity he didn't have more powerful friends."

Abruptly he hurled the book against the rock wall beside the alcove where they had found the skull. The pages stuck to the wall, and suddenly sparks crackled along the rock surface, a cascade of brightness that drew everyone's unblinking attention. Even Flayze watched, yellow eyes hooded, long fangs partially bared.

And letters were written there on the cave wall, words of magic and power. Foryth slowly knelt and began to pray. His hands went to Emilo's bleeding chest, and the magic and the healing flowed from his hands.

Danyal watched in astonishment as the gaping wound in the kender's chest slowly knit. The blood ceased pulsing, and the heart, and then the ribs, swiftly vanished beneath clean, smooth skin. The scratching of the strange observer's quill was, in the lad's ears, an unnaturally loud sound.

Foryth looked up. "And now, my Lord of Neutrality, grant me the power to drive this foul force from my friend's body and soul. Exorcise the spirit that seeks to claim him. Drive it from the innocent flesh of Emilo Haversack."

Like the explosion of a sewer, stinking, sulfurous gas erupted from the motionless figure. Green mist swirled through the air, forming a cloud that surrounded Foryth Teel and seemed to seep upward from the still motionless kender.

Only then did Danyal notice that the bloodstone of Fistandantilus glowed bright green and pulsed more strongly than ever.

Chapter 43

Powers Competing

Reapember, 374 AC

He was free!

Fueled by the bloodstone and the stored might of the many lives it had absorbed, the essence of Fistandantilus rushed toward the skull, drawn into the vacuum of power with an exultant, stormy force. He felt an exultation and an explosive swelling of hunger. He was desperate to take on a physical shell.

And then came unspeakable pain as the essence of the wizard swirled into the bony artifact. The spirit was abruptly torn, cruelly twisted, the cloud of mist ripped into two parts in an explosion of agony.

One of those halves settled into the hungry, welcoming skull; in moments the spirit and the bony artifact had

merged, swelling into a creature of undeath. Fistandantilus had been torn apart by the convulsion of Skullcap,
but now the shards of his existence came together in the
form of a lich, a creature of remembered humanity and
insatiable hunger. The skeletal body was ready to cast
mighty spells, to work magic of death and violence.

The other tendril of mist was pulled away as it tore
part of the life and the soul of the wizard from himself.
The lich could only watch as a great piece of him roared,
relentless and unstoppable, toward the human boy.

Chapter 44

Fistandantilus Reborn

Third Bakukal, Reapember
374 AC

Like a small green cyclone, the gas cloud swirled in the air, rising from the vortex of the bloodstone, coiling into a translucent shape as it leaned toward the skull.

But something held it back.

A *whoosh* of air tugged at Dan, whipped at his hair and clothes. The gust was so strong that it threatened to pull him off his feet, to drag him across the floor.

Danyal felt the tugging hardest at his belt. When he reached for the buckle, he was astounded to feel that the metal was warm, vibrating beneath his fingers. It tugged fiercely at his waist as the force tried to pull the belt away from him.

And then, in a flash, he understood: The ancient heirloom, the buckle worn by his Thwait ancestors, was somehow drawn to the magic!

With a sound like a thunderclap, the whirlwind separated, twin columns of spiraling air wrenching apart with supernatural violence. One of the cyclonic shapes swirled toward the skull, lifting the bone from the floor, raising it eerily through the hazy curtain of the amorphous shape.

It was the second whirlwind that swept toward Danyal. The lad scrambled backward, recoiling from the roaring approach, but the gale pulled him closer, the miasma strangling, suffocating him, tightening around his throat like the belt cinched at his waist. Sensing the irresistible desire in that stinking fog, he fumbled with the clasp, cursing the suddenly stubborn bracket of silver, burning his hands on the unnaturally hot metal.

Finally the belt buckle released. Frantically he flipped open the clasp, and friction burned his skin as the strap of leather was snatched from his grip by the consuming force of the storm. Dan tumbled to the floor and lay there shaking as he watched.

The belt itself hissed into nothingness, burned to ashes by the unnatural touch of the green cloud. The buckle floated in the air, suspended amid the cyclone, and the silver metal began to glow brightly.

And then the silver spattered downward, drops of glowing metal flowing across the floor. Before the lad's disbelieving eyes, the molten droplets merged and rose into the air. Bending and flowing, they formed into a shining, perfect shape: a silver hourglass.

Dan wasn't really sure when the change came about, but suddenly the twin whirlwinds faded and softened, the space within each of them growing solid and distinct.

And then the cyclones were gone, and two black-robed figures stood in their places. Their features were invisible within deep cowls of inky, velvet hoods, but Dan had little doubt as to their nature: These were wizards of black magic, drawn here by the abiding enchantments of the bloodstone, the skull of Fistandantilus, and the silver belt buckle of Paulus Thwait.

It was the dragon who reacted first. Flayze roared loudly and reared with a great flapping of his wings. A blast of air struck Dan and the companions in the face, and the lad threw up an arm to screen himself. At the same time, he saw the dragon's jaws gape and sensed the inferno building in that massive, scarlet belly.

Mirabeth took his arm, and he dropped to the floor, pulling her down, trying to shelter her beneath his arms from the killing cloud that must inevitably follow. He remembered the charred bodies in his village and the slain bandits on the bridge at Loreloch; somehow it seemed almost a certain destiny that now he, too, would meet his death by fiery dragonbreath.

He heard another sound, an utterance of short, barking words, but that noise was quickly swallowed by the roaring blaze of an infernal furnace. Danyal was reminded of the sound of a blacksmith's forge, when the fire had been stoked and the bellows were pumping. This was that same hungry, crackling howl, except magnified to an impossible extent, as if he himself were watching the fire from within the chimney.

But he wasn't getting burned!

The truth penetrated his numb sense of shock with an almost diffident appeal to his senses. Danyal blinked, feeling Mirabeth trembling underneath him. He looked up and saw a wall of fire before them. Above, oily flames crackled and raged and on both sides as well. He felt the heat against his skin, as if he was staring into a hot fireplace, but neither he nor Mirabeth was being touched by the lethal blaze.

Nor, he saw, were Foryth, Emilo, Kelryn, or the two black-robed wizards. One of the latter held up a hand that looked like a skeleton's, clothed in sickly skin; it was the force of that gesture, Dan suddenly knew, that was parting the flames, carrying the dragon's lethal breath to either side.

Abruptly the fire ceased, and in its absence, the cavern felt utterly cold and dark. Though the air was still baked and illuminated by the streams of fiery lava flowing throughout the vast enclosure, it might have been a winter's night by comparison to the dragonfire.

The other wizard extended a hand toward the monster, the gesture swift and menacing. Dan had time to notice that the limb was more manlike than the first mage's skeletal digits. The fingers that now extended were long, slender, and clearly dexterous, but they were undeniably cloaked in flesh and pink, living skin.

Another word split the air within the cavern, a barking cry that sent a shiver down the lad's spine, and he knew that he was witness to still more powerful magic. The arcane sounds were harsh against his ears, and the feeling they left in his belly was not unlike the sensation of getting kicked very hard.

A wash of pale light expanded outward from the wizard's hand, a growing cone that encompassed much of the dragon and cast its chilly glow onto an expanse of bubbling lava and the smoking wall of the cavern beyond. The liquid rock instantly darkened, frozen hard, cracks wrenching violently outward across the floor.

And in the eerie glow of that spell, Danyal felt a bitter, piercing chill, a coldness that seeped through his clothes and his skin, striking so deep that it seemed to ice the blood in his veins. Even as he felt that cold, the youth understood another thing: He absorbed this penetrating effect from *watching* the spell—the real cold was a force of powerful magic attacking everything that was caught in the wash of that pale, icy light.

Blasted full in the chest by the arcane onslaught, the dragon reared backward with a shrill cry of pain and rage. Red scales, strangely rimed in thick frost, tumbled free from the monstrous shape as the serpent writhed away from the hateful chill. Flayze tried to strike with a massive wing, to brush the wizard away, but the leathery membrane was brittle and clumsy, crippled by the attack of cold magic.

Dan was vaguely aware of the gray-robed stranger in the background. The man was still making notes, though he showed little interest in the events being enacted before him. He had turned the silver hourglass over; now sand, glowing like powdered diamonds, filtered slowly through the glass's neck.

And still, except for Danyal, no one else in the cavern had seemed to notice him.

But it was the dragon who again commanded their attention. Flayze roared, the sound like the crash of a massive thundercloud, sending the companions and Kelryn Darewind reeling back from the onslaught of sound. Only the two wizards held their ground, black robes flapping around their legs as they regarded the crouching form of the infuriated dragon.

The whiplike tail lashed around, a crimson tendril of crushing power, but the fleshly mage pointed and barked a command. A spear of crackling lightning ripped through the air, striking the dragon's tail and shattering the last half of the supple limb. With a howl, Flayze pulled the bleeding stump into a coil around his feet.

But the dragon's wings were flexing now as the slowing effects of the ice magic wore off. The great head lashed forward, jaws gaping as it snapped toward the nearest of the two black-robed shapes.

The wizard blinked out of sight just before the serpent's jaws clamped shut. Danyal whirled in surprise, seeing that the mage had transported himself to the other side of the cavern. There he raised a hand and sent another searing bolt of lightning hissing and sparking into the dragon's side.

Still roaring, Flayze whirled back, but Danyal sensed that the dragon moved purely in reaction to the attacks of the two wizards. Indeed, as the crimson jaws lashed toward the target who had just released the lightning bolt, the other magic-user pointed a finger—this one, Dan saw clearly now, as bony and thin as any skeleton's—and released a great barrage of glowing, sparking balls of magic.

The arcane missiles struck the dragon's neck, one after another searing through the layer of armored scales. The great serpent moaned, the sound curiously plaintive emerging from such a monstrous being. Flayze thrashed again, more weakly this time, and tried to extend a reaching forelimb, only to have the leg blasted by another onslaught of magic missiles.

Finally, with a shuddering groan, the massive red dragon collapsed to the floor and lay still, dead.

Chapter 45

The Ambitious Priest

Third Bakukal, Reapember
374 AC

"My lord Fistandantilus!" cried Kelryn, throwing himself at the feet of the nearest of the wizards. "You have appeared in answer to my prayers!" He reached out as if to wrap his arms around the figure's legs, but then hesitated, rising to his knees, staring hopefully upward.

The black-robed figure ignored the man, turning a shadowy face toward the other gaunt, shrouded form. Though the two were dressed alike and approximately the same size, the nearer sorcerer was somehow more substantial, more solid than the other.

Both, Dan realized, were equally frightening.

The second wizard drew back its hood to reveal a visage of ghastly horror. Danyal recognized the skull of Fistandantilus, except that now that bony visage was attached to a skeletal neck, extending out of a corpselike body. The arms that moved the sleeves of the robe seemed vaporous and incorporeal, while the face bore that same, teeth-baring grimace that the companions had seen on the inanimate skull. The hands were skin stretched taut over bone and seemed to float, unattached physically, at the ends of the wide sleeves.

And the eyes of the skull had changed, Dan saw with a dull throb of horror. Instead of cold shadows within the empty sockets, there glowed a spark of heat in place of each eye, a crimson spot of burning fire that seemed to penetrate Danyal's skin, to shrivel his insides with the force of hatred, violence, and cruelty. It was as if the pure evil of this creature had somehow been condensed into illumination, and that vile brightness now glittered wickedly from the dead sockets.

Only vaguely did the lad become aware that the flaming, hellish inspection was not specifically directed at himself. Indeed, though the eyes seemed to see everywhere, the posture of the skeletal body showed that the creature's attention was fixed upon the other black-robed magic-user.

"Who are you?" asked the death's-head wizard of its counterpart, the voice a rumbling growl that shivered through the bedrock of the mountain.

"I am Fistandantilus!" crowed the other, the flesh-cloaked sorcerer, his tone exultant. This archmage threw back his hood, and Danyal saw the stern face of a mature, but not old, man. His hair was long and black, and his stern features were centered around a hawklike nose. Cold, dark eyes blazed with intensity as he raised a finger and pointed at the image of death.

"Now name yourself!" he demanded.

"*I* am Fistandantilus! I am the lich of Skullcap, survivor of the Dark Queen's foul challenges." The cry roared from the skull as the fleshless jaws spread wide. "It is you who are the imposter—and you who are doomed!"

Danyal tore his eyes away, saw Kelryn looking wildly back and forth between the two black figures. Mirabeth and Foryth watched with awestruck expressions, while Emilo Haversack observed the conflict with a look of intrigued curiosity. Looking around, the lad saw that the gray-robed observer remained in place, scribing diligently. The dust still trickled through the hourglass, though the level of sand in the timepiece hadn't appreciably changed.

"Dispassionate." Dan suddenly remembered the word Foryth Teel had used, the ideal that he strived for—and he knew that it fit perfectly this silent, aloof figure.

"Wait!" the command came from Kelryn Darewind. The Seeker priest, still on his knees, crept around the side of the human Fistandantilus. "You have both come in answer to my plea. Both of you together are the archmage!"

"I have no need of together, or of any intrusive assistance!" declared the man in black robes. His eyes never left the apparition of death, which likewise maintained a tight focus on its opposite number. "I am myself, powerful and invulnerable. I have returned to Krynn, and now I am ready to commence my vengeance."

"Wow—will you have a look at that?" Emilo's voice, calmly speaking into Danyal's ear, was like a dousing of cold water on the numbed young man. Grateful for any indication of normalcy, Dan turned to see what the kender was talking about.

Emilo was pointing at the floor, where the bloodstone of Fistandantilus lay, temporarily forgotten. Danyal saw that the green gem was pulsing, radiating its sickly illumination through the darkness, the seeping, misty light apparently unnoticed by the great figures debating nearby. That vague illumination swirled in the air, slowly congealing into a flat disk, suspended perpendicular to the floor. The hourglass was below the disk, and the foggy image seemed to be centered above the silver timepiece.

As he watched, Danyal saw a vaporous essence take

firmer shape, whirling into an image that looked like nothing so much as a window, a view through space into a place of gray mist, like the dew-laden air of a foggy morning. The representation solidified above the hourglass, and Dan knew he was looking at an entirely different place.

"It's the power of the stone and the skull. It has opened a window to other planes, other worlds!" Foryth gasped. "A gate into space and time."

The bandit remained focused on the twin sorcerers. "You have come because I called you! I *summoned* you!" cried Kelryn Darewind, rising to his feet, turning to confront one, then the other of the two mages.

"Silence!" snapped the human version of Fistandantilus. He stared at Kelryn Darewind for a moment; then his eyes flickered, attracted to something else. "Ah, my bloodstone!" declared the archmage, spotting the gem on the cavern floor. He stepped toward the pulsing artifact.

Danyal watched the shimmering window take firmer shape in the air.

"Hold!" cried the skeletal Fistandantilus. Abruptly the grotesque personage vanished, reappearing directly before his counterpart. Kelryn Darewind stepped after it, forming the third point of a triangle.

"I remember!" It was Emilo Haversack who spoke, his voice a whisper of wonder. "I recall everything that happened to me. It started with the skull, a very, very long time ago. I saw it there, in the darkness. . . . The dwarf struck me with it, and my memories were gone."

He looked at Dan, his eyes wide with awe and dawning understanding. "That's where my sickness came from—and it took away my memories, too! My life, my whole past! But now they've come back!"

Emilo skipped a little step, as if he were ready to break into a dance. "I come from Kendermore, and . . . and I remember a time before the Cataclysm! And . . . and I thank you all for helping me, for keeping me alive, for letting me get better!"

"You saved us, too, if you don't remember," Danyal

replied.

The kender scowled. "But that stone and skull—they shouldn't be together, should they?"

"No, they shouldn't!" Mirabeth wrapped the kender in a hug as Danyal continued to watch the two magic-users and their prophet. Kelryn was raving, his voice shrill as he made demands of first one, then the other Fistandantilus.

And all the time the bloodstone lay on the floor, pulsing in time with the flaring image of that green-framed window. The mysterious portal whirled in the air, still suspended above the silver hourglass.

"The power was *mine*—the bloodstone belongs to me!" Kelryn's voice was shrill but futile.

"*You* are mine!" the lich declared in a voice like the wind from a newly opened crypt, finally turning to regard the bandit lord with its flaring, horrifying eyes. "For too long you have used my talisman as your toy, playing your role as a priest. My strength sustained you, and now *you* will sustain *me!*"

Kelryn recoiled, his face draining of color under the inspection of the ghastly undead mage.

"His life belongs to me!" the other wizard interjected. "It was *my* essence that held back the effects of age, that allowed him to survive for so long."

Each of the black-robed figures took one of the bandit's arms. Light seared the air, a sizzling aura that outlined the twisting, writhing figure in cold brightness. Danyal, watching in awe, saw the illumination as power, and he observed the power divided.

The essence of Kelryn Darewind's life was sucked from his body as the bandit lord writhed and screamed in unspeakable agony. He weakened quickly, moaning, slumping between the two mighty sorcerers. Vitality faded from the man's eyes, and Dan could almost see the warmth of his blood being pulled from his flesh, flowing in equal portions into the two versions of the black-robed archmage.

Finally the sorcerers released the clawlike hands of

their shriveled victim, and Kelryn Darewind crumpled to the ground, the shell of his skin drained of blood, of vitality and life. The corpse lay motionless on the floor while the two images of Fistandantilus stood trembling under the onslaught of renewed life and restored power.

A web of green light flared, sparking and firing between the two archmages. Tendrils of ghostly power connected into a glowing net of supernatural, sinister force.

"Together—they've absorbed him together!" Foryth Teel whispered, awed.

"What does it mean? What will happen?" Danyal asked.

"I don't know, but see: Neither archmage can break away from his counterpart. I think that whichever one prevails will either be very powerful, so much so that he becomes in fact invulnerable, or he will be doomed."

The mountain itself trembled under the onslaught of barely contained power. Pieces of rock broke from the ceiling, tumbling down to shatter on the floor. Sharp-edged shards of stone flew here and there, several whizzing past dangerously close, but Danyal's attention was rapt, still focused on the two wizards. They strained visibly to tear themselves apart, but with the violence of the collapsing mountain forming a convulsive backdrop, the two black-robed forms were pulled inexorably closer together.

At the same time, vibrations of power continued to seethe and to rumble in the ground itself. Spatters of gravel tumbled from the ceiling, and tongues of flame flared upward, breaking through the crust of the floor. The cavern rocked back and forth, filling with smoke and dust, thundering with the violent noise of collapse and destruction.

And Danyal knew that Flayze's mountain was dying.

Chapter 46

Departures, Alive and Dead

Third Bakukal, Reapember
374 AC

The green vortex of magic still hung over the hourglass, swirling like a liquid mirror. Now, instead of a pure reflection, the companions caught glimpses of actual places. Dan saw a forest, and then a swath of smooth, wave-swept beach. The two wizards grappled magically, taut within the web of green magic.

Another convulsion shook the lair of Flayzeranyx, and Danyal nearly lost his balance as a piece of the ceiling smashed to the floor nearby. Already the corridor by which the companions had entered was gone, vanished beneath a crushing barrier of rubble.

"Go!" Foryth Teel cried amid the chaos, pointing

toward the glowing aperture. "This place is doomed! It's your only chance!"

Dan saw the diamondlike sand still sparkling magically as it tumbled through the narrow neck of the hourglass. The gray-robed man had lowered his pen, and his eyes were fixed upon the companions. He would write, Danyal sensed, when they acted.

But what should they do?

A hiss of energy crackled loudly as the Fistandantiluslich tried to pull his counterpart to the side. The human version of the archmage set his feet and spread his fingers, summoning a roaring spiral of greenish fire that flared high and momentarily blocked the two figures from view. The screams that emerged from within the cocoon of magic were chilling and unnatural, each sound intense with unchained fury and violence.

The vortex to the worlds wheeled like a kaleidoscopic image, and the kender stared into the space, obviously fascinated. "What a place to wander—so *many* places," he declared in amazement. "There's a range of blue mountains—and look! A city, the whole thing crammed into one big tower!"

"Go, then. See all those places!" urged the historian. "Escape while you can, to survive and wander!"

"My friends, I shall do just that!" declared Emilo, suddenly decisive.

Mirabeth clasped her arms around him in a crushing hug. "Go *now!*" she demanded through her tears.

"Farewell, then, all of you—and thank you!" cried Emilo Haversack, turning to wave a jaunty farewell to the three humans. The two mages, still enshrouded by magic, took no note of the companions.

Before Dan could shout any kind of reply, the kender dived into—and *through*—the mirror. The lad caught a glimpse of a crowded street, a city with strange, lofty walls, and then the image had moved on to display a vault of cold, starry sky.

The visions in the arcane window continued to change. The next place was familiar—a mountain valley,

scored by a small, babbling stream. Dan recognized the
road they had followed near Loreloch, and then he saw
the blackened ruin itself. In another moment he saw
something moving, a familiar equine shape.

"There's the horse!" he cried as the image of the black
mare, cantering gracefully along the road, came into
view.

"Nightmare!" Mirabeth shouted. "Can you hear us?
Come here!"

Suddenly the scene shifted, whirling closer in a dizzying rush, and then the horse was right before them. With
a kicking, plunging jump, the animal leaped, and
abruptly Nightmare passed through the shimmering
window and was in the cave alongside them, rearing
amidst the crumbling stone.

"She will carry the two of you to safety. You must go
after the kender!" Foryth declared sternly, taking Mirabeth and Danyal firmly by their arms. "Leave Fistandantilus to me!"

"No!" Dan shouted. "I'm not leaving you!" Though he
sensed it was foolish to remain in the collapsing mountain, he felt a fierce loyalty to the historian, who had so
clearly proved himself a friend.

"I'm staying, too!" declared Mirabeth, taking the lad's
arm, watching in awe.

The mountain rocked with growing violence. A shard
of stone scored a deep gash in Foryth Teel's head, drawing an immediate shower of blood and sending the man
staggering backward.

Abruptly the green shroud fell from the two images of
Fistandantilus, and the archmages staggered apart. The
human gasped for breath, while the lich slowly drew
itself into a tall, utterly rigid posture.

"Go—before it's too late!" the historian insisted,
angrily gesturing to Danyal and Mirabeth.

But the two young humans merely shook their heads,
locking their arms around each other as they shared their
intention to stay behind with the historian and see the
matter to its conclusion. With one hand, Mirabeth

reached out to grab onto Nightmare's halter, and under her soothing touch, the horse grew strangely calm amid the chaos and destruction.

Ignoring his stubborn companions, Foryth turned back to the two archmages. Inflamed by their consumption of Kelryn Darewind's essence, they stared at him with the light of hunger banked only slightly in their eyes. The web of green light still glowed between them, and Dan could plainly see the tension, the strain that the connection placed on the two figures. The balance of power between them was tenuous, and the lad sensed that neither could relax, or the other's victory would be absolute.

"You can become what you want, you know," Foryth ventured. "A true fusion of your selves, through the bloodstone, will result in a being of truly godlike power."

"I will not yield to a corpse!" sneered the fleshly version of the archmage.

"Nor I surrender to mortality!" cried the other.

"But you already have—both of you," Foryth Teel replied, his scholarly tone utterly reasonable. "In truth, you are the same being, but you have been brought here from different segments of the River of Time. If you think about it, the chance to merge with yourself is a unique opportunity, a combination that has never been attempted in all the history of Krynn."

As the wizards glared at each other, Danyal noticed that Foryth Teel had picked up the golden chain and its green stone pendant.

"The key, of course, is that only one of you can wield the bloodstone. Here!"

Foryth suddenly flipped the gem into the air, tossing it between the two mages, and for an instant it seemed to Danyal that time stood still. The artifact tumbled and careened in space, the gold chain flashing through a dizzying whirl, and then the two images of the wizard reached forward. Each of them seized a portion of the chain, pulling on the treasured artifact.

The links pulled taut as the power of twin sorcerers raged through the ancient metal. The sound of a thunderstorm rocked through the chamber. Bright flashes of light, like green spears of lightning, crackled outward from the two figures and sent the watching humans staggering backward. The air in the cavern was instantly fouled, thick with the stench of death.

The whirling storm exploded around them, louder than anything Dan had ever heard. He pulled Mirabeth close, and the two of them hunched down, wincing against the unnatural gale, grimacing as the wind lashed like a physical force against their hair, clothes, and skin.

And then the black-shrouded wizards were gone, both of them vanishing in a crackle of green smoke. The storm vanished with them, though the tremors of the dying mountain still rocked the floor and dropped showers of rubble and boulders from the ceiling.

"What—what happened?" Dan asked, stunned. Even though the cavern was still jolted and rocked by subterranean convulsions, it seemed strangely silent in the wake of the sorcerous departures.

"The two versions of Fistandantilus are scattered again, shards of them tossed along the length of the River of Time. It should be many centuries before that power is mustered into the world again." Foryth's tone was wistful, almost as if he regretted that the archmages had departed before they could be fully interviewed.

"But how did they . . . why were there two? And why did one of them come for my belt buckle?"

Foryth Teel nodded confidently. "I've been thinking about that, and I have an idea. But first, tell me: Was your ancestor a silversmith in Haven, and did he wear that belt of yours when he faced a wizard in battle?"

"That was the family legend, yes."

"I think Fistandantilus arranged to store himself in a metal object, and that belt buckle was handy when his original host—a black-robed mage named Whastryk—was killed. That spirit of the archmage must have been stored in the silver, dormant for centuries.

"Then, after the violence of Skullcap, Fistandantilus survived in another, undead, form. That was the lich. When the spiritual essence was exorcised from our kender friend, it entered the skull and created that creature. But at the same time it split, torn in two by the ancient spell stored in your silver buckle.

"The two wizards were perhaps the only beings on Krynn powerful enough to defeat each other. Fortunately competition between them was inevitable, since they both needed the same artifact. And that battle insured their mutual destruction."

Another rumble shook the cavern, and a great section of the roof collapsed, nearly crushing them all. The three humans ducked, covering their heads against splintering shards of stone.

The vortex, the window to the planes, continued to whirl before the trio. The hourglass still stood beneath it, and there had been no appreciable change in the level of the dust trickling through its narrow neck.

"You two should go as well. Chase after Emilo, or take your own road. This portal is the only safe way out of here. Leave while you still can!"

"What about you?" Mirabeth asked insistently.

"I will stay. It is essential that I record the events of the last days—"

"I know . . . for history," Dan interjected. "But can't you come with us and write somewhere else where it's safe?"

"I think if one of us goes through that window, he won't be coming back here. But there will be new worlds, new adventures waiting, and both of you are well prepared to face those."

"But you'll die here!"

"Perhaps . . . if my god wants me to. If not, I'll live—and write."

Nightmare whinnied loudly, rearing as another jolt rocked the cavern. On the other side of the horse, the gray-robed man came forward, standing and watching with an expression of serene patience.

And Danyal understood that Foryth Teel would be all right.

"The window won't last much longer. *Go!*" cried the historian, and this time the lad agreed. He clasped Foryth in a quick hug and waited as Mirabeth did the same, then joined the lass in scrambling onto the back of the prancing horse.

As tremors shook the floor underfoot, the window of space seemed to waver. Mirabeth put her heels to the mare's flanks. With a powerful leap, Nighmare bolted forward, and they were through—gone into the whirling mists of time and space.

In another instant the chaos vanished. Danyal and Mirabeth found themselves on a roadway, a well-paved path of smooth stones. The lad looked over his shoulder immediately, but there was no sign of the magical window behind them.

Nightmare advanced at an easy walk, approaching a wide ford across a clear stream. A castle more beautiful than any they had ever seen rose on the far side of the river. Silver towers rose into the sky, and banners of multiple bright hues fluttered and glowed in the springlike breeze.

"Let's go see who lives there," said the lad, gently nudging the mare into the shallow ford.

Epilogue

To His Excellency Astinus,
Lorekeeper of Krynn

Excellency, as you have requested, I have tried to recall my specific impressions as the matter of the skull and stone came to a head.

The two young humans departed, and I saw them riding into a pastoral realm. Both orphans, they left little behind, and I knew they would prosper there. The knowledge gave me some comfort as the mountain continued to shudder around me. The kender I never saw again, but I presume that he fared well. He had much of the survivor about him and was at least freed from the terrible burden he had unwittingly borne for so many years.

In the shattered debris of the destruction, I saw the figure of a mature, dignified man approaching me. He was dressed all in gray, and by this I immediately recognized Gilean. The god of neutrality held up one hand, disavowing my initial intention to kneel in reverence.

"You have proved your worth many times over, my faithful chronicler," said the benign image. "Know that you have proved yourself capable of serving in my priesthood should you wish to return to the monastery."

"Should I wish . . ." I was puzzled until, after a moment, I perceived what my lord had already recognized. "And if I do not choose to make this choice? Suppose my destiny is not to be found in the priesthood?"

The old man smiled. "Then I have other work for you. Important work, and it is in an area for which you are well suited."

I waited.

"You must go to Palanthas, and thence to the Great Library."

I felt my heart quicken, for there was no place on Krynn that offered such excitement and opportunity to a dedicated historian.

He reached down and picked up a silver hourglass from the floor—an object I had failed to notice before, though it was midway through the course of its sands— and he offered it to me.

"You have earned this. It is an historian's treasure, a priceless tool that will allow you to travel into the realms of the past. There you will be able to observe history as it happens, to ride the currents of the great river through its course."

"My lord, I am not worthy of such a treasure!" I was aghast, and powerfully moved by the awesome responsibility inherent in such a treasure.

The god waved aside my protests. "My chronicler, Astinus, is in need of a skilled field historian, a researcher who can travel abroad in the world, not only in this time but also in times past, and report accurately upon that which he discovers."

"But, my lord . . ." I was indeed humbled by the honor but could not believe myself worthy. "Have I not failed to display the level of objectivity, the dispassionate aloofness, that is the creed of the true historian?"

"Bah," Gilean said with a soft chuckle. "Aloofness is much overrated. No, my son, you have learned that the true historian *must* become a part of his story, else he will inevitably fail to understand the underlying truths of the tale."

And so, Excellency, I arrive at the Great Library and await your commands.

In devotion to the truth,
Foryth Teel

THE LOST GODS BOOKS

FORGOTTEN REALMS®
Harpers #15
Finder's Bane
by Kate Novak and Jeff Grubb

DRAGONLANCE®
Fistandantilus Reborn
by Douglas Niles

FORGOTTEN REALMS®
Tymora's Luck
by Kate Novak and Jeff Grubb
(October 1997)